The Wives

of

Henry Oades

The Wives

of

Henry Oades

A NOVEL

Johanna Moran

BALLANTINE BOOKS
Trade Paperbacks
New York

A Ballantine Books Trade Paperback Original

Copyright © 2010 by Johanna Moran
Random House reading group guide copyright © 2010 by Random House, Inc.

Published in the United States by Ballantine Books, an imprint of
The Random House Publishing Group, a division of
Random House, Inc., New York.

BALLANTINE and colophon are registered trademarks of Random House, Inc.
RANDOM HOUSE READER'S CIRCLE and colophon are trademarks of
Random House, Inc.

ISBN 978-0-345-51095-2

Printed in the United States of America

www.randomhousereaderscircle.com

2 4 6 8 9 7 5 3 1

Book design by Caroline Cunningham

For my husband, John Moran

And for my parents, June Ray and John Campbell Chommie

Tena, ki te riro ko ta te teina ki mua whanau mai ai, hei muri ko ta te tuakana whanau ai, na, he iwi kino taua iwi hou, ina tae mai ki tenei Motu.

But, if it happens that the child of the younger is born first, and of the elder afterward, then the newcomers will be an evil people, when they arrive in this Land.

—A Maori premonition of disorder

PART ONE

The Newcomers

1890

A COMMON BAT on the other side of the world elects to sink its rabid fangs, and one's cozy existence is finished.

Margaret Oades knew her husband was up to something the moment he came through the door with a bottle of wine. It was late. The children had gone up hours ago. "What's the occasion?" she asked, laying out a plain supper of shirred eggs and lardy cakes.

Henry kissed the nape of her neck, giving her a shiver. "I've an announcement," he said.

Margaret expected him to say he'd found a collie for their son. John, nearly eight now—her big boy, her pride—had been wheedling without letup for weeks. She took down two goblets, hoping the dog was an old one and not some frisky crocus lover.

"A senior passed in New Zealand," he said instead. "Of a bat bite, poor bloke. I'm to complete his stint. We're due as soon as possible. You'll want to prepare."

Margaret set the goblets aside. "Henry."

"Two years, sweetheart." He'd proposed marriage with the

same pleading look. "The time shall sail by, you'll see. It's a grand opportunity, a flying leap forward. I could hardly say no thanks."

Three weeks later, boarding the steamer tender that was to take them down the Thames and bring them up alongside the *Lady Ophelia*, Margaret could not recall what she'd said next. Nothing perhaps, stunned as she'd been.

On board the crowded tender, a child each by the hand, Henry and Margaret jockeyed for position at the rail. Already the narrow boat was moving, spewing gray smoke. Margaret waved to her parents on the quay below, flapping her hankie, straining to pick them out through tears and drizzle. She'd not told them she was expecting again, thinking it too soon. She regretted now not making an exception, cutting the sadness with a bit of happy news. Henry wrapped an arm about her, kissing her brow, his beard grazing her cheek. He'd been made a ship's constable, issued a red-lettered guernsey too small for him. The bulky knit pulled across his broad shoulders and chest. Pale knobby wrists jutted between glove and cuff. He was to be paid seven pounds for patrolling the single-women's section, which appealed to the latent cop in him. He'd had other aspirations before settling upon an accountant's stool. There was a time when he thought himself bound for the opera stage, but that was years ago, before he knew what it took.

He kissed her again. "It's not forever."

"The new baby shall be walking," she said, rising up on her toes, waving wide arcs.

Behind her a woman said, "They cannot see us anymore. We're too far off."

Margaret turned to face the lady in the gaudy checked cape, a pixie of a woman with a sprinkle of reddish brown freckles to match her hair. Earlier, Margaret and her father had been standing on the wharf, monitoring the loading of their trunks. The cheeky woman sashayed up like a long-lost relation, saying, "Your wife has such a serious look about her, sir."

"I beg your pardon," Margaret had said. "You're addressing my *father*."

"You don't remember me," the woman said now, fingering a dangling ear bob.

"I do, madam." How could she forget?

"Where's your lovely da?"

"My father isn't sailing," said Margaret. "He was there to see us off."

"A pity," she said, turning to Henry, smiling, dimpling. "I'm Mrs. Martha Randolph, Constable. One of your charges. Who might the wee lady and gentleman be?"

Henry introduced the children, clapping a proud hand to John's shoulder, prying six-year-old Josephine from Margaret's leg. Margaret turned back to the watery haze that was her parents, spreading her feet for balance, her pretty going-away shoes pinching. She'd been told the river was calm. "Smooth as glass," her favorite uncle had claimed.

"Your children are charming, Mr. Oades," said Mrs. Randolph. Meaning, presumably, *Your wife is utterly lacking*. The woman sauntered off not holding the rail, flaunting her superior sea legs, a cockiness won by being on one's own, no doubt.

London was behind them now, the hawkers and filth, the soot-belching chimney pots, the piles of manure in the streets, the raw sewage in the black water. Margaret had visited once before. It's good to get to know other things and places, Henry had said on the train. She'd agreed aloud, but not in her heart. At thirty-two she was a contented homebody, John and Josephine's mum, Henry's wife. It was enough, more than enough. She knew all she needed to know about other things and places.

The tender rounded a rocky promontory. A row of small cottages went by, lighted from within, the mothers in them tucked away, minding their worlds, starting their suppers.

Henry spoke close to her ear, his breath warm as toast. "Think of the grand stories we'll tell in our sapless dotage."

She laughed a little. "Assuming we've the sap to see us to dotage."

He laughed too, releasing pent-up excitement. "That's my girl." He was as keen to go as she was not. He hoisted John and put a fist, a make-believe telescope, to John's eye. "Now watch for our ship, boy. She'll come into view any moment now."

A shout came from above. "Ahoy! There she is!"

The passengers stampeded toward the bow. Henry and the children fell in, joining the stream. Margaret stood rigid, the blood quickening in her veins. The *Lady Ophelia* was enormous, majestic. She came with sails as well as steam. Four towering masts swayed against a pewter sky, as if unstable.

Henry called to Margaret. She scanned the throng, spotting them ahead, larky children shrieking, Henry waving her forward. She gripped the burnished rail and began to inch her way toward them, the deck seesawing beneath her feet, her insides turning. "Like walking about in your own best room," the prevaricating uncle had said.

❖❖

THEY'D NOT BEEN on board the *Lady Ophelia* five minutes when John stumbled over a coil of rope and fell, scraping his knee. A uniformed officer was on him immediately, setting him to. The deck was positively littered with ropes, with winches and chains, drums and casks, all manner of object designed to draw a curious boy close to the rail. She'd need to watch the children every second of the day.

"There's some confusion in the ladies' section, sir," the officer said to Henry. "You're wanted straightaway."

The ship's doctor came up, offering Margaret and the children a tour in Henry's absence.

Henry cheerfully accepted on Margaret's behalf, before she could decide or get the first word out. They were led down a narrow corridor and shown the maple-paneled library, and then a card room, and yet another social room with a piano, an Oriental rug, and plush velvet drapery.

"It's all quite impressive," said Margaret, calmer now. It helped to be inside, away from the rail. By the time they reached the hectic dining hall she was feeling rather human again. The roast lamb smelled delicious. How novel to sit down to a meal she hadn't so much as pared a potato for.

Dr. Pritchard escorted them to their cabin afterward, passing the animal pen along the way, where chickens mingled with pigs, and sheep stood with sad-looking dewlappy cows.

"We've the best of butchers aboard," said the doctor.

"Nice piggy," said Josephine, squatting, putting herself face-to-snout with a homely sow having her brown supper.

The grizzled old sailor inside the pen approached her. "You mustn't ever utter the word *pig* on board a ship, lassie. 'Twill bring the worst of luck. You're to say *swiney* instead."

"Come away, Pheeny," said Margaret, giving the frightening man a stern eye.

At the opposite rail two young African sailors struggled to unlatch a wooden lifeboat. "They're required to practice," said the doctor, "before each sailing."

The inept lads looked no older than twelve or thirteen. She would have to study the latching apparatus and teach herself how to unlock and release a boat. God help them should they need to rely on tots.

The women's section was located just behind the animal pen. Male passengers, the doctor said, were strictly forbidden here. Margaret looked for Henry, but saw only women coming and going, old and young and in between, all laden with sacks and baskets. Off to the side, four women stood in a close huddle, Mrs. Randolph obviously presiding, one hand holding her fancy cape closed, the other gesturing wildly.

"Your husband will have earned his stipend," said the doctor, reading Margaret's mind.

She asked, "Do you have any idea when we might expect him?"

"I don't. Sorry." He brought them as far as their cabin door and left, saying that he was overdue.

She entered thinking, *Henry, Henry, wait until you see.* They'd both imagined a fairly spacious cabin, anticipated a small sitting area at least. In fact, the room offered only three places to sit: upon one of the two lower berths or upon the stool beneath the writing shelf. Lamps and washstand were bolted to the wall, virtually promising heavy seas. A shout came from outside, along with a grating rattle of chain. The ship shuddered and began to move. John begged to go to the bow, but Margaret said no, Father wouldn't find them in the crowd. They waited for Henry inside, the dim little cabin rocking like an elephant's cradle. When he didn't come, she prepared the children for bed. "It's been a long day, hasn't it?" She changed into her nightdress and climbed the six-rung ladder to her berth, crouching at the top, proceeding on her hands and knees. There was no other way. The Queen herself would access the bed with her bottom in the air. Below, John kept up a steady stream of chatter.

"We're bound to see whales tomorrow," he said. "And sea pigs too."

"The wobbly man told us not to say pig," said Josephine. "You're to say sea swiney instead."

"Porpoise then," said John. "That's their other name." Margaret fell asleep to their voices, dreaming that Henry had snuck off the ship and gone home on his own.

He showed up just after ten, whispering apologies. The captain had detained him, along with the other constables, treating them all to brandy and cigars. "The skipper's a dyed-in-the-wool bachelor," he said, "with no appreciation of a lovely girl waiting." He attempted to squeeze his large self in beside Margaret, but even with her backside flush against the wall, the berth would not hold them both. He climbed down and then up again, settling in the opposite upper with a loud sigh. They were to sleep like celibates for the duration then, something they'd never done. A lonely, hemmed-in feeling came over her. In the dark, she touched the ceiling, calculating the distance—eight inches, ten at the most. A near-term woman wouldn't fit. "'Night, Henry."

"It'll be all right, Meg," he said.

She closed her eyes. "It will."

❖❖

HENRY WAS CALLED away to duty the next afternoon, missing the last spit of England. Margaret bundled the children and took them up top. A few dozen others stood somberly at the rail, a westerly whipping their clothes, blowing hats from heads. Cornwall's jagged cliffs rose somewhere off the stern, no longer visible without a glass. Ahead lay nothing, absolutely nothing but an alarming expanse of churning sea and dull winter sky. A man began to play the anthem on his flute, slow and mournful. Some of the passengers locked arms and sang. The women sounded especially sad, their voices cracking. Margaret wasn't the only one, then. There were others whose bones wouldn't warm, others thinking: *What in God's name have we done?*

❖❖

THEY ENTERED the Bay of Biscay that evening and came along the edge of a storm. An hour into the weather, Henry complained of dizziness and blurred vision. Margaret went to fetch Dr. Pritchard, finding his tight quarters filled with patients. He gave her an orange and instructions to have Henry go up on deck. "I think you should come have a look," she said. The doctor promised he would first chance. But he didn't, and Henry was left to rally on his own.

On the sixth morning, in sight of the African coast, the seas placid, Margaret awoke feeling queer herself, quaky and nauseous. The doctor gave her an exasperated look when she came in, one that said: *You, again.* He asked straight off, "Are you in a family way?" Margaret said yes, and he shrugged, as if to say the symptoms were to be expected. He advised her to keep a full stomach.

"Much easier said than done," she said.

The doctor laughed, showing another side of himself. "You're a droll one. I like that."

Mrs. Randolph was passing the infirmary just as Margaret came out. "Mrs. Oades! You're well, I hope?"

"I am." The lady's eyes were glassy, fevered-looking. She was younger than Margaret first thought, probably Margaret's own age, give or take a year. "And you, madam?"

Mrs. Randolph put a hand to her middle. "The lamb stew of two nights ago nearly killed me. Mind what you eat."

"I shall," said Margaret. "Pardon my saying so, but you appear a bit peaked still. Perhaps you should see the doctor."

"I've seen the no-good," said Mrs. Randolph. "Once was enough, thank you. A baby died last evening, you know."

Margaret's eyes filled. "Oh, dear God. Of what?"

"Whatever the cause," said Mrs. Randolph, "the quack inside made not the first bloody attempt to save it. He's a dentist, by the by, not a bona fide *doctor.* The purser informed me." She touched Margaret's hand with trembling fingers, her voice softening. "The child was the mum's one and only. She is beside herself with grief, poor wretch. She's not left her berth even to relieve herself. Some of the others and I plan to attend the service at four. Will you come, Mrs. Oades?"

"Of course."

"We'll show she's not alone in the world, won't we?"

"Yes," said Margaret. "Though we won't begin to solace."

❖❖

THE BABY'S NAME was Homer Brown. Someone whispered, "Barely a year old."

Prayers were said, and then the shrouded child was let over the rail, into gray water, beneath a gray sky. The bereft mother faltered as the baby was released, grasping the rail in lieu of a husband. There was no man present, no kin at all.

Above, Margaret could hear the rowdy drunks in the men's hatch, Norsemen, a good many of them. Someone shouted in English, "Show a bit of respect for the baby's mum." But they did not let up for a moment.

Kindness Itself

MARGARET BEGAN to miscarry on the eleventh morning out. A strong wind had come up during the night and was only now abating. A keen howl continued, along with straining-timber noises, hideous, ungodly sounds to die by.

Henry brought her down to John's berth, and then went for Dr. Pritchard, returning instead with Mrs. Randolph. She carried a sack and something wrapped in blue flannel.

"Dr. Pritchard is ill," said Henry.

"He's utterly worthless is what he is," said Mrs. Randolph, placing the flanneled package upon Margaret's abdomen. "A brick hot from the oven," she said. "Just the thing."

Mrs. Randolph turned to Henry. "Take the children up top, why don't you?"

"Yes, do please, Henry," said Margaret.

Henry began snatching the children's clothes from pegs. He dressed them, consoling all the while. "Mum is fine, Mum is perfectly fine." With sleepy Josephine riding his hip, he bent and kissed Margaret's forehead. "I'm sorry, sweetheart," he whispered.

The ship rolled to port. A stir of odor rose from the chamber pot. Margaret turned to the wall, cramping still. The heat from the brick helped some. She drew up her knees, the sheet falling away, exposing her stained nightgown.

John cried out, "Mum's bleeding!"

"Lady's blood," said Henry in a low voice, though not so low as to frighten John with seriousness. "Nothing more natural, boy."

"Her eyes are closed," wailed John. "She's dead."

"She's not, son, she's not. She's resting. Let's let her be now."

She'd marry him all over, Margaret thought vaguely, for his fathering alone. "Go look for whales, John," she murmured. "This may be your lucky day."

Mrs. Randolph went to work the moment they left, preparing a basin of cool water and fishing a bar of scented soap from her bag. "Were you very far along?"

"Not quite three months." She'd lost two others. It never got easier. The first, a full-term boy, was stillborn. That was the unspeakable worst.

Mrs. Randolph sighed. "It's a terrible bleak feeling, isn't it?"

Margaret sat up and began to wash. "Have you children?"

"None living."

"I'm sorry."

"Tut, tut, Mrs. Oades. No need for the long pussy face. I've not dried on the vine quite yet." Through the wall came a male groan, a ghoulish sound. "So many ill," said Mrs. Randolph. "Especially down in the women's hatch. It isn't right the way they have us situated alongside the animals. The girl under me is ailing. Spinster sisters both have a fever."

"They should be quarantined," said Margaret.

"The ship is chock full. Where would you have them go?"

"Hammocks might be slung in Dr. Pritchard's quarters."

Mrs. Randolph swatted the air. "And have the quack incommoded? He'd force oranges on the poor women and then fault them for dying, the same way he blamed Homer's mum."

"He didn't," said Margaret.

"He did," said Mrs. Randolph. "The baby was fed tinned milk instead of mother's. He'd be alive if not for that. The charlatan said it straight to the grieving woman's face. I was there."

"How cruel," said Margaret.

"Men are."

"What would a dentist know about babies?"

"What would any man, Mrs. Oades? Now where might I find a fresh nightgown?"

Margaret pointed toward the corner. "In the trunk. Near the bottom."

Mrs. Randolph crossed the rolling floor, her arms spread for balance. She wore big, bold rings on both hands. Margaret had never owned a ring other than her wedding band. Her grandmother had been the same plain way, her mother was, all the aunts and cousins. Each generation bequeathed the austerity to the next, passed it sideways.

Mrs. Randolph knelt and opened the trunk, picking up the porcelain ginger jar inside. "Here's a lovely thing."

"A parting gift from my mum," said Margaret. "A keepsake from home. It's been sitting on her chimneypiece for as long as I can remember."

"My mum was the sentimental sort, too," said Mrs. Randolph. She gently returned the jar to the trunk, pulling out the other nightgown and bringing it to Margaret. There were bloodstains on that gown too, flecks of Margaret's mother's, thanks to a lost thimble. They'd both sewed furiously preparing for the journey, talking without respite as they worked, trying to get everything said.

Margaret slowly dressed herself. She and Henry had thought of names—Anne for a girl, after Margaret's mother, Walter for a boy, after Mr. Whitman. "The dentist couldn't have known for certain," she said, setting the cold brick on the floor and lying back again. "Any number of ailments might have taken the child."

Mrs. Randolph said softly, "Just rest, Mrs. Oades."

Margaret closed her eyes. Never name a child before the christening. She'd heard it said often enough, but didn't see how it mitigated the loss. Name or no name, Margaret loved them completely from the moment she knew. She fell asleep weeping, waking an hour later to Mrs. Randolph's close whisper.

"How is it now?"

Margaret turned to face her. "You are kindness itself."

Mrs. Randolph arched an eyebrow. "You didn't think so at first. Mounting your high horse the way you did down on the docks."

"Oh, forgive me, please. I shouldn't be so touchy about my age. My husband is nearly two years younger. He likes to tease."

"I assumed the gentleman was your da," said Mrs. Randolph. "I was merely making certain."

"Why?"

"I took a slight fancy to him."

"You don't mean it!" Margaret's unsuspecting papa would have fainted dead away had she made an overture. "He's an old man."

Mrs. Randolph shrugged. "I prefer a mature gentleman."

"My mum would have run you through with her umbrella."

They laughed a little, Mrs. Randolph's hand brushing close, her dazzling red-stone ring glinting. Margaret felt an odd urge to try it on for size. "Captain Burns would be more your sort," she said. "I happen to know he's an eligible bachelor."

Mrs. Randolph waved off the suggestion, pulling a hankie from a side pocket, wiping her perspiring brow and neck. "No, thank you. His breath is foul, and he has a tremendous backside for a man. It's every bit as broad as my own." Her watery eyes shifted about. "The wind has died down, hasn't it? Perhaps it's time I fetched your husband."

Margaret sat up a bit. "Please visit a moment longer."

The cabin air was inhospitable, as warm and muggy as a coop's. Still, Mrs. Randolph didn't hesitate. She pulled the stool close and sat, buffing the ring with a sleeve and splaying her fingers. "Pretty, isn't it? I noticed you looking."

"It's lovely. A ruby?"

"A garnet, actually. You should see how it does in a good light." She tugged the ring free and pushed it down Margaret's middle finger. "There now. Hold your hand to your cheek." Margaret shyly complied. "Yes, like that. Isn't it striking next to your dark hair? Christmas is coming. I'll make a mention to Mr. Oades."

"He'd think us both daft," Margaret said, studying the ring. Henry was always saying that she was a natural, a born beauty. She denied that she was, though of course she liked to hear him say it. Oh, she wasn't a scare. Her features were arranged nicely enough. She was a tall woman, a bit too tall, though she walked erect as she'd been taught, in fear of growing a hump. Her wasp waist, considering the children, drew the occasional flattering comment from other women. Her eyes were clear, more gray than blue, and her complexion was even, unblemished. But her mannish hands weren't right. The knuckles were too large, unworthy of the ring's glamour.

"You may borrow it one evening," said Mrs. Randolph.

Margaret removed the ring and returned it. "Oh, I couldn't possibly."

"It was given to me by a circus performer," said Mrs. Randolph. "A wild-animal trainer, a Persian living in Paris, a splendid masculine specimen."

"How romantic," said Margaret. "And the blue ring? A sapphire, is it?"

Mrs. Randolph nodded, smiling as if with fond memory. "An English gent surprised me with this one, a charming old dear from London. Rich as Midas. George. I don't recall the surname. We'd just been to the Lyceum to see Sarah Bernhardt onstage."

"Sarah Bernhardt. Really."

"It was the highlight of my life. She sleeps in a satin-lined coffin, you know."

"I didn't know."

"Am I tiring you, Mrs. Oades?"

"Not in the least," said Margaret. "Was she as vulgar as they say?"

Mrs. Randolph leaned in. "She was *sensual.* She embodied the *complete* woman, if you know what I mean." She closed her eyes and threw back her head, embracing the air, an invisible lover. A warm flutter passed through Margaret. She felt herself blushing. Mrs. Randolph let out a dreamy moan, her back arching, the stool teetering. She toppled off sideways, hitting her head with a solid thud.

"Mrs. Randolph! Are you all right?"

The cabin door flew open. Storming in ahead of the children, clumsy Henry nearly stepped on Mrs. Randolph's outstretched hand. She rolled out of his range and stood awkwardly, brushing herself off, starting to laugh. Margaret laughed too. She couldn't help herself.

Henry stood staring, looking as if he'd happened upon a cell of loons. "I heard the noise. What are you up to here? I thought my wife had fallen out of bed."

"It was nothing," said Mrs. Randolph, breathing hard. "Just a bit of cheer."

She left a moment later, with a sisterly kiss to Margaret's cheek and a promise to look in on her later. When Mrs. Randolph knocked at two, Margaret was sleeping, and Henry didn't wake her.

"I hadn't the heart," he said.

They put in at Malta the next morning. Margaret looked for Mrs. Randolph at breakfast, but then the ship began taking on coal, a filthy process. A dry black dust rained down on the decks, their faces, their clothes. She and the children were forced below because of it. Soon after leaving tranquil Malta they were in rolling seas again. Henry ventured out toward the end of the day, bringing back cheese and warm milk that was to be their supper. The captain had ordered the decks cleared and the hatches closed.

"It's expected to get worse before it gets better," said Henry, breaking up the cheese with his hands.

They remained penned for the better part of two days. It fell to Henry to dump the pot and fetch the food. Margaret stayed with the children, entertaining them with stories and spillikins, a simple game when played on land. Players take turns selecting a jackstraw from a scattered pile, losing if another straw is disturbed. Margaret should have known that the ship's movement would spoil the game, although the children didn't seem to mind. They spent hours playing, riding John's lower berth together.

On the third morning Henry returned later than usual from his constable's duties. "Your Mrs. Randolph is gravely ill, I'm afraid."

Margaret stood to leave. "You'll mind the children?"

"I'm sorry, Meg. I cannot allow you to go. She might be contagious."

"Think of all she's done for me, Henry. I'll stay no more than a minute, I promise. I'll simply peek in to show I've come."

He shook his head. "I'm sorry."

She kicked the stool instead of him. "Imagine my preventing *you* from going to a friend in need!" John quit playing suddenly, gathering up the jackstraws. Josephine began nibbling her thumb, her wary eyes darting from parent to parent.

"Never mind," Margaret said to the children. "Carry on with your game. Or would you rather a story? Shall I read some *Tom Sawyer*?" Henry hovered too close, looking infuriatingly contrite. There was no place to turn with her anger.

❖❖

MRS. RANDOLPH DIED the next day. Margaret left John and Josephine with Henry and attended the service alone, joining a clutch of women on the lower deck. The cause of death was internal convulsions. So said the dentist. He volunteered the information straightaway, before anyone might think to inquire.

"I did everything within my power," he said.

Margaret spoke up. "She didn't respond to the orange cure?"

The dentist turned, glaring at her, drawing up his collar. As if her remark had sharpened the day's gray bite. "I beg your pardon?"

"Mrs. Randolph complained to you of a stomach disorder early on, did she not?"

The dentist cupped a hand to his ear, feigning deafness. Margaret was about to repeat herself when Mrs. Randolph's sailcloth-wrapped body arrived. She made a heartbreakingly paltry package. Margaret wept. There was so little to her in death.

Two African sailors brought her. The somber, broad-beamed Captain Burns—the bounder who'd allowed the dentist to pose as physician—followed behind, Bible in hand. Margaret bowed her head and prayed curses. *God blast them both.*

When she lifted her eyes, the sailors were in position at the rail. The Africans shivered in the damp air, awaiting their cue from the captain, who appeared impervious, both to weather and death. Almighty Burns began with a great heave of his shoulders, a world-weary glance skyward. A minute was given Mrs. Randolph, two at the most.

"We therefore commit Martha's body to the deep. . . ."

The mourners were forced aside to allow the crew room. Her body fell with a flat splash into the choppy sea, floating only a moment inside the weighted shroud.

"Looking for the general Resurrection in the last day, and the life of the world to come, through our Lord Jesus Christ, at whose second coming in glorious majesty to judge the world, the sea shall give up her dead. . . ."

All sails were full. She was already gone, behind them. Somewhere off the stern, in the Mediterranean Sea, east of Malta, out of sight of land. Margaret imagined meeting Mrs. Randolph's relations one day, or George from London, and having only these few unlovely facts to offer.

A week later, approaching Aden, Margaret pulled her own aching tooth with a string. She'd extract every tooth in her head, she told Henry, before she'd betray Mrs. Randolph by seeking out Dr. Pritchard.

"What does one have to do with the other?" said Henry. "Besides, you hardly knew the poor woman."

Margaret tried, but she couldn't make him understand an affection forged in a single morning. The small transactions between women, particularly mothers, cannot adequately be explained to a man. Some, like hers with Mrs. Randolph, will bind women for life.

❖❖

CHRISTMAS CAME. Carols were sung. A plum pudding was served. They were nearly halfway quit of this wretched, murderous bark.

Wellington
February, 1891

SOMETHING HAD GNAWED a shilling-size hole straight through the trunk. Margaret stepped back and gave the contents tentative pokes with the umbrella. Nothing stirred. The vermin was gone. She leaned in again and unfolded the teal-blue arrival frock, a ridiculously expensive thing with exquisite glass buttons. Her family slept on, oblivious to the shouts and clomping boots above, the lovely symphony of men preparing to anchor. At her back, Henry shifted fitfully, thrashing his sheet to the floor. He'd been seasick two days running now. She retrieved the sheet and covered him, feeling his warm forehead, stroking his shoulder. "Today's the day, dear heart."

He murmured something unintelligible and turned on his side.

"I'll wake you when it's time," she said, returning to the business of their wardrobe, brimming with energy and health. She felt exhilaratingly liberated, like a servant just released from indenture. Let the sailors request her assistance with the heavy mooring lines. She'd have a go at it.

She roused the children before they were ready and dressed them as she would two posts, putting them in the twin costumes sewn up for the occasion, black-and-white-checked ensembles with sweet sailor collars. "Perfect," she said. "Now make believe you've just been introduced to the governor."

John made a lackluster bow and sat back down on the edge of his berth. Josephine curtsied and did the same. Margaret clapped her hands sharply. "On your feet. Today's the day. What did Tom Sawyer say to his mates? Shake out that maintogalans'l! Sheets and braces! *Now,* my hearties!" She bent and kissed them, turning her cheek to their cool foreheads. "Time for breakfast, my darlings."

"What about poor dad?" said John.

"He'll come round once on land, son. You'll see."

Up top the warm wind lifted Margaret's hat from her head. Perspiration streamed from her temples, her underarms, pasting her fine new overcorset to her flesh.

"My word," she said, coming abreast of the first officer. "Such unusual weather."

"Not at all, madam," he said. "'Tis summer here, you know."

She hadn't known. Nor had Henry. He was dressed when they returned, decked out in the handsome wool purchased with the governor's welcoming party in mind. Even now he was unhealthily florid, panting.

"You'll roast alive," said Margaret.

"I've nothing else," he said, gesturing toward the corner. The cabin boys had already come for the trunk.

She brushed a bit of lint from his sleeve. "Well, never mind then. We've arrived. That's all that matters, isn't it? Tonight we'll enjoy supper in our own cozy flat. Won't that be lovely at long last? I might start a pot of cow-heel soup if we're settled early enough and there's a decent butcher on hand. How does that strike you?"

He touched her cheek. "You're the best girl."

❖❖

THE *LADY OPHELIA* was anchored some distance from the wharf. A queue to board her tenders wound around one deck and down a flight. The line moved at an encouragingly swift pace and then abruptly stalled.

Margaret gazed landward. After eight weeks aboard, the Arctic steppes would have been a welcoming sight. Still, she hadn't expected such an idyllic storybook place. They were moored in a perfect bowl. Small houses dotted the rocky shore. Farther back stood lush blue-green hills.

A man spoke behind her. "The head of the fish. It's hardly a fair description, is it?"

Margaret turned, smiling at the bespectacled officer. "Sir?" She knew him by sight, not by name. He'd been particularly kind to the children on board, winning them over with small treats from his pocket.

"North Island is shaped rather like a fish," he said, "or so the Maori legend goes. Wellington is its head, the sweetest part."

"Maori, sir?"

"The indigenous peoples, madam. Did you not attend the captain's lecture Friday last? He went into some detail on the subject."

"I'm afraid not," said Margaret. She'd had no interest in anything the captain had to say. "I couldn't leave the children." The officer tipped his cap and wished her good day, good luck.

To the west a double rainbow arced, a thrilling spectacle, the best of all omens. "Lovely," she murmured, more to herself. Henry had been right. It *is* good to get to know other things and places. Beside her, Henry bowed over the rail, as if about to pray or die.

"Why not take off your coat?" He shook his head, not opening his eyes. She gave him a pet. "Just think of the luxury coming. I've been dreaming of a real bath for weeks now." The queue started up again. He pulled himself from the rail and shepherded his family forward.

Boarding was a tricky proposition, given the swell in the harbor. The secured tender came and went sideways, banging against the ship's hull. The tender's skipper stood waiting inside the narrow open boat. Fashionable ladies stepped down cautiously, clumsily, into his large grimy hands. Margaret stood single-file behind John and Josephine, who were behind the corpulent vicar and his wife, and about to go on. In the next moment, Henry made a strangled noise and vomited between ship and tender, into the water and down his brass-buttoned front.

The children cried out in unison. "Dad!" The mangy skipper snatched them up, John first, and then Josephine, sitting them down hard on the tender's wooden bench. He beckoned 'to Margaret, growling that he didn't have all day. Margaret pulled Henry free of the soiled coat. They boarded the tender, she shakily, bulky coat and satchel on one arm.

Onshore the soft ground swayed. Her legs wobbled, felt about to give way. People swarmed, meeting in raucous reunion, kissing and hugging. Margaret and Henry scanned the wharf in all directions, looking for the governor's welcoming committee. They stood for half an hour, smiling at various clutches of well-dressed men. No one approached except a yellow-eyed mongrel with an oozing gash in place of an ear. Josephine stood in the dog's path, howling. Margaret put herself between child and beast and stamped her feet. The dog fled. Josephine blubbered on. Henry collapsed onto a cask. "Where could they be?"

"Never mind," said Margaret. She adjusted the brim of his good hat, shielding his face from the beating sun. "Stay with the children. I'll find a hack." She bent and whispered to John and Josephine. "Keep an eye on your dad." They gave dull nods, John boring a finger into a red ear, Josephine snuffling up, her nose running like an urchin's. It was just as well that they were on their own. The governor's pomp would have done her family in completely.

She headed toward the road, asking the first woman she encountered, a plump lady in an everyday dress, about to drive off in an open rig. "Oh, I don't imagine you'll find a hack this time of day," the woman said. "They'll still be in church, or gambling their babies' milk money away. One of the two."

Margaret thanked her and turned to resume her search.

The woman called after her. "I can take you where you're going."

The unexpected kindness brought Martha Randolph to mind. "We'll gladly pay."

The woman laughed. "Did you bring anything for bunions?"

"Sorry, madam. No."

"You'll owe me then," said the woman, introducing herself. Mrs. Anamim Bell.

"A lovely name," said Margaret. "Biblical."

"It's a horrid name," said Mrs. Bell. "You'll call me Mim or I won't take you."

"Mim, then. Thank you, Mim. Thank you very much indeed. And you'll call me Margaret. Or Meg if you prefer." Her earlier energy had leaked away. She was tired now, wishing only to be settled. And here came her bedraggled family. "My husband, Henry Oades. My children, John and Josephine. We call her Pheeny."

"The poor lambs," said Mrs. Bell. "Step up now. You'll send for your things. I know a reliable man. Though you won't get him to work on the Sabbath."

So be it, thought Margaret. They'd make do one night, sleep in their underclothes. All she asked for was a stable floor and a stationary bed. She sat up front, next to Mrs. Bell. Henry dozed behind them, an arm curled about the limp children.

"You're nearly dead, aren't you," said Mrs. Bell. "Poor girl."

Margaret smiled, beginning to drowse. She pictured a nice big bed with crisp dry linens, her husband sleeping beside her for the first time in months. Supper first, though. "Can you recommend a butcher, Mrs. Bell?"

"Can you recommend a butcher, *Mim.*"

"Of course. Sorry. *Mim.*"

"The most handy is a blackguard from whom I wouldn't buy a bone for my dog."

"Oh, dear."

"Jones is the best of the lot. His gristle at least comes with a morsel of flesh. You'll want to keep watch on his fat thumb, though. His wife's as well. They cheat for sport here."

Mim began to list the town's shops, describing the goods within each, naming the slippery-fingered sneak-thieves to be avoided. "You'll find everything you need, but it's not like home."

"I don't imagine," said Margaret, fighting to stay awake. The woman's drone would put an insomnious owl to sleep.

After a while, Mim asked, "What's your man to do here?"

"He's been asked to take over the new accounting system at Her Majesty's distillery."

Mim nodded. "Quite the cap feather for one so young."

Henry cleared his throat. Margaret turned around. He smiled, waggling bushy eyebrows, vindicated. Margaret smiled too, rolling her eyes.

They came over a wooden bridge, passing a broad orchard. "What's grown here?"

"Pip fruit, mainly," said Mim, "Apples and grapes. And tedium."

⟡⟡

THEY ARRIVED in late afternoon, tying up the horse in front of a dull brown building with small windows. A cheese shop and a sneak-thief bookbinder occupied the ground floor. "His paste doesn't last a week," said Mim. The flats were located above the shops, eight homes in all. Mim offered a hand with the children and satchels, bustling about, not waiting for an answer. Margaret started up the building's stone steps behind John, thinking mainly about relieving herself.

Theirs was number four, two steep stories up. John opened the front door. "It reeks," he said, looking around.

He was right. The air was stale and musty. A chamber pot sat in full view, in it a desiccated mess. Margaret scraped the pot along the gritty floor with her foot, moving it behind the coarse curtain separating the sleeping alcove. She summoned the children, saying don't look, feeling their foreheads for fever as they squatted, opening her reticule then, dealing out a toilet square each. An aunt had presented her with a generous supply before sailing, saying you never know what you'll find. Margaret took a square for herself and loosened her drawers, hovering over the putrid pot. Henry the camel feigned no urgent need, shy of Mim Bell, no doubt.

Henry led the tour. The main room contained a green divan, an empty curio cabinet, and three straight-back chairs, one with elegant tapered legs. There were no books, no paintings, no vases for flowers. The stove was greasy, the tub beside it filthy with private hairs and insect husks. There was no oil for the lamps. The kitchen curtains were dreadful, dirty and tattered, and they were one bed short. Margaret hung her head after a brief inspection, defeated. Henry came to her, springy, as if with a second wind. It was how they were, how they'd always been. When one tottered, the other rallied.

"We'll hire a girl," he said. "There's no need to lift a finger."

His beard was crusted with salt; his fetid breath turned her stomach and weakened her knees. "I'm a bit dizzy," she said.

Mim produced a hankie and began flogging the worn divan. "Sit now, why don't you?"

"Just for a moment perhaps," said Margaret, grateful. "I seem made of rubber."

"Mr. Bell and I arrived five years ago Saturday," said Mim. "I remember the wretched day all too well. It's the queerest feeling being on land again, the bobbing and weaving, the addled thinking. It'll be with you awhile, I'm afraid. You'll go to take the bread from the oven and find the raw loaf still sitting in the bowl."

"*Five* years," said Margaret. "I cannot begin to imagine."

Henry dipped behind the curtain and picked up the chipped chamber pot. "Come along," he said to the children. "We'll let Mum have a rest." The three traipsed out. Mim followed on their heels. "I'm just round the corner," she said before leaving.

Margaret closed her eyes, stupid with exhaustion. Moments later, on the other side of the wall, there came a clatter of pans, an angry man bellowing, "Get to it!"

A woman screeched, "Not on *your* bloody say-so." He was a toad, an idler, a no-good. Her mother was right about him. She was a cow, a common draggletail. His brother was right about *her*. Margaret removed the pretty slipper meant to impress the governor and threw it against the wall. The man sneezed a blustery sneeze. Then all went silent. She retrieved the shoe and closed her eyes again.

She had wondered about the neighbors, never having lived where people were above, below, all around. She'd looked forward to it actually, had imagined a warren of like-minded women her own age, all helping one another, exchanging recipes and such. She nodded off, her head heavy as a melon. The next thing she knew a woman was letting herself in, butting the door open with a broad hip, a bulging sack in one arm, a limp tick folded over the other. Margaret came to disoriented, assuming herself at sea. "Hello."

The woman grinned. "Your boy happened upon a little playmate."

"He's a friendly one," murmured Margaret. She recognized the moldy place now, the stout woman with the overbite. "Where are they, Mim?"

"In the yard. No need to worry. Your mister's minding them just fine. Lucky you, landing such a prize. Otherwise you'd string him up here and now, wouldn't you?" Mim proffered the sack. "Give us a hand, will you?"

They laid out the supplies on the kitchen table, their backs to the one dirty window. Mim had brought back a sleeping pallet, lamp oil, tea and supper things. There were cheeses, sausages, toffees for the children, and a bottle of red wine.

"You shouldn't have," said Margaret, overwhelmed. "You're much too generous." The cracked linoleum rolled beneath her feet. The cupboards shifted with every turn of her head. "You'll stay for supper, won't you?" It shamed her to offer hospitality from such a cesspit. "If you can bear it, that is."

"Don't be discouraged," said Mim, slicing the sausage, laying it out on the clean plate she'd thought to bring. "Elbow grease is all. A good scrubbing, a new curtain or two."

"I suppose," said Margaret, looking about. There was nothing to see out the filmy panes but brick. "There's a horrid smell."

"Like mutton left cold and forgotten," said Mim.

"More on the order of entrails," said Margaret. "An old goat's viscera."

"Or an old man's work drawers," said Mim.

Margaret laughed. "After a bout with the trots."

Mim pulled a corkscrew from her pocket. "A wee drop to sweeten the stench?"

"No, thank . . . yes, thank you. Thank you very much indeed. It couldn't hurt."

Mim took a throttlehold on the bottle. "You're dying to wring his dear neck, aren't you?"

The children were coming up the stairs, chattering in healthy voices. Margaret thought yellow curtains might be nice, a cheery color to stand in for the light.

Mim wrestled with the corkscrew, perspiration collecting above her lip. "You'd like nothing better than to put a pillow to his darling face and murder him in his sleep for carting you and the little ones halfway round the world."

Henry came in. Mim's scorched cheeks blazed brighter with embarrassment. "A figure of speech, Mr. Oades."

"She's offered to wring my neck for less," he said, folding an arm about Margaret, kissing her temple. "Haven't you?"

"I don't recall it," Margaret said, swaying against his side. If only the dingy room would still itself. He spoke close to her ear.

"Imagine us crabbed old sots before the fire, telling our spoiled grandchildren about the days spent here." He bent over in parody, an ancient on a walking stick. He felt and looked feverish, in need of a bath and sleep. He took a bit of cut sausage and put it to her lips. "Have a taste, Granny. Or haven't you any teeth to enjoy it?"

She ate the sausage to please him, to allow him to quit the nonsense.

"It's quite delicious, Grandpapa."

He kissed her again. "It's not forever."

Mim said, "I didn't speak to my husband for the longest time after we came."

Margaret looked at Henry. "Do you promise?"

Wellington
March, 1892

Dearest Parents,

We have moved at long last, loved ones. Henry borrowed a dray from Mr. Sweeny. ("Leased," I should say. The miserly man charged us for the use of his rickety conveyance & sickly mule. He wasn't in need of either at the time, I might add.) But no matter, we have arrived. We have traded our cramped flat for a lovely cottage by the water & are glad for having done so. There's not another soul within sight. Instead of rowing neighbors one hears only the rushing river and the wind blowing through the trees. It is the perfect tucked-away place.

We are swiftly moving into autumn, though our world is still abloom. The former tenants, Dr. Garrett and his wife (returned to England due to old-fashioned homesickness), left healthy roses behind, yellow mainly, & some red. We have gardenias as well, sweet violets, fuchsia & blue hydrangea as big as a baby's head!

The cottage itself sits upon a gentle rise & is quite suitable, but for an infestation of moths. Henry treated the problem with turpentine, but it has not done much good. He says I must give it time. (I say I must give it every last frock!) Too, we've a leak directly over our bed. Henry promised to repair the roof, but has yet to get round to it. I lack the heart to keep *after him. We would have remained in town, had he had his way. Now that we're here he is obligated to rise long before the sun & start out in the dark, on primitive clay roads.*

You asked about Henry's duties. He is the one to calculate the distillery's every last expense, which is no small feat. It is not merely a matter of keeping count of the pencils & pens & kegs. He must also keep a close eye on the workers. If a man is tardy or loafs, Henry must determine and assign a cost. He likens Mr. Freylock, his supervisor, to the English master at Kings School who left him in charge of the younger boys & then popped in every ten minutes to see that Henry was running things properly. You know the sort. Henry tolerates Mr. Freylock far better than I would.

'Tis the mud season. Henry will often stay in town after a big rain, rather than risk becoming stuck. Then too, he is both bakeryman & dairyman, as no one will make deliveries this far north. He's made his fair share of sacrifice. I shall learn to live in harmony with the moths & drips. The tranquillity is more than worth it.

Mum, I picture you reading this letter aloud to Dad. You are situated on the green chair, cup at your left, the tea in it gone cold. Dad sits across from you, old Grazer snoring at his feet. Have I drawn an accurate picture? Is Dad grousing: "Flowers & moths & muddy roads! Will she ever come round to mentioning the children?"

Patience, Father dear. (Is he rolling his eyes to the heavens now?)

By now you have received the photograph. It is not a bad likeness, though the sun was in our eyes. You must forgive my lunatic's smile. Our precious twins put it there. (Martha in Henry's arms, Mary in mine.) They are the dearest of baby girls. I cannot wait for you to meet them. They are feeding well & sleeping four hours at a stretch. Do put the photograph in a safe place, by the by, as we shall not be sitting for another. Every mother wants a photograph to send home, & so the photographer gets away with charging a ludicrous fee. "A solid gold frame should be included in the price," I said. The pompous dandy suggested I take my business elsewhere, knowing full well I wouldn't, as he has no competitors worth considering in Wellington. At the end, I found myself cajoling him, much to my shame. I not only paid his ridiculous fee, but laid out supper as well! The blackguard enjoyed my kowtowing. He relished every last minute of it.

Were you shocked to see how Josephine has shot up? She so appreciated the embroidered apron her granny sent, but is close to outgrowing it already. Such a joy she is, & such a fine & willing helper! Sunday last she prepared a potted hare that I'd be proud to serve the governor. I'm enclosing the recipe. The more butter you add the better it will taste. It should keep nicely in a cool place for several weeks. Her sewing is coming along as well. Pheeny shall make a splendid wife one day. I'd worry were she ten years older. Dr. Garrett's handsome daughter married a local lad. It broke Mrs. Garrett's heart to leave her child so far behind. I had her to tea before they sailed. She had quite the long sob, believing she'd never see her daughter again. I offered to keep an eye on the young woman, but what good does that do Mrs. Garrett, really? It's an unnatural business, putting impossible distance between parent and child. I, for one, have had my fill of it. I plan to stay put once home. You have my word, & Henry's word as well.

John is kept in books & so is thriving. He is particularly keen on the stars & planets these days & has recently struck up a correspondence with a member of the Royal Astronomy Society. He'll no doubt meet boys his own age once enrolled at the new school. In the meantime, our son's closest chum is a pensioner of eighty-four!

Good news: You'll remember my mentioning Anamim Bell, the sailmaker's wife. I am happy to report that she has talked her husband into moving up this way. Mim is grand company. She is cheery & not one bit overdone about it. She vows we shall sit our husbands down & teach them to play euchre. Now if only I might magic you dears over for a hand or two. I miss you both so. As of today, ten months and three weeks remain. Pray the time flies.

> *Your always loving & devoted daughter,*
> *Margaret*

◇◇

On Wednesday Henry returned home with a bottle of wine and a sack of hard candies for the children. Margaret followed him into their bedroom, where he hung his hat and coat, and followed him out again. "What's the occasion?"

He laughed a nervous laugh and ran a hand through his hair. "You'll never guess."

In the front room he bent over the babies in their cradles and made foolish noises. John came in, bombarding Henry. "Dad! I've taught the dogs seven new tricks. Come round back and see." Josephine continued laying out the soup plates. She called to her father, competing for attention.

"Give your father a moment's peace," said Margaret. She met his eyes. "What is it, Henry?"

His gaze shifted to the ceiling. "I've been promoted."

"Oh, Henry. What does that mean precisely?"

"It means I've 'a dozen men below me now. It means another ten quid per week."

"In terms of time," she said. "Tell me we're not staying on indefinitely."

John and Josephine stood silently watching. Henry took his place at the table and motioned the children to take theirs. "It's an honor, Meg."

"I've no doubt," said Margaret, striving for calm. She brought out pea soup and a platter of ham and sat. "Let us be family now." It was what she said every evening. Henry and the children bowed their heads for grace. "Are we staying on, Henry? Just tell us that much."

"Not indefinitely," he said, looking up briefly.

"Oh, Henry." Margaret bowed her head and pressed her fingers to her burning eyes.

The twins were three months old now, a demanding set at times. The move from the flat to the cottage had been fraught with frustrations great and small. Granted, she was tired, overly prone to dark moods these days. Still. They'd been less than a year shy of their return. How could he?

❖❖

"A MAORI LAD was publicly flogged today," Henry said after grace.

"That's hardly a subject for the table," said Margaret. It was like him to negate one problem with another more dramatic.

John's face was vivid with interest. "What was his crime?"

"Please," said Margaret. Mary started up, the fussier of the two. Margaret went to her and rocked the cradle with her foot.

"He pinched a keg of rum," said Henry. "Or so it was charged. He didn't look the sort. A grand display was made of it. Several dozen Maori were lined up, forced to witness the lashing. As a lesson, I presume. A tribesman from the church was there. The lovely tenor? What's his name, Meg?"

Mary squawked, waking Martha. "Bring a cross lass to me," Henry said. Margaret brought Mary, intentionally handing over the more sour-smelling and cranky. He held her in the crook of one arm, smiling down, transformed as always. "Turns out the lad was a royal. The governor says there's bound to be trouble."

"That's enough now," said Margaret.

❖❖

"FORGIVE ME, HENRY," she said next morning. He was dressing in the far corner by wavering lamplight. Her voice gave him a start. "I was purely selfish."

He came to her just as she sat up, cracking his forehead against hers, swearing. "Christ! Hardheaded woman."

"Irreverent man! You shall be struck down by lightning."

Both laughed softly. She stroked his beard, the back of his bristly neck. "I'm quite proud of you."

He took her face between his hands and kissed her lips. "And I of you, my girl."

"I'll post your letter this morning," he said, standing, pulling his coat from the peg.

"I need to add a few lines," she said.

He nodded. "I'll wait, then."

Margaret hugged herself, thinking of home. "What shall I say about our return?"

"I wish I could tell you. I'll know more next month."

"Forever?" she asked.

He bent and kissed her again. "Not forever."

PS: We have only just learned of Henry's promotion to senior inspector. He has twelve men below him now, two of whom have just arrived. It is an unexpected honor, one that requires an extended stay here. We hope to start for home before next Christmas, but no assurances have been made as of yet. I shall write again soon with the particulars.

Taken

T HE IRRITABLE BABIES kept Margaret from going herself. She sent John in his dog cart to Mim's, returning the six borrowed eggs, plus one as interest. A note went along, telling of the promotion.

It's an honor, indeed, though I wish with all my heart we were preparing to sail. This morning I could no longer hear my father's voice in my head.

She'd stopped writing and fed the note to the fire, starting another. You'd never hear such sob-baby blather leaving Mim's pen or lips. "I'll escape this godforsaken place when Cyril croaks," Mim once said. "Not a day before. There's no point in stewing in the meantime."

Mim rode out two days later, her dull-witted boy, Oscar, driving. Margaret was watching for Henry at the front window. She came out to greet them, lantern in hand. The reddening sky was already fading.

Something spooked Mim's horse, causing it to rear and Oscar

to shriek. Mim seized the abandoned reins, yanking hard. Margaret took hold of the cheekpiece and tied the shuddering animal to a fence post, smiling up at Mim's only child. "Hello, Oscar. Fine evening, isn't it?"

Oscar stared off into the middle distance, a thin stream of drool coursing from the corner of his slack mouth. He was eight now, a stocky boy, too fond of boiled sweets, and fearful of everything, horses in particular.

Mim, as myopic as any mother, thought him exceptional. "You should have seen him coming over," she said. "Calm as a rutabaga, weren't you, sweetheart? And every bit as brave."

Margaret took his slippery fat hand and assisted him down from the open rig. "What do we have here?" she asked of the dish towel knotted at his neck.

"He fancies himself a cowboy," said Mim, climbing down. The mare let out an odd squeal, straining against her tether, baring yellow teeth. Mim slapped a broad rump. "Mind your manners."

"You're a fine cowboy indeed," said Margaret. She stroked Oscar's round head, a terrain of scabs and bumps she couldn't see.

He thrust out his chest and bowed his chubby legs. "I'm off to America."

It may have been the longest sentence he'd ever uttered in her presence. Margaret wrapped an arm about him, grateful for her sound-minded children. "You're not sailing straightaway, are you, Sir Cowboy? I've a lovely goulash cooking. You'll stay for supper, won't you?"

"Grub," said Oscar, shrugging off her hand.

"That's a cowboy's supper," said Mim, rolling her eyes. "He's been down on the docks with his dad all week. There's a Yank ship in port. The blokes sport with him, fill his ears with cowboy rubbish."

Oscar drew an imaginary pistol from an imaginary holster and aimed thumb and forefinger, shooting first his mother, and then Margaret. Mim clutched her heart and reeled a bit.

Margaret laughed and passed the lantern to him. "Lead us in, cowboy. I've grub burning on the stove."

"You're in jolly spirits, considering," said Mim.

"Jolly enough," said Margaret. "What choice is there, really?"

"Have you considered returning early with the children?"

"Certainly not." Though Margaret had, privately. Yesterday while shelling peas she'd given the idea long selfish thought. She'd imagined herself standing on the dock, the ship bobbing in the bright distance. She saw the leather trunk being loaded onto the tender. She saw too her morose and confused children, falling on Henry, refusing to be separated.

Margaret and Mim started up the path behind Oscar. Mim caught Margaret's hand, swinging to and fro, like a schoolgirl. "It shall be a sad day for me when you go."

Margaret squeezed Mim's hand. "Misery loves her company, doesn't she?"

✧✧

JOSEPHINE STOOD at the stove, humming under her breath. "Auntie Mim! I didn't know you were coming."

"Hello, my darling girl." Mim came into the light, struggling from her too small coat. "Your lamb smells divine. Where's your brother? He promised to show Oscar a rope trick."

"He's round back with the dogs." Josephine left the stove, picking up her embroidery and settling on the divan. "We're training them for the circus. I'm to hold the hoop. I'll wear a special costume done up in spangles."

Margaret smiled, picturing her freckled twig-thin girl done up in spangles. Josephine gave a haughty toss of braids, as if reading her mother's thoughts. "We plan to make our fortune."

Mim gave Oscar a swat to his trousers. "Run along outside now, and I do mean *run,* precious slug. It'll do you some good."

"I'm hankering for grub," said Oscar, moving out of her reach.

"Hanker outside then," said Mim.

Determined Oscar started toward the goulash, like a poky sow toward her trough. "I reckon it's too dark out."

Mim took him by the shoulders and turned him about. "I don't reckon the dark will harm you any."

"Grub shan't be long," said Margaret.

Oscar took the lantern and shuffled outside, calling John's name.

Mim went to the babies, asleep in their cradles. "Oh, the loves," she whispered, gazing down. "What I'd give for a tidy girl."

Margaret came up behind. "Their ears are tidier, certainly. Was Oscar born with dirty ears?"

"Filthy. Chock full of crusty muck, his nostrils no better."

Margaret shook her head. "I don't know what it is. John was a little wax factory from the start." Martha suckled in her sleep, creating a sweet milky foam. Their beauty never ceased to amaze. There was no love like it, not in this world.

"And mine?" asked Josephine.

"You were born with angel ears," said Margaret.

Josephine nodded, as if to say "of course."

"What I'd give," murmured Mim. "Every mother needs a girl of her own." She bent and lightly traced the rim of Mary's perfect pink ear. "Where's the promoted one?"

"He's due any time. Come sit. The water's on. We'll have a quick hand and a cup."

At the table, Margaret dealt a hand of euchre to Mim and herself, and two invisible players. The dogs started up a frantic barking just as she turned up trump, spades, the jack, right bower. Mim glanced at the dark window. "Henry?"

Margaret was already standing, collecting the cards, returning them to the case. Henry would come in ravenous as always. She was searching out the jam when the shots rang out, silencing the dogs. The jar slipped from her hand, shattering. People were coming, heavy footsteps pounding the earth. Mim rose from the table, drawing a long breath of audible panic. Josephine sat suspended, her eyes unnaturally brilliant, needle drawn up. The front door blew open, driving in a raft of brown-skinned males.

Josephine cried out. "Mama!"

Margaret shouted, her heart roaring with fear, "Into the bedroom!" But there was no time.

The Maori filled the room, brandishing rifles and whips, a hideous tattooed four, with mouths yawning wide, tongues wagging obscenely.

The babies wailed in high-pitched unison. Josephine still hadn't moved. Margaret crooned to her petrified girl, her voice crackling. "Don't be afraid, darling. Mama's here. Father's coming." *Please, God. I beg you. Bring him now.*

She backed toward the cradles, considering weapons—the finely honed butcher knife, Henry's black pistol in the bedroom. "What do you want? Get out. You've the wrong house. I insist you leave immediately. My husband will have your bloody heads on a pike."

Mim ducked toward the door. A squat one blocked her path, latching onto her arm. She screeched, spittle flying. "If you've harmed my boy, so help me God, I shall pull your misbegotten cock out by the root and make a dog's supper of it!"

Margaret bent and scooped up Mary. In the next instant the howling baby was wrenched from her arms and stuffed inside a flax sack. She fell on the sweating creature, clawing, drawing blood. He shoved her off. She staggered, knocking back Henry's chair. Margaret shrieked, searing her throat. "Please, God! My baby!"

The squat one went for Martha, doing the unspeakable same with her.

"In the name of our Lord Jesus! Have mercy. Is it money you want?"

Her arms were yanked back, her wrists bound with rough twine.

Two wrestled with Mim, but she evaded them, flailing wildly, screaming. "Animals! Lowly stinking shit-eating swine!" She threw back her head and delivered a shrill hog-call of a racket.

The one by the door came forward, leaving an unguarded opening behind him.

Margaret shouted, "Run, Pheeny, run!"

Josephine came alive and bolted for the door. The man lunged, yanking Josephine back by a braid. She squealed in pain and sank her teeth into his hand. He raised his rifle, as if to strike. Mim lowered her head and charged, ramming him from behind. "Leave her be, ye sodding savage!"

The monster spun around without releasing Josephine. He caught Mim beneath the chin with the butt of his rifle. Her head snapped back, eyes rolling white, blood streaming from her nostrils. She fell in a heap, one plump arm crossing her face, the other beneath her.

Margaret whispered Mim's name, choking on phlegm and tears. She pleaded with God, with Jesus. But Mim did not stir. Margaret started for Josephine. The youngest-looking bastard, barely older than John, came between them. He caught Margaret's forearm and marched her toward the door. He was a full head shorter. Nits crawled in his greasy hair. She begged the wretched child. "Please, sir. Allow me my babies."

He balled up a foul-tasting rag and forced it past her teeth.

"Mama," sobbed Josephine. Then she too was gagged.

They were goaded forward, out the door. Margaret strained, searching out her babies in the dark, the sacks that held them. Behind them a torch was lit and put to the curtains she'd only just hemmed and hung.

Outside, Oscar was trussed like a lamb and positioned belly down on the back of a horse. He looked up expectantly as Margaret and Josephine were brought out of the burning cottage, letting out a heartbreaking keen when his mother did not appear. John was tied, but on his feet, wet horror gleaming in his eyes. He mouthed to Margaret as she passed, "They murdered the dogs." The nit-boy jerked her forward. *Oh Jesus, please.*

A rant of prayer coursed on in her brain. Margaret fixed her gaze on the pitted road from town. She beseeched God to intervene, to spare her children, to bring Henry now. The fear was a salty, blinding, viscous thing, clogging her throat and ears. They started toward the river, she, John, and Josephine on foot, a Maori each between them. The men chattered among themselves, speaking their bastard tongue, laughing now and again, drowning out her babies' muffled cries. For a time she heard both Mary and Martha, and then, eventually, only Mary.

Inconceivable

THE MOON APPEARED between two slow clouds. Margaret told herself Martha was sleeping. The child slept sounder than most, did she not? Like a bear cub in winter, as Henry would say. He'd sung operatic cradle songs to her. He'd sung to them all. It's a lovely thing, a man singing to a baby. Surely he was on his way.

The air had turned colder by degrees. Her feet were soaked, icy. A numbness had developed in her right leg and hip. How far had they walked? Ten, fifteen miles? Twenty? Christ, Lord. She had no way of gauging distance or time. Hours had passed, it seemed. John and Josephine would be out of their minds with exhaustion and hunger.

Margaret was second in line, shivering behind the lead savage. Two on horseback followed at some distance. John and Josephine were farther back still, beyond her view now. She glanced over her shoulder again. The Maori behind bared his teeth and thrust his chin forward. *Please, God. Help us.* They'd all come away wearing next to nothing—no gloves, no coats, summer stockings and thin soles. The damp seeped right through. Her heel caught on a slimy river stone. She teetered, letting out a ragged cry. The brute ahead turned and glared. How hateful, how menacing his look. As though he were the one so horribly wronged. His wretched animosity was unfathomable.

She bowed her head against the chill. She must concentrate, keep her wits about her. She'd be needed when Henry came. Above, in the trees, a horse snorted. *Henry!* There was a snap of branches, a rush of hooves. She turned around, seeking out her children, just as another five tribesmen rode down the hill and fell in with the others. In her despair she wet herself. They were so many now. Almost simultaneously she realized that Henry would not have proceeded alone. He'd have Mr. Bell alongside, and, at the very least, Messrs. Clark, Sully, Reed, and Freylock, all strong and strapping men, all excellent shots. It would have taken time to rally them. Though by now they would be assembled and on their way. Margaret worked on producing saliva, softening the putrid rag in her mouth. The weave was stiff, inflexible. She sawed with her jaw and bottom teeth. Broom-straw slivers broke away. She spit them out quietly, marking the trail for Henry.

They continued along the black river. Her cold wet drawers chafed. Both the children had wet their beds from time to time, and Josephine, poor mortified Josephine, had wet her white Easter frock in church. She'd not been to blame. The garrulous old vicar had gone on far too long. God, how her little girl had suffered.

A savage in the rear shouted out. Two dismounted and disappeared into the trees. The broad-faced one ran up to her, gesturing toward the ground. "Down."

She filled her lungs with air and pushed hard, expelling the blasted rag finally. "Please untie me." She spoke with difficulty, her ribs throbbing painfully. "Bring my babies. They'll suffocate."

The man jabbed a finger. "Down!"

"Have you blankets to spare? My big boy and girl are surely

freezing to death." Her teeth clattered in her head. "Have mercy, please. They're only children."

He advanced. "Down!"

She sank to her knees, her breasts aching. "Mightn't you allow us to walk together? Surely that's not asking too much, is it?"

He picked up the rag and rammed it to the back of her throat. She gagged, her eyes watering. He walked away, joining the clutch of low-speaking brethren.

Alone she lost balance and fell sideways. She saw with one eye the men returning from the bush. A boy pulled her up by the apron strings. They resumed walking, making first one confusing turn and then another. Hadn't Henry maneuvered similarly on the way to his aunt's viewing? Round and round he drove, passing the same public house twice. They'd missed the entire wake. The man had no sense of direction. But he'd have others with him now, men who knew the land by heart.

Toward daybreak the Maori paused to water the horses. One approached, chewing on something gristly. He pulled down on her chin with his dirty fingers and extracted the rag, tossing it aside. She worked her sore jaw and pleaded in a rusty voice.

"Please sir. I beg of you. Bring my babies. They'll be in need of me."

He grunted and pushed on her shoulder. She swayed and fell to a hard sit, her back to the children. A lanky lad, no more than twelve or thirteen, swaggered her way. She met his sleepy gaze and spoke slowly, distinctly. *"Bay-Bees.* Fetch them, please." Nothing registered in his flat eyes. He put a wedge of cold sweet potato to her mouth and yawned. She hawked out the potato. "My babies, damn you!"

He scowled, understanding at least her tone. He picked up the rag and roughly gagged her again.

They were allowed no privacy before setting off again. She voided herself while walking, with no more grace than a horse.

She acknowledged the fetid act, but did not agonize. As if her parts, her cramped hips and legs, her leaking breasts, her bleeding soles, her filthy drawers, belonged to someone else.

Morning passed. The river was no longer visible. There was bright light above, blinding splinters of sun between the branches. They were tramping through dense growth, traveling in a north-westerly direction, she guessed. It was two o'clock at least. Though she could not be certain of that either.

The voices were like those inside a dream. She heard them throughout the afternoon, a steady running throb. Her father appeared, oddly clean shaven, as did Mim with her clothes ablaze. Unintelligible hymns were sung, incomprehensible advice given. Mim came and went throughout, crackling and burning and screaming obscenities.

The smell of smoke brought her around. Margaret broke from thick reverie, sensing Henry's presence. There was a break in the trees ahead, where Henry and his men, every ambulatory towns-man, she imagined, lay in wait. She grew giddy with anticipation. Leave it to her methodical husband. He would not put his family at risk by moving in with but a handful of men. No, praise God. He would have rallied a cavalry. The bastards would be surrounded, forced to put down their arms. Henry the pacifist would no doubt take them prisoner rather than shoot them, which meant endur-ing their murderous company on the return journey. So be it.

The village wall and moat came into view minutes later. Joy broke out among the Maori, rapturous barking and shouting. The lead bastard picked up the pace, throwing back his head, shaking his rifle. Chimerical Henry and the other figments of her imagi-nation allowed him to pass with impunity. Her legs turned liquid and gave way beneath her. She fell face forward.

"Up!" Someone seized her forearm, yanking hard. "Up, up, up!"

She staggered to her feet and faltered against him, the same de-testable linguist who knew the word "down." He pushed her off.

She heard a sound then, a single fluted note, a bird or her baby, and cried out. He slapped her. She barely felt his hand.

They were brought over a bridge, and through carved wooden gates. Maori came running from all corners—tattooed men, bare-breasted women, children, and dogs. They swamped the returning murderers. Margaret listened hard for her babies, looking every-where for the flax sacks containing them. Oscar was pulled from the horse. He took two drunken steps and fell. His face was red, swollen from crying. She spotted John and Josephine—standing huddled, hand in hand—and then lost sight of them again in the shrieking mayhem. The mob led them to a clearing, a common area, bordered by huts, low, sturdy-looking dwellings, beamed and thatched. Margaret turned in search of Henry. But the gates be-hind were already closed.

The smoke she'd been smelling came from their cooking fire. Flesh of some sort was being roasted, a nauseating smell. She and the children were herded together, their gags removed, their hands unbound. She petted them and kissed their matted hair, pressing hard against their scalps, battling lurid thoughts of dying, of having the children see her go first.

The sacks were brought forward, unceremoniously dumped in a heap. The men stood back while the tribeswomen flocked. They drew her clean sheets from one sack, a pair of Henry's drawers, her good blue apron, stockings and shirts, everything that had been hanging on the line down to the pegs. A young girl squatted and pulled Mary from another sack. Simultaneously, an older woman cried out, taking Mary from the child, cradling her in her arms. The women converged, softly cooing. Margaret rushed into their midst and snatched up her baby. A dry breeze moved Mary's fine hair. She was stiff, but otherwise undisturbed. Margaret put a gentle thumb to her eyelid and eased it up, exposing a pearly crack. She breathed a frantic breath into the tiny mouth and nostrils. A dozen brown hands reached. She backed away clumsily, her mouth still cleaved to her lifeless baby. They closed in, prying Mary from her. Margaret sank to the ground in a sick numbness. At the same moment, Martha was placed in her arms, suckling air. Margaret quickly unbuttoned her blouse and put the living baby to her breast, a shiver of joy coursing. Martha pulled at her nipple greedily, noisily. Margaret's shoulders sagged with the relief. A band of murmuring women came closer, hovering above. Margaret vaguely felt their presence.

"Up."

She did not look to see which murderer spoke, but continued to nurse, moving Martha to the other breast, stroking and kissing her warm head. "We're not finished."

"Up!"

Margaret took her time, shifting Martha again and rising slowly, thinking of Henry. She pictured his lined forehead, the agony in his eyes. He loved his babies so.

❖❖

THEIR THATCHED HUTS were but single rooms with a cooking fire in the center, and sleeping mats all around. Margaret, Josephine, and Martha were taken to one hut, John and Oscar to another.

"Leave the boys with me," she pleaded, when it became obvious that they were to be separated. "Keep us together." The flanking Maori did not respond.

Ahead, John was following Oscar inside. She called after her son. "Courage, John." He glanced over his shoulder and mouthed the word "Father." Margaret flicked a smile for her sturdy boy, a lad who should be home in England, romping in the meadow with the collie he'd pined for.

She bent to enter the neighboring hut, pulling Josephine

along. A half-naked granny, a guard presumably, sat motionless in a dark corner. Margaret spoke as she would to any elder, politely, deferentially. "Can you tell us why we're here, madam?"

The old lady looked at them, then looked away, saying nothing. A girl came in with a gourd bowl of wash water. Another brought rough skirts and swaddling of the same material. They scurried off, and no wonder. She stank; Josephine and Martha stank. Margaret pulled away Martha's filthy napkin to discover insects both dead and crawling. She folded the napkin in quarters and set it aside.

Josephine sidled up close and whispered, "Did Mary croak?"

She would have heard the horrible word from Mim. Margaret kissed her and said without conviction, "Mary's safe with Jesus now."

A long time ago, before Margaret's own children were born, a Surrey woman hanged herself with a bedsheet after her child's drowning. Margaret understood completely now.

She took the coarse rag from the water and tested its roughness on her own arm. She started with Martha's feet, moving up each squatty leg. Next she stripped and scoured Josephine, turning the wash water brown in her zeal, working up a madwoman's sweat. Every fingernail, every bodily crease, required her attention. Their undergarments were ruined. It was good to be rid of them. Josephine struggled with the strange skirt, gathering excess fabric in her fists. "It scratches."

"It's clean," said Margaret. She washed herself last, then crouched awkwardly and exchanged her feculent skirt for the dry one. "Now listen closely, little miss." She cupped her daughter's head and whispered directly into her ear. "All shall be fine. Do you understand?" Josephine nodded. "Father is coming for us. In the meantime you must do as I say. It's not the same now. You must mind me absolutely. Without question."

Josephine's chin trembled. "Mary."

Margaret closed her eyes and rocked her.

A girl brought food, a basket of sweet potatoes, corn, pork, and some reddish elongated pieces, dried past identification. Josephine took the meat with her fingers, chewing listlessly.

Margaret put restless Martha to her breast. "I'm very thirsty," said Josephine. Margaret turned to the old woman and pantomimed drinking from a beaker. "Water, please?"

The rooted woman did not speak.

"Have you no children of your own, madam?"

The woman farted, a noxious bleat.

Margaret clucked. "Why, you rude old trout!"

"Mama, please."

Margaret laid Martha in the scoop of her skirt. "You'll have a little of my milk."

Josephine scowled. "I'm much too big."

Margaret stroked her child. "Let's pretend you're not." Josephine came reluctantly. Margaret pushed on her breast to aid the flow, taking the hard teeth like a she-wolf. "Gently does it now."

The desiccated woman looked their way. Margaret met the beady black eyes. "Sodding old hag with your dried up dugs." The woman blinked. "Useless childless thing." The woman looked away again. "Warts to you," Margaret hissed.

Josephine stopped suckling. She nestled against Margaret's side, raking her tongue along her teeth as if to rid her mouth of the taste. Margaret adjusted her blouse and covered sleeping Martha with her apron. The crone came alive, pointing toward the mats along the opposite wall.

They crawled over, sharing a mat, Martha beneath one arm, Josephine beneath the other. Insects scuttled in the thatched ceiling above. Margaret drew up the hide of some long dead creature, tucking her big girl close. She ached for John, imagining him frightened and thirsty, biting his bottom lip raw.

"There's another matter, Pheeny."

Josephine moaned sleepily.

"When Father comes you are not to call out to him. Do you understand?"

"He may arrive in secret," said Josephine.

"That's right."

"Will he come in the morning?"

Margaret whispered, "It's quite possible, sweetheart."

"May I ride home with him?"

"You may." A gutter of voices could be heard outside, a baby's far-off cry. They'd sail straight home once this ordeal was over. Promotions, money, and honors be damned. They'd leave on the first ship. Four cots in steerage would do.

Josephine murmured, "Perhaps he'll bring the buggy."

"He won't. It's too large."

Josephine yawned a sticky yawn. "The branches won't allow it through."

"Yes. That's right. Sleep now, my love."

"He'll come," said Josephine.

"He will."

The grief pressed on Margaret's chest like a third child. Once her girls were asleep she wept without cessation. Never before had she loathed the world or herself so thoroughly. It had been her idea to move so far out. The fresh country air will be good for the children. Over and over she'd said it, wearing her husband down, getting her tyrannical way finally.

It was still dark when they came, and bitterly cold. If Margaret had slept she did not recall it. Her body was stiff. She could barely stand. Two short, sullen women led her to the latrine, and with a series of gestures instructed her to clean it.

Alone

HENRY SMELLED SMOKE and put the whip to Katie's rump. A tramp's cook fire started in the bushes, he figured, with the perfect breeze to bring it straight to his roof. *Christ Almighty*. He'd be up all night sopping down the bloody timbers. Rounding a stand of karaka trees, the smoldering destruction came into view. Henry called out, expecting his wife to appear, their homeless children clinging. He left the old nag and rig in the road and ran the last distance.

The fire was giving off the last of its heat. He entered where the door had been this morning. "Meg!" He stood stock still and listened for his family. "Meg, sweetheart." He said it softly now, taking in the blackened wreckage, his eyes adjusting. In the same moment he saw a few cookpots, John's lucky horseshoe, Meg's mother's ginger jar, and a human body. "Oh, Jesus, please." He approached disbelieving, falling to one knee. The body was hairless, faceless, and long-limbed, not a child. "Oh God." He removed his coat and laid it over her, then drew it away again and touched her head. An ashy wet bit of her came away on his fingers.

He stood in a stupor and called to his children. "John. Pheeny, darling. Dad's here."

He took careful steps, using his hat to gently rake the ashes. He paced off the length, and then the width. Here was something. He bent over, sweat pouring, soaking his beard. He rubbed the shard between his fingers—glass, not bone, a trembling joyous discovery. He started over. Inch by cautious inch he combed the floor for his children's remains. He went outside and did the same without finding a trace. They were alive then. A fire will always leave something behind. "Kids!" he shouted. They were lurking in the woods above, having fled the fire in time. They'd be freezing, frightened out of their wits. He ran uphill without a lamp, bellowing their names.

The forest floor was damp and slippery. Henry searched along the quiet periphery, entering the bush from the south. He'd been up here during the day with John often enough, gathering kindling, debating which dogs were best. At night the black trees loomed the same in every direction. Henry ran north; he ran west, climbing deep into the interior. It was after midnight when he quit, exhausted and hoarse. He started down, still calling to them, spotting Mim Bell's empty rig in the road then, a surge of love and relief rushing through him. The body inside had to be Mim's.

Henry untied Mim's skittish mare from the post and turned her and the buggy around. Meg and the children had somehow managed to escape. They would have found their way to the Bells', their closest neighbor. Henry rode south a grateful man, a man redeemed. He could not fathom a life without them. He would take them home to England now. They'd endured enough. He planned to tell Meg first thing, the moment he saw her.

❖❖

FEAR AND CONFUSION were fully restored by the time Henry reached the Bells'. Meg would not have set out in the cold and hiked the twenty miles with four children in tow, not with Bell's horse and buggy at her disposal. He pounded Bell's front door, hearing footsteps after an eternity, muffled cursing.

Cyril Bell appeared in his nightshirt, holding a lamp. He reached behind the door and brought out a crude cudgel. "Who the devil is it at this hour?"

Henry stepped into the wreath of light, listening for sounds in the house. "Oades. Henry Oades. We've met, sir." He spoke fast, wheezing like a hound. "I'm Margaret's husband. Your wife's friend. My wife and children have gone missing."

Bell frowned, scratching his privates with the club.

Henry demanded, "Are they here?"

"What's this all about?"

"Are you bloody hard of hearing? I'm looking for my family."

Bell craned, sniffing the air. "You're about three sheets to it, aren't you?" He lifted the club. "Go on home before I give you the beating of your life."

Henry shoved him aside, shouting into the interior. "Meg!"

Bell recovered from the surprise, raising the club higher. Henry had the advantage of thirty more pounds and at least ten fewer years. He grabbed Bell's wrist, locking the man against the door-jamb. "Where's *your* wife?"

Bell struggled. "What do you want with her?"

"Where is she?"

"She's not here, you buggering idiot. There's nobody here but me and the dog. She's a mean one, too. She'll bite. One word from me and—"

Henry wrenched the club from Bell's flaccid grip and sent it sailing into the dark yard. Bell ducked back inside. Henry put himself between door and jamb. "Help me, please."

"Why should—"

"Your wife visited mine last evening?"

Bell swiped his nose on a sleeve. "If you say so. Walked out with a bee in her bonnet. Not for the first time. She and the boy. Pig-headed woman. Didn't bother to say where they were headed."

"I found your rig on my property." Henry pointed vaguely. "I've returned it."

"I owe you then. I thought . . ."

Henry ran a hand through his dry hair, still scanning the interior, half expecting Meg and the children to suddenly show themselves. "My house burned to the ground last night."

"That's terrible news."

Henry stood shivering, the dread rising in his chest, constricting his breathing. "My children are nowhere to be found."

"Ah, for the love of—"

There had to be a rational answer. They couldn't simply disappear. "I came upon a body."

"Oh, no, was—"

"My wife, I thought at first."

"Oh Christ."

"Or your wife, sir. I'm sorry." Henry was anxious to leave. He'd given up the search too soon. There were miles still to cover. John would have constructed a shelter of some sort, far away from the smoke and fire.

Bell began to weep. "Jesus, Mary, and—"

"There's no way of knowing," said Henry. "I couldn't tell."

"My boy?" Bell's tears streamed. "Oscar?"

Henry shook his head. "I'm sorry. No sign of him either."

"Oh, sweet sacred heart. We'll want to inform the authorities."

"They can wait." On the way over Henry had considered and rejected the idea. No good would come of rousing the governor at this hour. He was a useless indecisive man; his sycophantic underlings were no better. Meg and the children were *his* family, *his* concern. He'd have the benefit of daylight soon. He'd start over looking. "Will you make a loan of a horse, Mr. Bell?"

"Have your choice of the two in the stable," said Bell. "I'll take the other."

They made good time, arriving by first light to a smoky quiet. Bell tied up the horses. Henry stood in the road making quarter turns, calling to his wife and children. The men tramped up to the bush and began searching, giving up after three hours, making their way down to the charred cottage. "Tucked away," Meg had called it. "A perfect place."

Bell had thought to bring a shovel and a bedsheet. The men labored with the delicate corpse. It collapsed in their hands, making red and yellow stains on the sheet. Daylight was no help, as Henry had hoped. "Can you tell anything?"

"Might be anyone," muttered Bell.

"Anyone."

"Mine wore a little gold locket on occasion," said Bell.

"Mine wore her ring," said Henry.

"With my likeness and Oscar's inside," said Bell.

Henry, the middle brother, had been the first in his family to present a wife with a wedding ring. His parents had disapproved, as had Meg's parents. The older set still regarded the ring an ostentatious pagan practice. "Unseemly," his mother had said. "Unchristian." She may have reconsidered had she seen the thrill in Meg's lovely eyes.

The men poked around and beneath the body for as long as they could bear it, finding nothing to prove who it was or wasn't. The lack of evidence meant little to Henry. Meg often took off the ring. She feared losing it in the wash, she'd said.

They took turns with the shovel, burying the body out back, where the hydrangea once bloomed. They fashioned a cross of scorched stones and walked away, both quaking with uncertainty.

Henry discovered the dogs beneath a thicket of broadleaf puka, flies and beetles feasting on the head wounds. "My boy's pets," he said, incredulous. "Who'd do such a thing?" Bell stalked off, disgusted. Henry stared, attempting to make sense of the grisly mess. These were John's harmless pups, pleasant, obedient animals, bound for the circus. His eyes burned. He craved sleep; he wished not to think anymore.

Bell called to him from below, waving an arm. Henry started down, his heart thundering with fear of finding a dead child. He came up on Bell, his breathing fast and shallow.

Bell held a white-tipped, black tail feather. "Huia," he said. "They wear the filthy things in their topknots." He pointed out the horse tracks leading down to the river, the droppings. "Goddamn Maori were here. I'd stake my last farthing on it."

Henry had heard stories about long-ago murders and snatchings. He'd chalked them up to apocryphal pub tales at the time. There'd been problems back in the sixties, blood shed on both sides over land, but nothing lately, not since he'd arrived, not that he knew or even heard of. What would provoke them? Why *his* house and family? "I'm going after them," he said.

"I'm going with you," said Bell.

"We'll need guns and rope," said Henry, wide awake now, full of seething energy. "I'll take a coat if you can spare it."

They raced back to Bell's for supplies. Henry was barely aware of the horse beneath him. He did not see what caused the animal to rear. He lost hold of the reins and fell back, striking the road hard, his leg audibly cracking. A dusty blur of hooves rose in his vision. Henry tucked his head and flung himself right, rolling down an embankment, his eyes filling with searing juices.

Bell came rushing, trampling leaves and twigs. "Close yer damn eye." Henry couldn't see him, but he could smell the man's peculiarly olid flesh. "Close it, I said. Don't try to use it." A dry cloth was pressed to his right eye. "Yer damn leg's broken. I can see the bloody bone. We'll get you straight to hospital. Can you hear me,

Oades? Put an arm about my neck. That's it. I've got you. Gently does it. That's a steady lad. Here we go then. On the count of three. One. Two. Here we go."

A fiery bolt shot up his spine. Henry screamed and slipped into black oblivion.

⋄⋄

THE DOCTOR SAID he was lucky. The leg was broken in three places, but both it and the eye had been saved. The doctor was a pale, walleyed man with cold hands. "You'll walk eventually," he said, "though it shan't be anytime soon."

The eye dressing would come off in two or three weeks, depending. Depending on what, the doctor did not say. Henry, in a laudanum fog, did not ask.

Bell's note was read aloud to him. *Dear Friend,* it started. *I'm off to see the governor. I haven't a Chinaman's chance on my own. Pray for us.* Henry had a rambling, fevered chat with the Lord, and then slept straight through four days. "A near coma," said the doctor. Henry brought a hand to his bandaged cheek and touched his shaved chin. He'd been bearded since twenty. He spent a drugged moment worrying that Meg and the children wouldn't recognize him, then closed his good eye and slept another three days.

He woke asking for his wife, his children, Cyril Bell. The aide on duty told him he was better off resting now.

All the staff cajoled. "'Tis always darkest before the dawn," said the Irish nurse with Meg's blue-gray eyes. She came on duty early and was the kindest of the lot. "We've a lovely porridge this morning, Mr. Oades. You'll do your poor children no favors by starving."

He asked, "Have you any news today?" The nurse took advantage of his open mouth and shoveled in the tepid, mealy paste. It came straight back up, along with his own sour bile.

"I'm not hungry just now," he said, embarrassed.

She clucked and mopped his gown with a rag. "I'm praying for you," she said.

Most gave up on him fairly quickly and went on to the next bed. The ward was full. The overflow suffered outside in the hall. The groaning and sobbing never ceased. Henry closed his eye, letting the din wash over and through his ineffectual self.

On Sunday he begged the homely missionary woman who came around to read Scripture, "Please, will you find Mr. Bell?" She promised she would. He, in turn, endured her biblical gush, feigning comfort. He did not see her again.

Mr. Freylock, Henry's immediate supervisor, came the following week. He entered the ward with his hat in his hands, his mouth twitching with sympathy. "They tell me you're not eating," he said.

Mr. Freylock was a career man, one of the first of the distillery men to arrive in New Zealand. "The place suits me," he'd once said. Henry recalled feeling both vaguely envious and disdainful of a man who found true contentment behind a desk.

He looked up at Mr. Freylock, his good eye filling. The eye wept constantly. He'd been given drops, but they did little good. A brown spider ran along the windowsill. He dabbed at the eye with a corner of sheet, thinking how spiders frightened Josephine.

Mr. Freylock touched Henry's sleeve. "You've had an abysmal time of it."

Henry cleared his throat. "Is there any news, sir?"

"Only that the scouting trip was unsuccessful." Mr. Freylock fiddled with his felt brim. "Six men went out, myself included. The governor sent out four more. We rode together for a day and then split from them, thinking we'd cover more ground that way. I'm sorry, Henry."

"My family could be anywhere then?" Henry's dry lips cracked with speech. "Anyone might have them?"

"If you mean white men, no, not likely. The arson, you see, the snatching itself. It smacks of *utu*."

"I beg your pardon?"

Mr. Freylock sighed. "It is the heathen's word for revenge. The governor believes your family was taken in retaliation for last month's flogging. The whipping would have brought dishonor to the entire bloody tribe. *Utu* of some sort was inevitable. I sincerely loathe being the one to tell you."

The Maori lad had been no more than fifteen. Henry had walked away before the lashing even began, repulsed by the gawking onlookers. "I assume another search is under way, sir?"

Mr. Freylock shook his head. "Not at present, I'm sorry to say."

"Why not?"

"Simply put, Henry, it would do no good. The trail went cold scant miles out. We were but a handful of family men against a sodding band of savages. Sorry to say it. The odds weigh too heavily."

"And the governor's men?"

"They've since returned empty-handed as well. That is not to say you should relinquish hope. That is not to say you shouldn't continue to pray. All of Wellington is praying for your wife and children."

Henry's eye ran, salting his stinging lips.

"Ah, Henry. I'm only adding to your distress."

Henry pleaded, "Will you help locate Cyril Bell?"

Mr. Freylock took out his watch and flicked open the lid with a thumbnail. "Poor fellow had a bit of a breakdown, smashed a good bottle at McFadden's, started a brawl. They locked him up for his own well-being."

"When will he be released?"

Mr. Freylock glanced down at his watch. "Sooner rather than later, I'm sure."

"Will you ask him to come round?"

"I shall, Henry. First chance. I must be off. I'm sorry the news isn't better. Your post is being held indefinitely, if it's any small consolation. That's what I came to tell you."

Henry struggled to remain civil, to issue his senior a proper farewell, but all before him had eclipsed. As if a cupboard door had just been nailed shut, and he'd found himself inside.

She Speaks to Me
Day and Night

*I*T WAS LOVELY HERE, green and tranquil. Meg was decked out in her wedding frock, an ivory lace and satin affair with complicated buttons that were hard to undo. She nattered quietly, asking after his tea. The light shifted, the temperature fell, just as she offered a fresh cup. Henry opened his good eye to find Cyril Bell standing over him. Bell sucked on his cigar and hacked a rough cough.

"Are you awake, mate? Are you in need of anything?" Bell's cheek was bruised, his swollen lip split in two places. "Shall I call the lazy nurse?" He clamped the cigar between his crooked yellow teeth and tugged on Henry's pillow. "It's caught in the rail. There now. Much better, isn't it?"

Henry sat up, groggy, dream-addled. "What brings you?"

"You asked for me," said Bell, looking wounded. "I came when I heard."

"I did, didn't I? Sorry. Thank you."

Bell smiled a sad smile. "Birds of a feather now, aren't we?"

Bell wore black gloves and a mourning armband; he carried Meg's mother's ginger jar as one would a baby, in the crook of his arm. He offered it now. "Thought you might like a memento of happier times."

Henry took the lidded jar, a grinding fear clenching his bowels.

"Not a crack, not a singe," said Bell. "Queer what a fire will leave behind."

"Is there news?"

Bell shook his head, soft cigar ash falling, breaking on the white sheet. "They've gone to a far better place, my friend."

A vision of his children laid out in death swamped him. Henry's pained cry roused the sleeping patient in the next bed. "They've been found?"

Bell put a finger to his lips. "Hush now, Oades. Calm yourself. No, they haven't been found. But where the tree is felled that's where the chippings are."

"Jesus Lord," said Henry. "What does that mean?"

"Do you recall the poor Hagstrom family?"

"No," said Henry. "What in God's name are you talking about?"

"Six or seven years ago," Bell went on. "There was a spate of snatchings around the same time. The Hagstrom children, eight little towheaded angels, were all the talk. The old grandfather looked for years. Then one fine day he put his rifle to his mouth and pulled the trigger with his toe." Bell bent close. Early as it was, he smelled of gin.

"I didn't quit, Mr. Oades. The others gave up. Not I. I covered miles of ground in every direction." He straightened, dropping his soggy cigar into the beaker of cold tea. "If they were let go alive I'd have found them."

"It's only been two weeks," said Henry.

"It's been nearly four, sir."

"It cannot possibly be." In his mind Henry attempted to line up the days and prove Bell wrong, but it was no use. Some days stood painfully sharp in his memory; others he couldn't begin to account for. "I'll pay you to go out again."

"You'd be wasting your money," said Bell. "You'll want to make peace with it is my advice. The sooner you do the better off you'll be."

Henry begged. "Please, sir." His good leg cramped. "They cannot all be gone. I refuse to believe it."

Bell regarded him with flat pity. He was clearly finished. He'd dispatched his family to heaven and now no doubt wished only to dispatch himself to the nearest public house.

"I still hear my wife!" Henry often felt her beside him, the pressure of her warm hip against his. "She speaks to me day and night."

"Mrs. Oades was your first?"

"She is," said Henry.

Bell nodded. "She'll do more than speak to you. Her face will show itself when you least expect it. You'll swear it's her down at the docks. She'll come to you at all hours, shed of her nightie. That's the worst. There'll be times you'll want to take a working gun to your own head and have it over with. That's how it was with Libby, my first. Mim's my second. Childbed fever took Libby. The baby didn't stand a chance with the top of his wee head missing." Bell's cut lip pulsed; his red-rimmed eyes puddled. "I was given a look. A boy."

John came to mind, fat and howling, a perfect lusty lad, missing nothing.

"I'm truly sorry for your loss, Mr. Bell."

"I'm sorry for yours," said Bell, blinking back tears. "You'll learn to live with it after a while. It's a promise, Oades. You'll learn to tolerate. You'll have no choice."

The amputee two beds away moaned, as if grieving for the baby with a missing head. The entire ward seemed to join in at once, caterwauling off-key. Behind the cacophony Meg soothed, whis-pered. *There now, sweetheart. Rest a bit. You'll be all right.*

Henry set the ginger jar on the medicine table and turned his cheek to the pillow. "I refuse to believe it." Meg went on coddling, telling him to sleep, just sleep.

Henry closed his eye, waiting for his family. "Forgive me, Mr. Bell. I'm rather tired right now."

Bell stood in silence a moment longer. "I'll be going then," he said finally. He left Henry with Josephine. She was reaching with the sweetest smile, putting her tender skinny arms about his burn-ing neck. *Dad,* was all she said, all he needed to hear.

Meg and the children rarely showed themselves again after that day. His dreams became peopled with misshapen intruders, no one he recognized. Drunk on laudanum, Henry called out to his wife. The night nurse regularly scolded him. "That'll be enough now. You're disturbing the others."

He was discharged from hospital on a sunny day in late May. He was ready to go. He'd had more than enough of the place. Mr. Freylock came for him, along with two grim-faced col-leagues. They brought a change of clothes, were seemingly pleased with their selection. "You're not an easy fellow to fit." There were grunts, a comment on his drawers. "Good God. It must be the same pair he arrived in." As if Henry weren't pres-ent. It didn't matter. He felt next to nothing.

They dressed him in a suit of mourning and fixed an armband to the sleeve. The doctor came in and wished him well. "My con-dolences, sir. You're to remain off the leg another month at least."

Outside, the doctor helped lift the wheelchair with Henry in it. They loaded him onto a buckboard that had had its seats re-moved. He sat above the other three men, like a freak of nature on parade. They said little. Henry said nothing.

He could not say how long they rode. A stream of foliage went by, shops and horses, dogs and people. He untied the armband and tucked it inside a breast pocket. If they were dead he'd know it; he'd know it in his bones.

They came to the Freylock home, where he and Meg had once gone to tea, fifty years ago it seemed. The wife and two children, a freckled boy and roly-poly girl, came out to greet them.

"You are welcome to stay as long as you wish," said Mrs. Freylock, an anxious woman. "We've prepared a room downstairs for you, Mr. Oades. It's rather small, but we cannot very well bring you up the stairs."

His vision cleared as she spoke. He became simultaneously aware of the potted geraniums, the pump of his own heart and lungs, the pimples and fuzz on the Freylock lad's chin. How he'd indulged himself in the sorrow. It was time to think straight, to plan. Henry doffed his hat, acutely sensitive to the cool breeze parting his hair. "Thank you. I shan't put you out a moment longer than necessary, kind lady."

The music room had been converted into a sickroom. Henry vaguely recalled the green and gold wallpaper border, painted to look like fringed drapery. The piano was gone now, replaced by a cot. There'd been other instruments on display at the time, two violins, and a lute perhaps. Meg had been delighted. "A musical family," she'd said. "How lovely the evenings must be." Those were her exact words. Henry remembered vividly everything she'd ever said.

He was left alone with Mr. Freylock. "Would you like to lie down now, Henry?" He spoke carefully, as if addressing an unpredictable lunatic. "I'll draw the curtains."

It was not yet two in the afternoon. "I'm fine here," said Henry. He sat close to the glassed bookcase. There were history books galore, biographies, books on animal husbandry, but no novels for Meg.

"Well then," said Mr. Freylock. "Duty calls. I'll be getting back to my desk. You know how it is." He gestured toward the small bell on the side table. "Don't hesitate to ring."

"I'd like to arrange a posse," said Henry.

Mr. Freylock removed his spectacles, blinking. "Henry, Henry, Henry."

"I'll pay."

Mr. Freylock brought out his handkerchief and polished the lenses. "That's not the issue."

The anger thickened Henry's voice. "What would you do in my place, sir?"

Mr. Freylock held the spectacles up to the window for inspection. "I'd be every bit as distraught, I'm sure. I'd propose infeasible schemes. It's only natural. We turned over every last bloody stone looking, Henry. Do you remember my telling you?"

"I do, sir."

"We almost lost Tom Flowers."

"I know Tom."

Mr. Freylock returned the spectacles to his face, blinking still. "Of course you do. Good lad. Quick with a joke. Fifth child on the way. I didn't tell you before. Didn't want to add to your distress. Nothing you could have done for him. Nothing any of us could have done, except perhaps turned back straightaway."

Perspiration trickled down Henry's spine. The room was warm, as stifling as a summer greenhouse. "About Tom?"

"He sliced his hand," said Mr. Freylock. "Nice and deep, but manageable. This was the fourth night out. We stayed gone a week, you'll remember, the better part of eight days, actually."

Henry heard a scratching outside the door and pictured his children standing on the other side, eager to surprise him. His mind playing tricks, he realized.

" . . . We weren't surgeons," Mr. Freylock was saying. "We wrapped the wound, thought, well, a cut's a cut, isn't it? None of us could have anticipated infection. They took his writing arm at the elbow. Poor man."

"Yes," murmured Henry. "Poor Tom. I'm sorry to hear it." Tom's pretty wife suffered a clubfoot, an odd thing to remember now.

A Freylock family photograph hung on the opposite wall, the parents and children posed as he and Meg had posed not long after the twins were born. Were his babies rolling over yet? Josephine was a veritable little acrobat at five months, their age now. God, how he missed them all.

Mr. Freylock came to him, laying a hand upon his shoulder. "We've done all we can, then. Everything within reason. Do you see that we have?"

Henry nodded. There'd be no help here.

"It wouldn't be disloyal to acknowledge their passing, Henry. I'll arrange a memory service if you're ready."

"I'm not," said Henry, beginning to plan his escape. He'd had enough of this place already.

✧✧

HE DREAMT of John that night. His son came walking out of the bush, steady and sure. Henry took it as a sign they'd be returned to him. He lay awake in the dark, cursing himself for having had doubt. In the morning he proposed rebuilding the cottage. "Just as it was," he said.

Curiously, Mr. Freylock heartily agreed. He slapped the breakfast table, rattling the cutlery. "Capital idea! Isn't it, darling?"

Mrs. Freylock smiled and passed the last rasher of bacon Henry's way. "Yes, indeed. It's a splendid plan. Aren't you smart to think of it, Mr. Oades."

"We'll get started straightaway," said Mr. Freylock, dribbling red jam.

Henry had not expected such enthusiasm. Perhaps they simply wished him gone. He gave it no further thought. Having the cottage restored was all that concerned him just now. Otherwise, how would they find their way back to him?

◇◇

THE OWNER of the property gave his permission. A new lease was signed. Dozens turned out to help, colleagues and strangers both. Henry had never laid eyes on some of them. He sat in his wheelchair, beneath the shade of a ladies' white parasol. The men sawed, hammered, and painted; the women served from overflowing hampers, vying to bring Henry a plate. The cottage was finished in six days. The donated furniture inside was different, but the outside was nearly identical, down to the green shutters and red door.

Mrs. Freylock asked about flowers.

"Roses," said Henry. "And blue hydrangea."

He watched the flowers go into the ground.

"He's smiling," someone whispered. "He's bearing up well."

On Sunday Henry attended evening services. Everyone seemed to expect it of him. He got through it. A bachelor colleague, Simon Reed, brought him back to the cottage afterward. "You're not equipped to see to yourself, Henry."

"I am, Simon," Henry insisted. His family would come. They'd see to him, and he to them. Things would right themselves. They'd all be fine. He believed it wholly.

Simon pushed him up the new ramp and inside, muttering under his breath. "A man in your state shouldn't be left alone."

"I shall get on fine here," said Henry.

Simon lighted a lamp and set it on the table.

"If you'll light the others, please."

Henry had him light every lamp, seven in all.

"Where would you like them, Henry?"

"I'll take care of it," said Henry. "You've done enough. Go on home now."

Alone, Henry maneuvered the wheelchair without difficulty. He put one lamp in his lap and rolled himself, setting the lamp in the side window, returning then for the next lamp. Lamp by lamp, he turned the room bright, as gay as a ballroom, making himself visible ten miles out.

He ate hard cheese and opened the brandy someone had left, putting out another goblet. Meg enjoyed a nice brandy. He rolled himself to the front window again, restless, excited. But they did not come. Not that night, nor the next. A quiet week passed, then another. He sat on the porch daily, his eyes fixed on the road. He went inside eventually and sat there, a useless stump by the window. *Sweet Jesus.* Every bloody day.

He rose one morning and limped unaided to the grave out back. He stood over the mound until his leg would no longer support him, then sat alongside and began to dig. He hadn't planned to do it; but once started he could not stop.

Almost before he pulled aside the sheet he knew. He brushed dirt from the skull, recognizing the sharp little tooth way back in her head, pointed, darker than the others. Henry cried out and began to cover her again. He scooped great handfuls as fast as he could, tamping down the crumbly dirt, beating it hard. He fell back exhausted, sobbing, struggling for air. He calmed after a while, but did not, could not, move. For months he'd felt her about, alive, and now he did not. He could no longer pretend. Meg was gone, lost to him forever. He lay stunned, face to the sun. He'd thought they had all the time in the world.

No Worse
than Here

*H*ENRY FOUND flat black seeds lying loose on a pantry shelf and planted a few at the foot of Meg's grave. He watched faithfully, witnessing the first shoot, the subsequent withering and dying. He gave thought to starting over, but knew the same would happen. He'd never had much luck in a garden. So he quit, and his days turned that much longer.

Mr. Freylock rode out at the end of June. "Good God," he said straight off. "Have a flock of filthy sheep been run through here?"

Henry said nothing. A bit of dust, a dried rat turd or two hardly warranted comment.

Mr. Freylock clucked like a woman. "There's no excuse for squalor. Even for a chap on his own." He dropped a slim packet of envelopes on the table. "A spot of comfort from home for you, Henry."

Henry didn't get up. "Her parents?"

"I wouldn't know." He picked up Henry's urinal and went outside to pour it over the porch rail. Henry watched without interest from his usual place by the front window. Recently he'd moved from the wheelchair to an armless ladder-back and felt less the invalid for it. He was able to move about as necessary, using the broom as a crutch.

Mr. Freylock came back in. "Have you written her loved ones?"

Henry studied his fingernails, broken and blackened from tending her grave. He hadn't written to her parents or his own. He hadn't the words. "I'll get round to it in due course."

"You should inform them immediately. They've a right to know."

"A right to know what precisely?"

"The facts, boy." Mr. Freylock pumped water and rinsed his hands, drying them on the only dish towel. "You know in your heart of hearts they're gone."

"I know nothing of the sort," said Henry. "Show me my dead children, sir!"

Mr. Freylock ran last night's plate under the water. What had he had to eat? Henry couldn't remember. "You're in a bad way, Henry. I'm sorry. I won't say any more about it."

Henry spoke to the window, the one thing he kept cleaned. "What do the savages do with them?" Hideous images too frequently rose from a black hell in his mind, visions of his maimed children screaming his name.

Mr. Freylock said softly, "What are you asking?"

Henry looked at him. "They wouldn't consume a tiny innocent, would they?"

"Oh, Christ, Henry. Please. Don't torture yourself. They're past their suffering now."

Henry's voice quaked. "They wouldn't."

"It isn't healthful, you know. Sitting out here all alone, with only your morbid thoughts for company. You'd be better off in town, in my opinion."

Henry turned back to the window, resuming his vigil.

Mr. Freylock offered to put the kettle on. Henry shook his head, willing the man gone. "Work is what you need," said Mr. Freylock. "Why not ride back with me now. Have you a decent shirt and trousers? You cannot go out as you are."

Hot tears rose in Henry's eyes. "Would they kill them first? Surely they wouldn't boil a live screaming child. . . ."

Mr. Freylock threw up his hands. "Henry, Henry. For the love of God, don't dwell on it. Think of them at peace with Jesus, will you? Think of your children quit of all adversity."

"They'd shoot them first," said Henry decisively.

Mr. Freylock sighed. "I'm sure you're right."

Henry put his face in his hands, depleted. "I'm going mad, sir. And it's not doing my kids the first bit of good. There's no reason to believe they didn't escape. My boy's as clever as they come."

"Ah, Henry. They—"

"You don't know him," said Henry, cutting him off. "John's sharp as a needle. The lad reads the night skies as well as you do the gazette." He stood with the aid of the broom and hobbled toward the back room, planning his next move. There were men in town he might call upon to help, resources he'd not yet thought of. It was merely a matter of keeping a rational mind, resisting the panic. That's all. He managed yesterday. He'd manage today.

He changed his clothes, and then wrote a note while Mr. Frey-lock waited.

Dearest children, you'll find a cord of good wood round the side and
a large ham in the larder. You're to contact the distillery
immediately. Your always loving and devoted father.

Outside he turned, scanning the forest, the road in both directions, looking for them.

◇◇

MR. FREYLOCK DROVE, breaking the silence with small talk every mile or two. His wife's brisket was mentioned, the new accountant with a penchant for the bottle. "Tom Flowers is coming along well," he said, interrupting Henry's reverie yet again. He'd been thinking about the babies, wondering what John was doing to feed them. It took a moment to recall Tom's amputation.

"That's very good news, sir."

"At his desk Monday last," said Mr. Freylock, casting a sidelong glance. "Taking it all in his stride."

"I've no doubt," said Henry.

Mr. Freylock's thin mouth tightened. "I can tell you don't find me particularly helpful."

Henry lied. "I do, sir." Roots or mussels mashed with river water. John would find a way.

They arrived on the outskirts toward dusk. Nothing had been said about where he might stay. "I won't impose on your family a second time," Henry said, expecting an argument.

"I know of a suitable bachelor's flat," said Mr. Freylock.

The word bachelor brought to mind an irresponsible, glib sort, no one like himself. He began to regret leaving the cottage, though he couldn't possibly endure a return trip. His leg throbbed from heel to groin. The day had gone on too long. And now the night was upon him. Nights were the worst with his kids out there.

◇◇

THE TIDY BEDSIT was located over a haberdasher. Mr. Freylock helped him up the two pair of stairs, and then went out again, bringing back a pasty and tea for one. He remained standing, driving gloves in hand.

"Will you be all right, Henry?"

"I shall get on fine, sir. Go on home now. Your wife will be waiting."

"I'll say it again," said Mr. Freylock in parting. "Work is what you need."

"Yes, sir," said Henry, and was rid of him at last.

The following Tuesday he returned to his desk, where he could not concentrate for the blinding headaches. On Friday he requested and was granted a leave of absence.

"You may as well go," said Mr. Freylock, signing the permission form. "You've no head for numbers these days."

That Sunday, in the social hall after services, Henry clapped his hands once and asked for volunteers. He'd hoped to find some of the Maori parishioners about, but everyone there was English, two dozen or so, prattling away.

"Who'll come with me to look?"

They stirred, scraping their feet. Someone offered to bring him tea.

"I'm posting a reward for their safe return. One hundred pounds sterling."

"Poor man," said a woman by the door.

Henry turned slowly, looking them in the eye individually. "I'd go without question were it any one of your children."

"God bless you, Mr. Oades," the same woman chirped.

"And God *blast* you, madam," said Henry, storming out. "God blast you one and all."

Someone called after him. "You're looking to get eaten, brother Oades."

❖❖

HENRY RODE NORTH, following the river, tying blue rags to tree limbs as he went, marking the places searched. He turned after a week, starting first south, and then west into the higher elevations. The pristine forest revealed nothing but the impossibility of survival. Sometime during the fourth week he lost what little hope remained and did not recover it. His children were gone. He stayed out looking another two weeks before finally giving up. Coming back, he saw that the blue rags had turned gray.

The return brought him past the cottage, where clothes hung on the line. Henry hitched the horse to a post and ran up the grassy rise, praying to find his children inside, feverishly calculating the chances. Miracles occurred every day. Anything was possible on this earth. A squat lady opened the door and his heart quieted. Behind her skirts a red-faced toddling child bawled, a glistening slime streaming from both nostrils. The woman did nothing to comfort or shush it. They both needed a hair combing.

"I had not expected to find the home occupied," he said.

Her fists went to ample hips. "I've papers to show we paid."

A spotted dog lapped at a pie on the table. The place was a mess, the walls and floor streaked with black God-knows-what. Even he'd been a better housekeeper. Henry gestured toward the back of the cottage. "Are you aware of the grave, madam?"

A look of horror came into her yellowish eyes.

"My wife," he said.

"Animals must have been digging," she said. "My husband spent a good portion of his day restoring it. He put up a wall of stones, did a fine job of it, too. Didn't want the little ones bothering it. You know how children can be, particularly curious boys. You're welcome to have a visit with her."

Henry declined, sickened by the idea of scavengers and brats. He shouldn't have been surprised to find the slovenly family there. He'd abandoned the place after all, without bothering to inform the owner. He rode back to town to discover that his bedsit had been leased as well, his clothes given to the Sisters of Mercy.

"You might give notice next time," said the landlord. "Was I supposed to hold the room indefinitely?"

On the man's cluttered mantel, next to a dusty shepherd-boy figurine, stood Meg's ginger jar. Henry noticed almost immediately and took it down. "It belonged to my wife."

"I was keeping it safe," the landlord said defensively.

Henry turned to go, not knowing where.

The landlord spoke up. "The Germans might have a room to spare. The old frau won't allow you in as you are, though. Five pence will buy you a hot bath. I'll toss in a trim free of charge, knowing your sorrow."

Henry paid double for a full tub, refusing the charity. There was sufficient money in the bank. The landlord sold him a threadbare suit, the sleeves of which were too short. The castoff got him to the tailor, where he was measured for a mourning suit, to the undertaker's after that, where he arranged for Meg's immediate unearthing. He went next to the Germans' and took the one available room without inspecting it.

Three days later, when the suit was ready, he hired a hack and rode out to the Freylocks'. He had in mind a simple graveside service. He meant only to ask Mr. Freylock for an extended leave.

Mrs. Freylock fell upon him weeping. She called her husband to the door. Together, with far too much chatter, they brought him inside, seating him in the best chair in the best room, feeding him tea and crumpets he could not taste.

"Shall we host the memory service here, Mr. Oades?" She glanced toward her husband, who nodded.

"I couldn't ask it of you," said Henry. "Just a marker might be best."

"Forgive me for saying so," said Mrs. Freylock. "But that hardly seems adequate."

Henry shook his head, his weary thoughts clashing. He was incapable of making the smallest decision lately. "I don't know."

Mrs. Freylock touched his sleeve. "For your wife and children."

Henry felt himself on the brink of tears. "All right. Thank you."

She smiled. "It's settled then. Is there a beloved photograph we might display?"

"The fire took everything, madam."

A little whimper escaped her lips. "I wasn't thinking."

Her nervous hands did not still for a second; they went to her throat, to her hair, to her ear bobs, and back to her throat. She pushed the plate of crumpets his way again. How unlike his Meg she was. His wife had possessed a certain feminine manliness all women could learn from.

Mrs. Freylock said something. He leaned toward her. "I beg your pardon?"

She pantomimed plucking. "*Flowers,* Mr. Oades. What sort would you prefer?"

"My wife enjoyed her roses," Henry said. For a light-headed half moment he thought to correct himself. *Enjoys.* My wife *enjoys* her roses. He was deliriously tired, and missing her so.

Something was said then about the funeral biscuits, but Henry did not retain it. He was allowed to leave finally. The same hackie drove him back to the Germans', where the stench of cooking cabbage reached even his small attic room. He vomited into the empty basin and swiped his mouth. Minutes later the downstairs girl knocked on his door. He vomited again, and then let her in to take the basin. Her elfin face pinched in disgust. But he was past caring what others might think.

◈◈

THE FOLLOWING WEDNESDAY he drove himself to the service. His hands trembled on the reins; they were freezing, despite the heavy black gloves, despite the unseasonably warm weather. He wished the day over and done with.

A large crepe bouquet with a card attached was fixed to the

Freylocks' front door. Henry approached, squinting to read the names of his wife and children. The loss flooded. He would never see them again, never touch them or be touched by them. His weakened leg bowed and began to give way. He clutched the knocker to keep from falling. The door opened. Mrs. Freylock caught him and ushered him inside, where the perfume of cut flowers—roses, daylilies, and glads—put sparks in his vision and started a jabbing headache behind his right eye. Good God, they were stashed in vases everywhere.

"Please sit, Mr. Oades. It's all so difficult, I know."

Henry sat, and then stood again. "I'm fine," he said. "If I may have a moment to collect myself, please, Mrs. Freylock."

She excused herself, leaving him alone in the sweet humid darkness. The heavy curtains were drawn, the clocks stopped at six o'clock, the imagined time of their deaths. The mirrors were covered in the old-fashioned superstitious manner, to prevent his family's spirits from becoming lost in their own reflections.

Meg's closed coffin lay on three straight-back chairs against the north wall. A pair of lighted candles had been placed at her head. He went to her, wondering if the Freylocks had looked inside, as he was tempted to do one last time. He had an aching need for her, a painful desire to see her whole and naked, with her hair loose and long. He wept, stroking the coffin lid as he might her lovely flank. "You're the best girl," he whispered. "The very best girl."

The mourners began arriving at eleven, in twos and fours. By half past the air was thick with their scented hush. Henry stood sentry alongside the coffin, accepting condolences. "Thank you," he murmured, over and over.

Cyril Bell took him by surprise. Henry had not seen him come in. Bell stepped up smart, bringing forth the simpering matron on his arm. "May I present Mrs. Wells." There was a lewd flush to

Bell, an obscene glint in his eye. "She's walked in our same sad shoes, Mr. Oades."

A widow then, evidently recovered quite nicely from her own grief. She clung to Bell as if he were a sweepstakes prize. Batting eyelashes and painted puckered lips. Would he marry her, take her to his wife's still warm bed? Look at the blatant creature. She'd accept in a wink, wouldn't she? Seeing them together deepened Henry's sadness. There was only rot everywhere he looked, both malignant and ordinary. He thought it time to leave these lawless islands, home to the Maori and the debauched pair standing before him.

❖❖

HE ORDERED A memory stone to be placed over Meg's grave. Two months later, Henry went alone to the cemetery. He saw that his wife's and children's names were spelled correctly and then he left. He didn't like the place, with its imposing spiked fence and brown grass. There was no comfort to be found among the blank-eyed stone cherubs, no peace. God knows, he did not feel his family there.

He returned to work, but still could not concentrate on the ledgers. On Monday, the distillery's caretaker quit his post. Henry impulsively asked to replace him.

"Fancy emptying the slops of your underlings, do you?" said Mr. Freylock.

Henry ignored the sarcasm. He knew what the lowly job entailed. "May I or may I not have the post, sir?"

Mr. Freylock sighed. "You'll last a week, if that."

❖❖

HENRY BEGAN coming in earlier and leaving later. He checked the rattraps first thing every morning, tossing the carcasses into the bin to be burned. Next he swept and cleaned the lavatories. He appreciated the mindless hard work; it allowed him not to think. Nights he spent at the Germans'. The old couple rarely bothered him. He ate supper in the frau's kitchen, and then went straight to bed, too tired to read. He stayed at the same routine for nearly six months, until the purposelessness won out. He presented his resignation in writing.

Mr. Freylock peered over his spectacles. "You're leaving altogether?"

"I am, sir."

"Returning home, then?"

Henry shook his head. He'd written to Meg's parents finally, and was not about to compound their anguish or his own by returning to England alone. "I'm off to America." How foreign it sounded said aloud. "To San Francisco, California, to be precise."

"Why there of all godforsaken places? I have an acquaintance who's been. It's a filthy city. Chock full of thieves and cutthroats. Nothing but the lowest class of humanity."

"No worse than here," Henry said flatly. "I sail on Saturday."

"What are your plans upon arrival?"

"I've none at present."

"You've truly gone round the bend, Henry."

"Perhaps, sir."

He might have gone to Mexico or Argentina; but the ship to America was due to leave port first. Had a ship sailed for China that morning, he'd be gone.

❖❖

ON SATURDAY, the Germans insisted on a hearty farewell breakfast, and Henry got off later than planned. The men's hatch was nearly full by the time he came on board. He walked the smoky narrow aisles between the tiers of bunks, searching out an empty.

"Here's one, mister." An American kid called from the across the way, pointing to the berth just beneath him. "Better come claim it."

The kid introduced himself. "Willy Morgan." He watched Henry take out Meg's jar and wrap it in his spare flannel. "What's in the jug?" He hung over the edge of his berth, exhaling a rotten onion stench. "Strange thing to be bringing along," he said.

Henry paid him no mind. He returned the jar to his satchel, placing the satchel at the foot end, where he could keep an eye on it.

Willy Morgan continued to study Henry. "You're not one of those funny types, are you? If you are, let's get one thing straight here and now."

"I'm not."

"I've come across a few in my travels. More girl than boy, some of them. Can't fault a genuine man for asking, mister. I was only making certain. The ladies' jug and all."

"It belonged to my wife, if it's any of your concern, which it decidedly is not."

The rancid lad laughed, mocking him. *"Which it decidedly is not."*

It took no time to discover that the boy was the cheery sort, with a lust for camaraderie equaling Henry's desire for solitude.

That first night at sea Willy thrashed above, nattering without letup. The lamps were out. The men were preparing to sleep. "They say," said Willy, "that a man can live two hundred and fifty years in California."

Henry punched his hard pillow and turned to the wall. "Who in God's name would wish it?"

"Just making conversation," said Willy. "Did I say I was foolish enough to believe it? There's plenty that do, though. I knew a crazy old man once. He was—"

"Jesus," hissed Henry. "Go to sleep now."

Somewhere in the dark a man gasped and began breathing heavily, with obvious building pleasure. Willy let out a nervous giggle and whispered, "Funny types. They're everywhere, I tell you."

Henry said nothing. He was sick to death of all types.

A Deal

STINKING MEN penned together will scrap out of boredom. They were three weeks out to sea. It didn't take much to incite them these days. Henry was lying on his berth reading when that night's brawl started. A dozen unwashed brutes fell in, cursing and hollering. Henry made his escape quickly, climbing up the ladder to the outside with Willy close behind.

They went around to the stern. Henry preferred it here, particularly on a starry phosphoric night like this. The wake had a mesmerizing effect, allowing him to drift from himself at times. He'd talked to the boatswain about a life at sea. "You don't strike me as the sort," the sailor said without explanation. Offended at first, Henry had gone away thinking perhaps he was right. There was precious little privacy aboard. He was forever seeking it out and failing.

Willy leaned precariously over the rail. "Idiots," he said, of their hatch mates.

"Cretins," Henry agreed. "Mind your footing, lad. I shan't be going in after you."

Willy fell back again and offered a cigarette.

Henry refused out of habit. He hadn't smoked since the deaths of his children. Nor had he touched spirits, not since killing a bottle waiting for them to return, that first night in the cottage. At the time he said no more, never again. It had seemed a sin to enjoy himself. But the Lenten sacrifice lacked meaning lately. Sot or saint, they weren't coming back either way.

He wondered if Mexico might have been the better choice. One can live on the cheap there, he'd been told. The natives aren't as bothersome, it was said, as rudely inquisitive as the Americans. He could always go. If California didn't suit him; if nothing purposeful turned up. Christ, did it gnaw. What was he to do next?

Willy cleared his throat. Henry willed him to keep his adolescent thoughts to himself. What did an untethered lad have to ponder? Twenty years old, if that. Henry was married at his age. The first, a stillborn boy, was on the way. John came next, beautiful lad.

Willy stared intently at the water. "Ever have the temptation to jump in headfirst?"

"No." But Henry had, more than once. He imagined a swift cold shock, the terror over in an instant.

Willy drew on his cigarette. "It's like those Siren beauties. Do you know about them?"

"Yes."

"I thought so. You're the bookish type. Let me guess. A schoolteacher?"

"No." A shooting star, first one, then another, arced and died in the southern sky. The grandeur brought a rise of tears to Henry's eyes. He thought of John running about the yard with his homemade sextant, taking sightings, meticulously jotting down his findings.

"Those Sirens will sing to a fellow," said Willy, "lure him right into the drink."

"I believe their primary occupation is shipwrecking," said Henry.

"I beg to differ, sir. Odysseus . . . do you know him?"

"Yes." Henry had found Homer too fanciful, Odysseus's exploits too preposterous. He was fifteen when he read *The Odyssey*, in love with Verdi and all things Italian.

"Well," said Willy, "Odysseus lashed himself to the mast because he feared the Siren would get to *him*, don't you see. I don't think he was all that worried about his ship."

"Perhaps," murmured Henry, recalling the sting of his father's strap against the back of his legs. The headmaster had reported him a daydreamer. Flighty thinking could be beaten from a boy. His bickering parents had agreed upon that much at least.

Willy asked, "Do you know much about wicked women, sir?"

A peculiar question from a peculiar boy. "Not a thing."

"You say things in your sleep. I thought you might."

Henry glanced sideways. "Such as?"

Willy whined, "*Please, Meg*," embarrassing Henry. "Things like that." He flicked his cigarette overboard. "Mine ran off. I miss her something fierce. I'd also like to shoot her dead. Her and the goddamned skunk that stole her."

"You're young," said Henry.

"Sure," Willy snapped. "I've got my whole life ahead. I'll find another. Is that what you're about to say? I'll find a sweet girl who will do right by me, is that it?" He spat an angry glob over the rail. "I don't want anyone else. I want my goddamned Polly."

Henry felt for him, though what was there to say? Yes, lad, I understand completely. There's no such thing as a settled life. Endure the day, get on to the next. Enjoy the sea if you can. Enjoy your smoke. Enjoy a grand void of the bowels. Try to sleep. Try not to dream. It's the best you can do.

A pleasant breeze was kicking up. Henry considered sleeping

on deck and inviting cuckolded Willy to do the same. He felt himself turning soft, involuntarily paternal. He patted the boy's narrow shoulder and changed the subject. "What shall you do in California?"

A resigned sadness passed over Willy's bony features. "My great-uncle owns a dairy farm in Berkeley. I'll be doing time there."

"Where is Berkeley?"

"Near San Francisco. Just across the bay. It's a dandy place if you happen to be a cow."

"Benign creatures, aren't they?" said Henry.

Willy snorted a laugh. *"Bay-nine?"*

"Placid," said Henry. "Tranquil."

Willy shrugged, lighting another cigarette. "If you say so. They sleep, they eat, they shit. I stayed a month. This was after I got out of jail. How can a man be punished for abducting his own goddamned wife? I didn't *abduct* her, anyway. I just put her in a wagon, tried to talk a little common sense into her deaf and dumb skull. So they locked me up. All right. I get out and can't find her anywhere. I was in a low position. I let my pap talk me into going down to the crazy uncle's farm. I stayed a month, like I say, then shipped out, got all the way to New Zealand. But that didn't work out. So here I am. I promised my folks I'd stay put this time, give the farm a year. I know what my pap's up to. He figures I'll forget all about her. He's wrong. I won't."

Henry closed his eyes. He appreciated the briny wind on his face and Willy's fragrant smoke wafting his way. "I want to go home," said Willy. "Show her the man I've become. Give her another chance. Pap says she's no good, not worth it."

Henry asked, "Did the girl not marry the skunk?"

"How could she? We're not divorced. She can't get it done by proxy, can she?" Willy answered himself. "Naw. Hell no, she can't. I have rights. I learned a thing or two at sea. I've been at it better than three months now, by the way." The information came with lifted chin and shoulders. The lad enjoyed a brief moment of pride before his shoulders sagged. "Goddamn," he whispered to himself, flicking another cigarette into the sea. "Turns out I don't have a seaman's constitution. The captain put me off in Wellington, told me to try something else."

"You needn't take one bloke's word for it," said Henry.

"He was right," said Willy. "I'm no damn good at it." He turned to go back down.

"Why not sleep on deck tonight."

"Naw," said Willy. "The stern's the worst place to be with a weak belly."

Alone, Henry stretched out, hugging himself. It was cold. The stars dazzled. He lay awake thinking about his family, holding their faces in his mind one by one, weeping for each individually. He saved John for last. His son loomed painfully large tonight.

✦✦

IN THE MORNING, over watery porridge, he asked Willy about dairy farming. The other men had breakfasted and left. They were alone but for a small platoon of Hindu coolies tidying up.

"There's not much to tell," said Willy, with his usual shrug. "They're milked, let out, run back in, milked again. Why are you asking?"

"Numbers," said Henry, scribbling down an imaginary column with his spoon. "It's all I've done, all I know. I fancy a change."

"Believe me, mister, there's nothing *fancy* about dairy farming. It's hard, backbreaking, putrid work. The strongest lye soap won't get rid of the evil shit stench."

"I don't expect I'd mind," said Henry, envisioning wide green acres.

Willy put the porridge bowl to his face and licked the interior clean. His wispy young billy goat beard came away with gray curds clinging. "I *expect* you would," he said. "It's downright miserable. No neighbors within spitting distance. The townies turn up their noses, cross to the other side of the street."

"I've no interest in a social life," said Henry. He pictured lowing, nodding animals, a serene absence of humanity.

Willy drummed his spoon on the rim of his tin bowl. "A man can get lonesome."

Henry shook his head. He was lonely for no one but his family.

Across the room, a coolie with a tub of dirty crockery stared their way, obviously wanting them gone. The men in the hatch were treated as nuisances, freight that required feeding. Henry met the lackey's eye and took a lazy bite of cold porridge. He was in no mood to be dictated to. "I keep my own company," he said to Willy.

Willy's chapped lips pursed in contemplation. "I've got a proposal for you." The sulky coolie approached. "Shoo fly," said Willy, flapping his hand in dismissal. "We're busy." The coolie retreated with a scowl, making a racket of collecting beakers and bowls at the next table. Willy leaned in.

"Out with it," said Henry.

"Say I set you up with my uncle. He's not as bad as I let on, by the way. You just have to get to know him, learn what to ignore. And the cows, they're just like you say. *Bay-nine*. Sweet things, named after flowers. Daffodil's the friendliest. So say I get him to take you on."

Henry felt a pump of excitement. "I suppose I'd catch on."

Willy rolled his milky-blue eyes. "Any numskull would." He blushed pink. "Sorry, sir."

Henry disregarded the slight. "I know nothing about farm life."

"Surely you've milked a cow or two in your time."

"I haven't."

"Well, Lord howdy, there's nothing to it." Willy pulled a black glove from a pocket and held it fingers down. "Looky here. Watch close." He took the middle wool finger into the palm of his hand and squeezed with thumb and forefinger. "See how I start at the top of the teat?" Henry nodded, absorbed. Willy laughed. "Look at that beautiful milk, will you? It's spilling all over the table."

It was a strangely optimistic, queerly buoyant, sort of feeling. Henry's palms moistened with the sensation, his ears rang. He'd had hunches, premonitions, but none as strong as this. His natural self belonged out of doors, not chained to a wooden stool in some blasted cubbyhole. Had he always known it? He thought so now. He believed it a fact of birth gone ignored.

Willy returned the glove to his pocket and ran a hand through his scraggly blond hair. "You'd be taking my job, see? No reason to tell Uncle Ned you've never met a cow. In return you'll give me two months' pay up front. One hand washes the other, right? What do you say?"

"What will *you* do?"

"I'll be on the first train to Polly, thanks to you staking me."

Henry hesitated. What right had he to undermine another father's wishes? "Your dad won't approve."

"I'm going anyway," Willy said, "with or without your help. I decided last night. I'm a man now. I'll be making my own decisions from here on." He played with his spoon, glancing up toward the open hatch. There was a smell of rain, the sound of flapping canvas above. "Thought I might do you and the uncle a favor," Willy murmured, more to himself.

Henry asked gently, "How old are you, son?"

Willy's apple throbbed in his young pimpled throat. "I'm eighteen years and two months old, sir."

Henry nodded. Had he not known everything there was to know at the same age? He knew by then there'd be no music conservatory in his future. Pretentious, impractical nonsense. Once married with a child on the way, Henry agreed with his father. Dreams don't butter the parsnips, his mother used to say.

Willy thrust out a hand. "What do you think? Do we have deal?"

Henry took his slim hand. "Two months up front?"

"Twenty-four American dollars, sir."

"Once the post is secured."

Willy grinned, pumping Henry's hand. "Let's smoke on it like the honest injuns do."

Henry accepted the cigarette, inhaling deeply. It was exhilarating, like a lungful of fresh new air.

Berkeley

*T*HE SAILOR IN CHARGE of the animals allowed him to milk. "Sure, guv. She's all yours." During the final week at sea, Henry went to the animal pen twice daily. "They don't care for surprises," said the sailor. "Pick the side of her you prefer and stick to it."

Henry chose the right side, resting his head against the warm agreeable flank as instructed. The stomachs gurgled in his ear. The cow chewed wetly, pissed hot streams, produced copious clods of yellow dung. By the third session he was milking with ease, falling a bit in love with the whole ripe enterprise. It was a world made up of just himself and an animal, a world he could somehow make sense of. The sailor in charge said he was born to it. Henry took it as a compliment.

Willy regularly looked on. "You've got the hang of it, Hank!" Henry let the nickname pass; he could afford to be tolerant. Their days together were numbered. Willy followed him everywhere now, as if in fear of losing him, or the twenty-four American dollars to come. He was at Henry's side the morning California appeared on the foggy horizon. Above them, a herd of first-class passengers trampled to the bow.

"There she is, Hank! Do you see her?" Henry nodded. There was land certainly, hilly and gray this far out. They might be anywhere. Willy threw open his arms, his eyes filming over. "America! Home of the brave, brother."

Willy had shaved his odd little beard and done something to quiet the halitosis, which may well have been what drove his Polly away in the first place. Henry hoped she'd receive Willy with open repentant arms. He wished them a long, happy life and a houseful of healthy children. He thought well enough of the boy, but would not miss his gregarious company. The youthful energy fatigued him. At thirty-three Henry felt too old for it all. He desired peace, only that. It was not asking too much.

Once docked, the passengers poured off the ship, all vying and pushing, including Henry. He was glad to be quit of the ship, and the men aboard her. A cold rain fell. His aching leg shook like a drunk's in bad weather.

"Hank!" Willy darted and weaved through the throng, calling over his shoulder. "This way. Follow me."

He and Willy carried only one satchel each. Within the first hour ashore they were on the ferry, crossing the bay to Berkeley. Henry sat in silence, huddled inside his greatcoat. He stared straight ahead, thinking of Meg, of arriving in New Zealand, the chaos, the peaked children, his ailing, useless self. How strong she was that day, how competent. She'd been gone from him nearly fifteen months now. At the moment it felt as if she'd just stepped out. Other times it seemed a century had passed.

"Don't fall asleep," said Willy, nudging his arm. "You'll sometimes see whales in the bay. A big launch was nearly overturned by one once."

Henry turned from him, feigning an interest in watching for whales. The world was solid gray outside the window. He could not tell which direction they were headed. It was impossible to get his bearings in a new place without her.

After a while he thought to ask, "Is there lodging nearby in the event something goes awry?"

Willy laughed. "You say the damnedest things, Hank."

"Your uncle may not be hiring."

"I told you the job's waiting. He'll have no choice."

Henry turned back to the monotony outside, miserable with doubt. Mexico may have been the better choice. Or perhaps he should have stayed put. There was always that faint chance. No, there wasn't. They were gone. Gone. Gone. Gone.

❖❖

"HER HAIR IS reddish gold," said Willy, on the way to the uncle's. "She wears it up like the grown-up ladies, but I prefer it down. She used to let me comb out the knots."

They'd leased a little rig and horse, which Willy planned to turn right around tonight. The lad drove too fast on the narrow road. He was afraid of missing the evening train to St. Louis, where he would surprise Polly. The promiscuous girl had sprouted wings and a halo. She was the prettiest by far of four sisters; her pies had won prizes. Not once since they had arrived had Willy goddamned her or threatened to harm her. Not once did he mention the other man, the skunk who stole her.

"You can think me nuts all you want," said Willy. "I can tell you do. She loved me once, you know. A man doesn't forget that, doesn't just say the hell with her."

"I don't think you nuts, lad."

"A good woman makes it all worthwhile," said Willy.

"It's true," said Henry. "It would behoove you never to forget the fact."

❖❖

THE UNCLE'S two-storied house was set far back from the road. Flowering trees made a bower leading up to a porch in need of repair. A floor plank was missing. The green paint was chipped and peeling. Willy rang the hanging bell, whispering, "Tell him you love the Lord if he asks."

The bald-headed uncle came to the door in his stocking feet. "Well, well," he said, baring a menacing set of false teeth. "The prodigal nephew has returned, has he?" There was no discernible affection in his voice, only sarcasm. Henry disliked him on sight. Willy greeted him with a hearty handshake.

"Good to see you, Uncle Ned. I won't be staying long. I'm taking the nine o'clock train to St. Louis. There's no use trying to talk me out of it. This here's your new man, Hank Oades. He's topnotch, milks with the best of them." He pointed to the gap in the porch and said, without knowing the first thing about Henry's abilities, "He's handy with a hammer and saw, too. You won't be sorry."

The old man looked up at Henry, cocking his head like a sparrow. His beady eyes were the same cloudy blue as the boy's. "Do you love the Lord, son?"

Henry had not given the Lord a great deal of thought lately and would not take up the subject with the old bloke in any event. "I do, sir," he said, keeping all doors ajar for now.

They were invited in and seated for refreshments. Henry was introduced to Portia, the girl of all tasks, a spindly woman of thirty or so. She stammered a shy hello and then left the room, returning after a bit wearing a different frock and a yellow ribbon in her brown hair. She served tea and plain shortcake, and then disappeared again. Henry had not eaten since early morning; it was half past three now. He devoured the dry cake and accepted with gratitude the old man's offer of more. The uncle shuffled off to the kitchen, humming a jolly tune under his breath. Willy grinned, slurping tea from his saucer. "He's taken a shine to you. We might as well settle up. A deal's a deal."

The uncle did not attempt to dissuade Willy from leaving. On the contrary, he congratulated the boy for going after what was rightfully his, for staking his proper claim. He slapped his armrest and turned village vicar. "For the husband is the head of the wife, even as Christ is the head of the Church!"

"Amen, Uncle," said Willy, nodding solemnly. He excused himself and went to wash up.

The uncle pushed himself to a stand, beckoning to Henry. "I'll give you the nickel tour while there's still light."

Henry presumed himself hired. He followed the uncle out the door. He didn't much care for the pious old man. But he was the head of himself. He could always leave, expensive lesson learned.

Outside, the damp ground was mush in places, uneven. Henry struggled some.

"Something wrong with your leg, Hank?"

"It was injured in a fall," said Henry, breathing hard. "Pay it no mind."

The spry old man slowed, allowing him to catch up. "I've got a turpentine liniment that'll bring some relief. We can go back now if you want. The cows will still be here tomorrow."

They'd come to the entrance of the barn. Henry craned to see inside. He could hear the animals, a contented mingle of nickers and snorts. "I'm all right," he said.

"You remind me of another Englishman I knew once," said the old man. "His name was Joseph Abbott. You wouldn't happen to be acquainted, would you?"

Henry smiled at the absurd improbability. "No, sir."

"He was a righteous man," said the uncle, crossing two fingers. "He and the Lord were like this." Henry nodded. They went inside.

The uncle introduced the cows one by one, telling little stories. Pansy socialized with the pigs, preferring their company over her own kind. Iris mooed in her sleep. Petunia was completely blind in one eye, partially so in the other. Hyacinth was in heat. The uncle stroked the blind cow, scratching beneath her black ears.

"She's not much good to me anymore," he said. "But I don't have the heart to beef her. She was my wife's favorite." He looked up at Henry, tears rising. "Belle . . . my wife passed last year."

Henry's throat clogged with sadness. "Mine as well," he said.

"It's a hard thing."

"It is."

The bereft uncle turned his back. He pulled on Petunia's wet chin and examined her slick yellow teeth, turning back composed. "I'm pleased you're here," he said. "The mule-headed nephew would just run off again. I'll pay fifteen dollars a month, plus a room of your own in the house. It's got a picture window."

"I'm new to this," said Henry.

"It doesn't take a college degree," said the uncle. "Hard work is all that's called for."

Henry petted Petunia. "All right, then," he said. "I'll have a go at it."

This life without them had to begin somewhere.

A Proposal

*T*HE UNCLE began to die in the spring of 1897. At eighty-four, Ned Barnhill was eager to join his beloved Belle in heaven. Henry and Portia discussed the situation. They both believed the old man had successfully willed himself ill. Henry had been with him just over three years by this time. Portia had lived in the little room off the kitchen for more than a decade, keeping house first for Mr. and Mrs. Barnhill, now mainly for Henry. Thoughts of marriage would naturally occur to her, he supposed, given the domestic setting. He should have been quicker to notice. She offered up her own supper one evening. "Seconds?" A cannier man would have guessed her objective then.

With the onset of cough and fever the old man took to his bed upstairs. Henry's room was just down the hall. The tortured hacking kept them both awake nights. The doctor said Mr. Barnhill might come around, given the proper regimen. The uncle accused the doctor of interfering with the Good Lord's plan. He stayed in bed, waiting impatiently.

Henry wrote to Willy Morgan in St. Louis, the only relative he knew of. Willy sent his regrets. His furniture store didn't allow him a day off, much less the time required to come all the way to California. Lucius, his firstborn, was already walking. The next was due any time. Polly, whom Henry had never laid eyes upon, sent her love. Henry didn't tell Mr. Barnhill they'd corresponded.

Henry was pretty much running the place now. The old man had slowed considerably over the last year and now he was useless. In June, Henry hired Titus Crump, a quiet fellow who didn't loaf. Titus went back to town at night, leaving Henry alone with Portia.

"It's strange," she said at supper. "Only the two of us downstairs now." She smiled, coyly twisting a lock of hair around her finger. It was clear she did not think the arrangement strange at all.

She chose to woo him on the sly, with charged gazes and food. Henry was uncomfortably aware of her fond feelings and did not encourage her in the least. He never lingered at the table, never said more than thank you for a succulent dish prepared just for him. She was a wonderfully inventive chef, turning out juicy roasts simmered with lady apples, crisp fowl stuffed with gooseberries and sage. There'd be no end to his compliments were she much older or much younger, or married. He'd bring tokens from town, lay chocolates and ribbons before her in honest appreciation, but he dared not. It would be neither decent nor smart.

They shared the nursing duties. Portia brought up oxtail broth and lemon tea on a tray. "He wants to starve himself," she said to Henry on Thursday. Her cheeks had been freshly rouged. She wore a butterfly gewgaw in her hair. "You should insist he put his teeth in and eat something solid, an egg at least."

"Portia thought you might enjoy an egg," he said, entering the old man's bedroom after supper. There was no response. He lay still as a mummy, the Bible opened on his chest, his bespectacled eyes open wide and staring. Henry felt a pang of sorrow for his passing and for the fact that he'd been alone. He approached reverently, intending to remove the spectacles and close the old man's lids. Inches from his face, a withered hand rose from the bed-clothes and swatted the air. Henry jerked back, his heart battering. "Christ Almighty!"

"Blasphemer," snapped the uncle. "What's the matter with you? Sneaking up on me like that."

"I was about to remove your specs," said Henry.

Mr. Barnhill closed his Bible. "I'm still capable of that much."

"About the egg, sir?"

"A dying man has no need for eggs."

"The pot, then?"

"If you please," he said. "Thank you, Hank."

Henry saw to the personal details, saving Portia and the uncle the embarrassment. He brought out the clean chamber pot and removed the lid. He lifted the frail old man beneath the arms and positioned him over the pot. He was light as cotton now, weighing no more than seven stone, if that. Henry turned his head, as if to draw a privacy curtain between them. A staccato of gas was passed, a pitiful trickle delivered. Another few moments went by unproductively. The old man shook himself off with a sigh.

"I'm finished now."

Henry returned him to bed and blew out the lamp. Some nights the old man asked him to read Scripture aloud, but not tonight. Henry went downstairs and settled in the front room with a brandy. He looked forward to the end of the day. Portia would be in the kitchen or in her tiny room. She wouldn't think of entering the best room except to clean. He might read or simply smoke his pipe before the fire. It was entirely up to him, whatever he fancied.

Some months later, in an unusually waggish mood, the uncle asked Henry if he was satisfied. *Content* was the word he used. Henry had just tucked him in and thought himself done for the evening. "Are you content here, Hank?"

"Why wouldn't I be?" Henry wasn't sure whether he meant

here on earth or here on the farm. Either way he was not in the mood for a philosophical debate. He had other concerns pressing. A heifer was expected to calve any day now. She was young and small; it wouldn't go easy.

The old man cocked his birdie head. "I'm leaving the farm to you." He laughed at Henry's stunned expression and broke into a fit of coughing. Henry went for the beaker of cold tea, putting it to Mr. Barnhill's toothless gums. The old man pushed it away, sputtering, choking, laughing. Merry tears streamed from his eyes. "I'm your gift horse, boy. So stop staring me in the mouth. She's all yours."

"It's a practical joke then," said Henry.

The old man shook his head. "I'm dead serious. Now there's a *practical* joke for you."

"What about your relations?"

The old man sobered. "I've no blood kin left."

"There's Willy Morgan."

"Except him and his no-good pap. They had their chance."

Henry had often considered a farm of his own. Twenty-five acres or so, nothing as grand as the uncle's sixty. "Perhaps a partial purchase could be arranged," he said.

"I can't take your money with me," said the uncle. "Any more than I can take the farm."

Henry went off in reverie, striding across his land, making improvements. The bloody bull would never accidentally get to any young heifer of *his*. "I don't know what to say, sir."

The uncle brightened, sitting up a bit. "Say you won't pitch the place into ruin. Say you'll get in solid with the Lord. Say you'll do right by Portia."

"How shall I do right by Portia?"

"She's a fine girl. Steadfast, sturdy. Not too hard on the eyes, is she?"

"No, sir."

"She's a wonder at the stove."

Henry agreed. "She is."

The uncle said slyly, "She's smitten by you, Hankie boy."

Henry did not hedge the truth. "As I am not by her."

The old man frowned, as if Henry had spoiled his happy game. "You might learn."

"I won't."

The scowl deepened. "Never mind then. Just forget I spoke. We won't discuss it again. Blow out the lamp, please. The glare is hurting my eyes."

Henry complied, angry at himself for snapping at the dangling chop without looking for sharp bones. Besides, the offer was likely a moot one. The uncle's color had improved recently. Twice this week he'd held down eggs. He was the sort to outlive them all.

The old man's voice quivered in the dark. "A soft, warm woman under your covers is a blessing, Hank, a precious gift from God. He means to compensate us for what we must endure on earth. Think about that."

Randy old coot, Henry thought, trying not to mind the disappointment. Everything comes with its cost.

❖❖

THE UNCLE kept his word. He never mentioned Portia or the farm again. He rallied a degree around Christmas, and then took another turn for the worse after the New Year. He died in his sleep in February, of a worn-out heart, the doctor said, not consumption.

The lawyer came out the following week, asking to speak to Henry and Portia both. Henry was shocked to learn that he'd been left the farm free and clear, without contingencies. He was humbled; he felt guiltily elated. Portia had been bequeathed Mrs. Barnhill's silver comb set, the old man's coin collection, and five hundred dollars.

"It would make a nice dowry," she said to the lawyer.

Henry pretended not to hear.

◆◆

PORTIA WORKED UP her nerve that same evening. Henry was seated at the kitchen table, finishing up delicious roast duck with creamed potatoes and peas. She hadn't sat with him before; she didn't now. She moved between table and stove as was her habit, looking serious, rather queenly, with her hair drawn back tight.

She said in an offhand manner, "Do you remember the day you came?"

He nodded to his plate. "Yes."

"I was mortified. There was no sauce for the cake."

He had no memory of cake without sauce. "It was lovely without," he said.

"You were every bit the gentleman," she said. "You didn't let on it was missing."

He smiled.

"Mr. Oades, I think it's time we married."

His insides clenched. He looked up at her. "I cannot. I'm sorry."

Tears flashed in her round eyes. "Just like that? Without a second's worth of thought?"

"I'm sorry." He *was* sorry, sorry to wound her, humiliate her; but he was glad, too, to be done with the pretense finally.

"You're not going to bother to say you're flattered at least?"

"I am, of course." He knew that was not what she wanted to hear.

"Ha! Sure you are." She tore off her apron and threw it at him. The skirt went to his lap, the bib into congealed duck grease. "Clean up your own mess, why don't you?" He folded the apron and stood.

"I shan't marry again," he said.

Her expression shifted, becoming a mix of longing and regret.

"Your poor wife would want that for you? She'd expect you to spend the rest of your days alone?"

"I don't know," he said truthfully.

She took the apron from him, picking at a loose thread, her bottom lip pulsing. "I can't stay on under the circumstances."

Henry nodded. "I understand."

Portia turned and went into her room, closing and latching the door.

Henry quickly washed the supper things and then retreated to the front room, relieved and ashamed. He should have spoken up a long time ago, found a way to act the man. He wasn't at ease with women anymore, or with himself for that matter, in their presence. It was best to steer clear, to simply leave them be altogether.

❖❖

On Monday, Henry went into town to inquire at the employment agency on Portia's behalf. He was immediately successful. The Charles Middletons were a prominent family with a grand house near the university. Dr. Charles Middleton, the bursar, came on Tuesday to fetch her himself.

She stood on the porch, clutching her battered brown case. "Good-bye, Mr. Oades."

"Good-bye, Portia. Good luck."

She held his gaze. He could not very well look away. "I'm a forgiving woman, should you have a change of heart." He had no proper response. They stood mute for an eternity. Finally she lifted her sturdy chin and made a smart turn. From the back, with those erect shoulders, she reminded him of Meg.

❖❖

He interviewed five domestics before settling on Dora McGinnis, a plump, uneducated girl of fifteen. She appeared a born workhorse and not bright enough to scheme without him catching first wind of it. "Fine, then," he said, stern as a dad, as a bloody granddad, no one a girl would take to. "You'll do." She turned out to be a rather dull cook, but that was all right. A dry rump roast seemed appropriate somehow. She spoke when addressed, staying out of sight for the most part. Eventually, happily, he began to forget she was even about.

In April he moved his belongings from the small room to the uncle's much larger one down the hall. Little else changed otherwise. The farm was thriving. Wright's on Center Street bragged in print that they used only the best and purest of cream in their ice cream—his. He grew wealthier by the month. He grew leaner as well, losing the soft flesh about the middle. He was lonely at times, but more often not, due to his schedule. A Sunday spent idle was not for him. He worked seven days, starting before dawn, continuing past dark. Only on Saturdays did he finish early. At half past two he cleared the kitchen of Dora and had his bath, then changed into a clean shirt and collar and rode into town. He visited the library, the tobacconist, the hardware shop, and occasionally the pharmacy, in that order. Afterward he treated himself to an oyster dinner at Smith's Chop House. He was typically home before nine, a dull creature of habit. Not that he craved change; he liked his life. He would say he was content if anyone cared to ask again.

❖❖

ON A SATURDAY in late summer of 1898 Henry drove in at his usual hour. Men in town, rooster-proud Americans, were still talking about the destruction of Spain's navy in Manila Bay. You'd think they'd had a personal hand in it.

The fire bells began sounding as he was leaving the Shattuck Avenue pharmacy. In the next moment the young assistant pharmacist came flying from his store. He ran past Henry, his white coat billowing behind him. Henry started after him, smelling the smoke, walking fast at first, and then breaking into a clumsy run. All of Berkeley seemed headed in the same direction. They carried buckets and cans, sped by on foot, on wheels, in buggies. Henry followed the pharmacist around one corner, another, a third, dropping library books along the way, a sack of tobacco.

Fire was already on the roof of the little house. Henry broke through the gabbling crowd, intent on going inside. He came up the walk just as the pharmacist emerged from the black smoke, an expectant woman in his arms. The pharmacist thrust the woman at Henry. "Watch her." Henry staggered back under the sudden weight. The pharmacist ran back inside. The fire wagon pulled up, horses snorting, bells clanging. Gawking neighbors scattered out of the way, reconvening again. Henry carried the woman across the street and lowered her to the grass. She was dazed, muzzy, mumbling incoherently. He removed his coat and made her warm, thinking of Meg, living her burning death for the ten-thousandth time.

Nancy

NANCY FORELAND opened her eyes. "Please, sir." Her throat felt scalded. The bearded man put a big rough palm to her forehead and stroked back her damp hair.

"Gently does it now," he said. "Help's on the way."

The shouting seemed far off. Closer to her ears and nostrils, whispering ladies hovered. Worse than their cloying sweetness was the smell of smoke and horse manure. The baby inside her turned, punching and kicking. Nancy felt on the verge of expelling it onto the wet grass. "Find my husband, will you?" She tapped her front teeth, speaking with difficulty. "He has a gap right here. His name is Francis Foreland. He'll be wearing a white pharmacy coat. Go now. Tell him the baby is coming."

"Mrs. Foreland!" Mrs. Tillman, the reverend's wife, appeared, shiny with sweat.

Nancy was relieved to see a familiar face. "I think the baby is coming."

Mrs. Tillman stooped at Nancy's side. "Nonsense. It's too soon."

The bearded man demanded, "Where's the bloody doctor?"

Mrs. Tillman fussed with the coat covering Nancy. "Who was called?"

He exploded. "Christ—"

Mrs. Tillman clapped her hands to her ears. "Sir!"

"—Almighty! I don't know."

"I'll thank you to keep a godly tongue in your head," said Mrs. Tillman.

"He was sent for a good ten minutes ago," said the man.

Mrs. Tillman stood, glaring down at him. "We'll take her to Dr. Wheeler."

Nancy latched on to his arm. "Francis will take me. Find him, please."

"You'll bring her to our buggy, sir," Mrs. Tillman said. "The reverend is in no condition."

He put his arms beneath Nancy and began a wobbly rise. She grasped his vest with both hands to keep from falling. He shifted her weight. "I have you, madam."

Mrs. Tillman pointed. "Over there, over there."

Nancy took hold of his neck, ashamed of her enormous self. "I'm sorry."

"It's no trouble," he said, clenching his teeth.

"Will you find my husband, sir? Tell him where I've gone?"

A glimmer of tears rose in his dark eyes. "You have my word."

He carried her through the murmuring crowd, across the street to the Tillmans' buggy, which was tied to a spared poplar in front of what was left of their first home together. Nancy tucked her chin and wept. It was entirely her fault. Clumsy and cramping, she'd tipped a lamp and fallen in the attempt to right it. She remembered seeing the front legs of Francis's chair catch fire and thinking her chair would be next. And then she found herself outside, looking up at a starless night sky and the soot-faced man. She'd thought he was a colored at first.

✧✧

IN THE BEGINNING, the Forelands thought themselves lucky to have found such a convenient place so close to the pharmacy, where Francis had just been entrusted to man the night-bell service by himself. The rent was sixteen dollars a month for a spacious four rooms and pantry; but, as the real-estate man said, what did they have to show for their money but a receipt?

For five hundred dollars, one third up front, and the balance due within two years, they could *own* a 50-by-135-foot lot in Berkeley Heights. The real-estate man promised unrivaled views. At an elevation of 350 feet, the outlook opposite the Golden Gate surpassed any scenery on the Pacific coast, he claimed. The persuasive gentleman made a window of his fingers.

"Just picture the daily majesty! And that's not all, young people!"

They'd hardly want to leave such a wonderful place, he said, though when the need arose they'd find the Berryman station just two short blocks away. The Oakland Electric railroad had extended its line to serve Berkeley Heights. And, as if that weren't incentive enough, they'd have complete sewer and water systems, macadamized streets, and curbs, gutters, and sidewalks of concrete.

"You can't afford not to afford it!" said the salesman.

Francis and Nancy began saving that afternoon. She let the housekeeper/plain-cook go, and he began working a long day on Saturday. Her father in Texas wired five dollars when he heard, and his heartiest congratulations.

Sundays became precious to them, the picnics on the beach off Delaware Street after church, the long strolls on campus among the oaks and eucalyptus. Nancy loved the sweet campus air; she loved all of Berkeley, with its rolling hills and canyons, its ever-changing bay. You can look, she'd say, but you won't find a prettier place anywhere. At times on campus she liked to playact, strut along the gravel paths like the brainy girls, carrying her Bible the way they carried their texts, pressed to her ribs just so. Francis said there was no harm in daydreaming. He never poked fun. Nancy adored him, to the point of madness sometimes.

The bearded man said his name. Oaks. Mr. Henry Oaks. She was blanketed still inside his scratchy coat. "I won't forget," she said weakly. "You remind me of one."

He arranged her ever so gently inside the Tillmans' buggy, next to Mrs. Tillman. The reverend sat opposite.

"Thank you, Mr. Oaks," said Nancy. "God bless you."

He smiled a little, closing the buggy door. The reverend gave the signal and they were off before she could think to return Mr. Oaks's coat.

"That one will be the last in line for God's blessing," said Mrs. Tillman, with her hot muttony breath. Nancy turned away, but there was no escaping the odor. The restless baby shifted downward. Nancy gasped, clamping her knees together and contracting every muscle in her body. It couldn't possibly happen now, in a moving buggy, with Rev. Tillman looking on. The baby rolled again, kicking hard, as if to let her know it certainly could. Already she felt herself no match for this child.

♢♢

THE DOCTOR's front windows were aglow. Dr. Wheeler himself came rushing down the front walk, lamp held high and swinging. "Mercy," he whispered, at the sight and smell of her.

Inside, the doctor's maid took her filthy housedress and apron first thing, bundling them up as if for the rag bag. She dressed Nancy in a man's robe, asking, "Is the hair on your legs growing normally? If it is, you're having a girl. Though I'd personally put my money on a boy, the way you're carrying high and round."

"That's what my husband thinks, too," said Nancy.

The doctor gave her an injection. She barely felt his clammy hands between her legs. "You're experiencing hysteria, not labor," he said. Nancy bowed her head and thanked the Lord for hysteria.

The burns on her right hand were salved and bandaged. She was taken to the parsonage afterward and led up to a small dark room. The baby was still at last. "Wake me when Francis comes, please." She closed her eyes and slept without dreaming.

✤✤

THE NEXT MORNING Mrs. Tillman came in with a tray.

"Is Francis waiting?"

Mrs. Tillman sat at the edge of the narrow bed and attempted to spoon-feed her.

"I can manage." Nancy picked up the spoon with her good left hand, testing the hot soup.

"Farina," said Mrs. Tillman.

"Tasty," Nancy lied, putting down the spoon. There were biscuits too, butter and a red jam, and tea to be poured into a pretty china cup, with honey and lemon. "Has anyone gone for him? Does he even know I'm here?"

Round-shouldered Mrs. Tillman inched closer. An oval mirror hung over the washstand. Nancy saw something of a gray vulture in the wavy reflection, as well as something of her own dead mother.

"Dear girl."

Nancy began stroking her belly in small circles. Very bad news was coming. *Your mother has gone to live with the angels.* Nancy had thought her father said *Engels.* Her mother had gone to live with the Engels, the grocer and his wife. Angels or Engels. Neither made any sense.

Mrs. Tillman petted Nancy's arm. "You must be brave now."

Nancy stroked wider circles, wishing on her fetus as she once wished on a lucky stone. She wished the woman gone, wished her not to say another word.

"Mr. Foreland certainly was," said Mrs. Tillman. Her bulbous nostrils quivered. "Your husband marched into that burning house like Shadrach himself."

If you say it aloud it won't come true. "Is he dead?"

Mrs. Tillman nodded, long tears starting down her mottled cheeks.

The wallpaper loomed, a dizzying cornflower pattern. Nancy stroked on, dazed and astonished. Why would God bother to bless them so exquisitely just to snatch it all away?

Mrs. Tillman dabbed at her eyes. "I was visiting Mrs. Louder two doors down, poor gouty woman. I saw Mr. Foreland bring you out. He ran right back into that black smoke. Why would he do that? Did you have a little dog? A little parakeet?"

"No, ma'am." Nancy pushed the tray to the end of the bed and rolled onto her side, facing the wall. *We had a little savings.*

There could be no other explanation. He'd gone back for their Berkeley Heights money. Close to fifty dollars last count. The greedy fool would have had to find the right tool and pry up the right floorboard.

Mrs. Tillman pulled Nancy to her gaunt bosom, murmuring something about God's will. Nancy hated her for it.

❖❖

DR. WHEELER arrived within the half hour and gave her another injection. Before he came Mrs. Tillman tried to get her to pray. Nancy refused. She wanted nothing more to do with God the thief. Mrs. Tillman said to the doctor, "She's suffering a crisis of faith just when she needs Him most."

"May He shine His Almighty light upon her," said the doctor.

"Amen," said Mrs. Tillman. They both looked at her hopefully. Nancy looked away. The injection was beginning to take hold. Her mouth felt as dry as her heart.

The doctor asked, "Whom shall we contact on your behalf, dear lady?"

"There's no one," said Nancy.

He insisted. "Surely there's *someone*. Try to think. An aunt you've forgotten? A second cousin?"

"My father's in Texas. I have a brother there, too, but he's not right in the head."

Dr. Wheeler pressed on. "No one close by? A friend perhaps, a helpful neighbor?"

Nancy shook her head. There had been no room or desire for anyone else.

She lay in a state of blankness for the longest time after they left, her eyes trained on the closed door. She was as tired as she'd ever been, but determined to be awake when Francis finally came.

Together Always

ANCY SLEPT WELL into the afternoon, thanks to the injection. She awoke in the parsonage bedroom sadly aware, her murky brain kinked with questions. Of course she'd return to Texas once the baby was born, but what to do in the meantime? There was the funeral to consider. At what expense? The Berkeley Heights money was surely gone, burned to a cinder. They didn't have a single red cent in the bank. Banks weren't to be trusted, Francis always said. "Banks are for suckers, kitten." *Kitten,* he called her. *Sweetheart. Pumpkin. Darling.* She could not bear the thought of leaving him behind in California.

She'd been sent west after her mother died. It pained him mightily to see her go, her father said. But a young lady needed a woman's guidance. That was six years ago. She was fourteen at the time.

She hadn't understood the permanence of the arrangement right away. She was too caught up in the adventure of going. Her father presented her with her mother's valise, which made her feel very grown up, and there were two new ready-made dresses, and a silk clutch purse with paper money inside. She wouldn't call it a sad leave-taking, not with all that, not with her daddy talking a mile a minute on the way to the station, describing the sights she'd see, the red Indians and buffalo and mountains, et cetera. She was the luckiest girl in east Texas, he said, and she believed him.

An elderly couple befriended her on the train. They sat opposite all the way to Berkeley, the gentleman teaching her to whittle. She carved a little horse with a wavy mane, a prized possession until the fire took it. So the journey itself was fine.

She could not say it often enough: Her great-aunt and -uncle had done their best. They were set in their ways, God rest their souls. She couldn't blame them. They were old, that was all. An Oriental cooked their strange meals, serving them up half raw. Dominos was their only form of entertainment outside of church. Of course Nancy was lonely. There were no neighbor girls her age, and her schooling was over, having graduated from the sixth in Texas. One bitterly cold summer day she asked to go home.

Her aunt said, "You *are* home."

Nancy had made herself fairly miserable with self-pity. You don't just banish a blood relation, your very own child. It didn't matter the reason. There was no decent reason.

She was due to return to Texas for a visit once. That was two years later. She was sixteen; she would have turned seventeen on the train. She remembered being plenty excited. But then her brother, Sanford, fell and hurt his head, a poor sick head not right to begin with. Her father wrote that it took every ounce of strength and every minute of the day to care for Sanford. He had no time to spare for her, apparently. Maybe next year, he said in the postscript. But it never happened. Nancy wondered how she and her father would be when they met again, if they'd even recognize one another right away.

Uncle Chester went first in '96, dying as her mother had, without a word of farewell, collapsing on the front walk in his case. Her auntie passed the following year.

Neither believed in doctors—God's usurpers, bound for hell, every last one of them. Aunt Gertrude had only Nancy at the end, to pray over her, to witness her heaving chest, with its horrible rasping noises. Nancy thought Satan had claimed her. She truly did. Auntie warned he might try. It was a fearsome display. The hands were the worst, twitching, clutching the air, grabbing for hours on end. Nancy slunk off when it was finally over, exhausted to the core. A full day passed before she could think what to do next. By that time the aunt's curled fingers could not be straightened. The undertaker eventually broke them in order to remove her rings. It was either that or cut the rings.

On the second day she ventured out. She had to tell someone about her aunt's passing. Mr. Jenkins, the pharmacist, seemed as good as anyone. Nancy went in and found Francis behind the counter. He later said it was love at first sight. She said the same, but couldn't honestly recall after what she'd just been through. Francis gave her a celery soda free of charge and told her to wait while he went to inform the undertaker. She crumbled some and he brought out his stool for her. He was her savior from the very beginning, as profane as that might sound.

❖❖

THE BABY TURNED and gave a listless kick. She should be grateful for his child; but she was only afraid, afraid of labor and delivery, afraid of the costly baby itself. How was she to dress it, feed it? What if it took ill, and needed a doctor and medicine before they arrived home? She didn't even have a bed for it. Francis had planned to build the crib himself, but never got started.

Nancy rose to use the pot, passing the mirror, taking note of but not caring about her pimply, sleep-creased complexion or her bushy, bird's-nest hair still smelling of smoke.

The irregular room looked out onto a green lawn and neat flower beds. Loudmouthed ragamuffins, stupid boys with stupid grins, played in the street, chasing each other with sticks. Nancy continued to watch. There was nowhere to go but back to bed, where every conscious minute took an hour to pass.

A tall gentleman with a limp, wearing a Sunday suit, opened the gate and came up the front walk. She heard the bell ring, and then a murmur of conversation below. Some moments later he was leaving again. Nancy recognized the man from the fire now. On impulse she heaved open the heavy pane and called down to him. "Mr. Oaks!"

He turned and looked up, smiling shyly when he spotted her at the window. "I was told you were resting." He started across the lawn, removing his hat. His hair was reddish and curly like her father's, like her father's in memory, anyway. "It's *Oades*, by the by," he said. "Henry Oades."

Nancy wrapped her arms about herself, suddenly aware of the shabby robe, the big belly it didn't conceal. She was embarrassed now that she'd called to him. "I'm not very good with names," she said as he neared. It was all she could think to say.

He stood beneath the big elm, partially hidden by a low branch. "I came to see how you were getting on."

Tears rose in her eyes. "My husband . . ."

He advanced a clumsy step and came into full view. "I'm aware, dear lady."

She sobbed, "I don't know where he is," immediately catching her irreverent-sounding self. "Of course he's in Heaven. No sweeter soul ever lived. I mean, what's left, you know."

"I could inquire about his remains on your behalf."

Francis would have been just as quick to volunteer. "Would you, sir?"

"Certainly, Mrs. Foreland. I'm at your service. You need only ask."

The bedroom door opened behind her. Nancy whirled around, expecting Francis for the briefest moment. Mrs. Tillman came in scowling, carrying black drapery over her arm. "Who are you talking to? Standing there for all the world to see in your nightclothes." She dumped the dark load on the unmade bed, and strode up to the window, peering out. "Mr. Oaks!"

"*Oades,*" Nancy whispered, mortified by the woman's shrill caw. You'd think she'd caught him making a bouquet of her hybrids.

Mrs. Tillman scolded, "I told you she was resting, sir."

"So you did, madam," he said, with a stiff bow.

"We were just having a conversation," said Nancy. "He offered to help."

"Say thank you then, and be done with it. Anyone passing by can see you."

All her young life she'd toed the line, never questioning an elder, certainly not a church elder. Be a good girl. Mind your manners. Sit up straight. Don't gulp your food. Don't sass. Yes ma'am, no sir. She'd been falsely led to believe that obedience would be rewarded. Comply and your precious husband won't die. Conform and you won't become a penniless expectant cow plagued with piles.

"We weren't finished," said Nancy.

"You are now," said Mrs. Tillman. "Get back to bed." She started to close the window, her sharp elbow jabbing Nancy in the side. "I'll not have you on display."

"Then kindly invite the gentleman in for a moment," said Nancy. Never had she spoken so defiantly. She hardly recognized herself.

"I'll do nothing of the kind," snapped Mrs. Tillman.

With that, her meek, indecisive self returned. Nancy hung her head and wept.

Mrs. Tillman latched on to Nancy's forearm and gave her a shake. "All right. We'll have him in. My goodness. Collect yourself." She poked her head out the window and motioned Mr. Oades toward the front door. "Just ring once, sir, and possess your soul with patience. The girl's busy in the kitchen." She took Nancy's hand and pulled her away from the window. Nancy was all of a sudden tired. She regretted now the demand to have him in.

Mrs. Tillman gathered up the black mound on the bed, holding the huge thing up by two corners. It was a dress, a tent of a thing.

"The girl and I were up half the night working on it. See? Just the one button in the front. On and off in a jiffy, and plenty of room to see you to the end. What do you think? You can't spend your waking hours in a man's dressing gown."

She forced the mourning dress into Nancy's arms. The fabric smelled strongly of moth balls. "Go ahead and put it on. You can't receive your guest as you are." Mrs. Tillman turned at the door. "Don't dawdle, hear? It's getting late. I don't want Mr. Oaks getting any ideas about staying for supper."

"*Oades,*" said Nancy wearily. Her neck and back ached. She undressed, avoiding looking at her hideous naked self. Her nipples had darkened considerably. An ugly brown line ran navel to pubis. Francis had thought the track an indication of twins. *What would he know?* He was barely twenty years old. *Oh, Francis. Why? How could you?* She put on the smelly black dress and checked herself in the mirror. Her hair was ratty, wild, shooting out in all directions. She licked her palm, attempting to tame the sides. Impossible, hopeless. All of it.

Downstairs, outside the parlor, Nancy heard Mrs. Tillman say there wouldn't be a viewing. *Who was she to decide?* Nancy entered, the somber canopy rustling like a party dress. "Much better," said Mrs. Tillman, interrupting herself, nodding approvingly.

Mr. Oades was seated alone on the velvet sofa. The Reverend and Mrs. Tillman flanked him on either side, a pair of pokers sitting perfectly straight. A fire was going, but no refreshments had been laid out. Mr. Oades stood as she came in, towering over the reverend, who popped up after him.

Dear God, how she wanted to go home and fix supper for Francis. He'd rub her swollen feet afterward and say how much he loved her. The gentlemen sat again. Nancy put the crumpled wad of damp hankie to her burning eyes and took the closest chair.

"Come sit by me, Mrs. Foreland," said Mrs. Tillman. Nancy rose numbly and did as she was told. Mrs. Tillman petted Nancy's knee, speaking as one would to a none-too-bright child. "We were discussing Mr. Foreland's service."

"What were you saying about a viewing?"

"We won't be having one," said Mrs. Tillman.

"Why not?"

Mrs. Tillman whispered, "He's simply not *viewable,* dear."

Nancy's nose began to bleed. Mr. Oades leapt up. He put his big hand to her forehead and gently pushed back, pressing his spicy-smelling handkerchief to her nostrils.

"I'm all right," she said, but his worried look didn't change. She took charge of the bloody handkerchief, waving him away. "I'm *all right,* sir." He retreated. "Where is he?" she demanded. "Who has my husband?"

Mrs. Tillman bent in again. "The Lord—"

"His *remains,*" said Nancy. "Where are his earthly remains?"

"He was taken to Fleming's," said the reverend.

"I know that scoundrel," cried Nancy, flecks of blood flying. "Mr. Fleming was my auntie's undertaker. He broke her fingers to remove her rings, and then charged extra for it! One ring turned up missing, too."

"Don't rile yourself," said Mrs. Tillman. "Think of the baby."

Nancy put a hand to her belly and apologized to the child in her heart. She took a deep breath, blotting her nostrils, examining the fresh blood on the hankie. "I can't afford him, anyway," she said quietly.

"I'm sure he'll allow you to pay something each week," said the reverend.

Nancy shook her head. "I'm in no position."

Mr. Oades leaned forward. He had such earnest eyes. "I could make a loan, madam."

"I couldn't possibly accept, sir. Thank you just the same."

"There's Potter's," said Mrs. Tillman.

"I will not put my husband in a pauper's unmarked grave."

"You might consider cremation," said Mr. Oades.

"Out of the question, sir," said Mrs. Tillman.

"How much does it cost?" asked Nancy. *Was he not as good as cremated already?*

"Two dollars," said Mr. Oades.

"God forbids it," thundered the reverend.

Mr. Oades clasped his hands and spoke directly to Nancy. "I saw to my former employer. Mr. Barnhill was a devout Christian. He believed cremation to be spiritually beneficial. *Purifying* was the term he used."

"Blasphemy," spat the reverend. "I'm going to ask you to leave, sir."

"A soul cannot be expected to rise from an unconsecrated urn," said Mrs. Tillman.

As if God would deny a soul so guileless. As if a moldering body would please Him that much more come Judgment Day.

It was the best decision under the circumstances. This way she could bring him along to Texas. They'd be together always.

"He'll rise just fine," said Nancy. "Don't you worry."

The Main Concern

MR. OADES TOOK Francis's remains to San Francisco, as Nancy was in no condition to go herself. He returned to the parsonage the following Tuesday and presented a lidded jar, a fancy expensive-looking vase, with a cabbage rose design.

"I was expecting something plain." She didn't mean to sound ungrateful, but she already owed him two dollars for the cremation. For all she knew the jar's gaudy trim was solid gold. Lord knows what it would set her back.

They were alone in the front room, though not really. The door to the rehearsal room had been intentionally left open. Mrs. Tillman and the choir's discordant sopranos made up an army of chaperones. Nancy accepted the jar; she was drawn to look inside, but didn't, for fear he'd think her ghoulish. She set the jar atop the reverend's credenza for the time being. Mr. Oades had come with flowers too, a small bunch of violets. These she arranged alongside the vase, and then turned around to thank him. The lamps were lighted, softening his ruddy cheeks. A sheen of tears stood in his sad brown eyes.

"What is it, Mr. Oades?"

"I wanted you to have it. . . ." he started.

"I'll pay for it, of course. I wired my father. He'll make good on my debts. I should be hearing from him any day now."

"It cost nothing, Mrs. Foreland. The jar's been in the family."

"Oh, then I couldn't possibly . . . oh dear. What have I said?"

He was weeping, making the quietest, strangest spectacle. She didn't know what to do. She gestured toward the sofa. "Won't you have a seat, Mr. Oades?"

He brought out a handkerchief and swiped his eyes. "The jar survived a fire," he said. "I thought it fitting somehow. It was terribly presumptuous of me. I apologize."

"No, no. It wasn't presumptuous at all. It's beautiful. I'll treasure it always. I mean it truly. Please take a seat."

He sat finally, as did she, across from him, smoothing the black folds that swamped her, smiling politely. "There. That's much better, isn't it?"

She'd never been good at parlor chat, especially with Francis in the room. Now *there* was a man with a gift, not a gift of gab so much, though he'd had that, too. His main talent was bringing people out, keeping the conversation light and merry. "Just ask folks about themselves," he used to say. "It's everyone's favorite topic."

In the next room the soloist started up "Jesus, Lover of My Soul." Why must worship music be sung so loud and mournfully? Nancy half shouted to be heard. "Where do you hail from, Mr. Oades? Not from east Texas, that's for sure."

He twitched a small smile. "I'm from England originally, by way of New Zealand."

"My, what a coincidence. My husband always wanted to see London. And I always wanted to see Paris, France. We said we'd visit both one day. I tell you, we made so many crazy plans." Burning grief washed over her. Nancy swallowed, trying to maintain a pleasant bent. She owed this kind gentleman so much more than money. "Do you have family, sir? Wife? Children?"

"They passed," he said. "Six years ago in New Zealand."

Her eyes brimmed with tears, the loss overwhelming, both his and her own. There was no such thing as true happiness. It was all a big hoax, a cruel tease. "Poor man," she whispered. "Poor, poor man."

Mr. Oades leaned forward, his expression full of anguish. "My wife perished in a fire, you see."

Her heart jumped a kindred beat. "Then you know."

"I do."

"It's a horrible death. You keep thinking about how it must have been."

He nodded.

"You say to yourself, how could it have happened? Why didn't he manage to escape? Was he trapped somehow? Did the roof fall on his head? Over and over and over, you think it. All the ways it might have been."

"Yes," said Mr. Oades, nodding still, a far-off look in his eyes. "I was away at the time."

He blamed himself; she could tell. They had that in common, too. Her raw nose ran, coating the back of her throat with the taste of rusty nails. She accepted his overstarched handkerchief. "And your dear children?"

He shook his head, tears welling again. "I cannot talk about them."

She laid a trembling hand on her belly. "Poor innocents. I don't understand." She crossed her arms and rocked herself, searching the dark ceiling for answers. The sopranos in the next room sang at the top of their lungs. *Help of the helpless, O abide with me.* "I don't understand one *damn* bit of it."

Mr. Oades reached, touching her hand briefly, creating in her a small serenity, a sense of surrender. Even the baby seemed to respond.

"It's impossible at first," he said. "You don't believe it now, but the days shall get easier in time. Don't punish yourself when they do, Mrs. Foreland; don't despair the first time you experience a bit of contentment."

Mrs. Tillman came in then, chattering sopranos in tow. Mr. Oades stood, nodding greetings. Only now did Nancy notice the singing had stopped. Wraps and hats were doled out. The ladies giggled, fussing over whose was whose, their careless arms flailing. Nancy got up and took the jar from its precarious perch at the edge of the credenza. Mrs. Tillman raised one eyebrow in her direction, as if to say, what is *that* doing here?

Nancy clutched the jar to her bosom, guarding Francis, shielding, too, the one possession to her name aside from the black dress and baggy drawstring drawers.

Mr. Oades said his good-byes shortly after the ladies did. Nancy followed him onto the porch, still cradling the ginger jar. "I can't begin to adequately thank you, sir. I know my father will want to thank you, too, for standing in for him, watching over me as you have."

"Will you be returning to Texas then?"

She nodded. "After the baby comes."

Mr. Oades fumbled behind a lapel for a pencil and paper scrap. He scribbled down his post office number. "Will you write once settled?"

"If you'd like. I wouldn't know what to say. My husband was the one. You'd think his letters were written by a college professor."

Mr. Oades looked away, squinting into the sun. "It'd do me some good to know that you and your baby arrived safely." He seemed on the verge of saying more, but didn't. He stepped off the porch, turning halfway down the walkway, tipping his hat in farewell. Nancy waved, sorry to see him go. He'd made her feel a degree less alone today.

✧✧

FINALLY. After weeks of queasy panic, imagining him ill, comatose, dead as a doornail, her father's letter arrived, along with twenty precious dollars and a promotional circus poster featuring nearly naked Serena, Peerless Fearless Queen of the Serpents. The advertisement put a shiver in Nancy's slippers. Black snakes slithered all over the tiny woman; a dozen were reared back with their jaws open, as if about to bite her placid, heart-shaped face.

Mrs. Tillman leaned across the breakfast table, her face pinched in revulsion. "What in the world?"

On the back of the poster, in his familiar loopy hand, her father had written: *The reptiles are old and have had their poison fangs removed.* Even so. How desperate would a lady have to be to take up with snakes?

"I guess my father is acquainted with her," murmured Nancy, scanning his letter. She started over, disbelieving. The letter was written six weeks ago. He was already long gone.

New York, NY, October 17, 1898

My dear daughter Nancy:

I know this letter will find you full of sorrow at the unexpected loss of your young husband. I regret to hear the news, and hasten to offer you the enclosed twenty dollars, which I hope will provide financial comfort in your time of distress.

By the time you read this I will be in Europe with the Barnum & Bailey circus. I signed on as a front man, which means I will travel ahead of the show, and see to a number of tasks. I will not bore you with

*the details at this sad juncture. Suffice it to say I am in no position to care
for you and my beloved grandchild. The contract with B & B is binding
for two years. My hands are legally tied. Would that I could better assist.*

*The Brenham house was sold eight months ago. Your brother Sanford
resides now at the Austin State Hospital. He gained a great deal of
weight over the years and became too large to manage on my own. He
appears much better off where he is.*

How would her father know he was better off? Sanford never
spoke. He grunted, squealed, but as hard as her mother tried, she
never got him to say the first word.

*Daughter, I know your optimistic nature too well to think that you
will remain buried in grief. I have suffered my own black days and have
learned firsthand that: "Weeping may endure for a night, but joy cometh
in the morning." Psalms 30:5.*

*I will write again soon. Meanwhile you are in my daily thoughts and
prayers.*

> *Your loving father,*
> *Herbert "Hick" Hickey*

Nancy excused herself from the table. She scooped up the
money, letter, and poster, and waddled up to her chilly little room.
Under the covers she read his letter again, still thinking she'd
missed the instructions regarding her future. But she had not.

Two weeks later, on December 16th, after a full day and night
of grueling labor, bald-headed, blue-eyed, red-faced Gertrude
came howling into the world. Five weeks after her birth, the Tillmans' son returned from missionary work in China and assumed
his room, Nancy's room until now. She and the cranky baby had
long since worn out their welcome, anyway. The reverend wrote a
letter of introduction, attesting to Nancy's good reputation, which
he gave to Mrs. Osgood, the owner of the boardinghouse. After

four nights there she was asked to leave due to the infant's endless squalling. Nancy begged Mrs. Osgood for time to make other arrangements. When the woman begrudgingly consented, Nancy sent a messenger to Mr. Oades.

Gertrude had just burped up her afternoon bottle when he arrived. Nancy ushered him inside, messy drooling baby on her shoulder. She couldn't afford to offer him anything. A greasy breakfast and supper came with the room. Beyond that, she was charged extra.

Mr. Oades held out his arms. "May I?"

"You want to hold her?"

"Oh, please," he said.

The fancy parlor was crammed with plush furniture. Nancy was afraid to put the baby down anywhere in the house for fear she'd leak or worse. She carried Gertrude around the livelong day, keeping her in a dresser drawer at night. "Oh, I don't know, Mr. Oades. Your nice suit."

"Not to worry," he said. He had a red mark on his neck, a shaving nick, probably. Francis was always nicking himself.

Nancy shifted Gertrude, frowning down on her baby, trying to read her wants. She was peaceful now, but that wouldn't last. "She's been bawling her head off all morning. Maybe I'm doing something wrong."

Mr. Oades eased the sticky baby from her hands. "Let's have a cross lass."

"Look at her poor splotched face."

"It'll fade in due course," he said. "My Josephine was the same."

"She looks all right to you then? She looks like a normal baby?"

He smiled. "She's a lovely girl, a perfect girl." Gertrude stared up at him, seemingly transfixed by his beard. He began humming to her.

With empty arms, Nancy collapsed on the settee, bone-weary and cockeyed from lack of sleep. She hadn't felt clean since before

Gertrude's birth. Her unproductive, sour-smelling breasts ached, and she was still wearing rags to sop the disgusting bloody discharge that wouldn't quit.

Mr. Oades paced to the far wall and turned, at home with her baby, singing a lullaby now.

She told him about her father. "Like a little boy running off to the join the circus! I'm at my wit's end, Mr. Oades. I didn't know what to do next. I thought on it and thought on it. Yesterday it came to me, and so I sent for you. You've been such a helpful friend, sir. I'll just come out and ask . . . could I come and keep house for you? I'm not the best cook in the world, but I'm not the worst either. You wouldn't have to pay much. Room and board are my main concern."

He came to her. "Mrs. Foreland."

"Never mind," she said. "Don't look at me that way, please. You think I'm off my rocker. I knew it was a crazy idea. I can't think straight anymore."

He sat down beside her. She studied her wedding band, refusing to meet his eyes. "Crazy ideas are my specialty these days," she murmured.

Gertrude gurgled, suckling a tiny fist. "Marry me, Mrs. Foreland." He said it so softly she almost didn't hear. She looked at him and knew at once the offer was sincere. He had a nice mouth and honest eyes, a hound dog's beseeching liquid eyes.

"You take your pity a step too far, Mr. Oades. But I thank you just the same."

"I realize I'm too old for you . . ."

Just how old was he? Thirty-five? Forty? Not impossibly old.

" . . . But I'd move mountains to make you and Gertrude happy."

"You don't mean it," she said. But she knew that he did.

"I do."

"We barely know each other."

He stroked Gertrude's bald head. "I feel as though we do," he said.

She liked him fine, gentle as he was, and she trusted him. But that was not saying she was even remotely in love with him. He couldn't suppose that she was. Though what did love mean or matter at this stage, anyway? Just a bunch of heart-fluttery nonsense. She was hot and confused, on the verge of yet more useless tears. What else in God's name was she to do?

His cheeks were flushed, his look hopeful. "Will you give it thought, madam?"

She whispered "yes," glancing toward the stairs. The house was full of busybodies, the queen of whom, with her razor-sharp voice, was salty Mrs. Osgood herself.

Mr. Oades returned sleepy Gertrude to her arms. He stood, taking his hat and coat from the tree. "Will you send word? Either way?"

"Of course, Mr. Oades."

They shook hands at the door, both smiling shyly.

That evening before bed she took it up with Francis, who rested inside his ornate jar on top of the chest of drawers. She swore he'd remain first in her heart always.

She married Mr. Oades the following week and moved to his farm, where a brand-new crib and highchair were waiting for Gertrude. It was a good-size house, with a spare room slated to become her sewing room. There was a garden, and a girl to help with the chores and the baby. Nancy found contentment eventually, and when she did, she took her new husband's advice and didn't despair.

PART TWO

North Island

1895

CANNIBALS, every last one of them, the women no exception."

The hyperbolic Mr. Wylie from Surrey, a man who shoe-blacked his whiskers, had claimed it of the Maori. Three years into their captivity, Margaret Oades still recalled his bluster.

They'd been in the social room after services. "The savage have a name for a human roast," he'd said, lowering his voice to a stage whisper. "Long pig, they call it."

"Ah, go on," said someone else. "That was then."

"They've come to know the Lord since," said another.

"Not all of them," Mr. Wylie said.

John had piped up. "Do they boil people alive, sir?"

Henry and Margaret had shushed him. Such an imagination, they murmured to each other. Such a brilliant curiosity. He gets it from you.

No, he most definitely gets it from *you*, Henry.

Later, alone with Henry, she'd asked, "There's no truth to it, is there?"

Henry laughed. "Not to worry. You haven't enough meat to make a decent roast."

Heading toward the latrine pits this afternoon, Margaret thought about that silly conversation, imposing upon it meaning, a sign that her husband would be coming for them soon. He began, not for the first time, turning up everywhere.

That same night he appeared dressed in a set of old drawers, the set she'd mended the day they were taken. He sat at the edge of her sleeping mat and spoke in his normal tone, engaging her in an ordinary conversation. Her roses were doing splendidly, he distinctly said, but sorry to say the gardenias were on the small and shriveled side.

Two mornings later, while tending the crops, Margaret heard him calling her name. She took a demented half moment to mourn her appearance before charging across the field in the direction of his voice. Josephine, hoeing thirty feet away, called to her. "Mum!" The old humpbacked woman stepped into her path, wooden spade raised like a spear. *"Kaati!"* Stay. Motes of vivid green light danced in Margaret's vision. She ducked to the side, with a laugh in her throat. Two of the nimble young ones were on her in the next instant, wrestling her back to work.

The hopelessness would set in soon enough, a long episode of it typically, followed by some semblance of acceptance, followed by more hopelessness, followed by yet another bout of arbitrary euphoria. Margaret recognized the periodic madness for what it was. She only regretted her ability to sustain it.

❖❖

SHE'D KNOWN Maori people in Wellington—not intimately, but well enough to discern profound differences between their tribes now. Several Maori families had attended church. One man in particular stood out in her memory. He sang in the choir, an angelic tenor, incapable, seemingly, of murder and enslavement.

Their captors were not Christians. The people were governed by various gods and by the promise of *Reinga,* a heavenly reward of a sort. Of tantamount importance were their *tapus*—taboos, more or less. All conduct was regulated by one *tapu* or another.

One cardinal *tapu* concerned property. A man's belongings, particularly a chieftain's belongings—his tools, his weapons, even the basket that held his food—were *tapu.* To come in contact with his personal property was to interfere with his *mana* and the *mana* of his family. *Mana,* as Margaret came to understand it, was a rather ethereal quality, critical to one's success and happiness, but not to be depended upon. One might lose one's *mana,* or be deserted by one's *mana,* as she once observed.

When two sons of a young warrior died within days of each other, it was said that the man's *mana,* his good fortune, had deserted him. The villagers were then free to pillage his house, which they did, taking everything of value, leaving him with a food basket and two sleeping mats.

To speak to certain people at critical times was also *tapu.* Not even his wife spoke to a man while he was having his facial tattoo, his *moko,* chiseled. Margaret never witnessed the actual surgery, but she'd glimpsed the crusty scabs often enough. The majority looked in need of a sugar tit afterward, or their mum's own.

The *moko* was done in stages, the procedure beginning as boy turned to man, and taking years to complete. The forehead was carved first, the cheeks last. The pattern applied to the cheeks was unique to the individual. It became his family crest in a manner of speaking. The same pattern was then carved on his doorpost with great ceremony.

Margaret and the children were never in any danger of breaking the speaking *tapu,* for at no time did they speak first. As slaves, they were the lowest of the low. Margaret made the mistake of straying too close to the burial ground once and was chastised, but that was the worst of it to date. She might have been whipped that time if not for a Maori child with an old woman's face. The wizened girl yanked on Margaret's skirt in warning, shaking a fist and stamping her feet. The small theatrics made the girl *tapu*, though she did not remain so for long. She was absolved in a cleansing rite down by the river. Margaret did not understand it all fully, any more than she understood the quid pro quo of her own faith. One takes communion every single Sunday for thirty-odd years. One humbles herself, embraces every last dogmatic note, and no good comes of it, no help when one needs it most. That is not to say she did not continue to pray. She prayed constantly, babbling both to God and Henry. *Please come today.* The fervency might vary depending on the degree of desperation, but the words did not. She breathed the selfsame mantra all day, every day, never once letting up. *Please come today.*

Escape was constantly on Margaret's mind in the beginning. About a month into their captivity she discovered a rotting spot in the wooden fence surrounding the settlement. She quickly jabbed her fist while backs were turned, creating a hole, a thrilling accomplishment. Some days later, she buried a sharp digging stone close by, to be used when the time came. She inspected the hole every chance. Weeks went by without repair, telling her the damage had gone unnoticed. She'd been about to take John into her confidence when a slave boy was caught and killed.

The child could not have been more than twelve or thirteen. He lived with other Maori slaves, relatives, Margaret surmised, given the ardent degree of their mourning. The boy had attempted to scale the wall and was brought down with a greenstone *mere*, the simplest and deadliest of hand weapons. Margaret remained prepared to move swiftly, to gather the children and rush toward their rescuers, but only in her most delirious moments did she contemplate escape on their own after that—the risk was too great.

The days ran together. She and the children toiled hard and

long, though no harder or longer than anyone else. Even the chief's wives did their share. Except for the gravely ill, all souls worked, even the ancient.

She rose before dawn every day to help with the fire and the cooking of the morning meal. Normally there was plenty to eat. The tribe grew potatoes and *kumara,* a tasty enough sweet potato. There were eel and fish, delicious perch, which were dried and eaten with the fingers. The clams and mussels were eaten raw, though not by Margaret and her children after the first day or two. The Maori ate the shellfish putrid, until they were gone, with seemingly no ill effect. They also made cakes, horrible little indigestible lumps extracted from fern root. And there was an abundance of wild pig, so much, too much, pig.

She thought it cruel the sneaky way the men went about the pig hunt, starting out after dark. They set fires, smoking the resting pigs from thickets and caves, falling upon the startled animals with spears. Mind, these were not the familiar docile farm creatures, but hideous beasts, grotesque beyond imagination, particularly the boars with their deadly tusks. Margaret and Josephine were regularly assigned the task of preparing the roasting pit. A solid day of digging was required for a monster so large, another three to lay the stones and cook it properly.

John was eventually made to go on the hunt. He was nearly thirteen the first time, a man by tribal standards. He stayed out all night, returning the next morning with a limp, stinking of sour swine, filthy with wet blood and gore—the pig's, John claimed, not his own. Margaret went straight to work washing him, picking coagulated matter from his hair and lashes.

"What were you made to do, precisely?"

"Run ahead of the pigs," he said.

Goddamn them all to eternal hell for using her child as bait. A miracle brought him back alive. The blasted tribesmen had not allowed him to carry so much as a knife. "Turn your head, please."

John calmly complied. As if dried viscera in his ears were an everyday event. "The sky was spectacular," he said. "Before the fires were lit. In all my days I've never seen Betelgeuse as bright."

"*All* your days indeed."

He laughed, full of a peculiar energy. "The pigs go mad once the fires are started," he said. "They come in a stampede all at once, making a shrieking racket. Some ran straight into the flames. The sows with their piglets, that's who you have to look out for. They scream like women. You've never heard anything like it. I'd sooner take my chances with a boar. The men eat the liver, did you know? They slash open the pig's belly and eat the steaming liver then and there." John jerked, twisting his head. "You're hurting me, Mum."

"Sorry." Margaret's hands cramped with rage. "Were you made to eat some as well?"

"I wasn't offered. They said I ran well, though. My *pakeha* legs are worthy."

"Don't tell me any more now, please. Lean forward so I might get at your neck."

He was made to go time and time again. Margaret never became used to it.

❖❖

AT NIGHT, weary as she was, Margaret faithfully schooled John, Josephine, Mim's son Oscar, and, after a time, Martha. They were living together now, sharing a hut with four other slaves, scheming female Maori from a South Island tribe, newly arrived. John had an obvious favorite among them, a shy adolescent he nicknamed "Beadie," because of her eyes Margaret supposed, but didn't know for certain.

The three older women plotted and gossiped while she conducted class. They picked constantly at their nostrils, teeth, and toes. Margaret didn't care a straw about them. At worst they were like mosquitoes, the very least of her problems.

The younger children enjoyed the stories, Aesop's especially. Ironically, Oscar Bell's favorite was *The Kid and the Wolf,* the story about a goat who is pursued by a hungry wolf. The goat tricks the wolf into playing his pipes, which attracts the hounds, who chase off the wolf. The tale taught how to outwit a formidable enemy, how to be clever in times of peril. But Oscar was only interested in a wolf playing pipes.

"Does the wolf stand on his hind legs to play?" he asked.

"I would think," said Margaret, petting him.

"What sort of tune do you suppose he plays, Mum?"

He'd begun calling her "Mum" six months into their captivity. He never mentioned Mim anymore. Poor slow babe. Named for Mr. Wilde, no less. How unlike his quick-witted mother he was.

The stories came last, after French and English grammar, after sums and letters practiced in the dirt with a stick, and after etiquette, the curriculum of which would vary. They might practice the manipulation of knife and fork (employing a smaller stick) one night, street deportment the next. They could not stand without bending due to the low ceiling. Margaret had them playact while seated.

"Fancy yourselves strolling along a fashionable London street."

They protested in English or French, shifting their eyes toward the chirruping, spitting Maori women huddled just a few feet away. The women often amused themselves by mimicking Margaret's gestures, mocking the children, snickering away. Margaret kept them at it regardless, as pointless and mortifying as it may have struck John and Josephine.

"Now Josephine, take John's arm, or Oscar's, but not both. A gentleman may take two ladies upon his arms, but under no circumstances may a lady take the arms of two gentlemen."

"Oh, Mum," they groaned. "Oh, Mum, please."

"You'll thank me one day," Margaret repeatedly said.

They were all exhausted at lesson's end. Some nights Margaret closed her eyes without worry, grateful for sleep alone. On her own she might manage. She'd learned to do without, did not waste away pining for sheets and soft blankets, for sweets and tea and tooth powder. Given sufficient food and rest, she'd likely rationalize her own lot. But the same could not be said of her children, and that is why she rode them night after night, regularly depriving them of an hour's more sleep. It was her duty to prepare them for their return. She refused to accept the possibility that they might grow old and die a natural death here. Margaret never once considered setting her children free to be slaves.

North Island

1897

Some Maori women give birth surrounded by their kinswomen. Others go it alone. Once labor has started, some will take their mats and find a quiet place in the open air. Margaret was gathering stones for the roasting pit when she came upon the laboring mum, partially hidden behind a thicket of ferns. The woman rocked on her haunches, mewling pitifully. Margaret came closer, letting herself be seen, thinking the woman would shoo her away. But the expectant looked up with wet, pleading eyes. Margaret put down the sack of stones and went to her, squatting alongside, encouraging her with gestures to lie back. Birth was not imminent. The perspiring woman rolled onto her side, keening still. Margaret began to rub the woman's tight neck, gingerly at first, uncertain about *tapu*. The woman jerked and then quieted. Margaret continued rubbing, kneading her shoulders with both hands, concentrating on the knotty spots, recalling the lovely relief. Henry had done the same for her during the long labor with the twins.

The woman in the ferns delivered a boy. Six months later she was pregnant again. When her time came she insisted that Margaret attend. Another live boy was born. Rumor started that Margaret's hands pleased the gods. All the women began requesting her presence at their births. Rows occurred, resulting in Margaret being awarded to the highest-ranking mother.

The following summer, Margaret attended the chief's niece, a big-breasted, pigeon-toed girl of about sixteen. Aroha was gigantic with her first child, long overdue according to her calendar stick. Margaret was summoned the moment she began wailing and went straight from the *kumara* field to the fetus house. Inside the crude shed, Aroha squatted, naked but for the *roimata* worn around her neck, a love token made of greenstone, most likely a gift from her husband. The girl clutched the *roimata*, her lips moving in prayer, her tattooed chin trembling. Other women were present, chanting, rocking to and fro. Margaret made her way through them, mute as a cob, her eyes cast down. In the next moment the girl's water bag burst, causing the others to yip with glee. Aroha threw back her head and emitted a long, piercing cry, like that of a boiling kettle. Between her legs the baby's head was already crowning. An old woman was on Aroha in an instant, pushing on her belly. Margaret gasped, fearing for the infant's soft skull. A baby boy with a head full of black hair slipped out like an eel and Aroha received him, panting happily. His cord was cut with an obsidian chip and the same old woman tenderly rubbed his stump with oil, bandaging it afterward, smiling an ecstatic gummy smile.

Margaret squatted before Aroha in preparation for the afterbirth. She was determined to stay put and protect the girl from further assault. She placed both hands on either side of the navel and felt first a slight wave of movement, then a good solid kick. Margaret patted Aroha's taut belly for attention, completely forgetting herself.

"Another baby! Another *peepe!*" She'd broken *tapu* by speaking, but the women were too excited to make anything of it.

The second wee warrior arrived as alert as the first, screaming lustily, waving his mucousy arms. A single afterbirth followed in a great bloody gush ten minutes later. Aroha sank back against Margaret, but the elders did not allow Margaret to linger. The grandmother began poking her with a long stick, prodding her toward the shed's opening.

A slave's presence during birth was traditionally *tapu*. Margaret vaguely understood that she was an exception. She was brought out of the fetus house and doused with rank water. She returned to the *kumara* field, released from the *tapu* earned by helping.

Two of the chief's daughters by different wives were due the following month, and there was some argument over who would have Margaret should their labors begin simultaneously. But the smallpox came that same month. Josephine was stricken first, then Margaret, Beadie, and two of the other South Island women living with them. Five tribesmen with rifles came to their hut in the night and summoned them all outside. The older slave, the sickest among them, refused to move and was shot in the head where she lay. Margaret cried out, fevered and confused. John spoke sharply. "Hush, Mum."

They were goaded forward in a tight knot and herded briskly through the village and across the dark field in the direction of the bush. John pulled Oscar and Martha along by the hands. Margaret had a lock on Josephine. She could not think for the slicing pain behind her eyes. She whispered to John, "Where are they taking us?"

He whispered back, "Be prepared to run."

Margaret stumbled on, blindly concentrating on not falling. From behind came footsteps and shrill female voices. Margaret glanced over her shoulder. In the moonlight the women seemed a single flailing, shrieking entity. The tribesmen stopped to listen to their magpie demands. The biggest, her chest heaving, pointed at Margaret and spoke stridently.

Margaret stood shivering, an arm wrapped around Josephine. John murmured close to her ear. "She says you're a favored one. Harm to you will bring harm to their sons."

One of the men argued. The big woman spoke louder, rivulets of sweat running down her breasts. The other women chimed in noisily. Another man spoke over them. The big woman launched into a heated speech. The lead man barked something and she went silent, crossing her arms triumphantly. The same man turned to John, giving an order, jabbing his rifle toward the bush. John snatched up limp Josephine and hoisted her onto his back. "They're letting us go," he said, corralling Oscar and Martha. "Come now, Mum. Quickly."

Margaret did as she was told, falling in behind John, bewildered and cold. He was moving too fast. They entered the trees and she lost her peripheral vision. A moment later shots were heard, three in a row.

"Beadie." John said her name and nothing more for the longest time.

North Island

Late 1898

*T*HEY WERE DESCENDING and therefore headed east, according to John. Margaret tried to make sense of the words. *Does a mountain not have a west face as well as an east?* Lucid thoughts reared within the dizziness, the headache, the confusion of seeing and then not seeing people in the trees. Once down, they'd follow the river to civilization, John said. It seemed at first logical, then utterly impossible.

John led them, carrying fever-addled Josephine on his back. Margaret had Martha and Oscar by the hand, until bawling Oscar broke off to trail behind. They tramped downhill long into the night, quitting finally, coming to a black thicket, spongy damp from the earlier rain, and collapsing there. Tall trees made a canopy above them, eclipsing moon and stars. Margaret found herself propped against rough bark, unable to move. John stooped and put a calloused palm to her forehead.

"Poor Mum. You're hot as a stove lid." He fanned her face with his hat, a black brimmed felt, already old when his father passed it down. "I'm going down a bit farther," he said. "You'll be all right here. I'll be back before you know it."

Her tongue was thick in her head. "You've taken very good care of your hat."

"That I have." His voice came from a distance. "It was Dad's. Do you remember? We'll be seeing him soon, won't we?" The fanning stopped. "We're going home, Mum! Do you believe it? Mum, please. Give a sign if you can hear me."

Margaret nodded, feeling weighty, pleasantly warm, as if melting. Then came a rustling, a meandering presence along her bare leg. Her body seized, cold perspiration breaking. "Snakes!"

The fanning started up again, causing the snakes to writhe in fury. "You're dreaming," said John, so very far away. "No snakes here, Mum. Come on, now. No snakes, no wolves, no bears. It's the lizards you hear scuttling." He drew a gritty thumb across her eyelids. "Get your rest." He stood. "I'll see to things."

She slept for a time, waking to Martha beating herself, fist to forehead, a common Maori gesture of worry. Margaret captured her tight little hand. "Sleep, my baby. Your mum loves you. Your dad loves you." They both drifted off again. The idea of dying occurred, but Margaret was too ill to fret over whether or not she was.

It was light when she woke with pain in her back. She was able to move her stiff arms, but not her legs. Oscar popped up like a turtle, putting his heavy head in her lap, and falling back to sleep. Martha did likewise. Margaret stroked their matted hair and called to Josephine.

"Wake up, Pheeny." Her big girl lay out of reach, knees to breast, hands tucked beneath her chin. "Wake up, wake up." High up, a bird screeched. John was nowhere in sight. Margaret attempted to whistle, but nothing came out. "Josephine Oades! Wake up this instant or I shall fetch a switch. Don't think I won't. Don't think you're too grown for it." Her chest hurt, as if weighted by rocks; her eyes felt misaligned, reversed in their sockets. "Pheeny, sweetheart, please."

John appeared. "Hush, Mum. Hush now. The area reeks of Maori."

She'd mistaken him for Henry for a moment, with his same thatch of ginger hair and something else. She couldn't say what. "Oh, thank God you're here. See to your sister."

He'd brought back a hat full of stinking mussels, rancid wet weed still clinging. He knelt beside Josephine and sprinkled river water across her forehead. Pheeny whimpered, lifting a hand in protest. The relief started Margaret quietly weeping.

John shook Josephine. "Come on, Pheeny. Open your eyes. You're scaring Mum. She imagines you dead."

"Leave her be," said Margaret. "Let her sleep."

"We haven't time to waste," he said.

"How far must we travel?"

"We're a good ten miles from the river," he said. "From there we'll turn south."

"Are you certain?"

John attempted to feed Josephine, poking extracted mussel meat to her lips. Josephine clamped a hand to her mouth, shaking her head. "Yes, I'm certain," he said, impatiently. He left Josephine and came to Martha. Martha turned a fat, ruddy cheek, accepting the mussel, chewing wetly, audibly swallowing. She opened her mouth for more. The smell was nauseating. Margaret dipped her head, her throat filling with acid bile.

"Ah, Mum," whispered John.

He'd been the sweetest of all babies, gleeful, responsive, a pure joy. From the moment they met he was more hers than Henry's. "John, if I should—"

He cut her off, his eyes pleading. "Please don't."

Margaret was struck by love for him. She'd only meant to tell him to do the practical thing. Bury her body swiftly and keep moving, for Josephine's sake. But she let it lie. Surely their resourceful son would do just that. *Don't you agree, Henry?* She closed her eyes. Her husband opened his arms to her and she fell right in.

❖❖

FOR THE NEXT THREE DAYS they lumbered along at a hideously slow pace, following the river. At dusk they climbed the wooded slope and moved up behind the trees, so as to be out of sight. Bloodthirsty sandflies descended the moment they settled. The Maori used the crushed leaves of the *ngaio* tree to repel them, but the *ngaio* grew only in the marsh. They swatted the air and each other, listlessly, futilely, trying not to mind them.

They built no fires for fear of attracting Maori. The children lived on wild celery and raw shellfish. John was the only one willing to consume wood grubs, picking them from the bark, closing his eyes and swallowing them whole. Margaret kept the river water down for the most part, but ate nothing of substance. Waking was a surprise each time.

She'd improved significantly by the fourth day, the day they became lost. They'd arrived at a narrow, seemingly shallow place in the river. "We should cross here," said John, studying the water, looking doubtful.

"We crossed no water coming," said Margaret.

"Your memory's not what it once was, Mum." He walked off a ways and stopped, surveying the lush, hilly surroundings. Next he removed his boots and rolled up his trousers and ventured into the rushing river. The water rose quickly. He returned to shore, cutting his heel along the way, swearing under his breath. Margaret started toward him, but he waved her off, and sat to nurse himself.

She examined Josephine while waiting. Her girl was still lethargic, but the fever had fallen, as had her own. A good sign. Pheeny's fresh rash was confined to her face, whereas Margaret's had already spread to the soles of her feet. The rash would turn to pustules, the pustules to crusts that would shed and leave deep pits. It was only a matter of time, assuming they survived it, and it seemed likely now that they would. They were fortunate then, scarred future notwithstanding.

Perhaps strides in medicine had been made. The thought occurred to Margaret while inspecting Josephine's scalp. Perhaps a salve had been invented that would repair a damaged complexion. Think of the demand for such a product. It would not come cheap, she imagined, and began mentally justifying the cost to Henry. He relented quickly within the same fantasy, so overjoyed was he to have them returned. Her heart thrummed like a bride's. He felt particularly close this afternoon.

John elected not to cross. "We'll forge ahead." He sounded dubious, but Margaret said nothing. They walked in silence for several hours, the river widening all the way. "We'll have to go back," he said finally, weary-eyed, his voice full of dejection. "I'll carry you over one at a time. Oscar can manage on his own."

They were perhaps two miles into their return when John began to limp. The sun had gone behind the clouds. Margaret judged it to be four o'clock, time to clean the village latrines, battle flies the size of ravens. John walked a little farther and staggered. He pried Josephine from his back and set her on the ground. He tottered off a few yards and folded, burying his face in his hands. Margaret so wished to go to him, to hold him and rock him, but she resisted. That sort of solace would likely strike him as *tapu* now. He stood after a bit, blotting his eyes and nose on his filthy sleeve, thrusting his chin toward the bush. "We'll rest now. Start out again later."

They arrived at the passable spot early the next afternoon. John carried Josephine over first, then Martha, and then Margaret. He toted them like infants, cradled in two ropy arms. They were easier to manage that way, he said. "Don't be embarrassed, Mum. You weigh no more than a feather."

But she was embarrassed, both by the helplessness and the intimacy. His odor was dank and musty pressed close, wholly masculine. She tried to joke. "The mum's meant to carry the child, not the other way round."

The next day they came to a salt marsh as wide as any ocean and were forced to turn around once again. Late the following day they crossed back over. John raged and wept in turns, cursing the fates one moment, beseeching God and His angels the next. He deposited the girls on the opposite shore, and then returned for Margaret, picking her up roughly, still raving on and on, like mad old Lear himself. He released her in shallow water, railing over the three lost days, a ludicrous lament considering the six lost years. She waded to shore and sat, pulling on her brown leather hightops, soles patched with flax, laces long gone—taken by the Maori for reasons unknown.

The girls were sprawled on flat rocks, eyes closed, faces to the sun. At least there was daylight left, progress yet to be made. Margaret went to Oscar, who was sitting by himself at water's edge, humming away like a loon. He was covered with red bites and warm to the touch. Her hand left streaks in the oily grime. His ear hole was packed; she could not see down it for the green-black stuff. The lad stank, as did they all. It was amazing to be so perfectly putrid and still continue to function. A believer might declare their beating hearts bona fide miracles, not one miracle, but five. She waged a small argument in her mind, but was hard pressed to arrive at a more satisfactory explanation. A doubter's creed is as confounding as any other.

She roused her girls. "Let's have a washup, shall we? For your father's sake?"

That night Margaret ate, managing three clams and four bites of wild celery. She kept it all down, too. If a miracle were in progress, she did not wish to queer it by starving.

THEY WERE FOUND on the eighth morning by a Caucasian man on horseback, a prospector in search of greenstone or gold, preferably the latter, he said. He might have ridden right on by, he claimed, if not for the snoring.

John sprang to his feet, licking the heel of his hand, slicking back his mangy mane. He greeted the man and began racing through the details of their ordeal.

The man gazed down, his rheumy blue eyes puddling. Certainly, of course, he'd carry one of them back to Wellington. "Not a sick one, no offense." He pulled taffy from a saddle bag. Martha and Oscar accepted shyly, putting the unfamiliar food to their nostrils, but not to their mouths. "I'll take one of you boys. You can bring a wagon back for your mam and the others."

John began gabbling instructions to Oscar. *Don't venture off. Share the sweets.* The gentle man reached again for taffy, saying he wished he had more. John's eyes were wet with elation. "You've been more than kind, sir."

The prospector offered a hand, a farewell, not a hand up, as John obviously thought, his foot slipping from the stirrup. He tried again to mount, his face flushed with confusion. The man put a boot to John's chest, pushing him off.

"I can't take you back today, son. I've work to do."

Martha threw the taffy to the ground, howling to the sky. John shushed her, staring up at the man, breathing hard.

"I'll try to get back tomorrow," the bounder said. "Day after at the latest. You have my word."

"Please reconsider, sir," said Margaret. "My husband will see that you're compensated."

"My mother and sister are sick," said John, incredulous.

The man gave a sympathetic cluck. "Look for me tomorrow."

"That's not good enough," said John, latching on to the saddle horn.

The man kneed John's hand, pulling sideways on the reins, trotting off. "It'll have to be, boy," he said over his shoulder.

John called after him. "How far to Wellington?"

"Thirty-five, forty miles."

"Follow this side of the river?"

The man hollered, "All the way into town," and was gone, swallowed up by the trees.

John picked up last night's clam shells and flung them hard against a tree. Above, unseen birds scattered noisily. Margaret touched his arm.

"We're nearly there, sweetheart."

John turned away, ignoring her completely.

Wellington

THEY'D BEEN ON the slow march all day when Thomas Straw, a squinting tinker, a whiskey-breathed seraph, approached in a cloud of dust, driving a rickety one-horse wagon piled high with tools. He was eighty if a day, and horribly pock-marked, with a good portion of his upper lip eaten away. He knew well their suffering, he said, referring to the smallpox. He'd lost two siblings to it, but those were not modern times. These days, a body stood a good chance of surviving the wretched affliction. He himself had come through it just fine.

"As ye can plainly see."

There's more to life than a handsome face. It's a fact, said Mr. Straw, not just words. He took a long pull on a silver flask, and came down, turning around horse and wagon, maneuvering gracefully on a wooden peg, responding all the while to John's rap of questions.

The year was 1898, the month December. The old girl was still on the throne; she'd yet to kick the bucket. Sure, he recalled hearing about the poor Oades family.

"'Twas all the talk for a while."

They'd be banner news again, he said, once he returned them. He wouldn't be surprised to find the reward still on the table. "There'd be interest paid, wouldn't you think?"

"I would," said Margaret, not wanting to scare him off.

Years back, one hundred quid had been offered. "A pair of weasels claimed to know right where ye were. Wanted the reward up front, the fiends. Went to jail, one of them. Died there of dysentery, ye'll be glad to learn."

Mr. Straw offered the seat next to himself, the place of honor, to John. "Step on up, son. Be my navigator."

John looked on the grateful verge of genuflection. "You'll want to stay on this road, sir."

Margaret and the children climbed up in the back and made a place among the rusty junk. There were dead clock parts galore, flour sifters, barrel hoops, gears, and hinges. They pushed it all aside and rode facing where they'd been, their legs dangling. It was dusk, balmy sweet. The weight had lifted from Margaret's shoulders, back, limbs, and soul. She had a living daughter tucked beneath each arm. They were headed home, nearly there. For the first time she truly believed. She could visualize Henry's wordless astonishment, almost feel the heat of his suffocating embrace.

Henry, dearest. You're not half as surprised as I.

She belonged in hospital, as did Josephine. Henry would take charge; he'd see to things straightaway. The realization flooded her with happiness. With any luck, they'd set sail within a fortnight.

❖❖

JOHN WAS THE FIRST to see the standing cottage. "Mum!"

Coming up the long gravel road, Margaret turned, straining to see. Smoke rose from the chimney. Her roses, yellow on the south side, red on the north, must have the bees in a swoon. And the hydrangea! They were breathtaking, blue as the sky, big as cabbages. Fire hadn't consumed the place as she'd always feared. It was just as they'd left it, with the same green shutters and red door, which was opening now. *Henry!* She tumbled from the back of the wagon and went running, conscious of her face, ripe with blisters. It wouldn't matter one whit to him. There was far more to life than a handsome face. The door was closing. She flew up the three porch steps, knocking then pounding with both fists. "Henry! Henry Oades!" Martha came running, clutching at Margaret's skirt, crying, frightened by her shrieking banshee of a mother. John went up to the front window and boldly peered inside, his hands to the side of his face. Oscar cowered behind John, craning left and right.

"There's a lady inside," said John.

Margaret pounded hard, splintering the wood. "Madam! We are Mrs. Henry Oades and children of England, returned from captivity. Please conduct yourself to the door this instant."

She heard approaching footsteps and stepped back, breathing hard, her heart thundering. The door cracked open, bringing a rich smell of onions cooking in butter. Worn gray eyes peeped around, a mottled hand held to nose and mouth. "I have children about," the woman said, clearly afraid. Margaret did not blame the quivering little hausfrau. She'd hesitate before opening the door to her own putrescent self.

"We've been so long gone," Margaret began, her voice a timid rasp, betraying her confusion. The cottage was not the same up close. The door with its ornate wolf's head knocker was not as she remembered it. "I am Mrs. Henry Oades."

The woman spoke behind her hand. "I know who you are, poor dear."

"Are you Mr. Oades's housekeeper then?"

The woman's shoulders flinched with regal offense. "I am the lady of the house."

"I beg your pardon," said Margaret, an eddy of morbid thought whirling. *Was he dead?* "Has he relocated then, gone back to town?"

John demanded, "Where's our father?"

"He's gone to America," said the woman. "Sorry to be the one to inform you."

America! "Impossible," said Margaret.

"When will he be returning?" asked John.

"I don't imagine ever. He left some time ago." The woman lowered her voice. "Everyone assumed you were d. e. a. d."

The crack in the door narrowed. Margaret stepped closer, panic rising. "We're very much alive, thank you. Did he leave instructions for us? Money for food and lodging?"

"Not with me, dear." The door began to close. "You belong in isolation," she whispered. "You and the big girl both. I'd have you in otherwise."

The first stars had come out. There was but streaky light left in the sky. This woman was their only prospect tonight. Margaret brought Martha forward. "Will you take my well ones in, kind lady? My youngest here and the two boys? Before dark sets in? It's turned quite chilly, hasn't it? They're quiet, well-mannered children, really. You'll hardly know they're about."

"Please, miss," said John.

It was no use. Margaret could see it in the harridan's hard little eyes. There'd be no pillows and blankets offered, nothing added to the onions and butter to make it go around. Still, she gave a last try.

"If you knew what my children have endured, madam. I'd do the same for you, certainly. My big girl and I shall make a bed on your porch. Just for the one night, of course."

The woman shook her head. "I'd rather you didn't," she said, closing the door. No amount of pounding would cause it to open again. Margaret turned in her sick despair and called to Mr. Straw, who was staggering up the front path, swaying lantern in hand.

"Are you acquainted with Mr. Cyril Bell, the sailmaker?"

Oscar fell to weeping at the mention of his father. It occurred to Margaret that Cyril Bell had run off to America as well, leaving her to rear his sob-baby son. She comforted Oscar as best she could, but her heart was not in the trying.

Mr. Straw said he knew of Mr. Bell and offered to take them down to the docks. "Ye'll be sure to tell who found ye?" Margaret promised she would. "We'll leave straightaway then," he said, shouting for Oscar's benefit. "Just as soon as the wee lass here dries her crocodile tears." Oscar glared and sloped off toward the wagon, softly blubbering.

John kicked hard, dirt flying. "How could he leave?"

Margaret took her girls by the hand. "At least we know his whereabouts."

"You start at the near end, Mum," said John. "I'll start at the far. We'll meet in the middle of America. Shouldn't take more than fifty years to find him, eh?"

"Gently does it, John." It was something her dad used to say when at a complete loss.

❖❖

THE ROUTE TO the docks felt only vaguely familiar. There was no nostalgia associated, no sense of having returned to a particular beloved place. Their travail was not over, not with Henry in America, a vast ocean separating them. She might have guessed that he'd feared them dead, but that did not satisfactorily explain his leaving. She would not have left had *he* vanished. Without absolute proof of death she would have waited, until her own dying day if necessary. The deserter would have expected no less of her.

They found Cyril Bell mending torn canvas. He threw himself

on Oscar, weeping into his hair. Oscar clung to his father, eyes closed in ecstasy, nose running. Margaret stepped back to allow them their reunion, thankful that the man had been found. Surely *he'd* help. She'd cared for his son all this time. Oscar might not have survived if not for her. Margaret was fully prepared to remind him.

Mr. Straw had her sign a paper stating that he'd found them first. He bowed, wishing them well, and disappeared into the starry night.

Mr. Bell pulled away from Oscar, looking at Margaret, shaking his head in disbelief.

Margaret flicked a smile. "Mim would expect you to assist us, Mr. Bell."

His droopy eyes were full of moist sorrow. "You and the children were sorely missed, Mrs. Oades," he said. "You were powerfully mourned."

"As was he," murmured Margaret, wondering how long Henry had waited before deciding them dead.

Mr. Bell brought them to his house and pulled out the copper tub first thing. He heated the water and rigged a privacy curtain. Margaret went last. The dirty water rose like a blanket of warm scum, entering her ears, drowning out sound and thought. She fell asleep in the tub, waking to Martha's solemn brown eyes peering down at her. "I thought you were d. e. a. d."

"Don't be silly." Margaret reached up and gently finger-combed Martha's wet tangles. Martha resumed her wandering, picking up a fork from the table and examining it closely, furrowing with curiosity.

"It's a dinner fork," said Margaret. "To be held in your left hand as I taught you."

Martha nodded and went again to sit in Mr. Bell's soft reading chair. She leaned back smiling. Her baby bottom had never known such luxury.

❖❖

MRS. VIRGINIA WELLS, Mr. Bell's intended, stopped by the next afternoon. "Bell's Wells," she joked. Mr. Bell did all but scatter rose petals in her path. He spanked her chair clean and delivered tea, hovering close like a whelping pup.

She was a widow with two daughters of her own, a rather formidable lady with startlingly blue eyes. "You'll make a fine, sturdy brother for my girls," she said, shaking Oscar's hand. He'd bathed, yes, but was still a far cry from presentable. His hair needed a scythe put to it. His fingernails and toenails were tinged with green fungus. "Will you call me Mother, son? And may I give you a mother's hug?" Oscar melted in her arms.

Margaret felt a hot pang of envy and was ashamed. Oscar was the first to find a home, when she'd thought all along he'd be the last.

"And you, madam," said Mrs. Wells, turning to Margaret, who stood in the far corner like a leper. "We must get you straight to hospital."

Margaret came forward, lifting her chin and displaying her ruined face. Mrs. Wells was obviously a patron of wretched cases. "I must first see my well ones properly situated," said Margaret.

Mrs. Wells frowned. "They cannot stay in this bachelor's hovel." Mr. Bell shook his head in agreement. "I'll take them," she said.

There was no other option. Mrs. Wells was her Hobson's choice. Margaret was relieved she hadn't had to beg.

❖❖

DEAR MIM was officially declared dead. On Sunday, after regular services, Mr. Bell and Mrs. Wells married, with Martha, John, and Oscar in attendance. Margaret and Josephine were still in the hospital, their faces masks of angry, painful pustules.

The worst was over, said the doctor, speaking from the doorway. He had remarkably flawless skin, which made Margaret feel all the more repulsive. Had they suffered tremors lately? Bouts of delirium? They hadn't, said Margaret. They'd been lucid from the onset. The doctor corrected her.

"You hallucinated nights on end. Your boy told me. It must have been dreadful under the circumstances."

Margaret remembered only the road's sharp stones, the sandflies, the headaches, and the ceaseless fantasies of Henry and home.

"Though you probably wouldn't recall," said the doctor. "Certainly not while in the throes of it. And it's just as well, now that the worst is over."

He said it twice, knowing that Henry was in America.

The point of crisis had passed. The pustules would soon begin to crust and shed. Once that occurred, and they were no longer contagious, the doctor would sign their discharge papers. The other children had been examined and pronounced uninfected.

"Thank God for that," said the doctor.

"I have," said Margaret. She'd considered inoculating Martha, John, and Oscar, picking a papule from her own body and applying it to an open nick or scrape, which they all had. She wouldn't have had to cut them. But a cousin in England had died that way, and Margaret had not been willing to take the risk.

They were to rest, the doctor said. They were to nourish themselves well and take frequent sun baths. That was the sum of treatment. No miracle remedy had been invented in her absence, no magic salve to restore the complexion.

She'd forgotten how delicious it was to sleep in a bed with sheets; even so, the isolation ward was a lonely, gloomy place, with windows too high to see out. There had been one other woman in residence when Margaret and Josephine arrived. She slept the entire time, or was unconscious. She died sometime during their third night there, and was taken away. After that, Margaret and Josephine were alone.

Visitors weren't permitted. The attendants were the only human faces they saw daily. The uniformed women were not without compassion, but neither did they linger. Meals came on a cart that was rolled as far as the doorway. Margaret and Josephine fetched for themselves, returning the dirty dishes to the cart. One evening, a piece of heavy muslin, a hoop, a needle, and three colors of embroidery thread were left with a note: *Something to wile away the hours. Best wishes.*

They took turns with the piece, working up some flowers that grew more elaborate by the day. When the thread was gone, Margaret carefully picked out the stitches, saving long strands so that they could start over. It was the most peaceful shared time in memory.

Josephine spoke of her dreams a great deal. One night she dreamt that she was a harem lady. She'd danced before a fire, wearing a bloomer costume and veil. She asked casually about other occupations that might require a veil. Some nurses wear them, Margaret said, her heart breaking. She'd give two limbs to have her beautiful daughter restored. She'd give all four.

One morning Josephine woke determined to become a stage actress. It was pouring rain outside, which cozied up the place and made them less restless. "A stage actress? Pheeny, really. Did you dream it?"

Josephine played with her thick braid, twisting the coil, holding the knot to the nape of her slender pocked neck. "No. I laid awake thinking."

The attendant with her rattling breakfast cart appeared in the doorway. Good-mornings were exchanged, comments on the dismal weather. Makes a person homesick, said the attendant. She left, and Margaret said, "How did you arrive at stage actress?"

"I fancy adventure," said Josephine. She got out of bed and headed toward the cart.

"A teacher's life is chock full of grand adventure."

Josephine turned, raising a skeptical eyebrow, already the little thespian.

Margaret said, "Stage actresses don't enjoy much in the way of reputation."

"Perhaps not." Josephine lifted the domed lid and inspected the breakfast. "Lovely! A poached egg today."

"They smoke cigarettes and paint their faces."

"You once mentioned it," said Josephine, bringing the plates, smiling a moony smile, her mind obviously made up for now. There'd be no pushing this one down an unwanted path. That much was certain.

❖❖

ON THE NINTH MORNING, red roses and a note from Mr. Frey-lock, Henry's former supervisor, arrived on the cart. He'd tried to visit apparently, but wasn't allowed in. He'd last heard from Henry three years ago. At that time Henry resided in Berkeley, California—post #32. Mr. Freylock hoped the pittance of information would be of some help. He hoped, too, that she'd come to tea soon.

Berkeley, California. A husband and father shouldn't go to a place his family has never heard of.

❖❖

VIRGINIA BELL didn't forget them. On Monday Margaret and Josephine received crisp nightgowns, smelling exquisitely new of the tissue they came in. Tuesday she sent a euchre deck, which evoked vivid images of Mim's last moments. Mrs. Bell could not have known. Wednesday, Mrs. Bell's own copy of *The Jumping Frog of Calaveras County* by Mr. Mark Twain arrived, inscribed on the flyleaf: *To our Calaveras County-bound friend, Mrs. Margaret Oades. She shall be missed.*

Mrs. Bell knew by now that they were Berkeley bound. It was all California to her, and to Margaret as well, for that matter. One town was just as foreign sounding as the next, and no less distant.

❖❖

THE ATTENDANT brought stationery, fountain pen, and ink at Margaret's request. Margaret began firing off letters to Henry while Josephine slept, tearing them up as she finished. The anger kept bleeding through. How dare he abandon them so far from home? Eventually she was down to a single leaf. She wrote on both sides and let it be done.

Wellington Hospital

Dearest Husband:

The news of our survival will no doubt come as a shock. I know the feeling well, having returned to our sweet cottage with hopes high only to find you gone. How I longed to see you, Henry. How I long to see you still.

Where do I begin? Suffice it to say, we are safely returned to civilization at last. You are aware, I now know, that we were taken by Maori. The details of our ordeal can wait until we meet. Pray God that day comes soon.

At present, Josephine & I are in hospital, recuperating from a relatively mild bout of smallpox. We are both expected to recover completely, our vision unaffected. John & Martha were spared, blessedly. They are being cared for by Cyril Bell, the sailmaker & his new wife, Virginia. (Our dear friend Anamim did not survive the horrible day. I miss her even now.)

I live for the moment you lay eyes on our children again. You will be proud of them, one & all. John has shot up like a weed this year. He is an honorable boy, brave of heart, a protector by nature. He remembers you well & fondly. You will barely recognize Josephine, who lately reminds me of your Aunt Bertie. Pheeny appears to have inherited Bertie's independent streak. We'll need to keep a close eye in the coming years. Martha, of course, is no longer a baby, but a precocious child, chock full of questions. She has described you to strangers on numerous occasions. One would think you had only just left the room. (I spoke of you long & often.) "He is bearded," she will boast. "He is quite tall & very handsome. He served as constable on the ship & was the very best of the lot." Prepare yourself, dear Henry. Our youngest is highly demonstrative. She will expect more than a pat on the head from her "very handsome" father.

I come now to the saddest news. Our precious Mary is gone. She died six years ago, just hours into the abduction. Our baby suffocated. I weep as I write it. I was allowed to bury her & say a prayer, but that is all. Nothing marks her little grave. I so wished to tell you in person. Shared grief is half the sorrow, they say. I can only close my eyes & pretend it is so.

I expect to be released from hospital next week, the following week at the latest. I'd entertained a grand fantasy that our family would be reunited by Christmas. Of course that is impossible. (If only I might magic this letter into your hands today, better yet, magic the four of us into your arms.) You left neither instructions nor funds with your office, & so I shall need both as soon as possible. Please write in care of Cyril Bell (addressed envelope enclosed). Mr. & Mrs. Bell have generously invited us to stay until we sail for America. I do not wish to insinuate ourselves upon the newlyweds, but I must, as I am penniless, plain & simple. I prefer you send money as opposed to booking passage on a scheduled sailing. Various trading vessels put in regularly without notice. Funds in hand, I shall have us on the first one.

I must warn you that illness & circumstances have taken their toll. Do

*not expect the same fresh-faced, short-tempered lady to waltz through
your front door. Expect only your devoted wife, your own Meg. I belong
with my husband, & he with me & our children.*

I miss you terribly, dearest.

> *Your loving wife, now & always,*
> *Meg*

She could not possibly know when the letter would leave, much
less when it would arrive. Would it go on the first vessel, or would
the sack containing it remain on the Wellington docks for weeks
and become a stool for a card-playing rummy? Would the letter
go by swift steamer? Or would it be put aboard a slow-moving
junk? Margaret couldn't begin to guess. She waited anxiously, expecting his response in the next delivery.

Christmas fell on a Sunday. They celebrated Boxing Day, Virginia Bell's favorite holiday, the next day, Monday. Margaret and
Virginia were in the midst of preparing the tea things; it was just
the two of them in Virginia's big kitchen. Virginia relished the
quiet, the sumptuous peace, of the holiday. She always had, she
said, even as a child, especially as a child. She'd come from servants who'd never known a Christmas free from duty, even if it fell
on a Sunday.

"Boxing Day was our special day." She was in a chatty mood,
which was not unusual. "They were very well off, you know, the
people Mum and Dad worked for. Boxes went not only to the
help, but to the help's children as well. All different, too. Good tobacco in Papa's box, fine linens in Mum's. I received a great many
figurines over the years, each representing a different country. It
grew to be quite a collection. Perhaps you'd like to see it sometime."

"I would indeed," said Margaret, spooning black currant into
the pretty glass jam jar. Virginia insisted on a minimum of two
jams.

Virginia poured hot water, turning to Margaret with a sorrowful look. "That's jam plenty," she said.

Virginia frequently paused mid task or sentence, looking at Margaret, cocking her head and smiling that piteous smile. She recently asked if Margaret had written to Henry about the smallpox, and Margaret said that she had, which seemed to worry Virginia. As if she feared he might not send money to a scarred wife. Margaret privately forgave Virginia because her generosity more than compensated, and because they would soon be gone. Today is Monday, she said to herself, better than half over, almost Tuesday then, which would go by quickly because they planned to wash their hair, a time-consuming monthly ritual. That brought them almost to Thursday, nearly to the end of another week.

In the parlor, Virginia drew the curtains against the harsh summer light. Margaret wondered if it snowed in Berkeley, California, if she'd ever again know the pleasure of a cold, white Yuletide.

They had the front room to themselves. The servants were off, of course. The children had scattered. Mr. Bell was down at the docks. Margaret and Virginia took their places on the gold and blue sofa, a baronial piece of furniture, a good ten feet long, with solid mahogany arms and legs. It had taken four men to lift it, Virginia said. She'd inherited the large house and all its grand furniture from her late husband, who'd died of a rupture before he could be brought to hospital. Over tea and scones, Virginia described his last moments, the violent vomiting, the agonizing writhing and sweating.

"It was a frightening spectacle," she said.

Margaret sympathized, thinking simultaneously that there were worse things than a husband's death. A child's death. That was the unspeakable worst.

Virginia shifted, sitting slightly closer, her knees angled in, brushing Margaret's. "A halfpenny for your thoughts."

Margaret managed a smile.

"You'll hear from him soon."

Margaret nodded. "I hope you're right."

Virginia seemed to hesitate before saying, "Mr. Oades did everything he could."

Everything but stay.

"Perhaps you'd rather not hear . . ."

"I would," said Margaret. "Please tell me what you know."

"We all saw how distraught he was. Everyone turned out to help the bereft man rebuild his house." There was a peculiar quiver to Virginia now, an eagerness to divulge all. "Some other ladies and I brought a picnic out to the site one Sunday, which is when I made Mr. Bell's formal acquaintance." Virginia dipped her chin to blush, touching Margaret's hand as she did, an unpleasant sensation, like that of a long-legged spider lighting. "Dear Mr. Oades," Virginia whispered. "He had such a time of it."

In that moment, Margaret resolved to truly forgive him for leaving, for her own sake as well as his. "How so after the fact?"

"They say he went nearly insane, that he kept the lamps burning all night long, often riding about in the wee hours, wailing for the children."

Tears rose in Margaret's eyes. No father loved his children more.

"Oh, dear. Forgive me, Margaret. I've said too much."

"It's all right, Virginia. I'm simply not myself today. Will you excuse me, please?" Margaret bent over the tea tray, intending to carry it to the kitchen. Virginia stopped her. Margaret was not to lift a finger. She was to march straight upstairs this very moment and have a nice lie-down.

The weeping began the moment Margaret closed the guest room door, six years' worth at once. Not since Mary's death had she wept so hard.

❖❖

JANUARY PASSED without word from Henry. The days became excruciatingly long. The house was overstaffed as it was. Any contribution on Margaret's part was regarded as intrusion. She read a great deal and worked with the children on their lessons; but there were still far too many hours in the day and too few ways to purposely fill them.

Evenings were spent in the front parlor, where Margaret was expected to accompany Virginia on the piano. Virginia's girls, studious towheads, fifteen and thirteen, acted as chorus, harmonizing softly, never upstaging their mother. The other children, Margaret's, and Oscar, were required to dress properly and serve as audience. Virginia's shrill voice sent an ice-water chill down the spine. Cyril Bell cheered his wife on, initiating round after round of applause. "Brava, Sweet Puss! Encore! Encore!"

Mrs. Barry, the cook, passed treacly refreshments afterward, biscuits oozing jam, or a trifle soaked in sherry. Margaret's children were still unaccustomed to such rich treats. The sweets undoubtedly contributed to Martha's nightmares. Her little girl regularly woke up screaming. "There's a man at the window!"

It was not unlike Margaret's own dreams, though the shadow at her window was more often welcoming. She held her perspiring child until she cooled again. "We're all dreaming of Dad."

❖❖

ANOTHER THREE WEEKS went by. Virginia said nothing directly, but Margaret knew she wished them gone. Fish and visitors stink after three days, according to Mr. Benjamin Franklin. They were long past spoiled. No one was more aware of the stench than Margaret.

Margaret was in the kitchen with Mrs. Barry one afternoon in late February, rolling out dough for kidney pasties. Virginia burst through the door, still wearing her good hat and coat. Margaret looked up, swiping her floury hands together. Virginia clutched a thick envelope, giggling like a girl. Margaret suspected her of tippling with the other Devoted-Friends-of-the-Library. "I went behind your back, Margaret."

Margaret smiled. "Did you now?"

Virginia opened the envelope, displaying the money inside. "What do you suppose it's for?"

"I have no idea," said Margaret.

"It's for you!" cried Virginia, fanning the notes. "For your passage to California!"

Margaret frowned, looking at Mrs. Barry, who shrugged and turned back to the stove. "Where did it come from?"

"From the lovely parishioners at St. Paul's. I took up a collection. They gave clothes, too. Wait until you see. There's one frock I wouldn't mind—"

"You shouldn't have," said Margaret, her flesh heating with embarrassment. She was enough of a charity case as it was. Mrs. Barry glanced her way, with a look that said: *Don't be a fool. Take it.* Margaret stared at the money. Dear God, how she wanted to leave. She and Henry would pay it back, every last cent, with interest.

"There's enough here for two," said Virginia, sobering some. "I thought perhaps John and Josephine might go ahead and then—"

"Out of the question!" said Margaret, shocked.

Virginia's blue eyes dulled. "John's nearly a grown man."

"He's not," said Margaret. "He's barely seventeen."

Virginia sighed. "Well, never mind then. I was afraid you'd feel this way." She turned to leave. "Don't look so forlorn, Margaret. We'll think of something else."

Margaret returned to the pasty crust, sprinkling water on the drying edges. It had seemed so real for a moment, so completely possible.

❖❖

VIRGINIA NEXT ORGANIZED a pie auction, which was held on St. Paul's green grounds. Margaret and the children were obliged to line up on the auctioneer's platform and face the bidders, a jolly crowd, quite boisterously pleased with their generous selves. The people waved huge wads of notes in the air, paying outrageous sums for the ladies' pies. At the end the auctioneer came for Margaret, taking her gently by the elbow, as if she might turn to powder, escorting her to his podium. He left her there alone to express her gratitude, which she did in an even voice, belying the humiliation she so keenly felt.

Virginia later remarked that Margaret might have tried to appear appreciative during the auction, offered a smile, a wave, a measly nod or two. Sufficient money would have been raised had she deigned to look half pleasant, not stood like a glowering post the entire time.

"I'm very disappointed in you, Margaret. Very disappointed indeed."

Virginia quite clearly had had enough. She augmented the donated funds with her own money, paying for steerage accommodations on board the *Sacramento*, which was due to sail in two days' time. Margaret searched out pen and paper, making a mess of the first letter and starting over, giddy with joy.

"You cannot count on your note arriving first," said Virginia. "Mr. Oades may not be on hand to meet you."

"Rest your mind," said Margaret. "I shall find him."

She began immediately to prepare, going through the boxes of donated clothes, setting aside two frocks apiece for the girls and herself, shirts for John, an extra pair of trousers. One lady had knitted bulky gray scarves which were meant to be wrapped across the lower half of a pitted face. Margaret kept the scarves from Josephine's sight, choosing instead wide-brimmed felt hats with fresh blue ribbons. Blue had always been Henry's favorite color.

March 1899

Unbeknownst to Margaret, Virginia Bell had bartered Margaret's services for a reduced fare. Margaret was expected in the galley twice daily, at five in the morning and again at three. In addition, she was to mind the captain's two young daughters. They were hours out to sea when the first mate came around to inform her. Virginia had also offered up John as a cabin boy, which suited her son just fine.

Except for Deborah and Lillith, the captain's motherless girls, Margaret and her children were the only passengers on board. They kept to themselves mainly, passing their nights in a dank hole. There was no piano to divert their attention, no singsongs, no library, no berths with sheets, only hammocks slung close together. John fell out of his when the all hands bellow came from above. He was due on deck during the most furious of gales, expected to reef the heavy flapping sails right alongside experienced, sure-footed men. Margaret lay swaying in the dark, nauseated, listening to the pounding boots overhead, the shouting, fearing in the next moment her boy would be swept overboard. For John it was adventure, high and pure.

"It was nothing, Mum," he said every time.

The *Sacramento,* formerly the *Governor Bartholomew,* was a creaking, shuddering old tub of an English brig. Margaret judged her to be at least thirty years old. She carried Australian wool and seal pelts that stank to high heaven, particularly on the leeward side of the ship. There was no getting used to the odor of decomposition, no getting used to the rats and cockroaches, the weevil-specked flour, the yellow water, and the rancid meat. There was only endurance, and the reward of a splendid sunset, signifying the end of another wretched day. Her stoic children did their best, as they had in captivity. There was little complaining to be heard. They simply kept at it, like the mindless cockroaches themselves, only without the same sense of urgency.

❖❖

ONE NIGHT in the galley Margaret learned that they were to put in at the Sandwich Islands within three or four days. Once there, the current lot of native sailors was to be let off and another set taken on. She asked the taciturn American cook how long they'd be in port, but he did not know. "Can't say," he said, with his usual paucity of words. "And the place is called Hawaii now. We took it last summer."

The captain and mate, Americans as well, were the same way, saying little unless the subject centered on America's military brilliance. The army would make mincemeat out of the Filipino gooks, said Mr. Grady, the mate. The navy had Guam sewed up.

"Took Wake Island while she was sleeping," he said, erupting in a rare laugh, thinking his little play on words extremely amusing. Mr. Grady scraped green mold from the last potato and pitched it into the pot. "China's next," he said. "Mark my words."

Mr. Grady looked for American men-of-war every day, but never did spot any. He'd come away from his watch like a lad who'd found coal in his Christmas stocking, treating everyone but the captain to a fit of the sulks.

The captain was another odd duck, though one of a different plumage. No display was made of it, but he had to be in mourning, having lost his wife to pleurisy only four months earlier. He was the indifferent sort, fairly ignoring his poor girls, who were naturally grieving themselves. They did not take to Margaret, perhaps because her pitted face frightened them, perhaps because she was alive and their mother was not. Who could guess the reason? They were ten and twelve, lithe little monkeys, at home on a slippery deck.

"Your stories are silly," the eldest said straight to her face. They needed no assistance braiding their hair or washing their frocks. "We're perfectly capable of minding ourselves." After a week of hovering, Margaret let out the tether, inviting them to come to her anytime. But they never once did.

❖❖

THE WINDS DIED DOWN on a Wednesday. It was another ten days before the lovely Honolulu harbor came into sight. By then the necessary rationing had begun to take a visible toll on them all.

The gaunt sailors sent up a rousing cheer. Their brown kin paddled out to meet them, bringing music and flowers and exotic women. The sailors dropped their lines one by one and commenced jumping overboard. The lucky lads were quit of this rat-infested bark. Envy made Margaret even hungrier.

The stinking cargo was unloaded first thing. The captain and crew then lowered a boat in preparation for a trip ashore. Fresh stores were sorely needed. Margaret stood watching, wondering when they might weigh anchor and be on their way again. Deborah and Lillith scrambled over the side without so much as a ta-ta for her. Captain Fisk followed, turning to Margaret at the last moment.

"Is there anything out of the ordinary you might require, madam?"

The offer took her by surprise, and so she said no at first, immediately changing her mind."A book or two would be lovely. How kind of you to ask, sir. Any sort, on any subject, will do."

"Consider it done," he said. With that the hellfires still ahead seemed quenched by a good ten degrees. If he brought back just one book she would divide the pages by days at sea to make it last. Two books and she'd be in her glory. More than two was asking too much.

◇◇

With the ship entirely to themselves, Margaret decided on a sea bath, thinking it would do them all a world of good. John had no interest, but kept watch, turning his gentlemanly back as she and the girls stripped down to chemise and drawers. Her modest girls hopped about, hugging themselves, poking each other in the ribs. Skimpy, bony things. As if Margaret had room to speak. She felt quite fit; she simply didn't look it. She'd like to say it was of no concern, but it was. A woman with a complexion as ravaged as hers was entitled to an ample pleasing figure. Fair's fair. A husband's eyes must have someplace to rest.

They climbed down the rope ladder and slipped into the warm water. There were fish of all colors, beautifully speckled and striped. The girls lathered each other with the last of the soap, splashing about, giggling. They were holding hands, dancing a watery minuet, when a long shadow passed behind them. Margaret put an immediate end to the frolicking, refusing their pleas. "A minute longer, please, Mum." She hadn't always been so fearful; though perhaps that wasn't true. She couldn't reliably recall her former self anymore.

The remainder of the day went by without sign of captain and crew. Just after dark a Kanakan boy paddled up in his canoe. A yellow lantern hung from a pole in his bow. Margaret and the children could see the boy quite clearly. His face was round, his teeth chalk-white. He banged on the side of the hull and lifted a large fish by the tail.

"From the captain!" he yelled in English.

John let down a basket and brought up the fish, along with a bowl of clay, which the boy demonstrated was edible, dipping two fingers into the gray stuff and licking them clean. He signaled for the basket and John dropped it again, pulling up a bar of soap, a tin of lamp oil, and kindling for the stove. Other canoes approached, curious boys in them, chattering happily in their musical tongue. A grand three-quarter moon hung low, throwing ripples of light on the calm water. John lowered the basket a third time. Margaret and her girls leaned over the side of the ship, eager to see what was coming next. They received another glistening fish, some rice, sugar, and flour. Then before her weak eyes a book was pulled from beneath a tarp and placed inside the basket.

"Gently does it now. Don't drop it, son."

It was only one, but it was nice and thick. Dickens perhaps. How silly to be so excited. Here it is, here it is. She plucked the book from the basket and turned it over, her shoulders sagging with disappointment. A Bible.

The boy pushed off and paddled away. Margaret made a megaphone of her hands. "Thackeray," she called. "Austen. Trollope. James." The boy waved, grinning, flashing his bright shark teeth.

"God bless you also," he hollered. "God bless you one thousand times."

Two days later, the boy returned, bringing fish and more taro mush, but no other books. Margaret shouted down, "Any word from the captain?" The boy shook his head no.

On the fourth day, Captain Fisk approached in the ship's boat. Margaret thought it peculiar that he was alone. At the same time she was hopeful. The winds were out of the west, a perfect day for sailing.

He came bearing gifts, strangely enough. She and the girls were presented with Kanakan dresses, calico frocks that went from neck to toe without a break. "How practical, sir," said Margaret. "Thank you."

John received a telescope, which he immediately trained on majestic Diamond Head. The back of his head looked afire in the sunlight, reminding Margaret of a young Henry in England, a walk down to the stables in winter, the Saturday before they married.

"I've sold the ship," said Captain Fisk. "My daughters and I are staying on."

Margaret broke from reverie. "Sir?"

There was a certain wildness in his gray eyes. "God has called me, Mrs. Oades. There was no mistaking it. My work is here now, among the Kanakans."

"All best wishes, sir," said Margaret, baffled by the news. What sort abandons passengers and crew mid journey? "Will the new master be sailing straightaway for America?"

The captain ran his hand along a teak rail in need of oil. "I'm afraid not."

Her underarms wetted.

"Mr. Bainbridge is a sealer," he said. "He'll be heading south. I cannot say when precisely."

John lowered the glass and moved to Margaret's side. Her girls stared up at God's newest servant, clutching their colorful frocks to their narrow chests.

Margaret found her voice. "And as for us, sir?"

"I've given your situation long, hard thought, Mrs. Oades."

Margaret nodded, needles of apprehension pricking. "And?"

"I believe you and your children will best be served by staying on as well. There's a great deal of work to be done."

"Sir, we cannot possibly consider . . ."

He raised his hand and closed his eyes, shaking his woolly head. "Don't dismiss me so readily, woman." He flung out an arm. "Look! Open your eyes and look, will you? Look at the sea! The beautiful bountiful sea! Have you ever in your life known any place like it? Here's latter-day Eden, I tell you. Every day is as now. You'll never again suffer an English blizzard, or a blistering, mosquito-infested summer. This is God's own sacred place. Do not suppose you are here by chance, good lady, by some mercurial quirk of fate. God brought you here, and he means you to stay. I prayed on it. Day and night I prayed on it."

He was breathing hard now, but still did not allow a word in. His daughters would benefit from Margaret's presence, he claimed, from her wise maternal comfort and guidance. His rabid tone shifted, becoming soft and courtly. "I myself would welcome your company. I try not to question the Lord's plan. But there is a dearth of eligible white women here."

"I am not an eligible white woman, sir. I am married."

"So you say."

Margaret looked him directly in the eye. "So I do indeed say."

He averted his gaze, heaving an impatient sigh. "Will you not give my proposal the least consideration?"

The warm harbor breeze brought a lovely scent from shore, a flower she could not name. "No sir, I cannot."

"Very well," he said coldly. "The *Golden State* is in port. I shall speak to the captain on your behalf."

"Thank you, sir. When does she sail?"

His jaw went hard. "Saturday. Will that be soon enough for you, madam?" He turned and strode off toward his quarters. Margaret felt a twinge of regret watching him go. For all she knew Henry was dead. She spent the afternoon stewing. It was not like her. She was a decisive person by nature, or so she once believed.

❖❖

ALL DOUBT VANISHED at first sight of the *Golden State*. She was a magnificent passenger ship, a fine, sleek steamer on the return leg of her maiden voyage. Margaret thrilled to see how clean and modern she was. She was more than delighted to accept the cook's helper and pot-scrubber post. She would have gladly signed on as a stoker had it been the only job available.

She was at work in the galley when they sailed and did not have a last look at Hawaii. They were busy laying out a seven-course meal for United States congressmen, a clamorous group. Upon arrival in San Francisco the congressmen presented Margaret with an envelope thick with American notes. This was the second of May, 1899, a Tuesday. They'd been at sea two months less four days.

Hello, Henry

S AN FRANCISCO, CALIFORNIA. A haven for the depraved, named for the kindliest of saints. Margaret corralled her children and kept them close. Seamen with knives swarmed the docks. They drank openly, staggering in and out of saloons and billiard parlors, shouting *fuck* this and *fuck* that at every turn. There were women, too, girls on the game, lingering in doorways, chatting up the reprobates. The atmosphere stank of fish, of whiskey, urine, and vomit.

"A reeking place," said John. They started down a damp alley that ended at a padlocked door, and turned around again. There was no obvious route, no signs to direct them to the ferry. A cook from the *Golden State* brushed by in a hurry. Margaret called to him.

"Mr. Mandina! Could you help us locate the Berkeley ferry?"

He had two knives himself, she noticed up close, one tucked inside each boot. Self-defense, she supposed. On board he'd seemed a gentler sort, with a special fondness for the seabirds he spoke to and fed. He guided Margaret and the children through the crush of men, past the ships and cargo, past an open crate of bananas with a small dead monkey inside. Softhearted Martha saw the poor creature and began to cry.

"It's sleeping," said Margaret, wondering what in God's name had drawn her husband to this miserable abyss.

On the ferry, John asked, "What shall be your very first words to Father?"

Margaret laughed a little, with a vague headache throbbing. "I suppose I shall say, 'Hello, Henry.'"

"Hello, Henry?"

His deep voice would astound his father. John had been ten, a squeaking whelp, the last time Henry laid eyes on him. He would be thrilled beyond expression, utterly bedazzled by their beautiful son.

"After all these years, Mum? That's the best you can do? A paltry *Hello, Henry?*"

Margaret cuffed him playfully. She had no idea what she'd say first, but was certain the right words would come naturally.

❖❖

WITH THE AMERICAN DOLLARS earned on board the *Golden State,* she hired a coach to deliver them to the Berkeley post office. Once there, Margaret asked the coachman to please wait, she wouldn't be long. John made a move as if to accompany her inside.

"Stay and mind the girls. I shan't be but a moment."

All she had of her husband was this box number. She'd not given voice to it, but it had occurred to her that he'd left again, returned to England perhaps. Or died. She wouldn't have her children hearing it first from a foreign stranger, not after all they'd been through.

The postmaster sorted envelopes behind a caged window. Margaret approached, introducing herself properly. He abandoned his task, his sleepy eyes widening. She ignored the rudeness. People will gawk, as if they'd paid their shilling to see the scarred lady and were entitled.

"Are you acquainted with Mr. Oades, sir?"

"Dairyman," said the postmaster.

"My husband is an accountant," said Margaret.

"Only Henry Oades around here is a dairyman. You're his missus, you say?" He wetted a pencil with the tip of his tongue and offered to draw a map to Henry's farm. "Is he expecting you?"

She'd heard about overcurious Americans, how they were keen to pry for the pure sport of it. She was not about to take up the long wretched tale with him, and so simply said, "Of course he is."

Outside, Margaret presented the map to the coachman, who offered a choice of a quick or scenic route.

"Oh, quick, please," she said, paying the agreed upon coins.

"Only two bits more for the scenic," he said, eyeing her bank notes.

She drew her reticule closed. "You shall take us directly." She climbed up without assistance and settled in beside John. The coachman slammed the door, muttering, "Foreigners."

"He's turned dairy farmer of all things," Margaret said to the children.

The news seemed to please John. He turned to the window with a smile. The coachman cracked his whip and they were off. Margaret rode facing her daughters, expectant-faced rag children in donated frocks. "He's a lovely man," she said, for perhaps the hundredth time.

"He's tall, bearded, and quite handsome," recited Martha.

Margaret nodded. "Quite."

"He thinks the world of us," said listless Josephine. She rubbed her eye with the heel of her hand. "We are Dad's all and all."

Margaret pulled down on Josephine's lower lid, checking for pinkeye. Her big girl had suffered two dripping bouts in captivity. Josephine twisted to the side, fending off her hand.

"Are you all right, sweetheart?"

"I'm just a bit nervous, is all," said Josephine. "It's been a very long time."

"Though he may be standoffish at first," said Martha, "due to the surprise. We shan't let it bother us."

John continued to stare out the window; he was having no part of the old game.

Margaret leaned forward again and fussed with Josephine's limp hat ribbons. "There's nothing to be nervous about. You *are* your father's all and all; you mustn't forget it."

The hats weren't the most grand. She'd thought them sufficiently suitable until she'd noticed all the women, on the ship and on the ferry, wearing extravagant feathered creations. Not that it would make a difference to Henry if she turned up wearing an entire swan.

Good God, Meg! Did you suppose I'd give your hat the first thought?

I wanted to look nice for you, Henry.

You could be wearing your drawers on your head for all I care. Come here now, lovely girl. Let me look at you.

She imagined the children already tucked in when he said it, her thoughts roaming to how they'd be once they were alone for the night. They would be fine, she decided, a thin shiver running. She knew her Henry. They would be lovely. Margaret sat back, happy for the first time in years.

❖❖

AN HOUR OUT Martha locked ankles and demanded a pot. They were in the countryside now, traveling over a rutted road, passing tranquil, hilly farmland. Margaret poked her head out the window and called up to the driver. "How much farther, sir?"

He hollered down, "Three or four miles, give or take. Just beyond this next rise."

"Will you stop, please?"

"What for?"

Never mind what for. "Only a moment."

"Two bits extra for the inconvenience," he yelled, expectorating a jawful of revolting black juice. Margaret ducked back inside. *The cheeky nerve!*

"Mama, please."

Margaret called to the driver. "We'll stop here."

He pulled on the reins. "Two bits extra."

They all got out to the driver's obvious surprise. "I shan't pay you another stiver," she said. "Please hand down our cases."

The sneak thief climbed up to the roof and threw their satchels to the ground, cursing under his breath. "Pinchpenny," he shouted, driving away, leaving them by the side of the road.

Pinchpenny, he called me. Margaret was already making light of it, forming the story for Henry, thinking a bit of humor would go a long way in mitigating the shock of their existence.

Martha finished her business and they set off walking. In her thoughts and dreams Margaret had imagined California flat, an arid prairie thick with bison and wapiti. Had she read it? She'd not expected the green hills and winding roads, a place so poignantly reminiscent of England, down to the dragonflies.

❖❖

JOHN WAS THE FIRST to see the start of a painted fence. They trudged on for some time, following the fence, scanning the acreage for signs of life. How peculiar that Henry had turned dairy farmer, but how like him to have such a pristine arrangement, a meadow so uninterruptedly verdant, a herd so storybook placid. Margaret spotted a male figure then, high on the horizon. She waved, sun and gladness watering her weak eyes. The children waved too, but the figure did not respond, and they all gave up.

Martha fell in alongside, taking Margaret's hand. "He'll have cake for us, don't you think, Mum?"

They'd missed the noon meal. Margaret wondered what he might have on hand, deciding surely there'd be eggs, and wouldn't eggs be perfect. A simple meal of toast and eggs. Bacon might be nice. Henry had always enjoyed his back bacon. She'd make a pud with the drippings, and cook his eggs without turning them. She hadn't forgotten the small details.

"He'll more likely have eggs," she said.

"I prefer cake," said Martha.

"You cannot count on it. Your father never had much of a tooth for sweets."

Long-legged John was a good way ahead when he turned, pointing. "There's Dad's house. Do you see it up there?" The girls broke into an unladylike run, overtaking John. Margaret strained to keep up. John hollered over his shoulder. "Do you see it, Mum?"

Her vision was poor, but yes, she could make out some sort of structure.

At the gate she reined them in, giving each a quick cat bath, spanking the dust from their clothes. "Let us be calm now," she said, a fresh wave of excitement running through her.

From the bottom of the porch steps she saw movement, a shadow passing behind the lace curtains. Margaret ascended and rang the hanging bell, her heart jumping with anticipation. A pretty girl opened the door and eyed them up and down suspiciously.

"Who are you? How did you get here? I didn't hear a buggy come up."

She was young, eighteen or nineteen perhaps, with thick brown hair sloppily pinned up. She was dressed in a work apron that had seen better days, though her milky blue-veined hands acknowledged no familiarity with hard work. Margaret had heard that American help was lazy, undependable. One had to stay on them. "Forgive us for startling you," she said. "Is this the home of Mr. Henry Oades?"

The girl poked at her unruly hair. "Who wants to know? Is it food you're after?"

The insolent lass could use a good caning. "We are Mrs. Henry Oades and children. We're not expected."

The girl scowled, cocking her head. As if she hadn't heard right. "You're his mother?"

"I am his *wife*, miss. If it's any concern of yours."

The loony thing clapped hands to ears and closed her eyes. Her lips moved rapidly for several moments, as if in prayer. With an audible "amen" her eyes opened wide, hands dropping to her sides, wedding band, gaudy new, winking with sunlight. "I'm sorry, but I don't know any other way of saying it but right out. I am Mr. Oades's wife now."

Margaret's children closed in, an arm encircling her waist, a little hand tugging on her skirts. They brought her down the steps just as a colicky baby started up inside, barking like a seal pup.

The girl shouted into the interior, "Dora! See to the baby!" She started down the stairs toward Margaret.

Margaret moved out of her range, trembling. "Father," said John, close to her ear. Margaret turned. Henry approached from the west, making long, lopsided strides. But for the limp he looked the same from this distance, leaner perhaps, but otherwise just as she remembered him. He stopped short just inside the gate, removing his shabby hat, staring, shifting his disbelieving gaze between Margaret and the girl.

"My God," he said.

John straightened through the shoulders. "Father?" Henry and John advanced toward each other, meeting in a powerful slapping embrace. Margaret wept openly at the sight. The baby inside was wailing now. *He had another family.* The sick circumstances wrapped about her hot and tight. She'd never once considered the possibility.

PART THREE

PART THREE

A Fly in the
Amber

Nancy's husband looked as if he'd suffered a sharp blow to the head. The woman, his heretofore dead wife, appeared no less stunned. Nancy approached her as she might a ghost, apologizing. "Forgive my atrocious manners earlier, ma'am. I thought you were someone else."

Nancy left it at that, unable to explain herself, confess that she'd mistaken Mrs. Oades for a Gypsy crone at first. West Berkeley teemed with those scary people. She took the woman's rickety arm, blurting, "Where have you been all this time?" The woman freed herself, rubbing her arm, blinking, as if bothered by sun or sty, saying nothing. Nancy was sorry she'd asked. It was a bad habit of hers, speaking before thinking. The poor woman had enough to contend with. That ravaged complexion, good Lord, and the dejection in those sore-looking eyes. She was a living, breathing heartbreak.

The little girl was the least intimidating of the four. Nancy beckoned to her. "Come inside, why don't you." The dog-eared family exchanged reluctant looks. "Let's all go inside where it's nice and cool. What do you say? There's lavender lemonade." It wasn't much in the way of comfort, but it was all she could think to do just then.

Mr. Oades came forward with his arm around the boy. They were nearly the same height. "John Oades," he said, introducing his son to Nancy, his voice quivering with emotion. He turned to the older girl, touching her cheek. "Pheeny, sweetheart. I cannot believe my eyes." The mud-plain girl curtsied, blushing behind a hectic constellation of brown freckles and pockmarks. "Please, Meg," he said to the woman. "Come inside now."

Mute Mrs. Oades lifted her chin and allowed herself to be escorted up the porch steps. Already Nancy felt her own world shrinking. This woman would fill every corner with her unhappiness.

"Well," said Nancy, once inside the narrow vestibule. It didn't matter which way she turned her head, the woman's steely eyes cut right through her. "Well, well."

The littlest girl asked, "Where are we to sleep?"

"You'll sleep upstairs," said Nancy. "You'll have a nice big room, with a nice big bed, with a crocheted spread. Say now, I made a rhyme, didn't I?"

The little girl nodded solemnly. They needed baths, the boy most of all. And with her sheets just off the line. But where else would they sleep? Of course they'd stay. For the time being, at least. You don't send kin away when they've only just arrived.

Mr. Oades squatted on his haunches, putting himself face-to-face with the little one. He'd come from the pigs and smelled as if he'd danced a waltz with them. His odor didn't seem to bother the child. She actually had the temerity to bob forward and touch her nose to his. The strange gesture filled Mr. Oades's eyes with tears. He stroked her hair gingerly, reverently, as if he were stroking fine silk. "Baby girl," he murmured.

"Martha," said Mrs. Oades, speaking at last.

Henry looked up at her. "And Mary?"

"Gone," Mrs. Oades whispered.

"Mary died," the child said. "She was my twin sister."

Mr. Oades glanced up again. "In the fire?"

Martha piped up before Mrs. Oades could respond. "She couldn't breathe where she was." Here in the failing light, at the base of the stairs, Mr. Oades buried his face in his hands and wept. Nancy touched his shoulder briefly, feeling the stony woman's resentful breath on her neck, imagining at the same time some chippie's hands on Francis. But that was not a fair comparison. Mrs. Oades was supposed to be dead and buried. *She,* not Nancy, was the out-of-place fly in the amber.

Mr. Oades composed himself and stood, the same stricken look on his face. Nancy couldn't begin to tell what he was thinking. "Meg and the girls will sleep upstairs," he said. "We'll give John the maid's room."

"What about Dora?" said Nancy.

"I'll go anywhere, Dad," said John.

"We'll send Dora home for the time being," said Mr. Oades.

"We can't do that," said Nancy. "Her father beats her regularly. Let's have John sleep on the davenport. It's comfortable enough." She spoke to the woman's mismatched shoelaces. "Will that be all right with you?"

"Whatever you decide, madam," she said, her voice flat as a fritter.

Nancy felt for her. How could she bear to stay?

"Show the ladies upstairs," she said to Mr. Oades. "Then fill the water pitcher and put out the rose petal soap. I'll see about refreshments. I assume they've had their main meal by now."

"We haven't, miss," said Martha.

Mrs. Oades shook the child's shoulder. "Please don't go to any bother," she said.

The older girl continued to glare. One look in the mirror would cure her. Nancy gestured toward the stairs. "The sheets are fresh. Just off the line."

Mr. Oades led Mrs. Oades and her daughters up to the spare room, Nancy's future sewing room only an hour ago.

Nancy brought John into the kitchen, not knowing what else to do with him. She introduced him to Dora, whispering for fear of waking Gertrude, who lay inside a blanketed crate on the floor. She'd all but forgotten her baby's existence in the bedlam.

Dora and John exchanged shy hellos, and the girl went back to oiling the tabletop.

"Our guests haven't eaten," said Nancy. "We'll be five . . . no we'll be six." She hadn't counted herself. "How about warming up this noon's fricassee. Are there any more dumplings? No? Well, make a batch of quick biscuits, please, and take down a jar of strawberry jam. All right? And please be quiet about it, hear? Please, please, please, don't wake the baby."

Nancy went to Gertrude.

John came up behind. "What's its name?"

"Gertrude Foreland, soon to be Gertrude Oades. Your father's preparing the papers. Why do you look surprised . . . oh, I see, you thought . . . well, no. I was married to another gentleman, Mr. Foreland, Gertrude's natural father. He passed before she was born."

"My condolences, ma'am."

"And mine for your sister, John."

He bore a striking resemblance to Mr. Oades. Nancy liked him already. A man needed a son. All by himself, John would make a welcome addition to the household.

❖❖

THE SIX GATHERED in the back room. In addition to the fricassee and biscuits, there were pickled beets and eggs, and some sweet lettuce from the garden, cooked in bacon. So the meal itself turned out fine. Grace was said. Henry thanked the Lord for the safe return of *our* loved ones, intending to include Nancy in the reunion, she supposed. He picked at his second dinner, looking at his children with wonderment, asking finally, "What happened?"

"We were taken by Maori," said John.

Mr. Oades nodded, as if he'd known all along.

"How awful," said Nancy. She thought to ask what a *maw-ree* was, but held back for a change.

Mrs. Oades spoke to her plate. "I wrote to you in detail, Henry."

Mr. Oades shook his head. "I never received a letter."

Martha said, "We looked for you everywhere, Dad."

Tears glistened in Mr. Oades's brown eyes. "Oh, baby girl. I'm so sorry."

"Oscar's dad stayed!" said the older girl, accusingly.

"That's quite enough, Pheeny," said Mrs. Oades, laying down her fork.

Nancy glanced her way. Mrs. Oades met her eyes for an instant and then looked away again. The greatest hatred is silent. Nancy's father once said so.

After the meal they retired to the front sitting room, Nancy's favorite room, Francis's room. She spent many an hour alone here, speaking to Francis aloud, polishing his jar and the pedestal it sat upon. Dora knew when to stay away.

Mrs. Oades noticed the ginger jar immediately. She stepped up to the marble pedestal with an outstretched hand. Nancy thought she was about to seize the jar. "Please be careful, Mrs. Oades. It's old, easily broken."

Mrs. Oades withdrew, looking at Mr. Oades, her eyes narrowing. He sat her in his reading chair, murmuring "sorry" and something else Nancy didn't catch. Nancy took her place on the settee, wondering why he'd apologized. The children went to the daven-port and sat wordlessly, three wan chicks on a roost.

"We want you to make yourself at home, Mrs. Oades," said Nancy.

Mrs. Oades stiffened visibly. "It's a bit difficult under the cir-cumstances, *Mrs. Oades.*"

What was Nancy supposed to do about the circumstances? Did the woman expect her to simply pack up her sickly baby, leave her husband, and go join the Gypsies?

"It's a peculiar situation I agree, but what can we do?" Nancy was babbling now. She heard her desperate-sounding self. "There's no one to blame. We must play the hand we've been dealt, as my daddy used to say."

Mrs. Oades looked at her children with such a forlorn expres-sion, tucking a stray strand behind an ear. Her hair was gray and thin; the scalp showed in places.

Nancy tried again. "The children have been reunited with their father. You're glad for that much at least, aren't you?"

"I am," said Mrs. Oades. "Of course I am."

"Well, all right then," said Nancy. "That's a good start." Mr. Oades sat down beside her, less close than he normally would. "We'll figure things out, Mrs. Oades." Nancy didn't know what she was saying. She had no answers, no idea of how to satisfacto-rily figure things out. "Don't you worry. It doesn't all have to be thought of today. Let's sleep on it. The children have had a long day. We've all had a long day. Let's turn in early. What do you say?"

Mrs. Oades was on her feet before Nancy finished speaking, looking as if she couldn't be up the stairs fast enough.

◈◈

HENRY STOOD TOO, his confounded gaze fixed high above the heads of both wives. His son was nearly a man. His baby was a little girl he shouldn't know, but somehow did. He felt snatched from a dream, having his beautiful children before him, the betrayal overtly displayed in Josephine's stiff posture, in her cold denunciative eyes. He'd replaced their mother. There was little a father might do to cause greater harm.

A Start

UPSTAIRS, MARGARET and her girls looked at one another and commenced undressing in silence. Margaret had never before worn the delicate nightgown given to her in the hospital. She'd kept the lovely garment in the original tissue, saving it for this night.

"You look like a bride, Mum," said Martha, stroking Margaret's sleeve, obviously trying to cheer her.

They got into bed, Margaret taking the outside. She wet her fingers and pinched out the flame. "He's still your same dad," she said in the dark. "Nothing's changed there."

Josephine said bitterly, "You're his *true* wife."

"He thought we'd passed," said Margaret. "He was horribly sad, dreadfully lonely. Let us sleep now."

Her girls drifted off. Next to them, Margaret tried to stay still. He clearly adored the woman, the *girl*. There was no getting around it. No getting around either the dry pounding in her ears, or the voices heard on the stairs, his and his wife's, the murmur fading as they neared their room down the hall. *Mr. Oades,* she called him. As if addressing the King of Egypt, as if she hardly knew him.

Toward morning Margaret slept, waking when the hammering started below, unsure of her whereabouts for a muddy half-moment. Her girls were gone, their frocks missing from the pegs. Light flooded in through the sheer curtains. It had to be late, far too late to make a reasonable appearance. She lay with her thoughts for a time, considering and rejecting a return to England. She'd spent years building up Henry, creating a near deity in the children's impressionable minds. The cruelest, most selfish mother wouldn't spirit them off now. John might even elect to stay. That she couldn't tolerate.

And how was she to explain the wretched situation? Telling her parents about the girl in a letter would be difficult enough. Facing them with the news would be next to impossible. They revered Henry, especially her mother. They would turn on him out of loyalty, alleviating nothing. Worse, they would drown Margaret in pity. It would be unbearable.

She rose and made the bed, moving slowly, bumping into things, smoothing the crocheted spread, patting the pillows, wasting time. She did not know what to do or where to go.

At the window, still in her nightdress, she saw John carrying lumber toward the house. He wore rough work clothes, Henry's, no doubt. He looked up and waved. She returned his wave and dropped her hand. An hour passed, two perhaps. The hammering downstairs continued, stopping at intervals and starting up again. The hacking baby could be heard from time to time. Margaret's back ached from standing in one spot, the pain fanning down both legs and up into her neck. Still, she couldn't bring herself to move away, sit, or lie down. The place was lovely, with long green views and flowering trees. She might have adapted to Berkeley, America. She might have gotten on quite nicely here.

The room was furnished with bed, rocker, a washstand and table, but nothing of a personal nature, no doilies or books, not even a clock. She heard Henry on the stairs, the clomp too heavy to be one of the children or his spurious wife, and guessed it to be noon. He knocked once and the deranged bird that was her heart began flapping in her chest.

"Are you all right in there?"

"Yes." The door wasn't locked. The besotted buzzard could easily enter and take her in his arms, say he was sorry, so very sorry, and vow to fix things straightaway. "Come in."

He cracked the door, taking two steps inside and coming no farther. She remained by the window, the light pouring in, silhouetting her nakedness beneath the gown. She made no move to cover herself. She'd overcome modesty early on in marriage and had no intention of returning to it now. He was her husband. He had every right to look.

"You missed breakfast," he said. "You must be famished."

"I'm not."

He looked tired, as if he hadn't slept. She hoped he hadn't. She hoped he'd suffered a long and torturous night as she had. He lowered his eyes. "I'd thought you gone."

She blinked. "I'm not."

He ran a hand through his hair, a familiar gesture of helplessness. His hair was silver at the edges now. Maturity became him. He was as handsome as ever, more so, perhaps. "I looked everywhere."

"Not everywhere, Henry," she said.

He looked up. "I'm sorry. Lord, Meg. I'm sorry."

She held his gaze. "How do you plan to right things?"

He took a step closer. "I don't know. But you needn't worry."

She felt a little flutter behind her ribs, a stir of hope. "I needn't?"

"I shall do right by you and the children."

"How so precisely?"

He threw up his hands. "By providing for you, of course, sweetheart!"

Sweetheart. Her stoic resolve broke. Margaret bowed her head and wept. Henry came to her, tears standing in his eyes. He touched her shoulder, creating such a surge of love in her. Her husband and children were all she wanted on this earth. Nothing more. Only that. He pressed his handkerchief into her hand. "Please don't cry." All wrongs could be righted here and now if he'd take her in his arms and hold her. But he did not.

He offered instead a cup of tea. "I could have a tray sent up."

Margaret shook her head, unable to speak or look at him.

He touched her arm again, briefly. "I'm sorry," he whispered. There was a pause. "You need to eat something, Meg."

Feed the gaping wound, give it tea. She looked at him then, with a desire to laugh, an urge to slap him hard, an impulse to throw off the gown and give her whole self to him.

"I'm all right, Henry. Just go now, please." He did.

◇◇

SHE WAITED OUT the dinner hour, then dressed and started down the back staircase. It took a lifetime to descend.

In the chaotic kitchen she found Josephine and Martha just out of the tub, with wet hair pulled back, sleek and plaited. They sat at the table, hands clasped in their laps, somber angels in a stranger's house. "You've bathed." Why did her clean children shock her, offend and shame her?

The stocky young maid, Dora, turned from a sink full of crockery with a bemused look on her face. Henry's wife paced the floorboards, bouncing her miserable raspy baby on a damp shoulder. She was quite pretty, even in her blowzy state; there was no pretending otherwise.

"Well, good gravy," she said. She had a strange, drawn-out accent, unlike other American accents Margaret had encountered.

"Mercy, yes, they've bathed. I'm sure you're dying to do the same, Mrs. Oades." The baby coughed a rough cough directly into her red ear.

"Colic," said Margaret, striving to maintain a calm façade for her children's sake. "What's being done for it?"

"Lately we've tried avocado juice," said Henry's wife.

Margaret stepped closer and peered at the baby, seeing Henry's flat ears and feeling a pang of jealous sorrow. She could hardly fault the scrawny infant. "Has it done any good?"

"As you can plainly see and hear," said his exasperated wife, "no."

Margaret resisted the temptation to poke a finger and scrape out the baby's caked left nostril. "May I suggest angelica root boiled in sugar?"

His wife heaved a sigh. "Nothing works. I'm at my wit's end here. I'm thinking about trying a brandy cocktail." She laughed a weary laugh. "On myself, not Gertrude."

"Oh," said Margaret, and twitched a smile. "I see." She stroked the baby's warm bald head. "A bit of honey perhaps. To coat the throat."

His wife shifted the baby, staring down into its pink face. "I don't think she likes me."

"Of course she does. All babies like their mums."

"I don't know about that," said Henry's wife. "She may be the world's first exception to the rule." She grasped the baby beneath her arms and thrust her toward Margaret. "Would you take her, please? I'm way behind schedule." Margaret had no choice but to accept the sour-smelling child. His wife flexed her free hands. "Dora and I were supposed to start the clothes soaking this morning. It'll be the middle of next week before I get to the ironing now."

"Put us to work," said Margaret. "My girls and I are quite capable."

"You're company," said his wife.

"We're not."

The baby squawked. His wife scowled and scratched some of the crust from the tiny nostril. "I never know what she wants. I never know what *anyone* wants." She brushed a hand across her apologetic face. "Never mind me. I didn't sleep a single wink last night." She hesitated. "I'm sure you didn't either, Mrs. Oades."

Margaret walked to the kitchen door and back again, rocking the peevish baby, saying nothing. How absurd it was to be having this asinine conversation with her husband's child bride.

His wife opened the door to the maid's room. "Look what Mr. Oades and John built this morning. I don't know what possessed them, really. The davenport isn't all that lumpy. But then no one asked for my opinion."

Margaret looked in, still jiggling the baby. A wall had been erected, another cot put in. There was a peg for John's clothes, a tiny table, and a lamp.

"It's not exactly the Palace Hotel," his wife said.

"I'm sure John will be comfortable," said Margaret.

"Mr. Oades is very grateful that you and the children have turned up alive," said his wife. Her eyes were hazel with flecks of gold; they were clear and well spaced. She had all her teeth and an unblemished complexion. She was fleshy, though. Years hence, she'd no doubt turn fat, carry a bosom large enough to accommodate teacup and saucer. But for now the advantages of youth and health were hers to enjoy.

"I'm truly sorry for . . . for things, Mrs. Oades," she went on. "But I don't know what you expect me to do. Well, maybe I do know. . . ."

"I don't expect anything from you," said Margaret, aware of Dora blatantly eavesdropping. She shifted her eyes toward Martha and Josephine. "Now wouldn't be the time to discuss it, in any event."

His wife sighed and held out her arms. "I'll take her now." Margaret returned the baby. "You don't even want to try, Mrs. Oades."

"I beg your pardon, madam?"

"You don't want to try and get along."

"Really, Mrs. Oades. I'm quite sure I don't know what you mean."

His wife rolled her eyes. "We can't run around calling each other Mrs. Oades day and night. It's too confusing, not to mention just plain unfriendly and dumb."

"What do you suggest?"

"You'll call me Nancy and I'll call you Margaret."

"As you wish," said Margaret, surrendering to the unwanted intimacy.

His wife shook her head. "It's a start, Margaret. We have to start someplace, don't we?"

"I suppose," said Margaret. Precisely what did this young imposter think they were *starting*?

Calling the
Same Man Husband

MARGARET AND HER CHILDREN had been living under their roof three weeks to the day when the sheriff's deputy rode up. It had started out a nice day too, warm, not too muggy. He arrived midmorning. Nancy saw him from the front room and came out onto the porch. The brim of his hat was angled, so she could not discern his mood at first. Though when, if ever, did the law bring *good* news?

He came as far as the bottom step and stopped, smelling like cheese gone bad. Some bachelors will go the entire winter without bathing.

"I have a warrant for the arrest of Mr. and Mrs. Henry Oades."

It took a moment for the crazy words to align themselves. "There must be some mistake, sir. My husband and I are law-abiding citizens."

He regarded her as one would a strange specimen under glass, leering after a moment, displaying large yellow teeth. "You Mrs. Margaret Oades?"

"I am Mrs. *Nancy* Oades."

A jaw muscle twitched. "I'm here for Mrs. *Margaret* Oades."

"What is the charge? I demand to know."

The arrogant mongrel consulted the paper in his hand, and said without emotion, "Open and notorious cohabitation and adultery."

She gasped, her insides sinking. "Outrageous!"

He worked up a cheekful of brown juice and spat. "I don't have all day, miss."

Nancy flew down the porch steps, running past him on watery legs, checking first the buggy shed, and then the henhouse and pigpen. She found Mr. Oades in the milking room with Titus, and fell upon him in broad daylight. "Oh, Mr. Oades." She got it out piecemeal, whispering in his ear the odious words *cohabitation* and *adultery*.

Together they went back to the house, Mr. Oades walking fast, Nancy straining to keep up. Margaret had come outside in the meantime. She stood on the bottom step, stiff as a queen, a glowering John Oades at her side.

"You're trespassing," said Mr. Oades, approaching.

The deputy scowled, putting a hand on his holstered gun. "Henry Oades? You're under arrest." He pointed to Margaret. "You and this here woman. I'm to take you in."

Mr. Oades extended a grimy hand. "Let's have a look." The deputy shrugged and surrendered the warrant. Nancy pictured Mr. Oades ripping the paper into tiny pieces and throwing the scraps down the well. But he only scanned the sheet, looking up once finished, thrusting his chin toward Margaret.

"The lady and I were legally married in England," he said.

A glaze, a love-shine, crossed Margaret's narrow features. Nancy didn't mistake it. "Three, February," said Mr. Oades, "1880."

They, she and Mr. Oades, were legally married, too, don't anyone forget. They married in the United States of America, before a judge and two sober witnesses. What God hath joined together, let no man turn asunder.

"I'll write for the wedding certificate today," said Mr. Oades. "And prove it."

"Tell it to the judge," said the deputy. He put a hand on Mr. Oades's arm, as if to goad him forward. Mr. Oades pulled away. He took Nancy's face between his hands and kissed her forehead.

"Take heart," he said. "Be a brave girl." Nancy nodded. He smiled. "The situation shall right itself, not to worry." He turned to John and ticked off some chores to be done, clapping the boy's shoulder.

Margaret took a tentative step into their midst, pulling on her hands. "When shall we be returning?"

Mr. Oades spoke gently. "Calm yourself, Meg. We'll be back before supper."

"Don't bet on it," said the deputy.

Margaret said to Nancy, "You'll look after my girls?"

"Of course," said Nancy, flicking a smile. "Like my own."

Margaret looked almost appreciative. "I'm in your debt," she said.

Without farewells, Mr. Oades and Margaret set off down the walk, the bowlegged deputy between them. Nancy stood watching until they were out of sight, thinking of Francis then, how quiet life had been with him, how sweet and peaceful. Had he not gone after the money, had he not died, she never would have met Mr. Oades, much less married him. He and Margaret would have surely resumed their life together. There'd be no trouble, no deputy at the door. It galled her to know what plain old greed had led to.

❖❖

THEY DID NOT RETURN that day. Alone in the front room after supper, a cold supper she'd barely touched, Nancy dipped into Mr. Oades's brandy and became almost instantly drunk. Still she couldn't sleep. Around three in the morning, Martha cried out.

Nancy threw on her robe and rushed into their darkened room, nicking her shin on the bedpost. "Damn it all!" She bent over, breathing hard, her leg throbbing with pain. "What is it? What's the matter?"

Josephine whispered in a tiny voice, "She had a bad dream, Mrs. Oades. We're sorry."

"There's nothing to be sorry about," said Nancy. "Who doesn't have a bad dream from time to time?" Martha had the covers pulled up to her eyes. Nancy touched the top of her head. "Are you all right now?"

Josephine answered for her sister. "Yes, ma'am."

"Come to my room if you need me," said Nancy, limping to the door. "And don't tell your mother I cursed."

Squally Gertrude was awake now. Nancy spent the next two hours rocking her, dozing intermittently, jerking to with cricks in her neck.

In the morning, groggy and bloated, she sent Titus into town to find out what was what. He was back before noon, tramping up the front steps and onto the porch, leaving a trail of dried mud in his wake. "They're in the clink," he said, hat in hand.

Nancy let the door slam in her fury, waking Gertrude inside. "This family has done nothing wrong!"

"Judge Billings came down with dropsy, ma'am. . . ."

"Serves him right," said Nancy. *May his privates swell and burst, fall down a trouser leg and into the gutter.*

"So the hearing was put off." Titus dug inside a coat pocket and proffered a folded note on dirty paper. "Until the 17th."

Nancy opened the note and read.

Dearest wife,

   Rest assured, this foolish debacle shall be put behind us soon. Do not get it into your head to attend the hearing. No possible good would come

of it. You and the children are better off on the farm. I shall be home
before you know it.

> Your husband,
> Henry Oades

Inside, the baby wailed, pining for Margaret most likely. Margaret had an almost magical soothing way with Gertrude. Maybe the baby preferred Margaret's voice over her own mother's. Nancy didn't know. She crumpled the note, thinking about the ironing and mending still to be done, about supper. Margaret's children woke hungry and stayed hungry the livelong day, especially John. He was always feeding, like a hog bent on a blue ribbon. She was not sure she wouldn't trade places with Margaret, given a choice. What was jail but a little room with service and no ravenous boys, no ironing or colicky babies. She was weary, too weary to think straight. What was a *debacle*, anyway?

❖❖

THE FOUR LADIES, led by Mrs. Charles Middleton herself, the bursar's wife, came the next day, a broody, rainy morning. Nancy was in the front room dusting Mr. Oades's Oriental carvings, ugly satanic-looking pieces, inherited from old Mr. Barnhill along with everything else. She heard the horses and went to the window, recognizing the women right away, of course: Mrs. Middleton, fat Mrs. Dooley, the dentist's wife, Mrs. Goodfriend, the professor's wife, and Mrs. Knox, the poundmaster's wife. Collectively and separately they served on dozens of committees. Their photographs, mainly Mrs. Middleton's, regularly appeared in the paper. The temperance brigade was their most vocal endeavor.

The old hags want to burn down every saloon in town, Francis once said, mounting his soap box, claiming the rich would hoard their whiskey and drink in the privacy of their homes, but the poor workingman would have no place to go. He must be turning in his jar to see them scurrying up the walk, shielding themselves against the rain with newspapers, a single open umbrella among them. Nancy tore off her work apron and stashed the ratty thing inside the liquor cabinet, and then went to let them in.

"We apologize for arriving without notice," said Mrs. Middleton. They left the umbrella and newspapers behind on the porch and entered single file, looking about. Nancy had nothing in the house to serve them. They'd probably expect one of those fancy frozen bombes.

She smiled. "To what do I owe the honor?"

Mrs. Middleton was elegant up close, tall and stately, with a pale complexion and kindly expression on her long horsey face. She reminded Nancy of the Catholics' Mary. "We represent the Daughters of Decency, Mrs. Foreland."

Nancy frowned, hairs prickling on the back of her neck. She was aware of someone lurking in the dining room, Dora probably, or Margaret's Josephine. "It's Mrs. Oades now."

The ladies exchanged knowing looks. "Not legally," said Mrs. Dooley.

Nancy put a hand to her chin, where a pimple was starting. "Mr. Oades and I are very much legally married. I can show you the license."

"We don't blame you, dear," said the poundmaster's wife, a mother of girl triplets. Mrs. Tillman had said that her bloodcurdling screams went on for days. Three times the ripping agony. *Merciful God, no thank you.*

"Blame me for what?"

"You're not the first naive girl to be taken in by a depraved hedonist," said Mrs. Dooley.

Nancy looked directly into her little black piggy eyes. "I beg your pardon. Are you referring to my husband?"

"We're not here to judge," said Mrs. Middleton, waving a perfumed hand. "We're here to offer you and your innocent child refuge, Mrs. Foreland. . . ."

"I told you it's *Oades*."

Mrs. Middleton gave a little push to Nancy's shoulder, as if to start her up the stairs. "Collect your things. You'll stay with us for the time being."

Us? Was she offering up her own magnificent mansion? She and Gertrude would probably have an entire wing to themselves in a place so huge. Nancy said as calmly as she knew how, "I'm not going anywhere. I have a house full of children under my care. Besides, you don't understand the circumstances."

"We understand perfectly," said Mrs. Dooley. "Two women are calling the same man husband. A Mormon in San Bernardino was hanged just this past Christmas. His wives—his widows, I should say, found themselves in the poorhouse."

"That's hardly our same situation," said Nancy, seething. She expected a personal thank you from Jesus one day for the tolerance shown Margaret Oades. The last thing she deserved was condemnation. "We're not Mormons, for your information. There is no funny business going on in our household, believe you me. The very idea! Really."

Mrs. Dooley, her ears obviously plugged with manure, repeated herself. "Two women are calling the same man husband."

Nancy could not contain the shrillness. "Would you have us put her out? Mrs. Oades doesn't have a dime to her name, you know. Her children are my husband's own flesh and blood! How can you suggest something so mean, so out-and-out heartless?"

Mrs. Dooley pointed a gloved finger. "What is preventing you yourself from leaving?"

Mrs. Middleton said softly, "You're living in grievous sin."

Nancy whirled on her. "I'm not! How dare you."

Dora came in from the dining room. "Will you be needing me, Mrs. *Oades*?"

Clearly she'd been eavesdropping, a habit Nancy normally deplored, but now appreciated. "Please show the ladies to the door," she said.

Dora spread wide her arms and herded the murmuring women forward.

"My offer stands," said Mrs. Middleton, over her shoulder.

The door closed on them. Good riddance to the sanctimonious, coldhearted hellcats. Nancy sank to the settee.

Josephine appeared on the stairs, clutching the banister. "Are they going to take us, Mrs. Oades?"

Nancy looked up. "Take you? Take you where? No one's going to take you anywhere. Not on your tintype."

Dora came back in carrying the damp newspapers left on the porch, ink running down her arm. "Dora, please. You're dripping all over creation."

Dora patted down a page with a corner of apron. "You'll want to read this."

Nancy took the soggy paper, the insides of her cheeks going sour with nausea.

DAUGHTERS OF DECENCY VS. LOCAL DAIRYMAN

Henry P. Oades, Berkeley dairy farmer, has been charged with having two wives. Oades is an Englishman of good education who came to Berkeley from New Zealand. In January last he married Mrs. Nancy Foreland, a young widow lady with a child. Postmaster Cleon Russell made it known that a second woman turned up recently, claiming to be none other than Mrs. Henry P. Oades. The three parties have been residing on Oades's farm since late last month. The Daughters of Decency organization, indignant at such open profligacy, put the matter before Justice Billings. On Monday, a criminal complaint was laid against

Oades, charging him with open and notorious cohabitation and adultery. A hearing has been scheduled for June 17th.

The words jumped incomprehensibly. It may as well have been a malicious story about somebody else. Better not to think about it, anyway, better to leave it be, leave the whole ugly mess to Mr. Oades.

Josephine turned to go back upstairs. She was regal in profile like her mother. Nancy called after her. She'd promised to look after them, and this one, this Pheeny, was a hard little nut to please. "Let's make something sweet to take the nasty taste out of our mouths. What do you say?"

Josephine nodded in compliance, obviously no more in the mood to make something sweet than Nancy was.

Beginning Today

"THE LAW IS ON OUR SIDE," said Henry. Margaret did not respond.

They'd been taken from their dingy cells and brought to a windowless room in the courthouse, where they were left to await the lawyer. The airless place was unpleasantly close. Her brown frock, the same drab frock she'd left the house in, worn four days and three nights running now, clung wetly to her back. Henry was dressed far more acceptably for public exposure. Someone had provided him a decent suit since the arrest. He hadn't said who. "Did you hear me, Meg?"

"Yes, Henry. The law is on our side."

He stood and opened the door to the hallway, peering out and ducking back in, closing the door again.

Margaret returned to quiet contemplation. There'd be no conviction. No one could deny the fact of their legal ceremony, to which she'd arrived late, knock-kneed with nerves and love, lilies of the valley clutched to her bosom. Indeed theirs was a blatantly lawful union, as his with Nancy was not, due to the fact. The first trumped the second. Common sense said so. Henry paced, a welter of tics and worry, having no doubt reached the same conclusion. What would he do? A man cannot be legally married to two women. It occurred to her that he might ask for a divorce. The answer would be an unequivocal no. He was her husband. She would not slink away; nor would she stigmatize her children by agreeing to it. That much was certain.

Henry crossed his arms and spoke to the framed portrait of William McKinley. "I sincerely wish I might have spared you, Meg."

Margaret glanced up briefly. Spared her what exactly? New Zealand? The Maori? His desertion? The miserable foolhardy journey to California? His fixation on Nancy? His inexorable passion for her?

"It cannot be helped," she said, equally enigmatically. Henry turned and faced the door, initiating a silence between them.

Minutes later, the lawyer burst in, florid and breathless, bringing with him a cacophony of voices. He closed the heavy door quickly, cutting off the noise in the hall.

"I'm late. Ever so sorry." He was a small man, particularly next to Henry, trim and dainty, with a cleric's shiny pink dome. He offered Margaret his hand. "Lewis Grimes, esquire, madam."

Henry said irritably, "How long should the bloody ordeal take? I've a farm to run."

Mr. Grimes began rummaging through a satchel of papers. "Hard to say, sir, hard to say. And don't bring that testiness inside. It'll get you nowhere lickety-split. Don't speak to anyone outside, Mrs. Oades."

Margaret nodded, a shiver of apprehension running along her spine. Why was Henry so certain that the law was on their side? What did either one of them know about the laws here?

"Don't give as much as a 'good-day' to the newspaper people," said Mr. Grimes. "Ned Bowman in particular. Speak to me or the judge. No one else."

Margaret nodded. For all she and Henry knew, an American marriage took precedence over a foreign one. "Our marriage is perfectly valid," she said, her voice shaky.

"Mr. Grimes is aware, Meg," said Henry. "Try not to worry."

The tidy lawyer dug out his pocket watch. "It's time to go."

◈◈

OUTSIDE IN THE HALL, a middle-aged woman came forward, shaking her finger in Margaret's face. "Shame on you!"

Mr. Grimes latched on to Margaret's arm. "Say nothing, Mrs. Oades."

Margaret was surprised to see so many women among the men, regular women, motherly sorts, who should be home with their children. She was worried sick about her own. Josephine had yet to warm to Nancy. Margaret took great care not to say the first denigrating word, but Pheeny was as stubborn as they came these days.

Mr. Grimes steered her toward a marble staircase lined with gawking people. Henry followed close behind. Together the three bored through the gabbling throng and made their way up the steps. Behind them came inspirational singing, a cappella.

Midway up the stairs an unseen woman screeched, "Let us have a turn! We want a look at her!" A female hand appeared, bearing an opal that caught the light. The hand snatched at Margaret's sleeve, tearing the cuff. Margaret cried out, "Henry!"

Henry moved up as if to guard her. Mr. Grimes pulled her forward. "Say nothing!"

A great handlebar mustache with foul breath above an unclean collar came into her peripheral vision. She did not look his way. "Please, Mrs. Oades," he said. "A few words?"

Margaret shook her head. The man was fat and warty, a jowly cock of the walk. "Are there other wives?" he asked. "Or just the two so far?"

"Leave her be, Bowman." The lawyer's bark belied his size. "Damn locusts. Every last one of you."

The newsman struggled to keep up, wheezing stink, pencil and black notebook in hand. "I'll wager you're the favorite," he said, his voice like oily sewage. Mr. Grimes tugged on her arm, just as she was jabbed from behind with an umbrella or cane. "You'd surely be mine," whispered Mr. Bowman.

"Bail out your filthy mouth, sir," she said, looking at him now, trembling with rage. "We're not Mormons."

Mr. Grimes's grip tightened. "Mrs. Oades!"

Someone yelled over the others, "Heathen polygamists! Worse yet."

Mr. Bowman bared a wicked smile, clearly pleased with himself for having goaded her to outburst.

Mr. Grimes opened the door to the courtroom and ushered her inside.

"It'll be all right, Meg," said Henry. *It won't,* she thought. *Ever again.*

◆◆

THE HEARING was shockingly brief, as if the judge and Mr. Grimes had rehearsed. Justice Billings certainly didn't seem surprised to hear that Henry couldn't produce a marriage certificate here and now.

"It's been sent for," said Mr. Grimes, with little zeal.

"You have my word that it exists," said Henry, nearly begging.

"Put the marriage certificate before me, sir," said the judge. "The court will decide the validity then. In the meantime, beginning today, you and Mrs. Margaret Oades will house yourselves separately." He gave a listless rap of his gavel and it was over. Henry and Mr. Grimes formed a lopsided phalanx and led Margaret away.

Henry's carriage and horse had been delivered to the stable six blocks down. Henry walked hurriedly, his face creased with worry.

"What is it, Henry?"

"I've put off burning the pasture too long as it is," he muttered.

"Why would you burn your own pasture?"

"Better grazing," he said.

"Perhaps I might take a room elsewhere," she said. "The judge said nothing about *how* we should house ourselves separately."

He glanced sideways. "You'd do that kindness?"

"You know I would," she said.

"I do," he said, looking relieved. "Thank you, Meg."

"In turn, promise that you'll keep a close eye on the children, Pheeny especially. She's at loose ends. She doesn't understand the arrangement." *And neither do I, for that matter.*

"I'll take her out riding before supper," he said.

"That would be lovely." It was rather like old times, discussing their children. Late at night, usually. In bed. One thousand years ago.

❖❖

Mrs. Osgood's boardinghouse was three-storied and painted robin's-egg blue, with white trim. The front porch had been swept clean, and there were wicker chairs about for reading or crocheting in pleasant weather. Henry removed his hat and rang the bell. Bread was baking inside. "You'll speak to the children?" said Margaret. "Explain the situation without alarming them?"

"Of course," he said. "Try not to worry."

Mrs. Osgood opened the front door, broom in hand. She had a face full of irregular moles and a large nose pricked solid with blackheads. Margaret's first and immediate feeling was one of kinship.

"I have no rooms," she said straight off.

"Your notice board indicates otherwise, madam," said Henry.

Mrs. Osgood advanced onto the porch, broom in both hands, held like a rifle. She lowered her voice. "I won't have your kind here." Margaret bristled, assuming an arbitrary loathing of the English. "This is a Christian house," she said.

"I'm prepared to pay twice the published rate," said Henry.

The woman seemed to hesitate before repeating herself. "I have no rooms. Good-day."

"Madam," said Henry, with a curt bob. He returned hat to head, taking Margaret's arm and turning her about. At the gate Margaret glanced back to see the woman furiously sweeping the spot where they'd stood.

Henry inquired at two more houses while Margaret waited in the carriage. Those rooms were allegedly taken as well. Henry then remembered a man who owed him a favor.

"Mr. Potter's twice borrowed my bull." He laughed softly, a sound she hadn't heard in years. "Sir Roger is quite the popular beast." She laughed too a little. It felt so nice.

They drove out of town, traveling in the opposite direction of the farm, eventually coming to a dilapidated house with a few stringy wet hens in the front yard. No smoke rose from the chimney. No smell of bread perfumed the air. "I'm sorry, Meg."

She touched his cuff. "I shall get on fine here."

"For all of it," he said, sitting back, the reins still in his hands. "Your letter came only Thursday last." He looked at her briefly and turned away again. "I don't know what to say to you."

"You once said that we'd have stories to tell in our old age," she said. "Do you recall it? 'Think of the grand stories we'll tell in our sapless dotage,' you said. The day we sailed, standing at the rail together. Those were your exact words. Do you remember, Henry?"

"Christ," he whispered. "It's been so long, Meg, so bloody long." He climbed down from the buggy. "I thought I'd never see my way through after you. . . ." He shook his head, not looking at her. "At some point I began to come round. I couldn't tell you when precisely." He looked at her then, wanting something, for-giveness, understanding at least. "It's a terrible thing to say," he said. "I'm sorry, but there it is."

Sitting in her cell, Margaret had imagined him sitting in his, pondering the situation without Nancy's influence and coming to his senses. But that hadn't happened.

She wept quietly, unable to stop. "I merely asked if you remem-bered how we once were."

"I do, of course," he said, offering up his handkerchief. "*Jesus, Meg. How could I forget?*"

There Was an
Old Woman

Nancy's monthly came that morning, around eleven, right about the time Mr. Oades and Margaret would have been standing before the judge. She thought at first she must be miscarrying because the cramping was so severe; but a miscarrying mother will deliver a tiny infant, the size of a tree frog, her mama said, perfect in every way, by and for God. Nancy inspected the pot afterward and saw that she'd delivered nothing but blood, more than a decapitated chicken would spill.

She called down to Dora, who came finally. Nancy climbed into bed, weak and perspiring, wanting only sleep. "Take the pot, please. Then bring the rags and pins."

Dora squatted to lift the porcelain pot, grunting, her knees spread wide. She was a hulking girl of sixteen, saddled with big feet and hands. Her eyes were pretty, though, bright and clear, with enviable long, dark lashes. "Oh, Mrs. Oades."

"Dora, please. Lower your voice. It's enough to wake the dead."

"Poor missus." Like a starved cat's wail, only twice as irritating.

"*Please,* Dora."

"How far along were you?"

Nancy sat up and peered into the rank pot again, becoming dizzy with the clotted sight and metallic stench of it. "There was no issue. Please take it away now."

The girl left, clucking sympathetically. Nancy slept, waking to Dora's work shoes ascending the stairs, the battering knock. She carried a cleaned pot and enough folded rags to staunch a dozen monthlies, piling them on the dressing table. "Poor missus," she murmured, making a coquettish face for the mirror. "'Tis a shame."

Nancy threw aside the bedclothes and stood. "'Tis *life,* dearie. We're all blessed by Eve's curse, every last one of us. So save your pity and leave me be now."

Sulky Dora stomped off. Nancy washed between her legs and pinned two folded rags to the belt, stabbing her thumb in the process and drawing more blood. She got under the covers, feeling empty, and wanting her mother. Her first monthly had come while her mother was still alive. Heaven knows what her father would have done if he'd been left to explain lady things. Nancy would still be in the dark to this day probably. He never would have thought to make black haw bark tea for the cramps, much less drink a cup of the nasty brew himself just to keep her company.

Nancy slept fitfully, waking to find her gown and sheets soaked through. A person could drown in all that disgusting blood. She washed again, turning the water in the basin bright pink, and dressed for supper, putting on the old gingham, the baggiest of her dresses. Her face was swollen, as if she'd been stung by a thousand angry wasps. She applied some cream, but it did little good, and she did not much care. She gathered up the sheets, rags, and ruined nightgown, leaving the unholy heap on the floor.

Margaret's door was ajar. Nancy announced herself. "Hello?" Martha was on the floor, playing spillikins by herself. She abandoned the game, looking up, wiping her chubby hands on her everyday smock. "Where's our mum, Mrs. Oades?"

"I thought I'd find her returned by now," said Nancy. Josephine sat in the rocker by the window, nestling sleeping Gertrude. "I told Dora to look after the baby this afternoon."

"Dora asked me to keep her up here," whispered Josephine. "I said I didn't mind."

"Well, thank you, Josephine. I can see she takes to you." Nancy stepped out again, hugging herself against the chill, picturing the wrecked buggy on its side, Mr. Oades and Margaret dead, their broken bodies lying in a ditch.

Downstairs she wandered into the front room and stood at the window. The mantel clock struck a sonorous four. Nancy imagined their coffin lids closing, the shoveled dirt raining down. Mr. Oades's pack of children would automatically become her sole responsibility. At least until she notified their relatives in England. How in the world would she manage? She was still shivering and so poured a brandy, then wrapped herself in the lap blanket and settled down to wait. When three quarters of an hour passed and they still hadn't come, she poured herself another, adding water to the decanter. Mr. Oades didn't mind her taking the occasional nightcap, but she did not think he'd like the idea of solitary drinking, even if cramps and frayed nerves called for it.

Eventually she got up to check on supper's progress. That's all she meant to do. It certainly was not her plan to spy on Dora, to listen to her groans of rapture. That was the last thing Nancy needed today.

The sink had been scoured to look like new; the floor had been swept. A strawberry pie with blackened edges cooled on the sideboard, and cow-heel soup, Henry's favorite, simmered on the stove. So Dora had seen to her chores before inviting a man to her room and latching the door. Nancy knocked once and the low moaning stopped. She knocked again, harder, and the wanton girl called out. "A moment, ma'am, please."

Nancy could hear their whispers, the panicky rustle of bed-clothes, the sounds of their hasty dressing. Lately, Dora had been keeping company with the neighbor's bulgy-eyed hand. Clarence was his Christian name. He had to be at least twenty. How many times had Nancy said to her: Don't let the sweet talk go to your head. The lower the intention, the higher the praise.

Nancy pounded the door. "Open up this minute." Dora was underage, an innocent. The misguided girl had probably lain beneath him thinking a wedding was coming; she'd probably conjured up an entire rosy future in the time it took.

Dora cracked the door and peeped out. "I'm sorry, ma'am. "'Twas all a—"

Nancy pushed on the door, letting herself in. There against the wall, red hair on end, eyes cast down, stood John Oades. "John!"

The boy's voice broke with remorse. "Please don't tell my father, Mrs. Oades."

"I'm ashamed of you both," said Nancy, with a twinge of longing. There was something of Francis in the boy, something pure and genuine and flawed. That type didn't think twice before running headlong into a burning house or a young girl's arms.

"We meant no harm, ma'am," said Dora, squeezing past into the kitchen. "No disrespect." She pulled her work apron over her head, pausing to sniff at the soup and toss in some salt. "Mr. Oades's favorite," she murmured, her lips pressed tight, as if suppressing a smile. "Nothing he likes better."

John remained trapped, his escape blocked by Nancy. Nancy sighed, not knowing what to say to him. "Are the cows in?"

"Yes, ma'am," he said, flush-faced still.

"Milked?"

He bobbed his head. "Yes, ma'am."

Nancy stepped aside to allow him room to pass. "Go have a

look at the latch on the henhouse door." He and Dora exchanged tragic looks on his way out, as if the world were plotting against them.

"It won't happen again, missus," said Dora.

"My advice to you," Nancy started, then stopped. She was tired, achy, and newly worried about Mr. Oades and Margaret. She turned to leave.

"Missus?"

"Yes, Dora?"

"The back of your pretty dress—"

John came running up to the back door, winded. "Mum and Dad have arrived . . . please, Mrs. Oades, don't tell my father."

"Blood's easy," said Dora. "Cold water, elbow grease. Don't you worry."

John clung to the door frame, arms raised, narrow chest heaving. "Please, Mrs. Oades."

"All right, John," said Nancy. "All right."

Relief washed over the boy's face. Nancy was once again reminded of Francis. How nervous he'd been that first time, how bumbling and precious. Thank you, he said afterward, holding her close. Their bodies had fit together perfectly. Nancy tied an apron on backward to hide the blood and went upstairs to change.

She thought it was Dora knocking twenty minutes later, but it was bedraggled Margaret, cracking the door tentatively. Nancy was seated at her dressing table, repairing her bloated face. "Come in, don't be shy, look at you, your sleeve is torn, close the door, will you, I don't want Mr. Oades to see the mess."

Margaret entered, sidestepping the mound of soiled linen, coming up behind Nancy, softly, reverently, gazing down with such sadness in her eyes.

Nancy spoke to Margaret's grief-stricken reflection in the mirror. "What happened? What's wrong?"

"I'm sorry, Nancy." Margaret's voice cracked.

"Whatever for?"

"Dora said you'd miscarried."

Nancy waved a hand in dismissal. "Dora doesn't know one end of the horse from the other."

"Sorry?"

"I didn't miscarry, Margaret. I'd be the first to know, wouldn't I? Now tell me about your day in court. Is it all over now?"

"It isn't. I've only returned to collect a few things, and then Henry or John or Titus shall drive me to Mr. Potter's. I'm to stay there until the marriage certificate arrives."

Mrs. Potter was rumored to be a bona fide spell-casting witch. "You can't stay there!"

"There are other ladies in residence," said Margaret.

"*Ladies*! San Francisco types maybe, but no real lady would stay there."

"Well, I must."

Nancy looked up at her. "I'm expected to mind both Gertrude *and* your children while you're gone?"

"My girls are capable of minding themselves," she said.

Nancy scooped out another finger of face cream. She closed her eyes and slowly massaged the cool oil, reciting under her breath, "There was an old woman who lived in a shoe. . . ." She opened her eyes, catching Margaret's bewildered expression. "Yes, Margaret, I'm going crazy, out and out cuckoo, if that's what you're thinking."

"Pheeny and Dora might take turns minding Gerty," said Margaret, pulling on her hands. "If you're not feeling up to it."

The smell of cow-heel soup wafted up the stairs. She'd added too many onions again, trying to please Mr. Oades. He was the one who told Dora about the soup in the first place. It tasted like home, he said once. "I'm thinking of letting Dora go."

"Why is that?" asked Margaret.

"Because I found her under the covers with John, that's why."
She regretted speaking mid sentence.

Margaret's thin shoulders jacked up. "The filthy little trout! I'll
box her ears."

"Oh, I'm sorry for opening my big trap, Margaret. I didn't mean
to say it."

"You're making it up then?"

"No," said Nancy. "I just didn't mean to tattle. I promised I
wouldn't. They said it wouldn't happen again. Please don't let John
know I told you."

Margaret's hands flexed and fisted at her sides. "I'd give her the
sack before she could say Jack Robinson if I were you. She's not
needed, Nancy. I'd manage this household just fine without her,
better in fact, if you gave me the chance. You needn't lift a finger.
Think how pleased Henry would be. Think of the money saved
him."

"I'm not the Queen of Sheba. I don't mind lifting a finger."

Margaret brightened. "Of course you don't! Let's then."

"Not now, not with you going away."

"I shan't be gone more than a fortnight, surely," said Margaret.

"I can't take care of Gertrude and your three, too."

"Josephine will mind the young ones. She'll cook as well. She
makes a lovely potted hare, a splendid livermush, a perfect potato.
Dora's a terrible cook, you've said so yourself more than once."

"You're badgering me," said Nancy. "You're giving me a terrible
headache."

"I'm sorry," said Margaret. "But I cannot bear the thought of
leaving John to her immoral devices."

Nancy gestured toward the heap on the floor. The blood had
set in. The torturous job would be hers should she send Dora
packing. All by herself, she'd be scrubbing, soaking, rinsing,
wringing, mangling and folding until doomsday. "This household

takes tremendous effort since you . . . since lately." Nancy shook her head. "Never mind, Margaret. I can't think straight tonight."

"The clothes might go to the steam laundry in town," said Margaret.

"Out of the question. They wash in cholera water."

"Then Josephine shall do it."

Nancy didn't picture skinny Josephine having the strength. "Does she know how?"

"A far sight better than Miss Dora McGinnis."

Nancy fiddled with a hairpin, wanting nothing but the dirty mound to disappear.

"He's little more than a lad," said Margaret, pleading. "She'll hoodwink him into eloping the moment I'm gone."

A terrible bleak feeling had settled upon Nancy. Maybe all the blood caused it. She never knew a person could lose so much and live. "I'll give Dora notice tonight," she said, willing to agree to anything in exchange for silence.

❖❖

John drove Margaret off before supper, leaving not one but two empty places at the table.

Mr. Oades explained to his daughters that there'd been a grown-up misunderstanding. "It shall be dealt with straightaway, don't you worry."

Martha looked on the brink of tears. "I asked Mum if we might visit. She said it wasn't a nice place for children. There'd be nothing for us to do there."

"She was right, sweetheart," said Mr. Oades. "Enjoy your pie now, or I shall enjoy it for you. Don't think I won't." Martha took a listless bite of cobbler. "See? Delicious! That's a brave girl, that's a love. Your mum shall be home before you know it."

Josephine glanced Nancy's way, as if looking for confirmation. "Before you know it," Nancy echoed. "Sooner." Children never know what's what. Parents were forever withholding the pertinent details.

◇◇

SHE WENT TO DORA after supper. Dora turned from the sink, eyes narrowing to slits, soapy fist going to a hip. "About to let me go, ain't you?"

"I'm sorry, Dora, but—"

"You're going to be, missus. You're going to be more than sorry. People are talking. Nobody else is going to work for you, I promise you that."

Nancy had planned to give her two weeks' severance and send her off with a letter of recommendation highlighting her ability to tote great weight. Instead she gave her one week's pay and instructions to be packed by breakfast. If not for the sink full of greasy dishes, Nancy would have put the brazen sass out tonight. She'd reached the scraggly end of her rope hours ago.

A Trip to the Quack

A MAN FROM THE HEALTH DEPARTMENT came out a few days later. Mr. Oades said he wasn't particularly surprised to see him. Everyone was in a dither over consumptive cows these days. Officials and doctors were scaring mothers half out of their minds with their pure-milk crusade.

"He claimed Rose looked suspicious," said Mr. Oades. It was late. He and Nancy were alone in the front room. "He was prepared to take her and two of the others. That's when I picked up the rifle and showed him the way out. I'll be damned if I'm going to allow some bloke with a badge to make off with my good animals." He settled back in his chair with a sigh. "I'm going on his list, he says."

"What sort of list, Mr. Oades?"

He smiled, putting his brandy glass aside and patting his thigh. Nancy went to him willingly, sleepily, arranging herself upon his lap. She loved the luxurious size of him. He went for her buttons, those of her shirtwaist, then those of her overcorset, taking his time about it. Francis had always been in too much of a rush.

"You may call me Henry," he said, teasingly. "We're well enough acquainted now, don't you think?"

Nancy stroked his beard. "Yes, Henry."

Lines of happiness appeared at the corners of his eyes. Such a sweet blessing of a man.

Their romance had been in full bloom this last week. Mr. Oades credited the warm weather, but they both knew Margaret's absence was the reason. For the first time since she arrived, they'd not had to be mindful of her feelings.

Nancy kissed his mouth, mentally combing the kitchen in search of a lemon. The last thing she wanted was another baby. She'd prayed over it. She'd also taken precautions, inserting a barrier just before bed, a new sponge dipped in lemon juice. (Some older wives were talking one Sunday after church, which is how she learned of the method.) Four children were plenty, more than enough. She didn't think he'd disagree with the number, only with the unnatural interference of the sponge itself.

Maybe the sponge alone did the trick. Hers were of a good dense quality, sturdy enough to repel a tiny seed, you'd think. What purpose did the juice serve? There ought to be a book to which a motherless lady might refer in private. Birth and the act should not be related, anyway. She'd long thought it. Another method of conception would make more sense, one not yoked to pleasurable sensations. The world would be a better place. The poorhouses wouldn't be filled to the rafters with unwed mothers if babies were brought about by a hearty handshake. A lady need never remove her glove.

The mantel clock bonged ten. Nancy gently extracted herself and stood, buttoning up, her stomach rumbling with the onions from supper.

"Cruel lass! Where are you off to?"

She remembered the health inspector then. "What sort of list?"

"A scare tactic was all it was," he said, rising with crackling joints. "Meg is ailing, by the by. I meant to make mention earlier." He turned his back to her, as if embarrassed by the announcement, picking up the newspaper he'd already read, scowling into it.

"Were you out at Potter's today?"

"I was," he said, glaring down at the front page photograph of Jerger Okoudek, a Zulu prince who had fallen in love with a Caucasian lady while attending Cambridge University. The prince went by Tommy Taylor now. He was a soldier in the United States Army, stationed at Fort Alcatraz. His lady was "fair and French" according to the paper, a Cambridge student herself, amazingly enough. She'd boldly married her "ebony prince," only to take ill and die soon after. Life lost all meaning for the prince then. Nancy had wept for them, reading.

"What's the matter with Margaret?" she asked.

"Her teeth are giving her fits. Bullheaded woman refuses to see the dentist."

"Poor Margaret. That's the worst pain in the world. A bad toothache is second only to childbirth. I wanted to kill myself once."

"I bought medicine in town," said Henry, somewhat defensively.

"Did it do any good?"

"I don't know. I suppose. The new pharmacist said it should."

"You didn't stay to see?"

"I was there to pay Potter. I did what I could. She needs to see a dentist."

"Well, she can't go to Dr. Dooley," said Nancy. "Not after what his wife put me through. Maybe you should take her to a dentist in San Francisco."

"Shall I show her the sights while we're there? I've a farm to run, Nan."

"I'll take her then," said Nancy, expecting a blustery protest. Instead his expression softened.

"You'd do that kindness?"

"Of course."

He rushed on, as if fearing she'd have a change of heart. "You'd want to take the ten o'clock ferry, not the eleven. The eleven is crowded with Gypsies."

She wondered aloud, "When would we go?"

"John will bring you to the ferry," said Henry. "I could spare him say, Tuesday next."

"And leave Margaret to suffer until then? No, that wouldn't be right, Mr. . . . Henry. I'll go see her tomorrow. We'll take the nine o'clock on Thursday. That'll give us a good early start."

Almost immediately, Nancy had second thoughts about signing herself up for an entire day alone with Margaret, without the buffer of family. But it was too late now.

❖❖

JOHN DROVE HER to Mr. Potter's eyesore the next morning. The porch was splotched with dried chicken dung; it sagged where they stood. Rusty nails stuck out everywhere. The grimy front windows looked as if they'd never been washed.

"Your poor mother," said Nancy. "It's bad enough that she has to stay in this awful pit, but to stay here with a bad tooth is just beyond the pale."

"She's had it worse," said John, breaking his long silence. He was still mourning Dora's departure. Nancy felt for him; the first heartbreak is the hardest. Maybe they should start going to church again, and give him a chance to meet some *good* girls.

Margaret looked happy to see them, happy to see John at least. She ushered them into a ratty front room. "What brings you? Not that you need a reason, sweetheart."

Her left jaw was three times the size of the right and looked hot to the touch. Margaret said nothing about it, acting as if she were in the rosiest of health. Nancy was reminded of a story she'd heard a long time ago, about men who carried ferocious animals, wolverines or badgers, beneath their shirts. The men were gnawed nearly to death, but didn't let on. Nancy never did understand the brave point.

The oily red davenport obviously served as a bed at night. Long gray hairs had been shed, Margaret's in all probability, but who could tell? Sitting, barely perching, Nancy came right to the point. "I'm going to take you to a dentist in San Francisco."

Margaret frowned, putting a hand to her swollen jaw as if to hide it. "I don't care for dentists."

Something scurried along the baseboard, a rodent or a very large bug, giving Nancy a shiver. "There's nothing to be afraid of."

"I'm not in the least bit afraid," said Margaret. "I simply loathe their existence. I'd sooner let a miner come near."

Nancy laughed. "A miner?"

"A miner wrests a gemstone as a dentist wrests a tooth, does he not? Yet one won't find the honest miner strutting about, claiming a physician's mantle."

Nancy didn't have the faintest idea what she was talking about. Despite the unpleasant purpose of the trip, a normal person would be champing at the bit to leave this decrepit shanty for a day. "Well, suit yourself, Margaret. If you want to be a martyr about it. I can't tie you up and force you to go."

Margaret stood, cradling her jaw in her trembling hand. "Tea?" A sheen of tears stood in her eyes.

"You should go to the dentist, Mum," said John. "It'll only get worse."

Margaret dropped her hand and raised it again, silent tears streaming. "All right, Nancy." Each syllable seemed a painful effort. "Thank you. When do we leave?"

NANCY AND JOHN set out on Thursday, directions to Dr. McTeague's dental parlors tucked inside Nancy's velvet bag. Titus's mother had recommended the dentist to Titus, who recommended him to Henry.

Margaret was waiting on the Potters' porch when they drove up. She wore the same old brown dress, which could use a little lace. Lace flattered the homeliest of ladies. Nancy's own blue wedding suit had lace everywhere it might go, real duchess lace at the sleeves, neck, and hem. There was even a cunning bow of lace at the waist. She didn't care about the rule of wearing one's shabbiest clothes when traveling. If not for this one measly outing it would never be seen. On the ferry, she took extreme care in choosing clean seats. Margaret plopped right down without as much as a glance behind.

Nancy had been to San Francisco once before. Francis took her to the Cliff House to see the seals on her birthday. Coming back, a floating log became caught up in the propeller, causing the ferry to pitch and roll. It turned out they were never in any real danger, but the passengers didn't know it at the time. Women were shrieking. Men were shouting, flinging life preservers. No one could have slept through the commotion, as Margaret, blessedly drunk on tooth medicine, was doing now. Nancy sat beside her, watching the human panorama, guessing at ages, at professions and wealth. She bought an orange drink after a while, tart and delicious, tipping the vendor a penny. She was feeling generous, grown-up, and happy. It had been ages since she'd set foot off the farm.

From the ferry they made their way through knots of chattering Chinese and boarded a cable car to Polk Street. They found the address with no trouble. The doctor's sign hung outside a bay window, over a post office.

Dr. McTeague. Dental Parlors. Gas Given.

The sign should have read Dental *Parlor*. That's all it was, a single room, overly warm, smelling of beer and pipesmoke, and faintly, unpleasantly, of gas. From the looks of things—a stack of newspapers, a dirty plate, a mute canary in a cage—the doctor lived in the unsanitary room. The muggy little place had to be teeming with germs. And the doctor himself, good gravy! He looked nothing like a medical man. He was an oaf, a big yellow-haired lummox, with redwoods for limbs. He had a patient in his chair, a young lady, who sat with her head back and her eyes closed, still as a cadaver.

"Sit yourselves," he said, gesturing with a silver instrument toward three straight-back chairs. "I'll only be another five minutes."

Margaret turned to Nancy and mouthed the word "Quack."

"Let's leave, then," whispered Nancy. "We'll find another dentist."

Margaret deliberated for a moment before whispering back, "They're all the same. This one comes with a recommendation at least." She sat, holding her jaw, letting out a gasp of pain. Dr. McTeague looked at them, his broad forehead creasing in sympathy. *Was that egg in his mustache?*

He called to Nancy, "I'll have your mother fixed right up."

"She's not my mother," snapped Nancy. In Margaret's shoes she would have marched straight out the door. Margaret just shook her head, dismissing the idiotic insult. Nancy began to seethe on Margaret's behalf, working herself up to a good boil by the time he was finished with his patient. Margaret was in no condition to take him on, but Nancy certainly was.

"Just where did you receive your training?" she asked, as Margaret was settling back in his operating chair. He scratched his chin, a fine yellow dust falling. The dried yolk might have been clinging to the yellow whiskers for days. Nancy took a position behind his dental engine, where Margaret could see her.

"I apprenticed with a good man," he said, peering intently into Margaret's open mouth. "Abscess," he murmured. "No saving it. Ether would be best."

"No," said Margaret. "I want my wits about me, thank you."

"It won't hurt," he said.

"Thank you, no," said Margaret.

Dr. McTeague poked at his instruments, looking dubious, as if he thought Margaret a big fool. Nancy thought her one. She'd take the offered relief without question. He examined a pair of forceps and then put them down again, leaning over Margaret. She stared up at him, her eyes big and bright, like a pig's before slaughter. He inserted a huge thumb and forefinger inside her mouth. Nancy turned her back, feigning interest in a steel engraving hanging on the wall. She tried for lightness, making an attempt to distract Margaret. "Can you recommend a nice place for dinner afterward?"

"There's a diner around the corner," he said. "They serve a tasty steak, cheap, but on the tough side. Your lady friend here wouldn't get far. We could do something about that, you know. I could fix her up with some fine teeth. Good as the real thing, better in some cases. It's just a matter of extracting these last few, then taking an impression."

Margaret whimpered, the smallest pitiful sound.

"I've done it hundreds of times," he said.

"Something soft would be better," said Nancy, not turning around. "Oysters, maybe." Gertrude adored mashed oysters from Smith's Chop House in town. Nancy wondered if her baby had noticed that her mother was missing today.

Margaret moaned. "We could stop here," the dentist said, "and take some gas."

Nancy looked over her shoulder. Margaret's eyes were closed. A trickle of blood ran from the corner of her mouth, giving Nancy a light-headed feeling. "Do as he says, Margaret. Please." Margaret shook her head, her features squeezed in emphatic refusal. Nancy turned her cowardly perspiring back again.

"Maybe you should try the Palace Hotel," he said, grunting like a common laborer. There was a sickening odor now, a hot alcohol smell emanating from his pores. "You'd get your oysters there. Cost you a pretty penny though."

"We don't mind this once," said Nancy. "Do we, Margaret?"

Margaret didn't respond. Long minutes went by, with his heavy breathing, the scraping and clicking, filling the room. Finally he let out a little yelp. "Here we go, here it comes!"

Nancy turned around, relieved and smiling. Margaret's face and arms had gone slack; her eyes were closed, her head cocked to one shoulder. The bloody handkerchief she'd been clutching lay on the floor. For a terrible moment Nancy thought she was dead. "What have you done to her?"

The dentist dropped Margaret's bloody tooth into the receptacle at his feet. "She's only fainted."

Nancy patted Margaret's ashen cheek, calling and cooing to her. "It happens when they don't take gas," he said.

Nancy looked him square in his beer-yellow eyes. "Don't stand there like a big nincompoop. Bring me a cold wet rag. Make sure it's clean and give it a good wringing." She turned back to Margaret, half singing to her. "Wake up, now. Wake up, wake up, wake up. Margaret? Can you hear me?"

At the Palace Hotel

Nancy ordered another bottle of champagne from the haughty waiter. The day called for it. Margaret needed cheering up. They both did. It had taken Nancy a good ten minutes to bring her around in the dentist's parlor. What if Margaret emerged from her faint not right in the head? There were fates aplenty worse than death. And besides, Nancy was still enjoying herself. That's the main reason she unhesitatingly summoned the man. She wanted to draw out the afternoon. The room was beautiful, with spectacular crystal chandeliers that grew more dazzling by the minute. She sat back, her shoulders heaving with woozy happiness.

"I've read about this place so many times in the *Chronicle*. To think I'm actually here in person!"

A twelve-piece orchestra played a moony waltz. Elegant couples danced extremely close, gliding past their table, looking as if they didn't have a care in the world.

"Have you ever in all your born days been anywhere this fancy, Margaret?"

Margaret managed a wobbly smile. "Never."

"You wouldn't believe how many famous people have dined here," said Nancy. "Presidents Harrison and McKinley, General Sherman, and the Emperor of Brazil. And let's see. Oscar Wilde the poet came. And Sarah Bernhardt. I wouldn't mind having her in my autograph book. She sleeps in a satin-lined coffin. If that doesn't give a person the willies, I don't know what does."

Tears rose in Margaret's eyes.

Nancy leaned in, raising her voice to be heard over the music. "Is it your tooth?"

Margaret shook her head, pulling the crumpled bloodstained hankie from her sleeve. Nancy brought out her clean spare and passed it across.

"Memories come when one least expects them," said Margaret, recovering some. "I was reminded of a lovely lady who once saw Sarah Bernhardt in person, in Paris."

"Lucky lady," said Nancy. "What I'd give to see Paris, France."

The waiter appeared, a foreigner of some kind, good-looking and seemingly very aware of it. He swept up the platter of empty oyster shells, asking in his provocative accent if they'd like some more.

"Please," said Nancy. He lifted the tray to one broad shoulder and turned to go.

"Don't forget the champagne," she called after him. "I'll have some explaining to do at home," she said to Margaret. "Henry probably thought we'd have our meal at a ten-cent diner." Margaret frowned. "I'm not saying he's a cheapskate, just watchful, you know. Oh, what am I saying? Of course you know."

"I cannot imagine him denying you a thing," said Margaret.

Nancy swallowed the last of the warm wine in her glass, blushing. "I'm sure he was the same with you."

Margaret shook her head. "He wasn't. Ours were straitened circumstances."

"Well, he was young then, just starting out."

"True," said Margaret, with a prim shrug.

"I don't have permission to spend like there's no tomorrow," said Nancy.

"It's none of my affair," said Margaret. "Please let's change the subject."

"Don't be like that, Margaret. Did I say something wrong? I thought we were starting to have a good time for a change."

"I'm sure I don't know what you mean."

Nancy slapped the table. "There you go again. You don't need to be so all-fired polite. There's no reason to live in fear of me."

"I don't," said Margaret.

"I think you do a little," Nancy insisted.

"I'm at your mercy," said Margaret, her eyes hard now, the watery nostalgia gone from them. "If that's what you mean to say."

"You're no such thing!" The waiter came up with the second bottle. Nancy reached for her glass before he finished pouring, brushing his hand and knocking over the vase of peony roses. He gave her such a look. *Clumsy drunkard,* she imagined him thinking, or however the insult translated in his language. Nancy laughed out of embarrassment, out of clumsy drunkenness. He busied himself tidying the table, and then went away testily, saying the oysters would be served shortly.

Nancy sighed. What did she care about his poor impression? She'd never see him again. A couple waltzed by, the young lady flushed-faced, clearly taken with her clean-shaven beau. It used to be said that unmarried ladies should not dance the waltz at all, in public or in private, as the dance itself was too loose a character.

On impulse, Nancy lifted her glass to Margaret, toasting modern times. "We're at the dawn of the twentieth century! You're at no one's mercy, leastwise not mine." Margaret touched the rim of her glass to Nancy's, her hand aquiver.

"It's kind of you to say."

"I want us to get along," said Nancy. "I mean it sincerely, Margaret. Do you think we ever could?"

Margaret lowered her gaze. "I'm not quite sure what you mean, really."

"You'll always have a place in our home. I hope you know that."

Margaret looked up. "Thank you, Nancy."

They sat back, saying nothing more for a while. The words had just popped out of her. Nancy didn't altogether regret making the offer; but neither could she picture themselves years from now, two old grannies, still sharing the same kitchen.

They picked at the second platter of oysters when it came. The taste was off now, Nancy thought, a little rancid.

Margaret turned her attention to the dance floor, wondering aloud if Henry had ever learned to dance. "He suffered two left feet when I knew him," she said.

"I've never danced with Henry," said Nancy. The fact depressed her. Why hadn't they danced at least once? They were still young enough. *She* certainly was anyway. "We didn't have much of a courtship, you know. There was Gertrude."

Margaret seemed not to hear. The orchestra had started up a lively polka. She was watching the dancers. After a long silence she said, "Did you mean what you said, Nancy . . . about our truly being welcome in your home?"

Nancy hesitated half a moment before yelling over the accordion coda. "Yes."

A crash of cymbals brought the deafening number to an end. "Suppose we went elsewhere then, the lot of us," said Margaret. "Suppose we left wretched Berkeley and its wretched Daughters of Decency altogether? I worry," she said, more to herself.

"The marriage certificate will come soon," said Nancy. "The

Daughters will go on to other causes. You'll see. A farm isn't disposed of that easily," she added, quoting Henry directly.

Early on he'd sat her down to discuss his will, providing her with a list of bankers and managers to contact upon his death. Nancy wasn't to *give* the farm away. She was to wait for the right time and hold out for a fair price. The property would fetch income to last her days if she didn't lose her head and sell too hastily, he said. The proceeds were to be put in certain stocks, an eighth here, a quarter there. Nancy didn't remember what all. It was too confusing. She didn't imagine holding out very long in any event. The farm was nothing but hard work. She'd never told him, but given a choice, she'd leave tomorrow and set up housekeeping in town, have the butcher's boy deliver wrapped sausages and chops to the door. The move would be good for Henry. His disposition turned pitch black on slaughtering day. Nancy often thought he should return to accounting and leave farming to the less tenderhearted. "Where would we go?" she asked.

"A sizable city might be best," said Margaret. "It wouldn't matter really, as long as no one knew us. We'd introduce ourselves as Henry's wife and his sister, the maiden aunt from England, come to help out."

Margaret's concession both surprised and shamed Nancy. There was no telling what she might do in Margaret's position.

The waiter approached. "You think me preposterous," said Margaret.

"Not entirely," said Nancy. "Henry's the one you'd need to convince."

Margaret was like most any other relative in need, she guessed. At worst, they take up too much room and you can't stand them. At best, they take up too much room and begin to grow on you. Either way, they're here, and you live with it. Those weren't his exact words. But that's more or less what Uncle Chester said to Nancy when she arrived in Berkeley.

❖❖

A BROMO SELTZER would have been Nancy's salvation, but was not on the menu at the Palace Hotel, according to the sarcastic waiter. She tipped him, anyway, leaving the dime by her plate as she'd originally planned.

"Thank you, madam," he said, without a trace of gratitude. She had half a mind to snatch up the dime and leave a penny instead. She would not be returning. That much was certain. They would take their business elsewhere next visit. There were plenty of fine restaurants in San Francisco; that was but one advantage of a city so large.

They found a druggist a block away, who sold Nancy a packet of Bromo Seltzer, and gave her water at no extra charge. "Have you always had the desire to live in a big city?"

"Not when I was younger certainly," said Margaret. "I think now the anonymity might be preferable. And you?"

"Well," said Nancy, taking a bitter sip. "There's the disease to consider. And the pickpockets. They're everywhere, I hear."

"One might choose their company over certain Berkeleyans," said Margaret.

Nancy watched the pharmacist mash something yellow in his sieve. Francis loved mixing and concocting. His hands had never smelled the same two days in a row. "Flowery sometimes, not like medicine at all."

"I beg your pardon?" said Margaret.

Nancy emerged from her fog, aware now that she'd spoken out loud. "Never mind," she said, laughing a little. "I took a trip back in time. You know how it is."

"If only one could pick and choose the memory," said Margaret, "and erase the rest."

JOHN OADES was on hand to meet them at the fish-stinking Berkeley docks, as expected. He approached with a serious look on his face. Margaret rushed him. "What is it? Is it one of the girls?"

"It's Father," he said, and Nancy's knees buckled.

"Oh, sweet Lord, no." She pictured Henry laid out in his Sunday suit, Francis's jar and pedestal moved to make room for the coffin.

"He's all right," said John. "It's the cows. Four good animals were charged with consumption and taken in."

"Is that all?" said Nancy, breathing hard. "Thank God."

Mrs. Potter was in the yard when they arrived, hanging patched sheets on the line, and looking like a hobo's sweetheart. She turned with pegs in her mouth and flapped a wave. Margaret and Nancy waved back.

"Thank you, Nancy," said Margaret, "for all you've done." She climbed down and started up the overgrown path to the door, gathering her shawl about herself.

Nancy called after her. "It won't be much longer."

The ride home took nearly two hours in the one-horse rig, sufficient time for John's fitful account. The health department had had the advantage of surprise. Earlier that day, around noon, five armed men showed up. Two held Henry, John, and Titus at gunpoint, while the others inspected the herd.

"It's not right, Mrs. Oades. It's just not right."

"Settle down, John," she had to say more than once. "It's not the end of the world." As it surely would have been had she lost Henry Oades. She hadn't loved him at first crack; but she did now. She especially loved the tender way he said, "I love you, Nan." It was a strange thing to realize at this particular moment, and while talking about sick cows. Nancy thought of Francis then, the loss more than the man.

At home she found Gertrude in the bedroom, asleep in her crib. The baby had been fed, as had Henry and the girls. Josephine had seen to it all. She made flapjacks at her father's request. "Dad wasn't in the mood for meat."

"I don't know what the family would do without you," said Nancy.

Josephine's ears colored with the compliment, her mouth flicking with something close to a smile. The girl was beginning to thaw some.

Nancy and Henry retired early, undressing in the expiring amber light, getting under the covers. They lay faceup, not speaking until he turned his head on the pillow and said, "Did she do all right at the dentist?"

"He pulled her tooth cold," said Nancy. "She refused to take gas. I can't decide if she's brave or just plain obstinate."

"She's both," he murmured, kissing her lips. "Thank you for taking her."

"I didn't mind."

"You are goodness personified," he said sleepily, shifting, facing the ceiling again.

She turned to him. "Henry?"

"Hmmm?"

"It's me you love, isn't it?"

"Good God." He came up on one elbow and stared down at her. "Don't ever begin to doubt it."

"Never mind," she said. "I just thought . . ."

"What? What did you think?"

"I just thought you might be a little confused."

"I'm not the least bit confused. You are my wife. Now and always."

"Unless some old judge decides we have no business being married," she said.

"That's not going to happen, Nan."

"Would you be willing to swear on the Bible?"

"I would."

Nancy rolled, tucking her head beneath his arm. He smelled of fresh clean hay. "I love you, Henry," she said, for the first time. "I truly do."

Pieces

NANCY AND JOSEPHINE started the laundry soaking on Monday night, a full day and a half late. After the soaking came the scrubbing, the rubbing with lye soap, the boiling, the stirring, lifting the heavy clothes with the splintery paddle, rinsing twice, once in plain water, once with bluing. Finally came the wringing and hanging. Nancy had hoped to get to the ironing by Wednesday night, but did not.

She and Josephine regularly stayed behind schedule. There was just too much work for one woman and a girl. They took turns with the slops, Gertrude, the feeding of the stove, and the emptying of ashes. Josephine continued to do most of the cooking since she was better at it. Nancy was left with the floors, walls, bric-a-brac, and furniture. The lamp wicks got trimmed today, but there was no time for a badly needed polishing. She neglected Francis but for a brief swipe of his jar. They never did get to the windows. That afternoon Nancy picked up Gertrude and begged her to smile, to be happy and cooperative, but the baby refused, squirming like a snake in her arms until Nancy put her down again. Gertrude almost always behaved sweetly with Josephine, proof positive that Nancy was a failure as a mother. She felt ashamed and defeated, but mainly exhausted, too weary lately to bother with a sponge. Twice this week she went without, lying awake afterward, worrying, resenting Henry's even snore. Yesterday she burst into tears for no earthly reason other than fatigue. Last night she spoke up and asked Henry for another maid-of-all-tasks.

"I wish you'd made mention sooner," he said.

"I thought Josephine and I could manage," said Nancy. "I was trying to save you money."

He kissed her. "Your health is worth more than the price of a girl."

On Friday, Henry rode into town to ask at the new employment agency on Shattuck Avenue, returning just before supper in a foul mood.

"How about a small brandy," said Nancy. They went into the front room and closed the door, pouring two, as was not their habit so early in the day.

First-class Help, said the sign on the door. Satisfaction Guaranteed. The clerk turned biggity and high-hat right away, telling Henry he had no one suitable. Henry had asked, "How would you know off the top of your head? Have you every last maid memorized? Is there no list to consult?"

"I'll run my business as I see fit, brother," the clerk had said. "And don't bother looking elsewhere."

No one of any persuasion, of reputation high or low, was willing to work for the Mormons. The talk was all over town apparently.

Nancy suspected Dora McGinnis of starting the ugliness. Dora worked for the Stricklands now, not the uppity Leopold Stricklands in town, but the *Horace* Stricklands of the next farm over.

Last Monday Dora sent their lovesick hand Clarence around to ask about a hair ribbon she'd left behind.

"Miss McGinnis would like to stop by, with your permission." Wouldn't she, though? Nancy could just picture the girl's gears turning, itching to get at John. Poor duped Clarence. Nancy had been tempted to shake some sense into him. But she held her tongue and gave the donkey-dumb man a nickel. "Tell her to buy a new one."

After leaving the employment agency, Henry went to the Health Department to see about the confiscated cows. All four had been shot and incinerated the day before.

"I asked how many other animals were done away with," said Henry. "The man informs me just our four. I said, am I to believe mine were the only sick animals in all of Berkeley? He said he did not give a *damn* what I believed or did not believe."

"They had no proof or right," said Nancy. "We should sue."

Henry settled back in his chair, closing his eyes. Nancy stood to refresh his glass. He pulled two envelopes from his breast pocket. "The marriage certificate came today," he said wearily. Nancy took the envelopes, turning them over, studying the exotic stamps and markings.

"Well, at least Margaret can leave that horrible Potter pigsty now," she said.

"I'll need to put the certificate before the judge first," said Henry.

"Do it soon, Henry. She could catch something there and bring it home."

"As soon as I can, love."

"Who is this other letter from?" she asked, analyzing the fine script, deciding it was a woman's hand.

"A cousin," said Henry. "A vicar."

"Margaret has royal relations?"

"More like one of your ministers."

"Oh."

"It's a birthday greeting, I expect. She'll turn, let's see . . . forty-two next week."

"What do you know," murmured Nancy. Her own mother would have been forty-two last month, a strange coincidence.

❖❖

On Saturday, Nancy, Josephine, and Martha washed every last window with vinegar and water. If any chore brought more satisfaction at the end, Nancy did not know what it was. On Sunday she had Henry and John move her sewing machine from the bedroom to the kitchen. Once Dora's cot was removed, Nancy had the sewing room she'd always wanted. The Lord closes one window (a spanking clean one in this case), and opens another. It was the sweetest of sights: her machine oiled and gleaming, threaded with white thread, extra bobbins at the ready. It was warm inside with the door closed, but private. Nancy pictured happy productive hours to herself.

Margaret was not allowed home on Monday, after Nancy had planned a pork roast and lemon pound cake. She was due home on Wednesday now, after a second mandatory appearance at the courthouse for the signing of this, that, or the other.

"And that will be the end of it?" asked Nancy. "They'll leave us be now?"

"They bloody well better," said Henry.

In a celebratory mood, Nancy decided to sew. She settled on a nightgown for Margaret, as the fancy gown she'd left behind was now stained yellow. Too big of a load had gone into the boil this last time; the clothes never got stirred right when that happened.

Nancy had had the three yards of good quality cotton for some time now, since before Margaret's arrival. She'd planned to sew up a nightgown for herself, but hadn't gotten around to it. The fabric still looked and smelled clean when she brought it out to show Josephine, who tried to talk Nancy out of adding a flounce or two. "Mum prefers plain."

"Too much so," said Nancy. At least one flounce was in order; it was Margaret's birthday, after all.

The girls were willing to help. Nancy put them to work at the kitchen table, pinning the pattern pieces to the cloth. They were using a McCall's pattern, a pretty empire model, calling for long full sleeves.

"She'll look like a queen," said Martha.

Nice little girl, seeing her mother through rose-colored specs.

✧✧

AT FOUR ON WEDNESDAY, Nancy and the girls were watching from the front room. The whole house smelled delicious from the baking. They heard the horses before they came into view and rushed out to greet Margaret.

"My," she said, breathless, an arm around each clinging daughter. "Such a fine reception."

Nancy noticed Henry's solemn expression as he drove the buggy off to the shed, but gave it no lingering thought. There was the new nightgown to admire and a perfect lemon pound cake to fuss over. It came as no surprise that he chose not to join the welcoming festivities. He did not strictly avoid Margaret as he did at first, but neither did he look for opportunities to socialize with her. She haunted him still, understandably. Nancy could not carry his burden. She'd thought about it often enough, imagining the knock at the door, finding eager-eyed Francis standing there. Six months ago, she would have gone off with him. Now she was no longer so certain. Sending Francis away would be like stabbing him in the heart, especially if he were disfigured; but to have him stay and witness her new happiness would be more than she could bear. Despite the fierce grieving, it's best for all concerned that the dead stay buried.

✧✧

THE LETTER had slipped Nancy's mind in all the gay hoopla. She finally thought to give it to Margaret at supper. Margaret examined the envelope briefly and slipped it inside her skirt pocket as Henry began grace. Later, after supper, she pulled the letter from her pocket. She and Nancy were alone in the kitchen. Margaret placed the letter on the table and went for her apron.

Nancy pumped water into the sink. "Why don't you read it?"

Margaret tied a swift bow. "I don't want to keep Henry waiting," she said.

He'd barely said two words at supper. When the meal was over he stood, looking as if he'd lost his entire herd. "Meg," he said. "Will you join us in the front room this evening?"

Nancy hadn't expected an invitation herself, he'd been so withdrawn. She and Margaret had leapt up like soldiers and begun clearing the table. Never mind the digestive process. Never mind that she might have preferred to read her new *Ladies' Home Journal* in bed.

"Let the grumpy bear wait," said Nancy. "Go ahead and read your letter."

"I wrote home some time ago," Margaret said, taking a bread knife to the flap. "A single leaf," she murmured, as though disappointed. She scanned the page, the corners of her mouth sagging. "Oh."

"What is it?"

"My parents," she said hoarsely, blinking back tears.

Nancy took a wooden step toward her, dread rising.

"How can it be? Mother has the constitution of an ox. She's a

McGregor! McGregors live well into old age, in wheelchairs some, but sharp as needles, able to boil an egg for themselves still, every last one of them. They're famous for it!"

"Oh, Margaret."

"My dad," she sobbed. "My lovely, lovely dad."

Nancy gently wrapped her arms around her shoulders. Margaret allowed it. She was scarcely more than trembling bones and a broken heart.

Henry came in half a moment later. "What is it?"

"Mother," said Margaret, pulling away from Nancy, turning to him. "And Dad. They're three years gone, Henry. Influenza both. Dad first, then Mum. They're laid side by side." Her chin dropped, tears streaming. "In the west corner of the churchyard."

He advanced toward her, his own eyes filling.

Margaret closed the space between them, collapsing against his vest. "Ah, Meg," he whispered, folding his arms around her. She was no more than two or three inches shorter than Henry. They looked disturbingly natural, like two pieces of a long-lost puzzle come together. Nancy stood watching, an odd feeling coming over her—a sense of not belonging in the same room with them. He spoke close to Margaret's ear, their cheeks brushing. "I loved them like my own."

Margaret nodded, her eyes closed. "And they you, Henry. Mother's undisputed darling."

Nancy asked, "What does that mean?"

They came apart, laughing softly over some shared memory. Margaret accepted Henry's handkerchief, dabbing at her eyes. "It's something Meg's dad used to say," he said.

"He was jealous of Mum's affection for Henry," said Margaret, looking at Henry. "Do you remember her silly button collection?"

Henry said that he did.

"I wonder what became of it?"

Nancy went to the sink. An overwhelming tower of greasy

crockery still waited. Supper with Francis had been so simple. Two plates, two cups, a single pot, a pan, no more. On special occasions they dined at Fonzo's café in town. Nothing beat a juicy porterhouse at Fonzo's. They should have gone every night, lived large while they could. He would have had no reason to run back inside if they had.

Dickering

Henry offered to write a letter to Margaret's cousin and inquire about the button collection. Margaret said bother the letter, she'd only been wondering aloud.

Nancy turned from the sink, oily dishwater dribbling down her sleeve. She heard the squeak of a door hinge upstairs, a muffled thump of footsteps. "What was it you wanted to speak to us about, Henry?"

"It will keep until morning," he said.

"We're bone-tired," said Nancy. "Just say what you have to say. Did something happen at the courthouse? Please tell us the charges were dropped."

"They were," he said, running a hand through his hair. "New charges were then laid. Against you and me, Nan."

Nancy struck out at nothing, lashing the air with the dish towel. "You swore to me, Henry Oades! You swore on the Bible that it wouldn't, it *couldn't*, happen. What is the bogus charge this time?"

"The same. Open and notorious cohabitation and adultery."

Margaret croaked out a noise. "Preposterous."

"You were there," said Nancy. "Have you known all day?"

"No indeed," said Margaret. "I was made to wait in the carriage."

"I plain refuse to accept this," said Nancy. "We were legally married, in both the state's eyes and Almighty God's!"

"Which we shall prove in no uncertain terms," said Henry, coming to her.

Nancy flung the dish towel and stormed up the back stairs, catching Josephine and Martha, sneaky little eavesdroppers, on the landing. The girls fled back into their room, pale nighties flapping. Nancy escaped to her bedroom, blind with rage. She tore off her housedress and apron, peering over Gertrude's crib—asleep, thank God. When Henry came in, Nancy was under the covers, facing the wall. "Nan, sweetheart?" She didn't respond. He slipped in beside her, saying nothing more. She was seething, breathing like a dog in heat. Hot sleepless hours passed before she calmed, before she remembered how much he loved her. He would see that they had to leave this hateful place. She would make him see.

❖❖

NANCY BLURTED out her plan the moment he stirred. "I think we should go to San Francisco."

Henry got out of bed, floorboards creaking beneath his huge feet. He went first to the baby as always, looking down at her in the dark.

"Margaret and I have already discussed the idea some," Nancy whispered. "We'll just go and send for the furniture later. Or we'll sell it all and buy new. That might be best. It fries me no end to turn tail when we've done nothing wrong, but what else are we supposed to do, Henry?"

He lit a lamp and took his drawers from the peg, the same pair he'd worn ten days running. Tomorrow would make eleven, for shame, for shame. Dora had produced a clean pair every week without fail. Fastidious Francis would have protested by the eighth day. Henry, though no less particular about his hygiene, hadn't made the first peep.

"I want nothing more than a return to relative normalcy," he said.

Nancy sat up in bed, hugging her knees. "Then we agree."

He buttoned up, pulling on the drawstring. "We cannot simply light out. The farm and animals would have to go first."

"Fine." She began mentally packing up the room, leaving the old farmer's ugly drapes behind. "Fine and dandy! Let them go. Sell the whole kit and caboodle to the highest bidder."

His dirty wool shirt came next, trousers and suspenders. He sat to pull on his boots. "I've had an offer to purchase."

"Why on earth didn't you tell me?"

"It was too soon," he said. "And there's still the matter of the impending charges."

"They won't come after us. Good riddance to the Mormons, they'll say. And let them try and find us, anyway. We'll change our name if necessary. Or go farther. Sacramento, maybe. Why not? Tell me about the offer."

"Sweetheart, please," he said. "You're getting ahead of yourself."

She drew up the blanket, shivering with determination. They were going. It was simply a matter of when. "Who made the offer?"

Henry sighed. "Horace Strickland."

"Mr. Strickland! Really."

John could be heard downstairs now, rattling around in the kitchen, making coffee for his father and himself. "The offer was far too low to consider," said Henry.

"Well, you have to dicker," said Nancy. "My father taught me that much, at least."

Henry stuffed his gloves inside his coat pocket. "You need to leave these matters to me, Nan. The bounder sees a ripe opportunity to capitalize."

Left to Henry, they'd still be here next month. "What are you asking?"

"Five thousand, with the animals. Now go back to sleep."

"Five thousand! My goodness. I had no idea. What did he offer?"

"Two."

"Maybe I'll call on Mildred Strickland."

"Don't. It will serve no purpose."

He put on his hat, pushing it cockeyed. "You tossed the night long. Try and get a little rest before Gerty wakes up."

"We should strike while the iron is hot, Henry."

He pinched out the flame and came to her in the dark, kissing the bridge of her nose. "Don't worry. It'll be all right. Close your eyes now."

Nancy had already made up her mind to pay Mildred a visit.

❖❖

"DON'T LET ON that we're leaving," said Margaret, when Nancy told her.

"I'm not a complete nincompoop," said Nancy.

Nancy set out for the Stricklands on foot because Henry had taken the small rig into town to see the lawyer. She didn't want to involve John in her plan, have him drive her in the barouche, which Mildred might regard as uppity on so nice a day. She wore a dowdy featherless hat, and carried a basket of red carrots and lettuce from the garden, just the type of humble hostess gift Mildred would appreciate.

The Stricklands didn't live far, about six miles north. She and Henry had once been invited to play cards with them. Mildred, too, was a widow who'd married an older gentleman, not recently, but the experience was the same. Nancy thought she'd found a friend for life because of the similar situation.

She arrived just after noon, perspiring and footsore, her speech running through her head. She'd written a note, in case Mildred wasn't receiving. Margaret had thought up most of it.

> . . . *In regards to our property, it would behoove you to act quickly. Other parties have expressed interest.*

Nancy covered the wilted lettuce with the carrots and rang the bell. The porch swing had been painted since she last visited. She reminded herself to compliment the nice finish.

Dora McGinnis came to the door with her chin in the air.

"Well, hello, Dora. My, you're looking well."

"Are you expected, ma'am?"

Mildred came bustling up behind. She was the fidgety, frenzied type, with sewing needles saved in her sleeve, a pencil caught up in her graying knot. She was expecting again. That would make six, or was it seven now? "Oh, dear, girl," she said. "I've been worried sick about you."

Nancy offered the basket. "I haven't been ill, Mildred."

"The domestic arrangement," she whispered, her eyes sliding toward Dora.

"We're managing," said Nancy, looking at Dora. *Make the first smart remark, little missy, and you'll feel the sting of my hand.*

"Refreshments, please," said Mildred. Dora arched an eyebrow and left.

"She's working out nicely," said Mildred, taking the basket, saying the carrots looked too good to eat. "You shouldn't have, Nancy. Come in out of the heat. Dollars to doughnuts you're here about the farm. Am I right? What if we hens came to an agreement on our own? Wouldn't that be something?"

Nancy followed Mildred inside, feeling light and confident.

The deal was as good as sealed already. She wouldn't wait. She'd tell him right away. *There's not much to say, Henry. We dickered awhile, but that's how it's done.*

They sat in the cramped front room, where a child's cot was pushed up against the piano. Dora brought in lemonade and gingerbread that Nancy picked apart but did not eat, fearing saliva or worse had been added.

Mildred moaned after eating a few bites, patting her rounded middle. "It's not the same, the second husband, is it?"

"Well, no," said Nancy, thinking the comment strange. There was nothing to compare to first love. "You couldn't expect it to be."

Mildred's expression softened. "Your first husband was young, too, wasn't he?"

"Yes," said Nancy. "Francis was only twenty when he passed, God rest his sweet soul."

"My Dicky had just turned twenty-two," said Mildred, tears glistening. "Lockjaw."

"I remember you telling me, Millie," said Nancy. "It was a terrible tragedy."

Mildred licked her finger and pressed it to the plate, attracting crumbs. "Do you recollect the time we had you to supper?"

"Of course. Henry and I had only been married a week. We played whist. I don't think I won a single trick all night."

Mildred waved a hand. "You played fine. I was just recalling our husbands, how they looked, sitting across from each other, Horace's bald head blazing away in the mirror. I remember thinking, what have we done to ourselves, you and I? Saddling ourselves with these old men. Older than Methuselah, but that doesn't stop them, does it?" She patted her middle again. "Do you know what I'm saying?"

"I can't say that I do," said Nancy.

Mildred clucked, rolling her eyes. "Never mind, Nancy. I'm bound for the madhouse. But then what wife with half a brain isn't? Let's get down to business, shall we? Why are you giving up that wonderful place?"

Nancy said they were moving into town for the children's sake. "The girls will be starting Miss Stanley's Academy soon. Driving into town every day would be too much of a hardship." Margaret had come up with the excuse, though their reason for leaving did not seem to matter to Mildred.

"I'd sell my soul for your spacious front room and kitchen," she said.

For the next half hour they negotiated back and forth politely. Obviously, they could not reach an agreement on their own, without their husbands' approval. They did all the preliminary work, though. A signature here and there, and that would be that.

"Will you be taking the furnishings?"

"Could you use them, Millie?"

Mildred practically fainted with delight, offering another fifty dollars. That brought the grand total to thirty-five hundred even, a fortune. Nancy couldn't wait to tell Henry and Margaret. Mildred brought out sherry to celebrate, pouring into tiny blue glasses, hardly bigger than thimbles. Nancy had had two before she knew it.

"If I may speak frankly," said Mildred, as Nancy stood to leave. Nancy pulled on her gloves. "Of course, Millie."

Mildred spoke carefully. "I continue to regard you as a Christian friend."

Something unpleasant was coming. "Likewise, I'm sure."

"I worry about you," said Mildred.

"Please, don't. I'm fine."

"You must do something about that woman, Nancy."

"Such as?"

"Such as shipping her straight back to her people."

"Her parents have passed. *We're* her people now." It was true.

There was no other place for Margaret to go. Why couldn't people get it through their thick skulls?

"I'm sure there are charitable services where she comes from," said Mildred. "Some equivalent to the Berkeley Benevolent Society."

Nancy folded her arms. "I'm sure you're right. What about the children?"

"What about them?"

Mildred was no better than Mrs. Dooley. "You'd ship them thousands of miles from their father? Never to see him again? That's your *Christian* proposal?"

"I'm not standing in judgment, Nancy. I'm only looking out for your best interests."

Nancy headed for the door. There was no point in carrying on.

"If I were in crisis I'd expect you to speak up, out of our old affection."

"I'm not in crisis, Mildred. Good-bye. Thank you for the refreshments."

Mildred followed her onto the porch, scanning the darkening sky. "It looks like rain. I could round up one of my boys, have him drive you."

Nancy started down the steps. "I'd much prefer to walk, thank you."

"You haven't changed your mind about selling your place?"

"A deal is a deal," said Nancy. "We shook hands, didn't we?"

It's what a man would say. They never seemed to confuse friendship with enterprise. A man would stroll away whistling, caring only about the hefty profit in his pocket.

The rain began a mile from home. Nancy trudged on. Chilblains and a ruined hat were a small price to pay for setting their departure in motion.

Margaret was in the kitchen with Martha and Josephine, giving French lessons at the table. "You met with success," she said, knowing right away.

❖❖

HENRY WAS SURPRISED by the price she'd wheedled, but he was not happy that she'd gone. "I specifically asked you not to." He went to see Mr. Strickland the next afternoon, returning without having sold the farm.

"Only twenty-three hundred? Mildred promised thirty-five!"

"She doesn't hold the purse strings, Nan."

The miserly offer was to include all tools, all animals, alive and butchered, the contents of larder and root cellar, and every last stick of furniture.

"It's still a great deal of money," said Nancy.

"The farm and livestock are worth much more."

His dismissive tone hurt. "You're mean, Henry, and you're greedy to boot."

He turned short with her. "I told you to leave business matters to me. He'll come around, you'll see. He's desperate for the land."

She drew a bath the way he liked it, cold water first. The peace offering did nothing to improve his mood. He got in, spreading out, hogging the whole tub, when he usually made room for her.

"Enjoy your old bath," she said, leaving the kitchen.

❖❖

THEY WERE ARRAIGNED the following Monday. The proceeding took all of ten minutes. Nancy and Henry stood before Judge Billings, their lawyer, Mr. Lewis Grimes, a bald gentleman with fleshy lips, between them.

"Absolutely not guilty!" The fury in Nancy's voice ricocheted off the paneled walls and put an exasperated look on the old judge. He sucked his teeth and consulted his pocket watch, concerned about his noontime meal, no doubt. She had not expected such indifference from a man thrice married himself.

He named a trial date two months off, but Nancy didn't retain the exact day. It didn't matter. They'd be long gone.

"In the meantime," said the judge, "beginning today, you and the lady will house yourselves separately."

Nancy let out a little cry. The worst she'd anticipated was a command to return to this churchy courtroom, with its domed ceiling painted to look like heaven. Fat cherubs cavorted among frescoed clouds, taunting the innocent below. "That's not fair, your honor!"

The bang of the gavel startled her. "Oh, my."

The beaky judge glared down. "I'll be the judge of what's fair and what isn't, *miss*."

"It's *Mrs! Mrs.* Henry P. Oades!" Nancy nearly bit her tongue in two getting the words out.

A Question of
Divorce

THE MOON-BLUE ROOM SWAYED. Somewhere glass was breaking. Nancy lifted her head from the pillow, perspiring freely, alone and confused, still drunk on the croup remedy she'd taken for sleep. Henry was gone, spending his nights at Mr. Potter's, who was charging double now, simply because he could. The lawyer said it would look better come trial time if she herself vacated the premises. Nancy had agreed, not with enthusiasm admittedly, but Henry wouldn't hear of it. Mr. Grimes then made special arrangements. Henry was allowed to return by day to work his farm, as long as he kept his distance from her. He was permitted to speak to Margaret, his lawfully wedded wife, as long and as much as he pleased. They could go out riding in an open buckboard in broad daylight if they felt so inclined. But the briefest exchange with Nancy meant jail. The anger knotted her. She felt it pulsing the livelong day. All tranquillity left with Henry.

A door slammed down the hall. Someone cried out, the words unintelligible. The dogs and cows kept on, barking and mooing in the dead of night. Nancy fell back on the damp pillow, groggy and sick. In the next instant the bed had shifted and she was on the floor. Margaret pounded on her door, shouting, "Earthquake!"

The door burst open and in she flew, long gray braid streaming behind her. "Get up, Nancy, get up, get up!"

She yanked Nancy to her feet and plucked wailing Gertrude from her crib. Somehow Nancy found her robe and slippers. They raced down the back stairs, glass from the fallen frames grinding beneath their thin soles. Outside, Margaret's girls stood shivering, their flimsy nightgowns fluttering about their bare ankles. Margaret began pacing the yard, crooning a foreign ditty, reducing Gertrude's cry to a whimper in a matter of seconds. Nancy might have taken her baby then, but she feared setting her off again. Instead she went with John to check on the bellowing cows. She managed to quiet Begonia, talking to her by lamplight, sleepily stroking her cheek.

"Shush, cow. Simmer down now." The heifer eventually responded, surrendering sweetly. If only Nancy had the same effect on her own child.

At first light they went back inside.

The front porch had buckled. Two front windows had shattered. A south section of chimney was gone. But the walls and roof had held, and the hall floor felt secure.

The girls crept upstairs, Gertrude asleep in Josephine's arms. Nancy and Margaret went into the front room, finding a glittering mess.

The damage to Francis's jar was complete. The shards themselves were cracked. They approached the irreparable ginger jar with reverence, as if approaching a sacristy. Nancy fell to her knees weeping. She scraped Francis's soft ashes into a heap, desecrating his remains with house dust and spider legs. Margaret went into the kitchen, returning with a mason jar for Francis, a hand broom, and a pail. She knelt beside Nancy, stretching to reach behind the pedestal for the broken lid, her chin trembling.

"The jar belonged to my mum, before it became Mr. Foreland's resting place."

"Oh, Margaret, I never knew. Henry said it had been in the family, but I didn't think to ask more. I'm sorry. I was in such a state at the time."

Margaret rubbed the piece of lid, her eyes dulling with sadness. "You couldn't have known."

They sat back on their heels, not looking at each other. Nancy pushed at tears with a knuckle. "You'd think God was conspiring against us."

"I cannot imagine God bothering to concern himself one way or the other."

"You don't mean it."

Margaret gave a little shrug.

"Maybe something for our nerves is in order. If the brandy bottle didn't bust."

"No thank you, Nancy," said Margaret, rising.

Nancy waited for Margaret to leave the room, pouring then more than she'd intended.

❖❖

HENRY DROVE UP later than usual and headed straight for the milk room. Nancy so wanted to go to him, but didn't dare take the risk. People rode by at all hours these days, hoping for a peek of the bigamist and his wives. If Henry was reported seen near the house he'd go to jail. For of course the judge would take a shameless rubbernecker's word over theirs.

"You go, Margaret. He'll want to know that we're all right." Margaret was gone almost two hours. Nancy was wound up tight by the time she returned. She met Margaret at the kitchen door. "What on earth kept you? No conversation could have lasted this long. Did he have you milking?"

Margaret gave her a bewildered scowl, her thin lips all but disappearing. She was homely as dishwater, true, particularly in this harsh light, but she was also smart and sturdy. A man needed an oak in troubled times, not some useless meadow flower.

Margaret took her apron from the nail, pulling it over her head. She stooped and picked up a missed sliver. Nancy had swept up the broken crockery by herself. She'd also dumped the cold ashes into the privy, fed the stove, got the fire going, picked and washed some carrots and put them on for soup. Margaret seemed not to notice any of it.

Nancy asked, "Did Henry mention Mr. Strickland?"

"He didn't." Margaret went to the sink and gazed out the window. "The butchering shed is in splinters."

The longing in her expression gave Nancy an uneasy feeling. "Did he ask about me?"

"He wasn't given time. I told him straightaway."

Nancy forked a hard carrot in the pot. "Told him what exactly?"

"That Mr. Foreland's jar had broken, that you were bereft over the loss."

Nancy put down the fork and turned to her. *"Bereft?"*

"Are the girls still up in our room, Nancy?"

Nancy brushed a damp curl from her eye. *"Bereft,* Margaret?"

Margaret said without emotion, "Are you not?"

"You left him thinking I was sobbing away over a vase? He pictures me inconsolable? Unable to come to my senses?" Nancy bobbed forward, coming nearly nose to nose. "Boo-hoo, Margaret!"

Margaret stepped back, staring without comment, working her wedding band up and down. Her composure set Nancy's back teeth on edge and caused her voice to rise another shrill octave. "Boo hoo hoo hoo!"

Margaret distanced herself farther. "You're overwrought."

"Overwrought! Heavens to Betsy! You'd best go run and tell Henry!"

"Whatever is the matter with you, Nancy?"

"*You* are, Mrs. Oades!" Nancy sank to a chair, instantly regretting the outburst. What was happening to her? "I'm sorry, Margaret. I don't know what gets into me."

Margaret sat down beside her, patting her shoulder in a motherly way. Nancy looked at her. "Would you consider giving Henry a divorce?"

Margaret calmly stopped petting, her expression as placid as a cow's. As if she'd been expecting the request all along. Such an obvious solution. Nancy congratulated herself. They'd have Mr. Grimes draw up the papers, and then put the entire sad past behind them. They'd go on as before. Nothing would change. Their situation could only improve. They'd do something special to celebrate the end of their problems, take a trip maybe, a long train trip to the East Coast. What she wouldn't give to visit New York City and Niagara Falls. Nancy had their future perfectly planned in the moment before Margaret said, "Most assuredly not."

Margaret stood and went to the stove.

"Do you loathe him that much?" asked Nancy

Margaret answered coldly, "I don't loathe him in the least. He is my husband."

"In name only," said Nancy.

"Granted."

"Do you still have feelings of affection?"

Margaret repeated herself. "He is my husband." She came away from the stove, the blood drawn from her pitted face. "Have you once considered our innocent children?" She leaned into the table, fists down. "Girls who have come to regard you as a second mother? You sewed with them, laughed and joked. They told me all about it. Such a gay afternoon, Martha said. I was beginning to think you truly cared for them."

"I do!"

"Yet you'd have them suffer the disgrace of divorce in order to appease the almighty Daughters of Decency?" She looked Nancy directly in the eye. "How about *you*, Mrs. Oades? Would *you* consider giving Henry a divorce? No? I thought not!"

The earth rumbled as she spoke. They stared at each other for half a moment, frozen, poised to flee. When nothing occurred, Margaret returned to the stove. She peered into the simmering soup and changed the subject by complimenting the aroma. They courteously discussed the ingredients like two strangers, debating whether or not to cut up an onion, which added nice piquancy but gave Nancy gas. Josephine came into the kitchen and went for her apron.

Nancy scraped back in her chair and started to rise. "Do you want me to stay? Or will I only be in the way?"

"Do stay," said Margaret, with some authority. Nancy sat back down like a schoolgirl. Margaret presented her with a knife and onion, having unilaterally decided to spike the soup with indigestion.

All She Knew
for Certain

THERE WAS A GOUGE in the side of the overturned privy, as if someone had used a crowbar. Nancy sent Josephine to Henry with a note.

A prankster knocked over the privy. I so wish you were home.

Word came back that the privy would be righted before supper, and it was. *It is killing me, this,* he wrote. *I miss you terribly.*

And Nancy missed him, more than she could have imagined. She said so in a subsequent note, asking at the same time about Mr. Strickland. *Has agreement been reached?*

Henry sent John to tell her in person. "You are to be patient, Father says."

"I've been nothing *but* patient, tell him."

John turned red, stammering, "Under no circumstances are you to call upon the Stricklands again."

"Tell my Lord and Master his bossy wish is my command."

"Yes, ma'am." John turned to go.

"Wait, John. Just tell him we are anxious to know the details, tell him in a nice way. And tell him I asked after his catarrh. Tell him I hope the honey and warm water solution brought some relief. Remember to say it as I said it, all right? Say it sweetly."

Nancy received no response that day.

The following Sunday, the privy was stolen and carted clean away. A wagon would have been necessary, some plotting and planning by more than one. Notes were again exchanged. Lumber was scarce because of the earthquake, Henry wrote, as were bricks and mortar. All supplies were at a premium, but there might be some old logs available soon. *Will that do, my love?*

Whatever you think best, she wrote. She and Margaret and the girls had pretty much resigned themselves to the inconvenience of chamber pots. All things considered, it was not the end of the world.

Mr. Grimes showed up the next morning unexpectedly, asking the same questions, confirming the date of Margaret's abduction, etcetera, etcetera. Nancy need not worry her pretty head, he said for the umpteenth time. As he was leaving, he told them that the trial date had been moved back. A portion of the courthouse roof had collapsed during the earthquake. It would be December at the earliest, he said apologetically. "If we're lucky."

"That's almost two months from now!" said Nancy.

"I know you want it over and done with, Mrs. Oades," he said. "So do I."

Nancy was glad for the extension. Mr. Grimes had mistaken shocked relief for disappointment. She'd begun to think that time was running out for them, that they might be made to suffer the trial after all. At dinner, she and Margaret discussed the wisdom of going to see Mildred Strickland again, speaking in couched terms in front of the children. They had not told them they were leaving. The girls missed their father. His absence, the glaring empty chair at the head of the table confused them. The situation was complicated enough already.

They ate in the kitchen that noon, as they often did now. John had raced through his meal in silence and then asked to be excused. The girls remained, dawdling over rhubarb pie.

"I might pay a call this afternoon," Nancy said to Margaret. "If you'll look after Gertrude."

"Perhaps tomorrow would be better," said Margaret, standing, beginning to clear the plates. "Henry was mending the fence down by the road only an hour ago. You'd risk rousing his . . ." she glanced down at Josephine ". . . interest."

"You think I don't know you're up to something," said Josephine. "But I do."

Nancy spent the afternoon in the front room instead, boxing up the surviving bric-a-brac, feeling better once finished, steps closer to their new life.

It rained the next two days, the skies clearing finally on Friday. That same morning John came to the back door with a note from Henry. Mr. Strickland had rescinded his offer due to the damage done by the earthquake.

Try not to worry, sweetheart. We shall prevail.

Margaret was in the kitchen too, on her knees, rubbing kerosene into the wood. Mildred Strickland coveted Nancy's wood floor over her own ugly linoleum. How many times had she said so?

"Try not to worry," muttered Nancy, tearing the note in two.

Margaret sat back on her heels. "Have faith. He means what he says."

Nancy rolled her eyes. "Not you, too, Margaret." She went upstairs, flinging herself on the bed. She stared at a Texas-shaped stain in the ceiling, smelling Gertrude in her crib, her dirty diaper. A man can't be married to two women. That was all Nancy knew for certain.

❖❖

SIX WEEKS WENT BY. Nancy slept past noon on the best days, didn't sleep at all on the worst. On the morning of the trial she was not able to fasten her blue wedding skirt. Margaret came in to help, tugging on both ends of the waistband. They stood before the cracked mirror in the bedroom, Nancy swearing under her breath. "Damn it all."

Margaret squatted, squinting directly at the problem. As if she might will away Nancy's thick middle by glaring at it. Moving the button an inch hadn't done any good. Nancy was simply too fat, and she had no one to blame but herself. She'd been like a sow at her trough these last weeks, living on flapjacks, butter, syrup, and bacon. Margaret and Josephine had kept to schedule, putting on a normal supper at five, coaxing Nancy to join them. Nancy sat down with them a few times, but mostly she'd cooked for herself, always flapjacks, because they required no concentration.

Margaret pressed on Nancy's corseted ribs, as if to move them inward. "Nice deep breath now."

Francis had always preferred a trim figure, threatening to padlock the cupboards should Nancy become as stout as Mrs. Jenkins, the pharmacist's enormous wife. Henry had never voiced his preference one way or the other. Francis was so youthful in memory, especially when compared to Henry. Nancy was actually older than Francis had been when he died, a strange realization. A boy's ashes reposed inside her top bureau drawer. And she'd thought him such a grown, worldly man.

Margaret gritted what teeth she had left, exposing sore-looking gums. "I've nearly got it. Gently does it. Hold your breath."

Nancy should have noticed the condition of Margaret's mouth before now and found another dentist. She was no good to anyone anymore. Two days ago she'd let Gertrude's first birthday pass without as much as a celebratory flapjack. She'd plain forgotten.

That was the day the hooligans drove by on a lark, at least a dozen on a straw ride.

"Hello, Mormons! Hot enough for you today? It's not half as hot as where you're going!"

There were females among the boys and men. Nancy heard them. They were the ones who should stand trial, not she and Henry. They threw rocks at the house and started Gertrude and Martha yowling their heads off. The whole gay raft of them should be put away for life, the ringleader hanged. Lord forgive her, she was that angry and frightened.

"It's no use," said Margaret, letting go with an apologetic wheeze.

Nancy stepped out of the cursed skirt and kicked it aside. "It's a sign."

"It's nothing of the sort," said Margaret, picking up the skirt. She shook it out and smoothed the pleats. "Perhaps a small brandy would steel your nerves. Shall I go downstairs and fetch it?"

"Will you have one, too?"

"If it would help," said Margaret.

"Never mind," said Nancy. "It's getting late. I'd need way yonder more than a small one, anyway." She decided on the suit coat, her last option, a hot vise of unforgiving garment.

John drove Nancy into town, escorting her up the courthouse steps, where Henry and Mr. Grimes stood waiting at the entrance, along with three-quarters of the Berkeley populace, it seemed. Henry's black broadcloth hung on him like a shroud; his cheekbones jutted. Their eyes met briefly before Mr. Grimes came between them, locking on to their forearms, steering them inside, speaking low and close. "Say nothing, Mrs. Oades." Someone called from behind, a friendly male voice.

"Mrs. Oades, over here, please."

Nancy turned, coming face-to-face with a horrible sweating

man. He pursed his lips as if to kiss her. *Disgusting*. "Ignore them," said Mr. Grimes. "Pretend they don't exist." She was walking much faster now, eyes cast down, marble floor swimming by in a blur.

They entered an anteroom just off the courtroom. Henry came to her the moment Mr. Grimes closed the door, embracing her and whispering husky endearments. "Darling girl, lovely girl."

"Oh, Henry." She was a heartsick, perspiring hippopotamus. There was nothing *lovely* about her.

"We haven't much time," said Mr. Grimes.

Nancy pulled away from Henry. She felt the room's warm air seeping inside her clothes, causing them to shrink. The suit coat was unbearably tight now.

"How long should the proceeding take?" asked Henry.

Mr. Grimes riffled through some papers. "I expect to be finished today."

Nancy pressed a hankie to the back of her neck. "Finished?"

He looked at her impatiently. "Finished. Done. Complete. *Fini*."

"And then?"

"And then you and your husband will go home, have a merry Christmas, and live happily ever after, as they say."

Henry took her hand. "Are you well, Nan?"

Nancy forgave him the idiotic question, probing Mr. Grimes. "Are you truly all that confident?"

"Madam, I am ninety-nine and forty-four hundredths confident. Just like the floating soap. Now with all due respect, I must advise you not to fidget as you've been doing. Don't tug on your earring; don't pull on your clothes. Sit up straight once inside, hold your chin high. You have been unjustly accused and you must act the part. Do you have any further questions?"

Festive sounds could be heard from the courtroom next door, a muffle of excited conversation and laughter. Almost as if a party was getting under way. "I guess not," she said. A man can't be married to two women. That's all she knew.

The three went in, taking their places at the defendant's table, Henry on one side of Mr. Grimes, Nancy on the other. The spectators were everywhere a body might go, packed in the aisle, perched on the windowsills like turkey vultures waiting. They were dressed nicely for the most part, as if for church or a hanging.

The judge entered and everyone stood. Nancy whispered, "Where's the jury?"

Mr. Grimes whispered back. "No jury."

Judge Billings alone held their fate. Why had no one bothered to inform her?

Mr. Hiram Teal, the district attorney, was a clean-shaven ham. He stood like Moses, his eyes fixed on the frescoed ceiling. "Bigamy is a sin against God."

"Amen," a woman shouted. The gavel came down. The audaciously calm Mr. Teal did not as much as blink. "There is no sense in belaboring the fact, no point in debating. It is as certain as the sun rises in the east and sets in the glorious west. Bigamy is a grievous sin against God." Mr. Teal paused to drink water. "Bigamy is also against the law."

From behind jackals began whispering. Judge Billings glared and they ceased. On Nancy's left, shiny-domed Mr. Grimes studied handwritten notes, penciling in something now, not paying attention. He was unfortunately homely, a frog-lipped troll of a man next to handsome Mr. Teal, whose honeyed baritone oozed like righteous music.

"In 1854 the Republican party declared polygamy and slavery the twin relics of barbarism. In 1862 Congress outlawed plural marriage. More acts forbidding polygamy were passed in 1882 and 1887." Mr. Teal ticked off the dates on his fingers, as if the spectators were to commit them to memory.

"In 1890 the Mormon Church advised members to abstain from polygamy. Why then? Why a full twenty-eight years after polygamy was outlawed? Not because they'd come to recognize the degenerate error of their ways at long last, I will assure you. No, it was because statehood would have otherwise been denied them, and because they wished certain properties returned to them. Those were the only two reasons. They had no intention of rebuking Satan, no intention of adhering to the law of the land. They went right on with their sordid debaucheries, just as the defendants here before us have. Mr. Henry Oades is lawfully married to Mrs. Margaret Oades, as it was recently proved in this very same courtroom." Mr. Teal looked their way for the first time, aiming a cocked thumb and forefinger. "He therefore cannot be married to this lady, Mrs. Nancy Foreland."

Nancy lifted her chin and stared him dead in the eye. To her surprise he smiled a boyish smile. "The state has no real issue with Mrs. Foreland," he said. "She is a widow with a child. We have no wish to see her incarcerated, so long as Henry Oades is dealt with swiftly and appropriately."

Again came whispering from behind, coughing, an audible belch, the scratching of a dozen pencils. Judge Billings brought down his gavel. "Get on with it. Call your first witness."

Trying to read the judge was like trying to read a slab of granite. He sucked continuously on his pipe, exhaling a clove-scented smoke. Nancy could smell it in her gloves and taste it in her throat.

"The state calls Miss Dora McGinnis."

Dora sashayed forward, taking the oath, raising the wrong hand at first. A demure smile thinned her lips, belying the rabid plan to fix Nancy's hash once and for all. She'd probably laid awake all night thinking about retribution. Mr. Teal bowed slightly before her. Dora leaned forward, her big black eyes widening in anticipation. Mr. Teal would validate her grievance and make public the comeuppance. Oh, it was a glorious moment for the amoral little saucepot. To add to the insult she was wearing Nancy's serge day skirt. Nancy had worn the skirt no more than a dozen times before letting it out and giving it to Dora.

Mr. Teal spoke softly. "Are you nervous, Dora?"

"No, your honor."

Laughter came from both sides of the courtroom. Mr. Teal glanced over his shoulder, frowning, and turned back to Dora, correcting her. "Only Judge Billings is referred to as your honor. I am merely Mr. Teal."

She nodded agreeably. "Yes, sir."

"Please state your relationship to the defendants." Dora puckered in confusion. "Please state your relationship to Mr. Oades and Mrs. Foreland."

"I was their girl-of-all-tasks for a time," said Dora. "I broke my back trying to please."

"You lived in?"

"Yes," said Dora. "I was assigned a tiny rathole."

Nancy's insides clenched. She'd saved Dora from a drunken brute of a father.

Mr. Teal touched Dora's shoulder. "And who else lived under the same roof while you were there, Dora?"

"Mr. and Mrs. Oades, old Mrs. Oades, John Oades, and the children, Gertrude and Martha. I forget the oldest girl's name, the afflicted one."

"Now you say Mrs. Oades and *old* Mrs. Oades. You were instructed to address both ladies by the same name?"

"I was."

"Would you say that either Mrs. Oades lived there under duress?" Again Dora looked as if she'd been asked to solve an impossible arithmetic problem. "Did they live there under their own free will, Dora? Did you ever witness either lady being whipped? Strapped? Beaten?"

"No, sir. They was both free to come and go as they pleased. Nobody laid a hand on them that I ever saw."

"Did you ever witness any religious rituals taking place, say any special lighting of candles, any chanting, any peculiar worship involving Mr. Oades and the two ladies?"

Dora chewed on the question for a moment, finally saying no, but that's not the same as saying it did not occur. "I might have been in the kitchen while it was going on," she said. "They kept me there day and night."

Nancy glared, her hands fisting. *Liar!* She'd had Sunday afternoons free and every other Wednesday.

"No further questions," said Mr. Teal.

Judge Billings thrust his chin toward Mr. Grimes. "Counselor?"

Mr. Grimes did not bother to stand. "Did you leave the household of your own volition, miss? Or were you let go?"

Dora looked at Nancy. "Let go. And I'm glad that I was."

She was excused. Their hand, Titus Crump, was called next. He was dressed in collar and tie, looking as if he'd just put down a favorite horse. Nancy could not imagine what Mr. Teal expected from his loyal lips. Nothing incriminating it turned out, as Nancy had expected.

"I would have no way of knowing, sir," he said, when asked the same questions.

Mr. Grimes declined to question Titus.

Mrs. Charles Middleton of the Daughters of Decency was called. She floated up the aisle, refined and stylish, wearing a beautiful polka-dotted silk, with leg-o'-mutton sleeves. Nancy had so admired her at one time, for all the good she did, working tirelessly for orphans and widows.

On the stand, Mrs. Middleton spoke in a quiet, affectionate tone, saying she felt for Nancy, calling her a motherless wayward who just hadn't known any better.

"I pray for her every day," she said. Nancy bowed her head,

mortified. She did not look up again until Mrs. Middleton had stepped down and gone beyond her ken.

Mrs. Knox, the poundmaster's wife, a woman known to horse-whip the strays, came next. "They are not denying the situation," she said. "Why are we wasting precious time and money on this ridiculous circus?"

She was followed by Deputy Ingram, who only repeated in different words her same testimony. Henry Oades was an unabashed bigamist, and Nancy Foreland was his willing partner in sin. It was simply a matter of determining the punishment.

Mr. Grimes looked up wearily and said for the fourth time, "No questions for the witness." Nancy and Henry turned to him at the same time. Why wasn't the lawyer speaking up in their defense, exposing the vicious, ugly lies?

The state rested then. It was their turn.

Mr. Grimes started to rise, not quickly, but slowly, arthritically. He bent, bracing himself against the table before coming to a full stand, allowing the spectators a broad view of his rumpled backside. They stirred, snickering and whispering, causing the gavel to come down. The judge scowled, clearly blaming the turtle-slow Mr. Grimes for the disorder.

"My clients," Mr. Grimes began, the words catching in a throat rusty from disuse.

Nancy felt a sharp pang in her side, along with an equally sharp sense of doom. She felt Mr. Teal's eyes on her and glanced his way. He began tapping a pencil to his temple, as if marking time, theirs, ticking by.

A Christmas Duck

M R. GRIMES CLEARED HIS THROAT and began again. "My clients are not Mormons." A woman close by whispered, "Prevaricator!" The gavel came down hard. Mr. Grimes gave no indication he'd heard her. He stood between Henry and Nancy, speaking to the judge alone. "Up until recently, they have been tithing members in good standing of First Congregational."

A partial truth. She, though not Henry, had been a tithing member in good standing, sliding after Francis died, quitting altogether once moving so far out. Nancy became aware of herself shaking her head with regret and stopped, clenching her teeth to keep her brain still, clasping her gloved hands in her lap. A brown spot stained the thumb tip, dirt or blood.

"Mr. Oades, an Englishman, was baptized in the Anglican Church," said Mr. Grimes. "I have the certificate here." The sleepy bailiff came alive and sauntered over to receive the document. Mr. Grimes pulled Nancy's baptismal certificate from his papers. "Take this, too."

If only he'd treated Dora to the same authoritative bite.

"Mrs. Nancy Oades was baptized a Baptist at age twelve in Brenham, Texas. Shortly thereafter, at age fourteen, she came to Berkeley, where she resided with Mr. and Mrs. C. D. Dwyer, her maternal great-uncle and -aunt until their deaths in 1896 and '97, respectively."

Mr. Grimes went on to cite her uncle's credentials. Chester D. Dwyer had been a deacon, an elder, the men's Sunday school teacher. His name was engraved on two church plaques.

Judge Billings sucked on his pipe as he studied the birth certificates.

"And so quite clearly," said Mr. Grimes, "my clients are not Mormons. Though if they were, it would not have the least bearing on this case."

The judge shifted, grimacing as if with pain. "We'll take a ten-minute recess."

Nancy, Henry, and Mr. Grimes escaped to the side room. Henry and Nancy sat, Henry scraping his chair close to hers. Mr. Grimes remained standing, reading his notes.

Nancy peeled off the soiled glove and inspected her ragged, bleeding thumbnail. "I thought it was important that you prove we're not Mormons."

Mr. Grimes murmured without looking up, "It's not."

Nancy sucked the tip of her thumb, cleaning away the blood. "Well, I don't really understand then. What will you say next, sir?"

The lawyer lowered the paper, his face creased with impatience. "The facts, madam. I will convey the legal facts. Now please cease and desist with that infernal fidgeting."

Henry bristled with insult. "Sir!"

Nancy petted his knee. "Never mind, dear, never mind." Henry's complexion was unhealthily red. A pulsing place close to his ear looked ready to burst. He could keel over dead here and now. Would that satisfy the bloodthirsty hellhounds?

Mr. Grimes put his ear to the courtroom door, listening for a moment, and turning back to Nancy. "Another point, Mrs. Oades. Please refrain from those constant sidelong glances in the court-room. You look my way every two minutes, and not with confidence, madam. You appear guilty, like black sin personified. I find it very distracting."

"I'll try not to do it again," said Nancy, detesting him completely.

Mr. Grimes offered his hand. Nancy reluctantly surrendered hers, which became sandwiched between his unpleasantly fleshy palms. "Try not to worry your pretty head, all right? Concern yourself with what you might prepare for supper this evening, why don't you? Leave the rest to me."

She pulled free of his mushy grip. "Promise me that my husband will be seated at the head of the table and I will do just that, sir."

Mr. Grimes smiled indulgently, saying nothing.

Nancy pitied his wife if he had one.

❖❖

BACK INSIDE the courtroom, Mr. Grimes stood as tall as his diminutive stature would allow and spoke to the judge in a clear monotone. "Six years ago, Mr. Oades was living in Wellington, on New Zealand's North Island. One day, in the spring of 1892, without warning, indigenous peoples, with whom the English were at relative peace, attacked the Oades home while Mr. Oades was away."

Henry bowed his head and closed his eyes.

"Mr. Oades returned to discover his home in ashes and his family gone. Human remains were found in the ruins. From this sad evidence, and from information gathered in the ensuing months, Mr. Oades was forced to accept the fact that his wife and children were dead."

Nancy dipped her chin, overcome with sadness.

Mr. Grimes glanced down, frowning, running a finger down the page to find his place again. "Loath to remain amid the sorrowful memories, Mr. Oades left New Zealand and came to California, where he became a contributing member of our community. Earlier this year, Mr. Oades married Mrs. Nancy Foreland, a widow lady with a child." Mr. Grimes paused to take a sip of water. "Mr. Oades presumed himself a widower. And rightfully, lawfully so. My clients' marriage was valid then and it is valid now under the second subdivision of the sixty-first section of the civil code, which provides that the marriage of a person having a former husband or wife living is void unless such former husband or wife was absent and not known to be living for five consecutive years preceding the subsequent marriage!"

The judge's rimless spectacles rode down his shiny broken-veined beak. "Bring me the law." A paper was handed to the bailiff. The judge snatched it up, standing, as did they all, making a great collective questioning noise about it. "We'll resume in an hour," he said, stalking off.

Mr. Grimes touched her elbow. "You may be seated now, Mrs. Oades. He's left."

Henry came around Mr. Grimes, pulling out Nancy's chair. "Sit, darling."

Nancy sat, dizzy with confusion, her ears ringing. Behind her a knot of angry spectators spewed curses. She and Henry would rot in hell. They'd burn for all eternity. Hanging was too good for them. From the back of the room came singing, "A mighty fortress is our God." Nancy buried her face in a fold of her arms and tried in vain to drown them out with prayer. *Please, God. Shut them up.*

The off-key singing grew louder. A man shouted, "Look at the adulteress talking to herself! She's mad, batty as a bedbug!" Someone, Henry or Mr. Grimes, patted her shoulder. Nancy went on praying, begging God for unconsciousness.

The judge returned, visibly angry. He didn't bother to sit. "I have no choice but to dismiss. Court adjourned."

A new din started up. Nancy raised her voice to be heard. "It's over?"

"It's over!" Mr. Grimes shouted. Above, in the balcony, a woman shrieked. Something red came flying over their heads. Nancy turned, ducking, narrowly avoiding the second tomato. Raw eggs were hurled, an apple core, a melon rind. She stooped and scooped up a rotten handful from the floor, preparing to return fire.

"Nan!" Henry caught her in a tight grip, squeezing her arms to her sides. Juices ran through her fingers, staining her skirt. "Come quickly, sweetheart. We're going home now."

Nancy stumbled forward numbly, her mind transporting her, giving her wings. The spectators were below her now. She stomped on their cruel, thick heads on the way out, not missing a single one.

◆◇◆

CHRISTMAS CAME the following week. Only the duck was delivered. They'd ordered a bushel of oranges too, and sugared filberts, candles, potatoes, coffee, and brandy. There'd been a long list of special things. Nancy could not recall what all now. They'd ordered most of it months ago, from various merchants. None of it came.

"We have the main feature at least," said Margaret, kneading dough for her apple crumble. The duck had been left in a basket out by the gate. The butcher's boy hadn't even come to the door to collect his holiday dime.

"The lad didn't want to be seen on the pariah's doorstep," said Margaret, laughing to herself.

"I don't find it one bit amusing," said Nancy, sampling Margaret's simmering cider. The duck was soaking in milk to draw out the strong taste. He was a big one, with nice fat breasts. "We deserve to be left alone just as much as the next law-abiding person."

"We do," said Margaret. Gertrude let out a contented noise. The baby stood inside her crate, clinging to the rim. She'd taken her first wobbly steps recently, making Nancy deliriously proud.

"Those were my exact words to Henry last night," said Nancy. "I'm not asking for the moon with a fence around it, I said. I simply want a little peace and quiet."

"And?"

"And he agreed wholeheartedly. He promised to have the roof and chimney repaired, the butchering shed and privy rebuilt. If there's time we'll give the house a fresh coat. I said you and I could paint the first floor ourselves."

"We could," said Margaret.

"And then so long, farewell, and *adios*, as my daddy used to say. Let Beelzebub himself buy the place. Won't that be a glorious day?"

Margaret nodded. "It will indeed."

◈◈

AN HOUR LATER, Nancy pulled the limp duck from its soak and gently dried it all over, vaguely recalling her mother cautioning not to bruise the breast. She minced celery to go inside, mixing it with sage leaves, mace, and nutmeg. She was feeling less melancholy by now. It was Christmas after all, her first with Henry. There was a hot festive smell in the air. Margaret began humming "Jingle Bells" under her breath. Nancy joined in, entertaining Gertrude. They were as merry as regular people until Nancy reached inside the duck and pulled out a trio of dead mice. They were pink-pawed babies, tied together with bright red ribbon. Nancy flung the bound vermin across the room, gray fur clinging to her sweating palm. They hit the wall, breaking apart, holiday ribbon fluttering. "Jesus," she breathed, pumping water, washing her hands. "Jesus, Jesus, Jesus."

Margaret pitched the duck and the mice out the back door. The mean brown dogs came running, barking excitedly. Margaret stepped back inside, wrapping herself in the old wool shawl, and taking the small ax hanging next to the door. "We'll have a pullet," she said. "It'll be every bit as good."

Gertrude fell back on her diapered rump and began a hiccupy cry. Margaret set the ax aside and went to her, plucking the baby from her crate.

"What if I hadn't planned a stuffing?" said Nancy. "What if I'd cooked the duck plain, come to the table proud as a peacock, having roasted the mice to a perfect turn? Our first Christmas! And what do I put before my husband? Piping hot rodents!"

"Please do stop," said Margaret, suppressing a smile.

"It's no laughing matter!"

Martha came in, bug-eyed curious. Gertrude wailed on. Nancy took the ax and went into the cold yard alone, terrifying dogs be damned. She meant to kill something. The ugly mongrels would be wise to keep their distance.

A True Wife

MARGARET AWOKE sticky-tongued and confused, still in the throes of a disturbing dream. Martha was pressed close, bony knees drawn up, jabbing the small of Margaret's back. Martha complained regularly of having to sleep in the middle. It's the lot of the youngest, Margaret told her. They'd have the bed to themselves soon enough, once Josephine married and left the nest. That hadn't been good enough for the little miss. She'd suggested rotating every third week. The situation wasn't democratic, she'd said. *Democratic*. Margaret had no idea where she got it.

She pushed gently. Martha rolled into snoring Josephine, who opened one cranky eye and gave a shove. Pheeny was bleeding for the first time, which made Margaret feel impossibly old. Margaret had prepared her, refraining from calling it curse or blessing. Her big girl knew all about cramps and pins and rags, but was still incredulously indignant when it came. As if she'd figured herself exempt somehow.

The dream had begun as a familiar one. It was dark. An open window allowed a breeze. She was naked beneath thick soft blankets with Henry, or a Henry hybrid. There was something of Captain Fisk in the man, as well as someone else she couldn't identify. They were kissing as usual, quite passionately. And here the dream typically ended. This time there was sudden light, horribly harsh and glaring. The man saw her face and was incensed. He began hitting her over and over, bellowing that she'd tricked him. She was shouting, *It is I! It is I!* But he went on beating and berating her. Margaret blamed the New Year's eggnog for the nightmare. One of Henry's eggnogs would intoxicate a rhinoceros. They'd all had two.

Today was the first of January 1900. Time had run out on the year and century both. Last week, on Christmas morning, Henry presented Margaret with a handsome calendar.

"Just a token," he'd said shyly.

"But I've nothing for you."

She'd given plenty, he'd said, or words to that effect. From Nancy she received a length of Duchess lace. "To smarten up your good dress, Margaret." Margaret accepted the gifts into her lap and made an appropriate fuss. Of course they hadn't intended to make her feel small.

She'd spent the last of her wages earned on board the *Golden State* months ago, at the Palace Hotel, proudly insisting on paying a share of the bill. Nancy had been too inebriated to notice the five-dollar note, and Margaret had been too inebriated to think prudently and ask for change. The money might have gone toward a reciprocal token of her own—handkerchiefs for Henry, gloves for Nancy, something of that nature. Instead she'd sat like a side of cold mutton, unable to contribute so much as a halfpenny sweet.

A true wife needed no purse of her own. She more than earned her allowance. But Margaret was not a true wife anymore. She resided in a peculiar limbo all her own. She'd considered hiring herself out as tutor or nanny, contemplated putting up seasonal jams, knitting booties and caps. The knitting idea had her spinning for days. She'd gone as far as designing a fancy label—her initials done in a monkish script, flanked by two winged sprites. It turned out rather nice, vaguely French. She'd shown the drawing to Martha, but to no one else. The entire idea was naturally ludicrous. She'd have no clientele, not here, not now. She had no choice but to wait until they arrived at the new place. Henry saw to the children's needs, so she didn't require much, just a small stipend of her own to hoard or squander as she saw fit.

Margaret slipped out of bed without waking her girls and went down the dark stairs to the kitchen. She scooped out the ashes and put on more wood. John was already gone, up and at his chores. He'd taken to this hardworking life as if born to it. Henry called John his right-hand *man*. Not a whisker on the lad's chin! Still, his own mother could not deny the obvious. He was nearly eighteen. And Pheeny was bleeding. How impossible to have two so close to grown. She wondered if Henry had considered John's tainted future. Eligible girls would not be queuing up to vie for the Mormon's son's attention. Margaret could not bear the thought of her son compromising, marrying a promiscuous guttersnipe the likes of Dora McGinnis. He would not resign himself to a bookish bachelorhood, that much was certain. He had already demonstrated his abject weakness there, with wanton Dora herself. Would that not be a feather in her slatternly cap? She'd have John jumping through flaming hoops simply because she could. And her randy son would gladly leap, of course. Off he'd go, with Josephine and Martha following like dominos. They'd leave, as she herself had, as all normal children do eventually, for good. Then Gerty would go. Good God, how would it be then, with just the three of them? What if Nancy were to die first? Would she and Henry come together in their dotage? Tears sprang to Margaret's eyes, recalling his embrace the night he was told about her mum and dad. She'd relived the brief encounter a thousand times since. *Stop it*, she told herself. *Enough of this now.* She blotted her eyes on a dish towel. Her brain was a maudlin hodgepodge this morning, thanks to the eggnog. It would be a long while before she had another.

She put the kettle on for tea. They'd been without coffee for more than a fortnight now.

Ten minutes later, Nancy came down, looking at odds with the universe. She was dressed for the day, wearing the winter house frock, a brown checked wool that looked on its second seam in places. Her engorged bosom strained at the fabric. "The water's boiling."

"And a very good morning to you, too, Nancy."

Nancy sat, drumming on the table. "Where are the eggs?"

Margaret moved the kettle and collected the tea things. "I've not been out yet."

Nancy came to her feet, snatching the egg basket from its peg. "I'll just do it myself."

"Are you having your monthly?"

Nancy snapped, "No."

Margaret turned from the stove, holding the kettle in a dish towel. Nancy was on the brink of tears. "The eggs can wait. Let's have a cup."

Nancy pulled out the chair and sat hard, like a sulky tot in need of a sugar tit. "My monthly hasn't come in a while."

Margaret set down the kettle. "Do you think?"

"I don't know what to think."

Margaret had been thrilled to learn from John that Gerty wasn't Henry's. She'd taken great pride in being the only mother to his children.

Nancy looked at Margaret. "I haven't been sick, not even once."

"That's a good thing."

"I still could be?"

Margaret brought two cups, tea sloshing at the rims. "Yes." She sat down beside Nancy and patted her cold hand, a mix of jealousy and sadness stirring. Without tangible proof, Margaret was typically able to banish unwanted thoughts, images of her husband and Nancy making love. "Does Henry know?"

Nancy's eyes filled with watery anguish. "No. I didn't think there was anything to tell."

Once, a long time ago in England, when Margaret was overdue with Josephine, Henry, in an attempt to cheer, popped into their room naked as a robin, and danced an Irish jig. A neighbor's maid caught him. "Draw yer curtains," she'd yelled from below. "I see yer old bum!"

"What's so funny, Margaret?"

"Not a thing," said Margaret, shaking her head. She took her shawl from the back of the chair and swathed Nancy in it. "You should tell him. He'll want to be in on it from the start."

"I suppose," said Nancy. "I still don't know for sure myself."

"I tended to know straight off," said Margaret.

Nancy slurped noisily, her loose scraggly hair falling forward. She muttered something about Margaret being an expert at it.

"I was fortunate that way," said Margaret, standing. "I'll fetch the eggs. You stay in, drink your tea. It'll settle you."

Nancy spoke to her cup. "Did you ever consider taking measures to reverse your fortune?"

"Never." Margaret had heard of desperate mothers. She was aware of herbal concoctions, of long carriage rides over hilly terrain, the use of toilet articles, hairpins and combs, knives and knitting needles. "What are you considering, Nancy?"

Nancy picked absentmindedly at a blemish. Blood appeared on her chin. She licked her finger and smeared a red circle. "It was terrifying last time. The pain was terrible. Nobody told me how bad it would be. I kept screaming for Francis." She looked up at Margaret. "I'd never felt so alone in my life."

Margaret sat again. "You won't be alone this time." The midwife's carriage had gotten stuck in the mud. Mary had already come by the time she arrived. Martha was on the way. "You'll have Henry."

"I know," said Nancy, nodding, rubbing her belly. "I didn't mean what I said about . . . you know. It's not the poor baby's fault."

Henry had held slippery Mary in his two big hands, staring down in ecstatic wonder. It was a sight few wives get to witness, a transformation Margaret would never forget.

"And you'll have me," she said softly. "If you need me."

Elsewhere

A s HEAVY AS SHE WAS, Nancy felt lighter than down. It was official. They *were* leaving. It was only a matter of selling the farm for the best price. Henry didn't even say *right* or *fair* price anymore, just best.

Several well-to-do gentlemen had come out to look. Recently, on a beautiful Sunday afternoon, a professor from the university rode up with his wife. Nancy spent a full hour giving Mrs. Meyer a tour of the house. The lady admired her clean kitchen aloud and fingered the lace curtains on the sly, clearly interested.

"Don't be so sure of yourself," Henry said afterward. "Professor Meyer said he wanted to sleep on it."

"That's just something men say," said Nancy. "His wife will have the last word, you'll see. She's that type."

They'd talked about other places. Henry suggested Colorado Springs, where a good many British had settled. (Nancy had said no to Colorado without explanation, feeling outnumbered enough as it was.) Henry also mentioned Los Angeles, where oil had opened up all sorts of opportunities. It was much warmer there, he said, more healthful.

"I only wish to see you content and thriving, darling girl," he said.

"I will be," said Nancy. "The moment we're gone from here."

They ultimately agreed upon San Francisco, a world away, and just across the bay.

To be elsewhere when this baby was born was all Nancy asked for.

A boy this time. She'd put good money on it. The hair on her legs was unusually coarse. He lay high (yet another sign) and quietly. Gertrude had thrashed without letup from the get-go. This baby was amazingly considerate, sleeping when she slept, moving with her rather than against her. Nancy had come to love him in a way she hadn't known was possible.

Henry was beside himself with happiness. He caressed her belly late at night, speaking to their son, telling him how courageous his *mum* was, how kind and lovely. The little conversations might be the reason for the baby's quietude. Gertrude had received no such gentleness. Nancy had wept and retched the entire time with her, which probably caused her rebellion. The womb would have been a tumultuous place for her little girl. And yet Gertrude seemed to hold none of it against her now. Margaret said just the other day, "See how her eyes light up when you come in."

Nancy was dead set on making amends. That is not to say she planned on spoiling her children rotten. She'd be every bit as strict as the next mother, as strict as Margaret herself. But she would also read with them nightly, as Margaret did with hers. She would pay close attention, remember every birthday. This she solemnly vowed. Gertrude need never know how her mother once was.

Today was the big shopping day. Nancy and Margaret were on their way to the ferry dock at last, with John driving. The blue sky dazzled. Nancy bounced along, feeling extravagantly weighty, and proud of it for a change.

They needed traveling bags, and at least one sturdy trunk. Gloves and shoes were on the list, and a big jar of Pond's extract to replace the jar that had broken. Her complexion had gone from bad to worse since the earthquake. Forget what they say about a glowing mother-to-be. She was as radiant as a warty toad. They also needed foodstuffs to see them to moving day. The local merchants couldn't be trusted after the mice.

They expected to find everything they needed at the Emporium in San Francisco. Nancy had read that if a product wasn't sold there, it didn't exist. She and Margaret were both keyed up, having waited like impatient children for nearly a month. The butchering was going on, and the men were moving the fodder from the fields to the barnyard. John could not be spared for the longest time.

She'd wheedled. "Let Margaret drive us."

Henry refused to budge. "I won't have you going down to the docks unescorted. It isn't safe."

"But it's perfectly safe for us to be roaming the streets of San Francisco unescorted, I suppose." That had started him worrying all over again. She'd come this close to forfeiting the trip altogether with the stupid remark.

Margaret claimed she needed nothing, which wasn't true. She needed shoes too, as did Josephine and Martha. They all needed winter hats. Nancy wanted pipe tobacco for Henry, drawers and a decent suit for John. And newspapers. The paper was once the highlight of Henry's evening. He'd canceled the subscription after the last editorial. The *Gazette* wrote that something needed to be done about the Oades family, that the law had been made a mockery of, that the three were thumbing their noses at decent society. The press was determined not to let the matter drop. To the devil with the lot of them, Henry said last night.

John flicked the whip lightly and Bonnie picked up the pace. Beside John lay a bouquet of yellow field flowers, dirt and roots still clinging. Margaret adjusted her collar and blanket and leaned forward. "Lovely posies," she said.

John murmured, "They're all right."

Margaret cleared her throat and spoke up. "Who might the fortunate recipient be?"

"Father allowed me the afternoon off."

"You deserve it, son. And how shall you spend it?"

John shrugged, saying nothing.

"Not with Dora McGinnis, I hope," said Margaret.

John rubbed the back of his neck.

"I say," said Margaret, raising her voice. "Not with Dora McGinnis, I hope."

"She's a lovely girl," said John.

"She's anything but," said Margaret, her thin gloved hands working with agitation. Poor John hunched over, a grown man's scowl creasing his forehead.

Nancy whispered to Margaret. "Let it be."

Margaret hissed back, loud enough for John to hear. "I suppose you'd like to see a son of *yours* take up with that sort."

John picked up the limp bouquet and threw it to the ground.

Margaret had him stop the buggy. She climbed down and walked the few yards back, gathering the scattered flowers as she went. She shook the flowers, as if to restore them, and offered the bunch to John.

"Forgive me," she said, blinking in the bright sunlight. He accepted the flowers without comment, straightening through the shoulders. And that was that.

On the ferry, Margaret said, "I went too far. He'll go and make an honest woman of her if only to prove me wrong."

Nancy said, "Should I have Henry speak to him?"

"Perish the thought, Nancy." Margaret asked to see the shopping list again, her way of changing the subject. Nancy brought out the list, sniffing at the briny air.

"One thing about San Francisco, it smells so fishy everywhere."

"No place on earth offends as highly as Berkeley," said Margaret.

From the ferry terminal they went by private carriage to the Emporium on Market Street. Once arrived, the driver came around to the door and assisted them down, treating them like royalty, warning them to mind their backs and watch their purses. The little kindnesses warmed Nancy. She'd forgotten how gentle strangers who don't know your business could be. She fumbled in her bag and took out an extra nickel for him. He bowed and offered to return for them at three.

The Emporium was jam-packed with red-faced customers and a staggering amount of merchandise. Booths stretched in every direction, all decorated with colorful signs, loud banners, and bunting. It was hectic, exciting, noisy, and confusing. Nancy and Margaret linked arms, zigzagging down one drafty corridor after another, spotting the high-top lace-ups on the fourth or fifth turn. "There," said Nancy, pointing. "Aren't they perfect?"

The salesman said she had impeccable taste. "Notice the smart stacked heel," he said, turning the shoe. Nancy ordered two pair, one in brown, and one in black. She was about to do the same for Margaret, but Margaret wouldn't hear of it.

"They're much too dear," she said, stubborn as a mule as usual. "They're priced well above their proper value."

Nancy argued. "They're only three dollars. I saw a pair just like them in the catalog, only not as nice, selling for three twenty-five."

"A pair each for the girls," said Margaret. "Mine will do a while longer."

"Suit yourself," said Nancy, scribbling out shipping instructions for the clerk, ordering two pair for all four of them. She purchased hats and gloves in the same surreptitious manner. Margaret desperately needed the things, Lord knows. Those raggedy patched shoes of hers looked as if they'd been to Hades and back on unpaved roads. Nancy wondered if she'd always been so tight, or had the *Maw-ree* done something to make her that way?

◆◆

THEY FOUND every last item on their list and were leaving the Emporium, headed for the restaurant they'd spotted earlier, when the baby booth caught Nancy's eye. "Oh, Margaret, look!"

Nancy lifted the porcelain display baby from its cradle. It wore a delicate lacy gown and tiny shoes, and an impractical bib trimmed in eyelet, the likes of which Gertrude had never worn, having started out life in yellowed donations. Gertrude hadn't known the difference, but Nancy certainly had. She selected a christening gown and matching cap for the new baby, some precious fleecy stockings, and a wooden duck pull toy for Gertrude. It was half past three before they were on their way again. Nancy assumed the driver had come and gone, that they'd have a leisurely supper and then hire another cab later. But he was waiting at the curb, looking angry. He opened the door to the carriage and let down the steps.

Nancy started up, clumsy-footed and resentful. "You had your heart set on steak and kidney pie," she said.

"Next time," said Margaret. "We shall have opportunity galore in the future. Besides, we had quite the hearty breakfast, didn't we?"

"That was hours and hours ago. I'm famished."

"Well, then," said Margaret, extending her hand, assisting Nancy down. "We shan't be requiring your services after all," she said to the driver.

He clutched his whip in a menacing way. "You owe me."

"Let me give him something," said Nancy, nervous, her fingers stiff on the clasp of her change purse.

"No more than a nickel," said Margaret.

"A dollar," he barked. "Half a buck for the ride, another half for waiting."

Margaret gasped. "Put away your purse, Nancy. Don't give this extortive blackguard the first stiver!"

His jowly face darkened. "What did you call me?"

Margaret took Nancy by the elbow and turned her about, steering her into the crowd. She had them scurrying like guilty thieves, weaving at such a clip.

"I'm going to the cops," the driver yelled, just as they rounded the corner.

Nancy heard a piercing whistle and glanced over her shoulder, expecting to see a squadron of police bearing down. She and Margaret turned another corner and ducked into a diner, a greasy dive. The fry cook waved his spatula toward a booth. Nancy slid close to the grimy window, eyeing the brutish men at the bar. "Henry would have a seizure if he knew we were here," she said, and started to laugh. "Why am I so chickenhearted? So what if that hack called the cops? Would they have put us in jail for changing our minds?"

Margaret mopped her perspiring forehead. "Bullies," she said. "The world abounds with them."

"Well, they're not going to get the best of me anymore," said Nancy, reading the chalkboard specials on the wall. "I'm in the mood for a great big porterhouse and steam beer." Hunger and confidence always seemed to go together somehow.

"I wish I might contribute," said Margaret, when the bill came.

"You're not expected to contribute," said Nancy, counting the coins in her purse.

Margaret shifted her gaze toward the window. "Still."

"It doesn't matter, Margaret."

"It does though, Nancy. I feel like a child."

They seemed to be talking about something else now. Nancy wasn't sure what. "I only meant you weren't expected to contribute *money*. You most certainly *contribute*. My goodness! You contribute more than I do, I'm ashamed to admit. The household would fall to pieces without you. I mean it sincerely." Margaret looked unconvinced. Nancy pushed the change purse toward her. "I'm not Madam Ruby at the Texas state fair. I can't read your mind, you know. Do you want to be the one to pay the man? Is that it?"

Margaret pushed the purse back. "No, that's not it."

The baby inside was protesting the fatty porterhouse. "Well, I'm at a loss then."

"Are you feeling unwell, Nancy?"

"I have a little indigestion," said Nancy. Margaret went to the counter packed with loudmouthed men and brought back a Bromo Seltzer in a dirty glass. Nancy closed her eyes and drank, forgiving Margaret her peculiar ways.

❖❖

THEY ARRIVED in Berkeley just before dark. John saw them stepping off the ferry and came running.

"Father's been arrested again," he said. "They took him off to jail."

For a frantic half moment Nancy couldn't recall Henry's face, and then he suddenly stood illuminated in her mind, his every pore and whisker vividly defined. This is what it meant to truly go crazy, she thought.

"Take us to him," she said.

Something Demonic

$\mathcal{M}$ ARGARET COULD NOT HELP but recoil at the stench emanating from the walls of the jail, a horrible combination of mold and feces. Henry rose from his cot. "I instructed you to take them straight home," he said to John.

Nancy tucked Gerty's toy duck beneath her arm. "Don't blame John. I insisted he bring us. I was not going to take no for an answer."

On the opposite cot a man lay dead or sleeping. Both he and Henry wore gloves, hats, and overcoats. A fire blazed in the pot-bellied stove, toasting the deputy at his desk, and no one else.

Margaret met Henry's eyes as Nancy approached the bars. She'd never seen him so haggard and defeated. "Titus is keeping an eye on the girls," he said. Margaret nodded, trusting Josephine to manage without Titus. Henry and Nancy kissed briefly. Margaret lowered her gaze, stepping back, endeavoring to make herself invisible. John stood quietly in the shadows, hat in hand, his head bowed. The deputy was the only one overtly watching, having made a show of turning his chair toward the cell. He'd yet to say the first civil word, rudely pointing when they came in, expectorating into the fire.

"Now tell us exactly what happened, Henry," said Nancy. "And to whom do I pay the bail? This officer here?" She began a frantic riffle through her bag.

"Don't," Henry whispered, looking toward the deputy, a charmless cur, the sort to feed on others' misery.

Nancy went on rummaging through her bag, fretting to herself, dropping Gerty's duck in the process. It fell to the floor with a sharp crack. Margaret snatched it up by the broken beak and hid it behind her skirts. The deputy snickered, striking a match and putting it to his pipe. He sucked and coughed, drawing harder. Let him draw the pipe stem straight down his gullet. Margaret wouldn't be the one to the rescue.

Henry pleaded with Nancy. "Go on home now. Do as I say, dear girl."

Nancy's forehead glistened with perspiration, despite the cold. "Certainly, *dear man*. We'll go right home, won't we, Margaret? We'll have a nice supper, tidy up, have a hand of cards if it's not too late, say our prayers, and go to bed. We'll sleep sound as can be, not a care in the world."

Henry looked at Margaret. "Meg. Please."

Nancy clamped on to Margaret's forearm and held firm. "Now tell us what happened," she said. "We demand to know."

Henry kept his voice low, though Margaret was certain the deputy could hear every word. He'd been down on the east slope with Titus, he said. He'd known they might come today.

Nancy interrupted. "Who are *they*? Is this why you allowed us to go into the city today of all days? Just how did you know *they'd* come?"

"The case went before the grand jury a week ago," said Henry. "I should have told you before. I'm sorry. I just didn't think—"

Nancy broke in. "What case?"

Henry pressed against the bars, his chafed lips barely inches from Nancy's. Margaret felt a sad rousing, trapped appendage that she was. She stood close enough to touch and comfort him.

"They claim to have a true case for bigamy," he whispered. He had orange on his breath. Beneath his cot, next to a tray of un-eaten food, lay a curl of desiccated peel. "They don't," he said. "Believe me, Nan, they haven't a leg to stand on. Please go on home now. Consider your condition. Meg, please. Please take her home."

Righteous tears stood in Nancy's eyes. "We'll go home when we're good and ready. This isn't right, Henry. There is something demonic going on. A person can't be tried over and over. Why didn't you tell us about the grand jury?"

"I would have worried you needlessly had the prosecutor not made his case."

The other prisoner called out for Susan and began whimpering in his sleep. Margaret freed herself from Nancy's grip. "Let's do as he says." Henry's unconcealed gratitude settled upon Margaret, allying her completely. Nancy was unpredictable these days, teary and raging one moment, euphoric the next. He couldn't be blamed for not wanting to set her off. On the other hand, he might have confided in *her*, Margaret. Margaret wished he knew that he still could.

Nancy whirled on the deputy. "How much is the bail?"

The little ferret coughed up a laugh and banged his pipe on the edge of the desk. He deserved a swift kick straight to the bollocks.

Henry sighed. "No bail was granted, Nan."

"I'll stand as surety then," said Nancy, advancing on the deputy. "Will that do, sir? My aunt and uncle were pillars in this commu-nity."

The deputy cracked another filthy laugh. "Lizzie Borden her-self enjoys a better reputation than you do, miss."

Henry fisted the bars hard, making no sound. "Sir!" Nancy held up, returning to Henry, bright as a crackpot in need of medicine. "Heads are going to roll," she declared, beginning to name the steps she would take. The deputy chuckled, mocking her every fevered word. Nancy paid him no mind. She would wire the Governor's office first thing, she said, and start up a petition while she was at it. Don't think she didn't still have an influential name or two up her sleeve. She would bring Henry a clean shirt and collar, and soup. "Would you like that, dear?"

"Please don't bother," said Henry.

Nancy seemed not to hear him. "Do you need reading material, Henry? Wait. The newspapers!" She fanned herself, laughing a bit. "Why didn't you remind me, Margaret? The *Call*, the *Examiner*, the *Chronicle*! We bought all three. They're in the buggy. John, run out and bring them in, please. I left them on the floor, beneath a long box tied with twine, not ribbon, you'll see it. Deputy, will you bring my husband a lamp to read by?"

A derisive snort was the answer.

"Please, Nan," said Henry.

In the end, Henry convinced Nancy to do none of it. She capitulated finally, nodding as he spoke softly, the fight in her spent. "All right, Henry."

They agreed to go straight home. Yes, they would stay inside and keep the doors and windows locked. Nancy hung her head. "Yes, yes. We promise."

"See to it, will you, Meg?" He looked so helpless in that cage, so utterly knocked off his pins. You must bear it, she'd say if he asked. Margaret knew firsthand. You must do as they say and bear it. Try not to go insane for the children's sake. It's all you can do.

On the way home Nancy complained that the baby was restless. "Kicking up a storm," she said.

"They'll do that," said Margaret, adjusting Nancy's blanket. "A hot bath will help."

Nancy began to weep, rubbing her belly as she did. "I just want to lie down. I just want to lie down and cry it all away."

Margaret moved closer. They rode huddled for miles, not speaking in the shivery, juddering dark. From behind, John's shoulders appeared so broad. Yet another reminder. She could not get used to the man he nearly was.

"Are you warm enough?" he asked, glancing around. Even his voice seemed octaves lower tonight.

At home, Nancy wanted to take the toy duck upstairs, and leave it next to Gerty's crib so that she would see it first thing. "That's the last straw!" Nancy cried, seeing it broken. "That's the last damn straw!" She refused offers of bath and tea, and stomped up to her room. Margaret went to check on Josephine and Martha. They were awake, roused by Nancy's tirade. "Go back to sleep," Margaret whispered. "It's all over now. Everything's fine."

"We saw the men take our dad," said Martha.

"We saw from the window," said Josephine.

"Oh, dear," said Margaret, wearily. She undressed without lighting a lamp and slipped in beside them. "I was going to wait and tell you in the morning. What little there is to tell."

"Tell us now," said Josephine. "And don't make up a story."

"No sass, please, Pheeny. Not tonight." Margaret closed her heavy eyes. Sleep, lovely oblivion, was close. "There are certain laws," she began, "that simply make no sense whatsoever. They're beyond our normal comprehension. That is why we entrust barristers to untangle the mess. Your father's man is excellent, one of the best in the land. Mr. Grimes will sort things out for us, you'll see." Margaret drifted off. Josephine woke her a moment later.

"And after that, Mum?"

"After it's over we shall leave this place for good. We'll be off to San Francisco, all of us. Mrs. Oades and I were there today. We passed a school and saw dozens of girls your age in the yard."

Josephine whispered across sleeping Martha. "It would be better if just the five of us went."

"And leave Mrs. Oades and Gerty behind?"

"I wouldn't mind too much."

The grand life that she'd drawn for them coming over from New Zealand, her *made-up* story, wasn't going to happen. It was high time to cobble a new story. If she only knew where to begin. "Try and grow a bigger heart, Josephine. I know you've got it in you. Let us sleep now."

❖❖

THE NEXT MORNING, just after nine, three men arrived, two on horseback, another driving an empty wagon. Margaret was washing the front windows and called out to Nancy, who rushed in from the kitchen. She took one look out the window and flew upstairs. While she was gone two others rode up and dismounted. The five converged in a blur, tying up horses and wagon. In a perspiring panic, Margaret seized the letter opener from Henry's desk and put the marble paperweight into her pocket. Either could kill a man put to the right spot. She rounded up Josephine and Martha and sent them upstairs. "Mind Gerty. Stay put. Don't move." Nancy came back down and headed for the door, a long-barreled pistol in her hand.

"No, Nancy. Don't go out. Stay inside and be quiet."

"*You* stay inside," she said, storming onto the porch. "I'm through taking orders." Margaret ran out behind her, straining, unable to make out the individual faces. Nancy took a warring stance, spreading her feet, aiming the gun at their center.

"This is private property," she hollered. "Kindly remove yourselves and your wagon this instant or I'll shoot."

There was laughter among them. Three men stalked off toward the pasture. Another man started up the front walk. Margaret scanned the horizon for John, putting her hand inside her pocket, testing again the cold heft. It would need to be fast and hard, to the bridge of the nose, directly between the eyes.

The man coming toward them was grubbily dressed in shabby trousers and scuffed boots. A silver badge with illegible markings was pinned to his stained shirt. "Put the gun down, missus."

"Who are you here for?" said Margaret, Mim rearing in her thoughts. She held the letter opener behind her skirts, not completely defenseless this time.

"We're not after anyone," he said. "Unless you're looking for extra trouble, in which case we'll be happy to oblige." Margaret's battering heart slowed. The man scowled at Nancy. "I *said*, put the gun down, missus."

"Do as he says, Nancy."

Nancy lowered the gun.

The three men were about to disappear over the foggy rise. The fifth leaned against the wagon, smoking, Margaret could smell it. "What are you doing here?"

"Official business," he said. His handlebar mustache jutted, the tips pasted to sharp points. "Now get inside, and put that gun away before you hurt someone."

"This is our property," said Nancy, glaring. "We'll stand right here until the cows come home if we please."

The man hacked a wet laugh and spat, swiping at his mouth. "That's a comical choice of words, ma'am."

Margaret spoke up. "What sort of official business?"

He squinted up at her, sucking his false teeth. None was better than that dreadful set of dentures. He thrust an unshaved chin toward the front window. "The little ones are in need of you."

Margaret and Nancy turned to see the girls peering out, Gerty in Josephine's arms, slack-jawed Martha, confused little waif, beside them. Margaret flapped a hand, shooing them off. "Go on in now," the man said, starting back down the walk.

Nancy wasn't finished with him. "You can't tell us what to do or where to go, mister."

Moments later, John came running over the rise, yelling something unintelligible. Behind him came the three men, herding six cows. Margaret and Nancy watched them load the bellowing animals onto the wagon.

"They're taking Rose and her calf," cried Nancy. "What are we going to tell Henry?"

The men used the butts of their rifles, pushing and slapping the cows, swearing in their ears. There was a great mooing, defecating frenzy and then they were off, the wagon driver shouting. "The well ones will be returned."

Inside, Margaret returned the opener and paperweight to Henry's desk, stunned to know that she had been prepared to kill a man. She supposed that made her capable of anything now.

That night after supper Nancy said, "Pray heaven he will not go to prison, but we must prepare for the worst." They were at the sink cleaning up. "You and I cannot manage this farm on our own."

"No, indeed."

Nancy glanced sideways with a worried look. "You wouldn't pack up and leave, would you, Margaret? If Henry were sent away for a long time?"

"Not before the baby comes," said Margaret.

Nancy seemed relieved. "He won't go to prison."

"He'll be home before we know it," said Margaret, adding something to the hope pot.

Hello, Little Bastard

THE FRONT ROOM was now off limits at night. Nancy and Margaret would be sitting ducks silhouetted against that big picture window, said Titus. A one-eyed drunk could pick them right off. His old grandmother could.

"And I suppose you think you're helping," Nancy had said. "Scaring us half to death."

He'd gone away in a wounded huff. "Just doing as I'm told, missus."

Titus had taken Henry's request to keep a close watch much too seriously, bunking in the buggy shed for the last week, right beneath Margaret's window. He snored like a bear, Margaret said. During the day he lurked about, trying the locks, peeping in the front windows. Nancy could not so much as adjust a stocking in peace. The other day he caught her dipping into Henry's brandy. She'd jumped seeing him, spilling what little she'd poured. He was worse than the bogeymen he'd been assigned to guard against.

❖❖

NANCY OR MARGARET made soup twice weekly, enough to last Henry and his widower cellmate three days. Tonight's first batch came to a boil while Nancy wasn't looking and the eggs had curdled. She'd had to throw it out and start over. "If I ruin this pot," she said to Margaret, "he's going to have to settle for biscuits and jam."

Margaret said nothing, her thoughts obviously elsewhere. She sat at the table darning Henry's socks, a woolen pile growing at her elbow.

It was late, past nine. When they spoke, it was softly, out of consideration for John, whose door was closed. He'd been avoiding the family lately, coming in at odd hours, making cold plates for himself. At least Margaret had stopped demeaning herself by begging him to sit down with them, but her hurt still showed, and John seemed not to notice. Boys were like that. Girls at least possessed a guilt bone. A girl might cause a mother heartache, but she typically had the good grace to feel and express shame. Nancy almost wished she was having a second one.

Margaret put down the darning mushroom. "That's enough for one night."

A sound came from John's room, a yawn or a moan. Margaret's face clouded. She stared at his door as if expecting him to come out. "You look done in, Nancy," she said. "Go on up. I'll mind the soup."

Nancy sighed, rubbing her belly. She missed Henry so, especially at night. The bed was enormous without him in it. "Do you want to sleep in my room tonight, Margaret? It's not fair that I hog a bed when you're tripled up."

"Don't give it another thought," said Margaret. "We're perfectly cozy."

"Are you sure?" said Nancy. "It's such a nice big bed, bigger than yours."

"The girls and I are fine, Nancy. Go on now, have your rest. I'll see to the lamps."

"All right then," said Nancy, disappointed. "I guess I'll turn in." Her back ached from standing at the stove too long. She felt older than Abraham's Sarah with this baby. "Don't forget that Mr. Grimes is coming in the morning."

Halfway up the back stairs Nancy heard the scrape of a chair, and Margaret's whisper. "John? Son? Are you awake, love?" Nancy lingered for a moment. If John replied, she didn't hear it.

◆◆

THE TRIAL was to begin in nine days, Mr. Grimes unnecessarily reminded them. He arrived on time, getting rid of Margaret immediately, saying it was *imperative* to the case that he speak with Nancy alone. Margaret went away scowling. Nancy sat Mr. Grimes in the front room, and took a chair across from him. "How is my husband? Did he request anything special?"

Mr. Grimes reached behind a breast pocket and passed a single folded sheet. Nancy unfolded the note, glancing first at the closing, warm tears rising.

I love you now & always, darling wife.

Mr. Grimes shifted in Henry's chair. "I've been working day and night on your behalf. Yours and Mr. Oades."

Nancy nodded. "We're grateful, of course, sir."

"Been down to Los Angeles, up to Sacramento. I consulted with two judges, knew them in school, brilliant men. Probably the best legal minds in the state."

Nancy slipped Henry's note inside her pocket and gave Mr. Grimes her full attention. He looked tired for so early in the day.

"Here it is in a nutshell," he said. "We can have the first marriage annulled, the stipulation being that the action must be brought about by one of the parties of the second marriage."

"Yourself or Mr. Oades," he said, when Nancy didn't respond.

"I understood that much," she said. "But I always thought an annulment meant that a married couple had never . . ." Nancy looked down, blushing. ". . . had remained chaste."

"An annulment can be obtained for various reasons, Mrs. Oades."

"Then why are you just now thinking of it?" said Nancy. "You might have saved our family endless grief."

"It's tricky," he said. "Unfortunately, the children of the first marriage lose legitimacy."

The anger brought her to her feet. "How dare you raise my hopes this way. How dare you come into our home and make such an indecent proposal! Just wait until my husband hears about it."

"I've approached him already," he said, wearily.

"And?"

"Mr. Oades says as long as the law allows him two wives his conscience is clear."

"As is my conscience, sir," said Nancy. "As is Margaret Oades's conscience."

"That is all well and fine, madam. I was attempting to spare Mr. Oades the indignity of another trial. It promises to be more unpleasant than the last. And that's putting it mildly. He could go to prison for a very long time."

"You mustn't let that happen," said Nancy.

"I'll try my very best not to," he said. "As for the children of the first marriage, I don't see how they are any less stigmatized by the present situation."

Nancy remained standing, her blood churning. "And whose fault is that, may I ask?"

He shrugged, shaking his head.

"I asked you a question, sir. Who would you say is to blame for our predicament? The Queen of England? The Maori Indians?"

Nancy could not contain the shrill fury. "Ourselves? Is that what you think? Should we have barred the door? Should we have sent Mrs. Oades and her children, my husband's children, away? They didn't have a red cent to their name, you know. How were they supposed to survive? What would *you* have done in my decent husband's shoes? I ask you, sir. I demand to know just what you—" A shadow slid by her peripheral vision. Titus at the window. She screeched, "Shoo!" flying at the window, flapping her arms. "Shoo, you! Get back to work, you lazy succotash!"

Titus went running, taking the porch steps in a single bound.

"Our hand," Nancy said, embarrassed by her outburst. "He's been a problem lately."

Mr. Grimes calmly went on, as if he came across shrieking crazies on a regular basis. "To answer your question, I'd have the first marriage annulled, were I in Mr. Oades's unfortunate shoes."

"You'd brand your own legitimate children illegitimate, would you?" Nancy put her fists to her hips and bent, speaking to an imaginary child. "Hello, little bastard. You say you'd like to make a good marriage? You're seeking employment at a reputable firm? I'm so sorry, dearest. It's simply out of the question. You might as well run along now."

The lawyer stood, hat in hand.

Nancy was breathing hard. "May I ask how many children you have, Mr. Grimes?"

"I've not been thus far blessed," he said.

"I thought as much, sir. No decent parent would ask another to permanently scar their children." The trembling sense of victory lasted less than a second. He settled the coldest look upon her and started for the door.

He would quit now, thanks to her mouthy ingratitude. Henry would have no advocate, and it would be her fault entirely. "Please, Mr. Grimes." He turned. "May I offer you something before you go? Forgive me. My manners are atrocious. We have coffee, wonderful Arabian coffee from the Emporium in San Francisco. How does that strike you?"

"I don't have the time," he said. "If you'd like to scribble a quick note to your husband, I'll deliver it this afternoon."

Nancy went to the desk, taking out the good stationery and dipping the pen. She wrote hurriedly, having nothing to say to Henry just then, wanting only to please Mr. Grimes.

We are all fine. I will send John with soup and socks today. You are in my thoughts and prayers.

Yrs truly, Nancy O.

She blotted and folded the note, handing it to him. "Please don't hold my ravings against my husband."

"The law impels me, madam. Not hysteria."

"It's just that I'm afraid for Mr. Oades," she said. "My nerves, you know. It's hard to think straight these days for the worry. I say things I don't mean."

He touched her arm, his stony expression softening. "I understand."

"Oh, thank you, Mr. Grimes."

"I must ask you to reconsider annulment," he said.

"I couldn't put Mrs. Oades through it," she said. "Surely you see how it is. Her children are her world. They've all suffered so much already."

He shook his head. "The trial could go on a week, maybe longer," he said. "Be prepared."

"It's not a hardship," she said, escorting him into the hallway, opening the front door to a moist gray chill. "John Oades will drive me in."

He frowned. "I must advise you to stay away, Mrs. Oades."

"Why?"

"Rightly or wrongly, people have their minds made up," he said.

"It's in Mr. Oades's best interest that you not attend. I'm afraid I must insist." He started down the walkway, turning at the gate and giving a prim bow. Nancy waved, fresh fear for Henry welling.

Josephine came around the side of the house, dogs in tow. She was speaking, practicing one of her dramatic scenes. Margaret often asked her to recite, but Josephine seemed to prefer an animal audience. Nancy nodded a greeting. Josephine did the same and turned, going back where she'd come from, the dogs following.

Inside, Margaret emerged from the shadows. She'd been standing in the dining room the entire time. "I heard every word," she said. "Thank you, Nancy."

Nancy sank to Henry's still warm chair, picturing him wasting away in prison, dying there years from now. The baby moved, putting pressure on low organs. If she'd calculated correctly, he'd come in three months, in June. "What are we going to do, Margaret? What in God's name are we going to do?"

The Party Most
Principally Injured

MARGARET SAW THE BLOOD when she went out for the eggs, dark drops of it in the grass. The craven murderers had used the chopping stump, leaving a sticky pool there. She followed the trail of gore around the side of the house and up the bloody front steps. The decapitated dog—Ham, John's and Henry's favorite—had been flung onto the front porch, blood and sinew splattering. The head, black eyes wide, gray tongue lolling, lay to the left of the door that was opening. Martha started out, cheerful, oblivious, humming a morning tune.

"Go back inside," Margaret shouted.

Martha stood mute at the threshold, wet shock in her eyes. Her mum so very rarely raised her voice. In the next moment she saw Ham's head and began to howl. Margaret stepped over the head and took Martha by the wrist, bringing her into the front room. She knelt, holding her convulsing child, whispering the first lie that came to mind.

"It was a mountain lion." Natural predators were nowhere near as terrifying as the unnatural. "It happened quite quickly. Poor Ham barely felt a thing."

Martha sobbed, "Did it have sharp teeth?"

"Yes," said Margaret, stroking Martha. "I imagine it did. But you needn't worry. The lion shan't come round again. Titus shot him dead."

Martha lifted her stricken face. "May I see it, Mum?"

"See what, darling?"

"The lion."

"No, I'm afraid not. It's already been disposed of."

It all made sad sense to Martha after a while, as the truth would not to Henry. Margaret had never known him to be without a dog for very long. He treated them all like special chums, carrying on one-sided conversations without the least bit of embarrassment. Henry hadn't changed, certainly not in the way he regarded animals. He held his cows in equally high esteem. He was the same man, really. As gentle as ever.

❖❖

MARGARET WAS GOING AT THE blood on the door when Mr. Grimes drove up. She had bits of offal on her work apron and hands from having gathered Ham. His carcass and matted head lay on old newspaper at her feet, waiting to be buried. Mr. Grimes came onto the porch, seeing immediately the stinking mound. He pulled a handkerchief from a breast pocket and put it to his nostrils.

"Was that a dog?" he asked, not pausing for her response. He apologized for arriving unannounced he said behind the handkerchief, though he was pleased to find Margaret.

"It's imperative to the case that we speak alone, Mrs. Oades."

"Your exact words to Mrs. Oades yesterday," she said.

"So they are," he said irritably. "Allow me a minute, will you? I'm pressed for time." He turned and started down the walkway. Margaret followed, scanning the pasture for Titus. She wanted Ham's body gone before John or Nancy discovered him. The mice had set Nancy back for weeks. A viciously slain dog might cause her to lose what little equilibrium remained.

Mr. Grimes led her around to the far side of his handsome carriage, as if to shield them from sight.

"There's no need for secrecy," she said.

He folded his handkerchief neatly and slipped it behind a lapel. "It's the odor."

Margaret scratched dried blood from the back of her hand. "We might have gone inside."

"What befell the poor dog?"

"He was butchered during the night," she said.

"By whom?"

A ludicrous question from an educated man. "No calling card was left," she said.

He ignored the sarcasm, changing the subject in the next breath. "Here it is in a nutshell. As the party most principally injured by the second marriage, you are in an excellent position to bring suit against Mr. Oades and his second wife. I strongly urge you to proceed at once."

Margaret recognized his little game. He was playing her against Nancy, seeing who would topple first. One way or the other he was determined to win Henry's freedom. It did not matter who was in the way or what became of them. "I cannot," she said.

He lowered his voice. "Bigamy is a hangable offense in California."

"Do you mean to frighten me, sir? You said nothing about hanging yesterday."

"I feared young Mrs. Oades might come apart if I did," he said. "She's a fragile lady. Unlike you, madam."

"I bleed when pricked," said Margaret. Her eyes watered to the brink of blindness. The stench was all around. It was warmer today than yesterday, and very still. "We have been acquitted twice now, Mr. Grimes. What has changed that would find him guilty?"

"It is up to the jury this time," he said. "One cannot predict the vagaries there. I will tell you the general mood is ugly. You'd be hard pressed to find a single sympathetic individual."

"Do *you* think us guilty?"

"I'm a monogamist," he said, "if that's what you're asking. But that is neither here nor there."

"It is very much indeed *here*. You should be standing solidly behind us. How will it look to the judge and jury if you're not?"

"Believe me," he said. "I've gone round after round with Mr. Oades on the subject. I've offered to retire myself over philosophical differences, but he wouldn't accept."

"As he wouldn't accept an annulment," said Margaret.

"That is correct."

"From neither Mrs. Oades nor myself."

"True."

Margaret wanted Henry returned of course. She did not for a moment wish him in prison, even though she breathed easier when he was not about; she lived more freely. It was a selfish fact.

"It is wrong of you to go behind his back this way," she said.

Mr. Grimes pulled a pair of fawn-colored driving gloves from his pocket. "Madam, I'm acting in his best interest. You're in a position to do the same."

"Even if I were willing, he wouldn't have it," said Margaret. "He'd disown me."

"At least he'd have that luxury."

"I could bring a dozen suits against him, it wouldn't change a—"

"It would reduce the number of wives to one."

"You don't know him very well," said Margaret. "He would continue to reside with Mrs. Oades, regardless. Nothing would—"

Mr. Grimes interrupted. "Oh, I doubt that very much. I don't envision young Mrs. Oades consenting to an immoral arrangement."

"There's a baby on the way," she said.

"I am aware."

I just couldn't put Mrs. Oades through it, Nancy had said. *Her children are her world.* Margaret had experienced an involuntary rush of kinship, eavesdropping. "A successful petition on my part would label her children illegitimate," she said.

He shrugged. "Unfortunately."

"Henry wouldn't have it!"

"He'd have no say."

"I cannot go against him," said Margaret. "Nor can I go against Mrs. Oades."

Mr. Grimes shook his head, climbing up onto the driver's seat. "You ladies make speeches, you clamor day and night for the vote, for this and that right, and I'm all for it. I sincerely am. But when it comes time to make a hard decision, a man's decision, you turn to mush. You'll never make progress because of it."

He collected the reins. "At least do me the favor of keeping young Mrs. Oades away from the trial. She'll only inflame the jury. People loathe her. You're the rightful wife as they see it."

"Who are *people* to say?"

"Keep her home, please," he said, exasperated. "For Mr. Oades's sake."

"I shall take it up with Mrs. Oades," Margaret said, seeing Titus striding past the barn.

Mr. Grimes clucked, shaking the reins. "Holy Moses, madam! Have you no jurisdiction over anyone at all?"

Margaret looked up at him, a hand to her forehead, shielding her face from the sun. "Only myself, sir, and my children. My two younger ones, anyway." Mr. Grimes apparently did not care a fig that John had slipped beyond her reach.

❖❖

SHE FOUND TITUS in the milk room, sitting on a stool, straining milk through a layer of gauze. His right arm was bandaged elbow to wrist, wrapped in a filthy rag, for which he'd be cited if the inspectors came around again. Henry demanded the utmost cleanliness in the milk room.

"What did you do to yourself?" she asked.

Titus turned a baleful profile. "It's nothing."

For sanitary purposes the straining should have been done hours before, right after the milk was drawn, but she kept her peace. His right trouser leg had been torn or chewed, as if an animal had been on him.

"The dog was killed last night," she said to his back.

He didn't bother to turn around. "Which one?"

"Ham. He's on the front porch. I'd like him disposed of straightaway."

"Just as soon as I'm done here," he muttered. "I've only got two hands."

"Out of curiosity," said Margaret. "Where were you last evening?"

He glanced over his shoulder. "What's it to you, missus?"

"Did you hear anything then, see anything untoward?"

"No ma'am." He squirmed, letting out a low moan.

"Are you in pain? Would you like me to see to your arm?"

"I said it's nothing."

"Were you bitten? Is that what happened?"

He came to his feet with a minacious look in his bloodshot eyes. Margaret took several steps back. "I was in town last night," he said. "Nobody 'preciates the way I keep an eye around here, so I stayed. I got into it with somebody, took a jab in the arm." He unwound the rag on his arm and offered up the wound for inspection. It was a ragged gash, as wide as it was long, with specks of black in the blood. Any number of things might have put it there. "See?" he said, redressing himself. "A rusty old bowie knife did it. Not no damn dog."

"I did not mean to imply—"

He kicked over the stool. "Sure you did! First you don't like the way I'm keeping watch, next you think I killed your old dog."

"I did not mean—"

"I'll tell you who done it," he said.

"Please do, sir."

"Clarence Hawks, that's who. Ain't he sweet on your boy's sweetheart?"

Anger sparked, thinking of Dora McGinnis. "My boy has no sweetheart."

Titus smirked and righted the stool. "Hawks was in town last night, drunk as a skunk. He didn't come out and say so directly, but he said enough. Had blood on his boots, too. He done it. I'd stake my last dollar." Titus tugged on the ear missing a lobe, looking at her in sullen silence for half a moment. "I can see you don't believe me, and that's fine by me."

Margaret didn't know what to believe. The deed was done. The dog needed to be off the porch and in the ground. "I have no reason not to believe you, Mr. Crump. If you're finished here, would you mind tending to Ham, please."

Titus kicked over the pail of strained milk and stalked out the door. "Bury your own damn dog."

Margaret started toward the house. John came running up behind, breathing hard. "I've been looking everywhere for you, Mum. What in Christ's name happened to Ham?"

"I don't know. I was hoping to have him buried before you—"

"The Maori were less brutal with the dogs!"

"I know, sweetheart," she said, petting his arm. "Go back to work now; try not to think about it. I'll see to poor Ham."

"He was my dog," said John, blinking back tears. "I'll see to him myself."

"I'll help then."

"No need."

She insisted, carrying the head in a bucket, the shovel in her free hand. John walked ahead, the stiff putrescent body in his arms. He chose a spot behind the coach shed and began digging.

"We've seen so little of you lately, John," she said. She'd noticed immediately the small blue bruise on his neck, and despaired that Dora had put it there recently. "Where have you been keeping yourself, son?"

"About," said John. He paused in his digging to wave the shovel across Ham's body and drive off the swarm of black flies.

"Will you join us for supper this evening?"

"If I can," he said.

Margaret sighed with sadness, and went in to check on Nancy.

Nancy was dressed but for shoes and stockings. "I can't find them anywhere." She sat at the edge of the unmade bed, looking about the darkened room in a dazed sort of way, rubbing her belly. Margaret opened the heavy curtains, dust flying. She searched out shoes and stockings and brought them to Nancy. Nancy slowly finished dressing. Her voice was thin, anxious.

"It's this place, Margaret. It's cursed. I swear it is. I'd give anything to leave today."

Margaret waited until after supper to tell her about Mr. Grimes's visit, saying only that he thought it best that she not attend the trial.

"He thinks it inadvisable, given your condition. He makes a very good point, you know."

"I will not leave Henry to face his hateful accusers alone," said Nancy, examining a torn thumbnail. "He's done nothing wrong. And neither have we, Margaret."

"We shall go together then."

Nancy chewed absentmindedly at a raw cuticle. "I assumed all along we would."

Margaret had assumed all along they wouldn't.

The Wives
of Henry Oades

S TANDING ON MRS. POTTER's warped front porch, waiting for someone to answer the door, Nancy counted seven mud-dauber nests. She held Gertrude in her arms, wishing she were leaving her baby with almost anyone else in the world. Beside her, Margaret stroked Martha's hair. "It will be all right, Nancy," she said.

"I'm much too old for a nanny," grumbled Josephine, who'd barely said two words coming over. She kicked at a cracked churn. "I'm nearly a grown lady."

"Consider your father," whispered Margaret. "We're doing this for him."

Josephine had begged to mind the younger ones herself for the duration of the trial. Margaret had refused to allow it, not with dog-killers running around loose. Nancy had been shocked to hear about Ham, but not bereft. She'd hated that scary animal. Martha had been the one to finally tell her. Left to Margaret, she probably never would have found out.

Mrs. Potter opened the front door. Martha gasped and began a low whimper. Nancy didn't blame her. Mrs. Potter looked as if she'd stepped right out of a gruesome fairy tale. There was a shimmer of movement along her frizzy hairline. Nancy imagined lice, an entire robust colony on the march. Mrs. Potter held out a withered claw of a hand. The nails were thick and yellowed; the fingers turned in on themselves. "I'll take my fee up front, if you please," she said.

Nancy had the silver dollar ready. Mrs. Potter pocketed the coin and went for Gertrude. Nancy reflexively clutched her baby. "Maybe I should come in and put her down."

"Nonsense," said Mrs. Potter. "She may as well get used to me right off, seeing as the trial could go on for a while." She took Gertrude from Nancy, hoisting her to a bony shoulder like a sack of sugar. Gertrude squirmed, twisting her little pink face, her baby brow furrowed in bewilderment.

"She'll be fine," said Mrs. Potter, bouncing Gertrude too roughly. "They'll all be jim-dandy." She beckoned to Josephine and Martha. "Come inside, small fry."

Margaret's dejected girls shuffled inside, as if entering the house of detention.

"Don't mind the smell," said Mrs. Potter. "I'm making okra relish. The first batch burned beyond redemption. I was just about to start another. If you're good girls, I'll let you help."

So she was going to put the children to work while charging Nancy a king's ransom. The door with its broken hinge closed. Nancy stepped off the porch with Margaret, feeling like Judas Iscariot.

John had been waiting in the barouche meanwhile, occupying himself with a book. He was always reading, just like his mother. He climbed down to assist them up, treating Nancy like a breakable. How handsome he looked in his new blue serge. Even Margaret was glad now that the suit had been purchased. He'd outgrown the things he'd come in, and his smelly old work clothes wouldn't do today. Margaret touched his sleeve.

"Up you go, Mum," he said, not looking at her.

The three arrived late, as they'd planned, wanting to avoid people, mainly the newspaper people. Their scheme worked. Two gentlemen stood on the courthouse steps. One spat in their general direction, but neither came close, or said anything within earshot. The Oadeses passed peaceably, Nancy between Margaret and John, perspiring inside her wool cloak, a cumbersome ugly thing, a big plaid horse blanket of a wrap. It did nothing to hide her big belly.

❖❖

THEY ENTERED TO the gavel banging. Dora McGinnis sat on the witness chair, wearing the skirt Nancy had let out for her. Mr. Teal, the prosecutor, was bent over her, saying something Nancy could not hear. Dora looked up, spotting John, her lips parting. She put a hand to her heart, and he did the same, his eyes misting over. Margaret didn't seem to catch the quick gesture, but Nancy did. They were obviously in love.

John offered Nancy his left arm, Margaret his right. They started up the long aisle to hisses and whispers. "Shame! Double shame on you!" Henry turned, looking over his shoulder briefly, obviously unhappy they'd come. Beside him, Mr. Grimes scribbled away, appearing calm enough from here, confident. But then he stood only to lose a case, no more. The fear ran through Nancy's body like a fever, soaking her.

The judge gestured to three men seated in the row behind Henry, two ushers and a deacon from First Congregational, all dressed somberly, as if for a funeral. The churchmen moved to the back of the courtroom. Nancy sat in a vacated chair, John on one side, Margaret on the other.

Mr. Teal glared their way, heaving an impatient sigh. The judge gave a thrust of his chin, a signal to proceed.

Mr. Teal cleared his throat. "Now let us go back, Miss McGinnis."

Dora sat like a lady, her gloved hands folded primly in her lap, her hair strained tightly behind, tidy for once. Her complexion was clear, free of visible blemishes. A stranger would call her pretty today. John Oades surely would. He could not take his eyes from her.

Mr. Teal turned his back on Dora, striding toward the jury. "You have the court completely baffled," he said. Several of the jurymen nodded in agreement. Two others, one most definitely, appeared to be sleeping. Nancy wished they'd come in at the start now. Mr. Teal returned to Dora, shaking his head in theatrical puzzlement. "I don't think you mean to lie, do you, Miss McGinnis?"

Dora shook her head. "I ain't lied, sir."

His hands went to his hips, an unflattering feminine pose. "Every word from your lips refutes your previous testimony. You are either lying now, Miss, or you lied before. Either way, you've perjured yourself."

Dora cast a shy look toward John. "No, sir."

"*No, sir,*" warbled Mr. Teal, mocking her. The rude man bent at the waist, putting himself face-to-face. "*Yes,* sir! Miss McGinnis. On December eighteenth of last year, right here, in this very same room, you swore on the Holy Bible to tell the truth."

Dora nodded. "Yes, sir."

"At the time you testified that the two Mrs. Oadeses were paragons of cruelty, that they engaged in debaucheries behind your back."

Dora twitched. "I don't think I said all that."

Mr. Teal stood back, crossing his arms. "Ah, but you did, Miss McGinnis. You said all that and more. You said that they assigned you a tiny rathole to live in. Those were your own harsh words, young lady, not mine. You also said that the debaucheries took place while you were in the kitchen." Dora shook her head in mute denial. Mr. Teal threw up his hands. "Now you'd have us believe that the wives of Henry Oades are kind and virtuous, good God-fearing Christian women, that the defendant here is the same, that he accepted both women into his home out of the goodness of his pure polygamous heart."

"Yes, sir," said Dora, to a rise of laughter.

"And what brought about this miraculous sea change?" asked Mr. Teal.

Nancy could barely hear Dora's meek response. "Sir?"

"Are they paying you for your testimony?"

Dora spoke up, "No, sir!"

"No need to be afraid, Dora," he said. "They can't hurt you now."

As if they ever had.

"Nobody's paying me a penny, sir," said Dora.

"Then how are we to account for your change in testimony?"

Nancy guessed it had everything to do with John.

Dora stared down. "I learnt some things between then and now."

"Don't equivocate," said Mr. Teal. "What sort of *things*?"

"No chicanery, miss," said the judge, shaking his gavel. "I've already warned you once."

Dora looked at John, her bottom lip pulsing. John came to the edge of his chair, his fists curling, like a boxer poised for fight. Dora lowered her gaze again.

"Mr. Oades has but one true wife," she said flatly, as if by rote. "Mrs. Nancy Oades is the one. Mr. Oades only took in old Mrs. Oades because she was destitute, because he did not want to see her go to the poorhouse, because he is an honorable man." She looked up. "Old Mrs. Oades is a loving mother, you know."

Nancy glanced sideways. If Margaret was hurt or insulted it didn't show.

"I see," said Mr. Teal, turning again to the jury, rolling his eyes in disbelief. "And how did the maid, who no longer resided in the household, become privy to such personal information?"

Dora frowned. "I rather not say, sir."

"I rather you *did*," said Judge Billings. "And don't quibble."

Dora's round cheeks flamed red, her scowl intensifying. "I learnt it from my fiancé." Margaret groaned. "If it's anybody's business," snapped Dora. "And it ain't."

Mr. Teal pulled on his chin, leering in a knowing way. "His name, Miss McGinnis?"

Nancy and Margaret simultaneously turned to John. If Margaret hadn't known before, she did now.

A Queer Life

MARGARET WONDERED what Henry was thinking, if he could even tell that Dora was expecting. Men typically were the last to take notice. Would he rage—it would serve no purpose—or give John and Dora his begrudging blessing? The girl was at least four months along, rosy aglow with it. Whether John was the legitimate father or not, Dora had named him, and he'd quite clearly accepted. The woolgathering lad was happily tossing his life away. Margaret could cry. She could weep a bloody river.

The tedious prosecutor came to a finish at last. "It bears repeating," he said. "Dora McGinnis is not a credible witness."

Mr. Grimes declined to cross-examine. Dora stepped down, bowing her head as she passed them. Lovesick John turned and watched her exit the courtroom. Henry looked over his shoulder then, his troubled eyes meeting hers. He had guessed.

Titus Crump was summoned to the stand.

Titus never did return that day, saving Margaret and Nancy the unpleasantness of sacking him. They could no longer afford him. He ate like a horse on top of his pay. The cows would need to go as well eventually, if a buyer could be found. No one was buying Oades milk. That some of the cows had been marked consumptive would bring the value down that much more. Henry would see pennies on the pound for the remaining herd, if he was fortunate enough to see that much.

She and Nancy planned to go to Henry first thing if there was a conviction, whether or not he granted permission. (Prison was the very worst they'd considered aloud. The other, the inconceivable, had not once been given voice.) He'd forbidden them to visit these past weeks, out of concern for their safety. Notes were exchanged, but Nancy had not kept him apprised.

"He can't do anything from his cell, Margaret," she'd said. "He'll only worry himself sick."

He would not like the idea of their leaving, but what choice was left them? They could not run a failing dairy farm on their own, plain and simple. And they could not live ostracized in town, where butcher, baker, and candlestick maker refused their business. Leaving was their last and only option. Margaret pictured a clean city flat near decent schools.

Nancy had fretted. "He'll think we're abandoning him."

"We'll be but a ferry ride away," Margaret had said. "Tell him that." Nancy had hunted down the ferry schedule then and there, circling the arrivals in ink to show him.

Margaret planned to look for work in San Francisco, which would bring some financial relief. With any luck, she'd find a good post straightaway. She might teach French to American girls, or English to foreigners. It probably wouldn't pay much, but they'd get by. Nancy was becoming better at stretching a penny. How could Henry oppose them? Particularly now that there were two babies, both child and grandchild, on the way. *Grandchild.* Good God. Her baby was having one of his own. She could scarcely believe it.

"THEY'RE NOT WHO THEY SEEM," said Titus, the earnest, damning witness. "I thought I knew 'em, but I don't. They're not like you and me, I'll say."

His testimony was a complete turnabout from his last. Mr. Grimes should have stood and said so, but he did not. He again waved off the offer to cross-examine, as if he couldn't be bothered. The judge brought down the gavel.

"We'll take a fifteen-minute recess. Latecomers will not be readmitted."

John was swift to his feet, hat in hand. "I shan't be long," he said, blending into the buzzing throng. Margaret followed him with her eyes. She used to think she knew John better than anyone, better than he knew himself. A mother's head is often chock full of illusion. As is a wife's. Husband and son were both lost to her now.

Henry was escorted through a side door, led past four jurymen who'd elected to stay behind. One juror nudged a drowsy colleague, gesturing toward Henry with the stem of his pipe. Henry walked tall, putting on a sturdy show for Nancy's benefit.

"It's not going well," said Nancy. Margaret said nothing, thinking the same. Nancy might need to learn to live without him as well.

John returned, breathless, bringing paper cones of lemonade, cold and sweet. Margaret passed a flimsy cone to Nancy. "Where did it come from?"

"Vendors on the steps outside," said John, sitting beside her, still breathing hard. "All sorts set up. Jugglers, games of chance. It's like a circus! I wasn't recognized until after I paid, then the man wanted his drinks back. I laughed straight to his old mug and came away."

Margaret touched his thigh, feeling a muscle contract beneath her fingers. "John," she said quietly, meeting his eyes.

He looked away quickly, his face reddening. "Not now, Mum."

Margaret folded her hands in her lap, ordering away the grief and tears. She didn't succeed. John wordlessly passed his handkerchief. "I have a bit of a cold," she whispered, pressing the hankie to her eyes. She kept it even after she'd composed herself. It smelled of him.

❖❖

MR. TEAL STARTED up again, facing the jury. "The law is to be construed according to its spirit and intent." The jurymen nodded, a dozen sage gibbons bobbing. At least they were all awake now. Margaret twisted John's handkerchief, unsure where the prosecutor was headed. Henry had been almost childlike in his spirit and intent. He'd tried to do right by everyone.

"Where the reason of a rule ceases, so should the rule itself," said Mr. Teal. "And again, where the reason is the same, the rule should be the same. He who considers merely the letter goes but skin deep into the meaning!"

A commotion started in the back of the room, a loud demand to "Speak up!" The gavel came down. Mr. Teal cleared his throat, striding closer to the jurors. "Now in this case," he said, gaining volume, pointing toward Henry. "The evident intention of the law was simply to provide against illegitimacy of the children of the second marriage." The prosecutor grasped the oak rail corralling the jurors and leaned in. "Believe me, gentlemen, it was certainly never intended to make bigamy lawful!"

Nancy put a hand to her stomach. "Oh, dear." Henry heard Nancy's tiny cry and turned around, distressed, as did Mr. Grimes, irritated. The judge tapped his gavel, peering down over his spectacles. "Is the lady ill?"

All glaring attention fell upon Margaret and Nancy. Margaret whispered close. "What is it? Shall we leave?"

"Tell them I'm fine," Nancy said, her pimpled cheeks on fire, her fevered eyes cast down. "Have them go on, please." Margaret adjusted Nancy's cloak, nodding to the judge, signaling that all was well. They'd done no one any good turning up today, least of all Henry.

Mr. Teal resumed, his features tight with contempt. As if they'd intentionally staged the interruption to thwart him. "Let us assume for a moment it is true," he said, putting a temple of fingertips to his handsome chin. "Supposing that on the date of the second marriage, Henry Oades thought his first wife had passed. Let us say he truly believed himself to be a poor lonely widower, that he only did what any man in his same situation would do, given the opportunity. Say it is so. Let us allow it, for it makes no difference. The *intent* of the law, gentlemen, does not permit Mr. Oades to cohabit with two women. Once learning the facts, he did willfully continue to do just that, which is conclusive proof of guilty *intention*! He's expressed no remorse while incarcerated, by the way. On the contrary. Let the defense convince you to set Mr. Oades free, and off he'll go, I guarantee you. He'll trot straight back to the *bosoms* of his family, no ifs, ands, or buts."

Margaret winced at the crude remark. Mr. Teal paused, his eyes sliding toward her. For half a moment Margaret thought him moved by the sight of Nancy weeping, and imagined he'd recant. But he simply said, "The state rests."

Mr. Grimes looked up from his notes, clearly surprised.

Mr. Teal made a stiff bow before the jury. "The law judges by the *quo animo*. The *intent*, gentlemen. It is what separates us from the beasts."

A restless murmur started up, along with the rudest of all personal rackets, knuckles cracking one by one, sharpened fingernails raking along dry scalps. Henry turned. Margaret lifted her chin, a gesture of encouragement. A brief flicker of light came into his eyes. Mr. Grimes whispered something to him. The gavel came down. The men straightened and faced forward.

"Is the defense ready?"

"We are," said Lewis Grimes, standing.

"He'll show the rotters," muttered John, giving Margaret's hand a pat, a brush of familial solidarity, causing her heart to seize with love. If they only knew how little it took.

Mr. Grimes wore a somber black broadcloth and immaculate collar that fit him well. His bald dome was quiet, without a sheen. He seemed taller, oddly enough, a good thing, unless the jury suspected lifts as Margaret did, in which case they'd make game of him when they went off to deliberate, and Henry would pay the price of his vanity.

"Your honor. Gentlemen of the jury." His voice was well modulated, an octave or two below normal, as if he'd rehearsed, aimed for a funereal air. He stood behind the defense table, a pale ringless hand resting lightly upon Henry's shoulder.

"Mr. Oades's marriage to Mrs. Margaret Oades was proved valid and lawful. The record reflects it. The record also reflects that his marriage to Mrs. Nancy Oades is no less valid and lawful. The second subdivision of the sixty-first section of the civil code provides that the marriage of a person having a former husband or wife living is void unless such former husband or wife was absent and not known to be living for five consecutive years preceding the subsequent marriage. That is the law in a nutshell, gentlemen. Let the law be changed. I, for one, would be all for it. But as it reads today, no man shall be held guilty of bigamy under the aforementioned circumstances, Mr. Oades's precise circumstances."

Mr. Grimes went on to cite the particulars of Margaret's death by fire in New Zealand, providing the dated death certificate, reading aloud the obituary ("loving wife and mother," etcetera). Margaret sat stunned at her own funeral, barely recognizing the eulogized woman. No one had the esteem of *all* who knew her. No one possessed uniform gentleness, or bore everything patiently. It embarrassed her to know the treacly rubbish had been published.

"She enjoyed sound health until the end," said Mr. Grimes, reading without emotion. "She leaves a husband to mourn her death." He laid the paper down, clasping his hands before himself. "However tempting it may be to do so," he said calmly, "the law says we are not to convict my client. We must stick to the letter of the law, no matter how intolerable, no matter how egregious it strikes us. It is true, as Mr. Teal contends, that the intention must govern, but the language *is* the evidence of the intention! It is wrongly called interpretation when we alter the words."

Margaret was astonished to see the old judge nod.

Mr. Grimes in his wisdom paused. A fly droned in the awful silence, on and on.

Judge Billings laid his pipe to rest and removed his spectacles. He rubbed his eyes for an eternity, saying finally, "I agree." An immediate din rose up in the room, a babel of curses and prayers. The judge gave a lackluster rap of the gavel, facing the jury with a pained expression. "I'm instructing you to acquit."

Henry turned around again, his tired eyes sparkling with happiness and relief, reminding Margaret of the night he delivered Mary.

The jury left, returning after a few minutes. The judge took a cursory look at the paper handed him and said, "You're free to go." No thoughtful homily was offered to Henry, no apology. Without the least bit of fanfare it was over.

Judge and prosecutor stalked off. The jurymen dispersed, grousing among themselves. Mr. Grimes gave Henry a perfunctory handshake, and then he too gathered his papers and left, without a single good word for his client. Henry came to his family, gathering them, herding them close. The sketch artist had made his way to the front of the room. He was watching them intently, drawing hurriedly. They'd be featured on the front page tomorrow, no doubt. No matter, no matter. It was finished.

"Oh, thank God," said Nancy, sagging against Henry, closing her eyes.

Margaret stood alone, her hands to herself. They'd been emancipated, set loose to resume their queer lives. With Henry gone, she hadn't dwelt daily on the particulars of their peculiar arrangement.

"Mind your mum," said Henry to John. Nancy took Henry's arm, and Margaret took John's, conscious of its adult hardness.

❖❖

THEY CAME OUT to a glaring sun, to a lawn and steps littered with paper cups and chewed cigar stubs, but not to the tar and feathers Margaret had feared. There were several dozen people still milling about, a listless lot, waiting for their buggies to arrive, most of them. One man who bore a striking resemblance to Benjamin Disraeli advised them to leave town if they knew what was good for them. Another jovial bloke said he pitied Henry. One wife was more than enough for *him*.

"Bet you're pecked from dawn to dusk, brother! Bet the pretty one doesn't let up."

"Oh, shut your old trap," said Nancy, linking arms with Margaret. Margaret smiled, unfazed by the fool's insult.

John went for the carriage, coming back on foot half an hour later. "Somebody stole a wheel and untied the horses," he said. "They're gone. I looked everywhere, Dad."

Eavesdropping Benjamin Disraeli with his long sloping forehead approached, offering to take them home for twenty dollars.

"Twenty dollars!" said Henry, incredulous. He looked left and then right, as if expecting the sibling bays to come trotting up on their own. He was as thin as Margaret had ever seen him, and he stank. It was disgraceful the way prisoners were left to ferment.

"You can always walk," said the man. "No hack will take you."

"I'd have to pay you at the end," said Henry.

"No deal," said the man, walking away.

"I've no money on my person," said Henry, fumbling with his watch and chain. The man shrugged and continued walking. Henry freed the watch, holding it aloft. "Here! Will you take a good watch instead?"

"The girls are at Potter's," said Nancy.

Henry shouted, "Solid gold, sir! And an additional stop will be necessary."

The man gave the watch a brief inspection before pocketing it. He brought them home in his raggedy carriage, refusing to exchange the watch for money once there. Henry offered twenty-five dollars and a broody hen. "Nope," said the man.

Henry started up the front walk behind Nancy and the children. Margaret remained in the road, pleading with the greedy bounder. "The watch belonged to his father, to his grandfather before that. It's all he has of them."

Henry called from the porch. "Bother the watch, Meg. He's not going to change his mind. Come inside now."

"A deal's a deal," said the man, riding away.

Margaret went inside finally, where the reunion was already starting without her.

At Home

Nancy said Henry looked exhausted. "You should rest." He said he could rest any time. "Whatever you say," said Nancy, settling down next to Margaret in the front room.

"Where's John?" Margaret whispered.

"I don't know," said Nancy. "He was here a minute ago."

Henry sat in his chair holding Gertrude, a weary king on his throne. Josephine and Martha brought their projects before him—a sea-green apron with tiny perfect stitches, a collaborative drawing of a family with two mothers and a dog with a halo, Ham, presumably. Josephine charged up the stairs to change for her solo recitation, descending again with deliberate grace, her hair swept up in a grown-up style. She stood beside the marble pedestal, upon which sat an empty vase that didn't go.

"My heart leaps up when I behold, a rainbow in the sky."

She managed Wordsworth's poem without once faltering. They clapped until their palms stung. Henry embraced his daughter, tears standing in red-rimmed eyes. "Lovely, Pheeny."

"Please call me Josephine, Father," she said.

"Josephine, sure. Sure, lovely girl."

"We should let your father rest now," said Nancy.

"I could do with a bath first," said Henry.

Margaret took the children upstairs while Nancy went to work in the kitchen, getting out the tub, heating and pouring the water, beating an egg for his hair. He got in and sat back, spreading wide his arms.

"I've missed you so, Nan."

She undressed quickly, her heart brimming with love. He drew up his knees, making room for her and her blue-veined girth. They simmered for the longest time, kissing, caressing, feeling for the baby's head, his fluttery movements. They did not discuss the days in jail, or the confiscated cows, or Ham's murder, or John and Dora, but all else under a lover's sun. The kitchen was dark by the time they emerged from the cold water, limbs and breasts solid gooseflesh. Drying off, Nancy thought of Margaret, self-banished to another room.

"What is it, darling? What's the matter?"

"Nothing," she said. "I'm just a little too happy, I guess."

❖❖

NANCY PUT THE TUB AWAY before calling Margaret down. Together they decided on flapjacks and Margaret's special syllabub. The punch was best when made with port, but they were out. Margaret cut the brandy with cider, sweetening the mix with brown sugar and nutmeg. Minutes later, John came in the back door with hay caught in his hair, looking surprised to see them.

"I came in for—" He laughed nervously. "I don't remember what I came in for now."

Margaret set down the nutmeg grater. "You'll join us for supper, won't you, John?"

"Of course, he will," said Nancy. "It's his father's homecoming night."

"I need to see to something in the barn first," he said.

"Wait," said Nancy. She poured the syllabub into her best company bowl and handed it to him. "It needs to be milked on. Try to be quick, all right? I'm about to start the flapjacks."

He took the bowl and left, returning an hour later. The syllabub should have been put in the icebox outside for a while, but the flapjacks and bacon had been sitting too long already. Nancy brought the punch to the table warm, placing the bowl in the center, arranging the new cups all around. "Supper's on!" Grace was brief, though heartfelt. Martha piped up the instant it was over.

"Are we going away soon?" she asked.

Nancy had had every good intention of giving Henry at least one night's peace, but she had forgotten to instruct the children.

Bright tears welled in Martha's eyes. "This is a very bad place, Dad."

Nancy and Margaret simultaneously shushed her. *Let your dad be. Let him enjoy his supper, his first night home. We'll discuss it later.*

Henry smiled, handsome as could be, at the head of the table where he belonged, his beard and hair clean and curly from the egg shampoo. "The next place will be a good place, sweetheart. I promise."

"We don't need a palace, Henry," said Nancy. "A nice house in a nice neighborhood. A room for you and me, one for John, one for the girls, and one for Margaret is all."

"Is *all*," teased Henry.

Nancy reached, helping herself to another ladle of punch. "Well, it's high time Margaret had a little privacy. And an allowance of her own too, come to think of it." She laughed, joy and syllabub gone to her head. "Don't pout. We won't bankrupt you. Just give her half of mine."

"That wouldn't be right, Nancy," said Margaret.

Margaret didn't know how she felt. Nancy had never expressed herself aloud.

And you'll have me, Margaret had said that morning. *If you need me.* Nancy had come to love her in a way she didn't have words for.

"It most certainly would be right," she said. "I can't think of anything more right, Margaret. We should have thought of it a long time ago."

Epilogue

Mr. Grimes rode out a day later, finalizing the sale of the farm to himself for services rendered plus fifteen hundred dollars. He and Henry had been in negotiations for more than a month now, but Henry hadn't wanted to get anyone's hopes up.

The Oades family moved the following week to a rented flat in San Francisco, where Nancy's baby, a girl named for Margaret's Mary, was born in May. She came in the dead of night as they liked to do, headfirst and fast. Margaret loved her immediately and without reservation; Mary was her own stepdaughter, after all. She cut the cord and washed the baby in warm water, taking her time. The child was an Oades, no doubt there, with that thatch of ginger hair.

Nancy lifted her head from the pillow. "Is she all right?"

Margaret swaddled the baby and put her to Nancy's breast. "See for yourself."

Mary latched on and began to greedily suckle. Nancy gasped with joy, long tears running. "It's coming, isn't it? I feel it. I have milk this time, don't I?"

"You're doing splendidly," said Margaret, looking down, her own eyes filling.

Henry knocked on the bedroom door. "May I come in now?"

❖❖

JOHN AND DORA had been married two months by the time Mary came. They shared the cramped flat, sleeping on the front room divan. Margaret regularly caught them sporting with each other. Dora would break away from John, feigning shock to see Margaret. Margaret would pretend to have noticed nothing. She took long city walks to escape, but Dora was always about when she returned.

"Soon," Nancy said almost daily. Henry was considering a lot on Elizabeth Street, upon which Nancy imagined having a grand house built. "Soon we'll all have room to spread out."

"We shall see," said Margaret, not picturing a house big enough.

Henry took no time in securing a good post with an American accounting firm. John was apprenticing there as well, though Margaret did not think it would last. Their son had begun complaining of claustrophobia, likening the office to a prison cell. Collar and tie choked him. On and on he went. He'd written letters of interest to vintners in the north and was eagerly waiting to hear back.

"We'll visit often, Mum," said Dora.

Mum. The girl did not let up.

❖❖

WORD OF MARGARET's inheritance came at the end of July. She'd been bequeathed a fortune, one thousand, four hundred and sixty-two pounds, the bulk of her parents' estate. Her frugal mother and father would have advised saving the money. Margaret had another idea.

"Perhaps it's time the girls and I struck out on our own," she said one night at supper. A new life had come to her in a daydream.

Nancy was emphatically against it. "No. You belong here."

Martha wholeheartedly agreed with Nancy. "Dad and Mrs. Oades would be too lonely without us," she said. Margaret's baby was nearly eight now, with firm opinions on just about any given subject.

Josephine was all for their leaving. "Why not go downtown, Mum? I know of a lovely building near the theaters. It's spanking clean, with well tended-to flowerboxes. I could inquire tomorrow, first thing."

John didn't care one way or the other. "A person has to make up his own mind," he said.

"Are you so terribly unhappy here, Meg?" asked Henry.

Margaret wasn't. Restless was more like it, jumpy, impatient.

Nancy said in a private moment afterward, "You didn't really mean it, did you?"

Margaret set aside the notion for the time being, and made a contribution to the lot on Elizabeth Street, putting the rest of the money in the Wells Fargo bank. For now, it was enough to know she had a choice.

The house, a turreted Queen Anne catalog house, began arriving in early September, coming shingle by shingle, nail by nail, in boxcars from Knoxville, Tennessee. That same month Margaret went to work for a milliner on Polk Street, a British widow originally of Sussex, who knew of Margaret's second cousin, once a headmaster there. The slender tie bound them from the start.

In November, John and Dora accompanied the family to the new house, along with their precious infant, William Oades—Billy, they called him.

"Begging your pardon, Mum," said Dora, "but I think those fancy choppers of yours scare Billy."

Margaret took out the new teeth the moment she arrived home now.

Nancy had egged her to get them. Margaret wore the hard plates to the milliner's shop, removing the dentures in the back room, where she spent peaceful hours alone, working with feathers and tulle. The teeth crowded her mouth and didn't keep a good grip. Nancy said a little pain was worth the youthful effect. "What lady doesn't make sacrifices, Margaret?" Margaret supposed she'd become accustomed to her mouth as it was.

"All the old actors wear false teeth," said Josephine. "Some of the younger ones, too."

Josephine was a dresser's assistant now. She sewed and fetched mainly, and in between memorized every part, even the male parts, just in case. She'd applied for the position on her own, after reading a notice on the stage door. Henry eventually came to allow it.

"I'm of two minds," said Margaret.

It was Margaret's night to cook. He'd come into the kitchen with a sack of pork chops and steam beer. "She's more grown than most her age, Meg," he said.

"I suppose," said Margaret, flouring the chops.

"She's a good girl."

Margaret nodded. "She is."

"A brave high-minded girl," he added.

Margaret looked at him, laughing. "Is she paying you, Henry?"

In the end, Margaret was persuaded to allow it as well. She'd never known her girl more exultant.

❖❖

HENRY. Margaret loved him still, for the same reasons she loved him once, for his courage, his sturdiness, his loyalty, his fathering. She no longer felt a wife's desire for him, not really, and it was a profound relief. She indulged in memories at times, but she did not mourn. One did not mourn that sort of loss forever. If Margaret left, *when* she left, Nancy would be the one most missed. Somewhere along the way her husband's wife had become a friend, as true a friend as any Margaret had ever known.

Margaret was in the bedroom when that stunning realization occurred, her bedroom, hers alone. It was a lovely room, with a large bay window and fireplace, though it was rather spartan in decor at the present time. That was due to change soon. New curtains were coming, the fabric for which she'd selected and paid for herself. She'd have a nice rug and reading chair eventually, and Henry promised to put up maple shelves for her books. Like those in the *Lady Ophelia*'s library. Next week, he said, at the latest.

It was nearly four o'clock. Margaret took off her shoes and lay down, this being Nancy's turn to prepare supper.

Acknowledgments

I am deeply grateful to many remarkable women. For bringing my story to light, I thank my agent, Barbara Braun, and my keen-eyed editors at Ballantine, Caitlin Alexander and Anika Streitfeld.

To my treasured sisters, Francie Knox and Karyn Wyce; my sagacious aunt, Jean Crump; my friends, Ginny Rorby, Ginny Wells, Elaine Waeber, Mary Ellen Woelfel, Susan Mckinney de Ortega, Phyllis Barry, Elsie Souza, Barbara Weibel, and Mary Marthaler—thanks for the sound advice and general good cheer along the way. I love you all.

The Wives
of
Henry Oades

Johanna Moran

A READER'S GUIDE

A Conversation with Johanna Moran

Random House Reader's Circle sat down with Johanna Moran to chat about the story behind the story of *The Wives of Henry Oades*. It was a breezy summer day in downtown Sarasota, Florida, and they each enjoyed a glass of wine at a café, just around the corner from Johanna's home.

Random House Reader's Circle: When I first heard the premise of your novel, it struck me as such a fascinating and unusual story that I thought there must be a family connection here. And indeed there is, though not the sort I would have guessed at. How did you come to write *The Wives of Henry Oades*?

Johanna Moran: More than a half century ago, my father, a law professor, came across an abstract on the Oades case and showed it to my mother, who was attempting to write short fiction in her nonexistent spare time. She was intrigued and gave thought to fleshing out the story, but that's as far as she got.

She might have had three kids down with mumps that week, or a spectacular birthday party for twins to host. In any event, five children and writing never did mesh. My mother squirreled the abstract away, perhaps thinking she'd get to it eventually. She gave it to me about ten years ago. I was drawn in immediately and went from there.

Fascinatingly, I've since learned from an Oades family descendant that the case, which was reported on in the *New York Times* and made its way into several legal texts, including *Readings in American Legal History (1949)*—70 plus years later!—may actually have been a hoax. There's some debate about whether the story was in fact invented by a California newspaper as a way for them to illustrate a loophole in the law that would have permitted bigamy.

RHRC: What in particular about the abstract drew you in? Did you and your mother discuss the narrative at all while you were writing?

JM: Well, I considered my own marriage. It's my first, but it's my husband's second. How outraged would I have been in Margaret's shoes? (She who didn't want to leave England in the first place.) My mother, two sisters, and I have discussed the narrative at length, from both women's perspective and from Henry's, never arriving at a perfect solution.

RHRC: What aspect of the story did you find most challenging to fictionalize?

JM: The greatest challenge was knowing Henry. I regularly interviewed my husband and other men. "Don't tell me what you think I want to hear," I'd say. "Tell me what you'd really do/say under these circumstances." Of course, no two men had the same answer. I came away with a mix of responses. My Henry Oades is a bit of a composite. I like and respect him. I also feel sorry for him at times.

RHRC: One of the things that's so compelling about your novel is how sympathetic the three main characters are: The reader can relate to each of them and understand their predicament and the choices they make—even if we don't always agree with them. While you were writing the novel, who did you feel most connected to or sympathetic toward—Margaret, Henry, or Nancy?

JM: Easily, Margaret. She's endured the most and is more entitled to Henry than Nancy. But then that's one first wife talking about another. Others will surely feel differently.

RHRC: How do you think the three Oadeses would have fared today?

JM: Good question. The women certainly would have had more options in the twenty-first century. Either one might have divorced without the social stigma attached. They might have gone on to fulfilling careers, in a different city of their choosing. They might have enjoyed the freedom of life on their own, or found new love(s), with or without the benefit of marriage. But that's assuming one or the other was willing to give up Henry, and that's not the case. Both consider him their rightful, lawful husband. A modern world would not have mitigated the heartache.

RHRC: There was a scene that didn't make it into the final draft—one in which Henry gives Nancy and Margaret a rather unusual gift, and it takes the women a bit of getting used to. Tell us about the earth closet and where that idea came from.

JM: I laugh thinking about that scene. I came across the earth closet in my reading. It was essentially a human litter box, consisting of a commode, pail, and dirt. Its popularity was very short lived. In the original draft, when an earthquake destroys their outdoor privy, Henry surprises the women with this indoor contraption. Nancy is particularly horrified. American women took some time getting used to the idea of any sort of indoor toilet. The "necessary" was associated with germs and disease, and naturally belonged outside.

RHRC: *The Wives of Henry Oades* seems like quite a wonderful tribute to a wide swath of your family—writers and lawyers. And in your previous career you traveled extensively, didn't you?

JM: That's right. My grandfather was a district judge; my father was a professor of law. I've long had a fascination with the law because of them. The love of writing came from both parents. My father was a published author, as was my maternal grandmother. Too restless to spend another four years in a classroom, I began my flying career at nineteen, first for National Airlines, a regional carrier, then for Pan Am. They were exhilarating years for the most part, interspersed with union strikes and the rare close call. I live a little more quietly now with my husband, John—for whom, in Margaret's or Nancy's situation, I would have fought tooth and nail.

RHRC: Had you been to any or all of the three locations the novel takes place in (London, England; Wellington, New Zealand; Berkeley, California) before you began writing? Did you visit afterward? Do you think your travel experience helped you create vivid portraits of each city?

JM: My husband and I visited all of the settings in the novel before I began writing. So, yes, actually being in a place is a huge help in creating a visual. We've been back to England and California since. We walked down Polk Street where Dr. McTeague's dental parlor is located. And we ate at the Cliff House and drank champagne at the Palace Hotel, though not as much as Margaret and Nancy did that day.

RHRC: Of the places you've traveled, where has been your favorite and why?

JM: For natural grandeur—hands down: New Zealand, particularly South Island. It is a spectacular country, and the people are lovely. An Air New Zealand pilot invited us to dinner simply because we were new to the place. I'd love to go back. And I will always hold San Francisco dear. John and I honeymooned there. It is one of the most romantic cities in the country.

RHRC: Can you tell us a little about what you are working on now?

JM: I'm working on a story about a friendship between two nineteenth-century prostitutes, one of whom was in fact murdered by Abraham Rothschild.

Reading Group Questions

and Topics for Discussion

1. On the voyage to New Zealand, Mrs. Randolph, a fellow passenger, cares for Margaret as she miscarries. Later, when Margaret tries to explain her grief over her new friend's death to Henry, she thinks, "the small transactions between women, particularly mothers, cannot adequately be explained to a man. Some, like hers with Mrs. Randolph, will bind women for life." Do you agree with Margaret? Can a strong relationship between women be forged in a matter of hours? With whom have you felt this connection?

2. Why do you think Mr. Oades misidentified Mim Bell as his wife? How could he have made such a grievous error?

3. Margaret refers to the quid pro quo of her faith: "One takes communion every single Sunday for thirty-odd years. One humbles herself, embraces every last dogmatic note, and no good comes of it, no help when one needs it most." Nancy, too, feels as though she has been cheated.

Have people's expectations of contemporary Christianity changed?

4. Margaret teaches her children lessons every evening: grammar, mathematics, and etiquette. "It was her duty to prepare them for their return. She refused to accept the possibility that they might grow old and die a natural death here. Margaret never once considered setting her children free to be slaves." She refuses to allow her children to live the life before them, planning, instead, for the life she hopes they will claim. Why does Margaret remain so steadfast during their captivity?

5. Henry finally accepts that his loved ones are dead, and eventually he marries another woman. What is the catalyst for this turning point? Do you agree with his actions?

6. Why do Margaret and the children receive such a chilly welcome when they finally return to the village from the Maori camp?

7. Several matches proposed in this book seem made for convenience: Portia and Henry, Margaret and Captain Fisk of the *Sacramento*, and even Nancy and Henry, at least in the beginning. Do you agree? If so, why do you think that is?

8. At what point do Margaret and Nancy start to get along? What sparks their friendship?

9. Though it's a wretched situation for everyone involved, which Mrs. Oades do you think suffers most? With which woman do you most identify?

10. Was there a better solution for Mr. Oades and his nontraditional family? Or did they make the best possible choice? Would there be a better solution today? What would it be?

11. The claims of the Daughters of Decency seem ridiculous to modern ears. Can you think of any recent court battles that might seem as hysteric and unnecessary a century from now?

12. Consider the Maori premonition in the beginning of the book. How does it relate to the story?

13. What, in the end, do you think was the main theme of this book? Were you surprised?

ABOUT THE AUTHOR

JOHANNA MORAN comes from a long line of writers and lawyers. She lives on the west coast of Florida with her husband, John. *The Wives of Henry Oades* is her first novel. Please visit her blog at www.johan namoran.com